Praise for the novels of Sherryl Woods

"Readers who adore family dramas will again dote on Woods' newest romance." —*Booklist* on *Wind Chime Point*

"A reunion story punctuated by family drama, Woods's first novel in her new Ocean Breeze series is touching, tense and tantalizing." —*RT Book Reviews* on *Sand Castle Bay*

"A whimsical, sweet scenario…the digressions have their own charm, and Woods never fails to come back to the romantic point." —*Publishers Weekly* on *Sweet Tea at Sunrise*

"Charming characters combine to create the interfering, yet lovable, O'Brien family…a satisfying, heartwarming conclusion to the Chesapeake Shores series." —*RT Book Reviews* on *The Summer Garden*

"Sparks fly in a lively tale that is overflowing with family conflict and warmth and the possibility of rekindled love." —*Library Journal* on *Flowers on Main*

"Sherryl Woods writes emotionally satisfying novels about family, friendship and home. Truly feel-great reads!" —#1 *New York Times* bestselling author Debbie Macomber

"Sherryl Woods gives her characters depth, intensity, and the right amount of humor." —*RT Book Reviews*

"Woods…is noted for appealing character-driven stories that are often infused with the flavor and fragrance of the South." —*Library Journal*

SHERRYL WOODS

SEA GLASS ISLAND

mira

mira™

Recycling programs for this product may not exist in your area.

ISBN-13: 978-0-7783-3385-2

Sea Glass Island

First published in 2013. This edition published in 2023.

Copyright © 2013 by Sherryl Woods

For questions and comments about the quality of this book, please contact us at CustomerService@Harlequin.com.

Mira
22 Adelaide St. West, 41st Floor
Toronto, Ontario M5H 4E3, Canada
www.Harlequin.com

Printed in U.S.A.

Dear Reader,

Most of us have come to accept that dreams change as we go through life. Sometimes this is the product of maturity and new life experiences. Sometimes we're simply forced to accept a harsh new reality.

That's the case with both Samantha Castle and Ethan Cole in *Sea Glass Island*. But while Ethan has embraced his new life running a small emergency clinic on the North Carolina coast, Samantha is still struggling to find a new focus for her future. She knows only that the acting career she once dreamed of is no longer as successful or fulfilling as she'd hoped. As readers have come to know, Sand Castle Bay is the perfect place to reevaluate goals and ambitions. And thanks to a little nudge from their grandmother, it's also been the ideal place for the Castle sisters to find love.

I hope you'll enjoy this final installment of the Ocean Breeze trilogy and that Samantha's story will remind you that there's often a new—and unexpected—dream right around the corner, if only you open your heart to the possibilities.

All best,

Sherryl

SEA GLASS
ISLAND

One

Samantha plunged a spoon into a pint of Ben & Jerry's Cherry Garcia, then sighed as the decadent ice cream melted in her mouth. Guilty pleasures like this were about all that kept her going these days. With enough Ben & Jerry's came hope that her acting career would pick up. A positive attitude had helped her to weather tough times in the past, after all.

It was getting harder and harder to believe, though. The silence of her phone lately had been deafening. In late spring, she'd had a minor role in a prime-time TV show that filmed in New York, but it hadn't led to other opportunities despite the enthusiasm of the director and the producers. Fall season shows were back in production, but she'd received none of the promised job offers, not even for bit parts.

She hadn't had a single callback for a commercial in weeks. If it weren't for her job as a hostess at a high-priced Upper East Side restaurant, she'd be in the most serious financial trouble she'd faced since coming to New York over fifteen years ago. Even with that, she'd had to dip into her savings already.

Though her sister Gabriella had mounted a terrific PR buzz campaign for her back in the spring, its effects had worn off in weeks, rather than months, and now, once again, she was struggling. She'd worn out her list of contacts. But with everything going on in Gabi's life these days, Samantha hadn't felt she could ask for more free publicity assistance. Gabi was adjusting to being a single mom and trying to work things out with the very patient man in her life, who'd agreed to postpone their own wedding until after their sister Emily's in a few weeks.

Ever the optimist, Samantha had survived discouraging times more than once since arriving in New York just out of high school as a fresh-faced girl with stars in her eyes. This dry spell, however, was the worst she could recall. More disturbing was that now it came with pitying looks from other actresses up for the same roles. Her once exuberant, supportive agent had started dodging her calls, then parted ways with her. His replacement, though enthusiastic, hadn't gotten promising results.

Samantha had been in New York long enough to read the handwriting on the wall. She was thirty-five, and while still beautiful, she was past her prime. Parts that once would have been hers for the asking were now going to women in their early twenties. It didn't seem to matter that the casting call was for someone her age, or even older. At the same time, she wasn't quite old enough for the burgeoning niche for older actresses. There wasn't enough optimism in the universe to counter that harsh reality.

When her phone rang, she lunged for it, which told

her just how desperate she'd become. She didn't like the feeling.

"Samantha, hey. I'm so glad I caught you," her youngest sister, Emily, said, as if finding her at home was a rarity, rather than commonplace these days. "We need to talk. Now that Gabi's had her baby, it's time to get serious about my wedding. It's just around the corner."

Despite her generally sour mood, Samantha smiled. "Does Boone have any idea you weren't *always* serious about the wedding?" she quipped. "Remind me, when is it again? Sometime next year?"

"Very funny. It's less than a month away."

"That soon?" Samantha teased.

"Soon? This has been forever in the making. How long were Boone and I apart? Years and years. We need to make up for lost time."

The excitement in Emily's voice was wonderful to hear, Samantha thought, trying not to envy her. She and Boone did deserve this long-delayed happiness.

"When are you coming to North Carolina?" Emily prodded. "You have to have another dress fitting, not that you ever gain an ounce. It's more of a show of solidarity with Gabi, who's still fighting baby weight. And there's the bridal shower Grandmother and Gabi are throwing, then the rehearsal dinner. I'm thinking we need a bachelorette night, just us girls. I want you here for every minute. This is going to be the absolute best summer the Castle sisters have ever had in Sand Castle Bay."

"I wouldn't miss any of it," Samantha assured her. "After all, wasn't I the one who predicted last August that you and Boone were going to get back together?"

"Yes, you demonstrated amazing insight, but it wouldn't be the first time that some irresistible part came through at the last second and you bailed on me. My college graduation comes to mind."

"Well, there's no way I'd bail on your wedding," Samantha reassured her. The likelihood of a plum role being offered was abysmally small. Besides, she'd never let Emily down after promising to be her maid of honor. The fact that Emily had even asked had come as a surprise. Their relationship had been tainted by some kind of sibling rivalry she'd never understood, but her sister seemed to be sincerely trying to leave that in the past.

"I'm driving south the day after tomorrow," she told Emily, not mentioning that the wedding was providing the perfect excuse to leave New York behind during these depressing dog days of summer. "I'll be there to do whatever you need."

"Are you bringing What's-his-face with you? The guy from the network or the producer? I lose track."

"Truthfully, so do I," Samantha admitted. "There's no one I'd want around for an occasion as important as my little sister's wedding."

There was a faint hesitation on the other end of the line and then Emily asked slyly, "Not even Ethan Cole?"

Samantha's heart did a predictable little stutter step. "Why on earth would you bring up Ethan? He's ancient history. Not even history, come to think of it. He never even knew I existed back in the day."

"Aha!" Emily said triumphantly. "You do still have feelings for him. I told Gabi you did. She thinks so, too. Our powers of observation are every bit as good as yours when it comes to romance."

"And you got that from my asking why you mentioned him?" Samantha inquired irritably, hating any possibility that at her age she could be wearing her heart on her sleeve for anyone to detect. Especially when the man in question probably wouldn't even recognize her if their paths crossed.

"I got that from your wearing his old football jersey around the house the whole time you were home after the hurricane last summer," Emily responded. "And, amazingly, it disappeared after you went back to New York. I'll bet it's in your closet up there right this minute."

"It is not," Samantha retorted, glancing down at the gold-and-green jersey she was currently wearing. So what if she still harbored a not-so-secret crush on the star quarterback from the high school? Three years older and surrounded by throngs of local girls, Ethan had never once noticed her back then. She was a summer kid, not even a blip on his radar. She seriously doubted he'd discovered deep feelings in the intervening years just from spotting her in some detergent commercial, and that was even assuming he knew it was her.

"You know he never married," Emily said casually. "And he and Boone play golf together. Boone's asked him to be in the wedding."

Samantha's stupid heart did another of those annoying little telltale hop, skip and jumps. "Not on my account, I hope."

"Of course not," Emily said. "But he is Boone's best man, which means you'll be seeing a lot of him."

Samantha groaned. She'd expected this sort of matchmaking from her grandmother, who'd actively campaigned to see that Emily and Boone were reunited and had done her share of manipulating to see that Gabi wound up with Wade Johnson. Samantha had been certain, though, that Cora Jane would show a little more respect for Samantha's ability to find her own man. Then, again, there wasn't much evidence that Samantha had made any particularly good choices up to now. The men she'd dated had been seriously lacking in staying power.

"Did Grandmother put you up to this?" she asked testily.

"Up to what?" Emily replied innocently. "I told you, Boone and Ethan have been friends forever. Their families go way back. It makes perfect sense that he'd want Ethan in the wedding."

"I suppose," Samantha conceded.

"Gotta run. I love you," Emily said. "See you soon."

"See you soon," Samantha echoed.

Suddenly going back to Sand Castle Bay for her sister's wedding had gotten a lot more interesting…and maybe just a little dangerous.

Gabi held Daniella Jane in her arms, rocking her gently as she studied the color in Emily's cheeks.

"Well, did you find out whatever it was you wanted to know when you spoke to Samantha?" she asked.

"Oh, Samantha still has it bad for Ethan, all right," Emily replied with a smirk.

"Which means you intend to meddle," Gabi guessed.

"Well, why not?" Emily inquired, reaching to take the baby from Gabi's arms and cooing to her. "Grandmother does it all the time."

"And gets away with it because she's Cora Jane and we love and respect her," Gabi reminded her. "You and

Samantha haven't always seen eye-to-eye on things, not that I've ever understood why that is."

Emily made a face that had the baby gurgling with what could have been delight...or a dire portent of something else entirely.

"I know that's all on me," Emily admitted. "And the worst part is that I honestly don't remember when it started. If I was going to feel this competitive nonsense, it should have been with you. We're the driven, ambitious ones. Or at least you were until you turned all mellow and had this beautiful baby. She's the one and only thing good to come out of your relationship with Paul the slimebag. Now you've fallen madly in love with Wade, and as much as it pains me to see, now you're just plain sappy."

"Hey, I have a thriving art gallery with a dozen temperamental artists working on-site. I'm trying to turn that into a tourist destination," Gabi protested. "I haven't exactly slacked off. I just redirected my goals."

"Yeah, yeah," Emily said. "You're missing my point. I can't figure out why I've always had this thing with Samantha, but I honestly do want to put it behind us. It's past time. I don't want any of those old lingering feelings to spoil what should be the happiest time of my life."

"Amen to that, and asking her to be your maid of honor was a really sweet gesture," Gabi said. "I know how much she appreciated it."

"It doesn't exactly make up for the way I've treated her over the years, as if her sole role in life was to annoy me." She tickled Daniella, then grinned as the baby squirmed. "Lordy, but she's cute. I think I want one."

Gabi laughed. "I have a hunch Boone will be more than willing to cooperate, but you might want to get this wedding behind you first."

"First, Boone and I have to be in the same place at the same time if we're going to make a baby," Emily grumbled. "He's checking in on all his restaurants on his way here from Los Angeles."

"So you'll be apart how long? A whole twenty-four hours?" Gabi teased.

"Two days actually," Emily replied with a dramatic sigh.

Gabi laughed. "You are pathetic. You were apart for years before you reconciled. Even after you got back together, your work kept you in different cities for quite a while."

"And now I'm spoiled," Emily conceded. "With Boone in Los Angeles with me while I work on those safe houses for abused women and families, I've discovered just how amazing living together can be. I had no idea I'd adapt so quickly to having someone in my life 24/7. Add in B.J. and instant motherhood, and it's been the most incredible few months ever."

"It really is wonderful to see you so ecstatically happy," Gabi told her. "It's great that you and B.J. formed this immediate bond. Not every stepmother is so lucky."

"Believe me, I've heard the stories," Emily said. "How about you? I can see what a contented mom you are, but what's the scoop with you and Wade? Why hasn't he moved in here?"

"As broad-minded as Cora Jane may be, I don't think I want to test her limits by suggesting that my boyfriend and I live together under her roof. Wade and I are committed to working things out. That's enough for now."

"You're really happy?" Emily asked, studying her worriedly. "Staying here in Sand Castle Bay is what you want? And the gallery's enough for you?"

"I have more than a job here, Em. I have family and a wonderful man and that little munchkin you're holding. My life is full. I don't need a ring on my finger just yet. I certainly don't need to go back to the stressful, demanding life I was leading in Raleigh. Besides, I think Dad would stroke out if I hit him with another wedding bill right now. You haven't been here when Grandmother's handed over the invoices for yours. Poor Dad's just grasping the reality that weddings don't come cheap, especially with a daughter who has very expensive taste."

"Hey, I'm not the one who insisted on inviting half the state of North Carolina. You can thank Dad and Grandmother for that. Boone and I would have been content with family and a few friends."

"So you say now," Gabi said, "but I never heard you putting up much of a fuss as the guest list grew and grew and started to include half of Los Angeles."

"Well, it is what it is now," Emily said blithely. "Let's get back to Samantha. Any idea what's going on with her? She didn't sound all that happy when we spoke just now. Is her career faltering again?"

Gabi winced. "I'm ashamed to say I haven't given it much thought. I've been a little distracted lately."

"Understandable," Emily said. "She hasn't asked for your PR help, has she?"

"No, but she wouldn't. I had to badger her into letting me help a few months ago. It seemed to be effective, so

I guess I just assumed that things kept on snowballing. In a good way, that is. That's how it is sometimes, one job leads to another, but I shouldn't have taken that for granted. I should have asked," she said, feeling guilty.

"Why? Not everything is up to you to fix," Emily said, an oddly defensive note in her voice. "If Samantha wanted help, she could have said something. That's her way, though. She just suffers in silence, then resents it when nobody jumps in to save the day."

Gabi regarded her younger sister with dismay. "That's not true, Emily. Samantha's not like that. Why would you even say something so cruel?"

Emily looked taken aback by Gabi's vehemence, then buried her face in her hands. "Because I'm mean and spiteful," she said in a small voice, then lifted her gaze to meet Gabi's. "What is the matter with me? I always see the worst in her, even when she's done nothing wrong."

"It's times like this when I really wish Mom were still around," Gabi said softly.

Emily blinked back instant tears at the unexpected reference to their mother, who'd died several years ago. "What does Mom have to do with this?"

"Maybe she would understand why you have this attitude toward our big sister. Dad certainly wouldn't have any idea. He was oblivious to everything going on at home when we were growing up. I doubt Grandmother was with us enough in the early years before Mom died to know the root of the problems between the two of you."

Emily sighed. "And it's increasingly obvious that it isn't something I can just wish away. These careless, hurtful words just pop out of my mouth sometimes, and I have no idea why."

"Then dig deeper and figure it out," Gabi advised. "You and Samantha both mean the world to me, and I don't want to be caught in the middle. I want us to be sisters, in every positive, loving sense of the word, okay? In fact, in my dream scenario, you and Boone eventually settle back here and Samantha marries a local, too, and we all live blocks apart so our kids can grow up together."

Emily nodded, her eyes still misty. "I want that, too," she insisted. "Well, maybe not moving back here full-time, but the rest. I will work this out, Gabi. I promise. Maybe once she's here, Samantha and I can sit down and hash this out. Who knows? Maybe she stole my favorite doll when I was two and I've blocked it from my memory."

Gabi smiled at the idea of something so innocuous causing a rivalry that had lasted for years. And Emily's earlier accusations about her sister harboring simmering resentments seemed to speak of something much more complicated.

"Just work it out, sweetie. Whatever it takes."

Emily settled Daniella back in Gabi's arms and gave her niece a last pat, then pressed a kiss to Gabi's cheek. "Done," she promised.

Gabi watched her sister leave and wondered if it could be that simple.

Ethan Cole had just seen his final patient of the day, a tourist who'd managed to slice open her foot on a rusty nail on one of the stray boards still around after a recent storm had ripped through the coastal areas of

North Carolina. Though most of the shoreline had been cleaned up immediately, debris still washed ashore from time to time, especially along a few more deserted areas of the beach. He'd given her a tetanus shot and four stitches and told her to come back if there was even a hint of any infection at the site of the injury.

He was just finishing up his notes when the door pushed open again and Boone Dorsett wandered into the small emergency clinic that Ethan had established with another doctor who'd also served in Iraq and Afghanistan. They'd agreed that the emergencies here in a small coastal community were unlikely to rise to the level of anything they'd coped with on their tours of duty in the military. Bumps, bruises and a few stitches were a day at the park compared to anything they'd seen, or in Ethan's case, experienced firsthand.

He'd lost his lower left leg to an IED explosion in Afghanistan. While that might not have kept him out of an operating room once he was back stateside, it had gone a long way toward changing his need for the adrenaline rush of spending hours in a trauma unit or performing complicated, high-risk surgical procedures.

"You busy?" Boone asked, his tone nonchalant but his expression harried.

Ethan studied his friend's face. "You look like you need to talk. Wedding jitters?"

Boone sat down, one leg bouncing up and down nervously, even though he uttered a denial.

"If it's not about the wedding, what's going on?" Ethan asked. He'd heard it was the best man's duty to keep the groom calm and focused and make sure he turned up at the church on time. Emily Castle had made that very clear to him. So had her grandmother. It's was Cora Jane's admonition that had resonated. She'd threatened him with bodily harm if he failed to deliver Boone precisely at ten-thirty two weeks from Saturday.

"There's something you maybe need to know," Boone admitted.

"Okay," Ethan replied slowly. "What?"

"You're the best man, right?"

"So you keep telling me."

"That means you have this sort of obligation to spend time with the maid of honor."

Ethan stilled. "What does that mean, 'spend time with'? We walk down the aisle together at the end of the service, right? Maybe sit next to each other at the head table and deliver our heartfelt toasts about how inevitable it all was that the two of you wound up together?"

"I think maybe Emily is expecting a little more than that," Boone acknowledged, squirming uncomfortably.

Ethan's gaze narrowed. "And why would Emily be expecting anything more? And why are you warning me?"

"Because I don't want you to be blindsided. I know how you are about dating. Ever since you got back from overseas, you've been this social recluse."

"I was still engaged when I came back," Ethan reminded him. At least he had been for about twenty minutes, until all the hero worship died down and Lisa had admitted she didn't think she could stay with someone "who's not whole." It was the first time Ethan had really seen himself as others probably saw him, as someone who was no longer quite the same man he used to be.

The only good thing to come out of that ugly breakup

was his increased determination not only to ensure that his injury put no limitations on his life, but to see that kids with physical disabilities learned to view themselves in a positive way. That mission to salvage his own dignity and help others had given his life a much-needed purpose. Project Pride filled hours that otherwise might have been spent on this so-called social life Boone—or more likely, Emily—thought he needed.

"It's been three years since you split with Lisa," Boone pointed out.

"Since she dumped me," Ethan corrected to keep the record straight.

"She was a self-absorbed twit," Boone said with feeling, "but let's not go there. My very low opinion of your ex is not the point."

"Then what is the point?" Ethan asked, frowning.

There was no mistaking his friend's discomfort as Boone finally muttered, "Heaven only knows why, but Emily seems to have gotten this idea that you and her sister Samantha are perfect for each other."

"Excuse me?" Ethan said, hoping he'd heard incorrectly.

"Come on, Ethan," Boone said impatiently, "you know exactly what I said. I didn't leave a lot of room for misinterpretation."

"Samantha, the maid of honor," Ethan said, finally getting all the implications of this little scheme of the bride-to-be. He shook his head and directed a warning look at his friend that he hoped would put the fear of God into him. "No way, Boone! You need to tell Emily to forget it. Being subjected to matchmaking, meddling or whatever you want to call it, that's definitely not part of what I signed on for."

Boone gave him an incredulous look. "Have you met Emily? She's got me in here spouting off like a blasted girl about stuff that is absolutely none of my business!"

"Okay, she's tough and determined. I'll give you that, but you're tougher," Ethan said.

Boone shrugged. "Not so much."

"I'll bail on you," Ethan threatened. "I swear I will."

Boone merely rolled his eyes in disbelief. "No, you won't. Besides, I can kind of see it. You and Samantha. She's beautiful. You're handsome. You'd make gorgeous babies, and that is a direct quote from Emily, by the way."

Ethan stared at him. "What has happened to you? Since when do you get involved in matchmaking, much less on the basis of how pretty any resulting babies would be?"

"Emily was very convincing," Boone said, then grinned. "Besides, she says Samantha had a crush on you back in the day. She seems to think this is destiny or something."

Ethan searched his memory, but no image came to mind, just bits and pieces of more recent gossip. "Isn't Samantha an actress? Younger than me by a couple of years at least? She went off to New York to be a star or something? Does that really sound like someone who'd be suited for life with a small-town doctor? The whole Lisa experience pretty much cured me of having unrealistic expectations when it comes to women."

"Emily believes Samantha is ready for a change of direction. She keeps talking about Samantha's summer of transformation or some such. Believe me, she has a plan."

Now Ethan couldn't hide his amusement. "And how does Samantha feel about that?"

"She might not have figured it out just yet," Boone admitted. "But she will, once Emily spends a little time with her. I have complete confidence in Emily's powers of persuasion. She's also highly motivated. She and Samantha haven't always been on the best terms. I think she sees this as a chance to turn that around and truly bond with her older sister."

"By delivering a man into her life?" Ethan asked incredulously. "One she may not even want?"

"Emily's convinced she has this right," Boone countered. "And just so you know, I think Cora Jane's on her side in this, too. She has an uncanny knack for these things. If you ask me, you're pretty much doomed. I'm just giving you fair warning."

"Just because Emily—or Cora Jane, for that matter—can obviously twist you around her little finger and get you to buy into all this sisterly bonding and destiny nonsense doesn't mean she'll have the same effect on the rest of us," Ethan said.

In fact, he could pretty much guarantee he wouldn't get with the program. He'd had his fill of silly, shallow women who thought looks were everything. His ex-fiancée had seen to that.

He realized exactly how bitter that made him sound. Well, he *was* bitter. In fact, he'd been counting on that for quite some time now to keep his heart safe, no matter who was scheming against him. Up to now it had worked like a charm.

Then, again, he hadn't tested it against the likes of Emily and Cora Jane Castle just yet. That, he was very sorry to admit, was just a little worrisome.

Two

Samantha wandered into the kitchen at her grand-mother's on her first morning back home wearing Ethan Cole's old football jersey and nothing else. Since the jersey reached practically to her knees, she considered it perfectly respectable to wear around the house, even if a little dangerous given the message it sent confirming her fascination with the man.

At least no one else was home at the moment and she was in serious need of a caffeine fix to jolt her out the lethargy she'd been feeling lately. The coffee would be better over at the restaurant, but it would take her at least a half hour to get there—even longer since she'd have to walk—and would require getting dressed, two huge strikes against that idea.

She'd just reached up into the cabinet for a mug when she heard a muttered curse. It came from a very masculine source, judging from the sound of it. It scared her so badly she dropped the mug on her foot, yelped as it shattered on the tile floor and then danced around the kitchen before even casting a glance toward the wide-open back door where none other than Ethan Cole stood with a dumbstruck yet surprisingly irritated expression on his face. It might have been years since she'd laid eyes on him, but she'd know those broad shoulders, that square jaw and those deep blue eyes anywhere.

"Well, this is awkward," she murmured, wrapping her arms around her middle in a probably futile attempt to keep him from identifying her nightwear as something that had once belonged to him.

He stepped closer and ordered tersely, "Sit."

Samantha couldn't believe the audacity, first for walking in uninvited and now for giving such abrupt orders. "Excuse me?"

He gave her an impatient look. "There are chips from the mug all over the floor." He adjusted his tone with apparent effort. "Please sit before you cut your feet and I have to stitch you up."

"Oh," she said, chagrined. As he stooped down and picked up the shards of china, she asked, "What are you doing here?"

He gave her a wry look. "According to Boone, I'm here to pick up something that Emily left for me, something that absolutely has to be delivered to downtown Sand Castle Bay this morning. He gave me Cora Jane's address. He also told me to come on in, that I'd probably find it in the kitchen. Just so you know, he neglected to mention that anyone might be home. Otherwise, I would have knocked."

"No problem," she said, despite the racing of her heart. "No other clues?" she asked, glancing around for a package of some sort. There was nothing in plain sight.

"He said I'd recognize it when I saw it," Ethan said, regarding her pointedly.

Samantha's mouth gaped as she put the pieces of the plot together. She was going to kill her baby sister. She really was. "You think he meant me?"

"I'd lay odds on it, if you're who I think you are."

"I'm Emily's sister," she said. "Samantha Castle."

Ethan sighed heavily. "Of course you are."

She frowned at the attitude, even though her own mood was deteriorating rapidly. "Meaning?"

"It's just that Boone gave me a heads-up about the meddling," he said. "I rather emphatically warned him and, through him, his bride-to-be and your grand-mother, to stay out of my life. Apparently I didn't get through to any of them."

Just great, Samantha thought wearily. She had no doubt at all about exactly the sort of meddling Boone had described. She just didn't want to believe that Emily would do anything this outrageous to embarrass her.

She opted to try to put a better spin on the situation, even though she was pretty sure it would take someone with Gabi's PR skills to pull it off successfully. Then, again, she hadn't lost all her acting skills, even if they weren't in much demand lately.

"Look, I don't know what kind of crazy idea you have about me," she said earnestly. "The truth is that I turned in my rental car yesterday, and everyone had to leave the house at some ungodly hour this morning, leaving me without transportation. Emily said she'd take care of it. That's all I know."

"Oh, I believe you," Ethan said, his tone resigned as he dumped the remains of the mug into the trash can.

"Meddling works most effectively when neither of the affected parties has a clue what's going on."

"In my experience it doesn't matter if they know," she said wryly. "In this family, we seem helpless to stop it." She gave him an apologetic look. "I'm really sorry, Ethan, especially if you've gone out of your way. As you can see, I'm nowhere near ready to go anywhere."

"I see," he said, his gaze raking over her in a thorough survey that heated her blood by several degrees. "Mind my asking how you wound up with my old high school football jersey?" He looked into her eyes. "It is mine, isn't it?"

She feigned surprise. "Is it? I picked it up at a yard sale down here years ago. I thought it would make a great nightshirt."

"It definitely makes a fashion statement of some kind," he confirmed, his gaze now frankly traveling up and down her very long, very bare legs. "So, are we going to do this or what?"

Samantha blinked and swallowed hard at the question. "Do this?" she asked, imagining every one of her teenage fantasies finally coming true.

An unexpected grin transformed his face. "Not *that*," he scolded, "though I might be open to negotiations down the road. I meant get you over to wherever your sister wants me to deposit you."

"A dress fitting," Samantha said, trying to hide her disappointment. She also saw the sense in taking him up on his offer. "Can you give me ten minutes?"

"Ten? Seriously?"

She laughed. "Trust me. In my world ten minutes

for a wardrobe change is an eternity. Help yourself to coffee. I'll be right back."

Of course, changing into something more presentable was only half the battle. She also had to catch her breath. That was going to be a whole lot trickier.

So this was what Boone had warned him about, Ethan thought as he watched Samantha practically race from the kitchen. Just the first tiny step in some campaign to hook him up with the maid of honor. Right this second he was having a little too much trouble seeing the downside of that. It had been a lot easier to rail indignantly when there had been no face—or body—to go with the name.

He wasn't sure what he'd expected, but it definitely hadn't been the sight that greeted him in Cora Jane's kitchen. Samantha Castle was a delectable handful. Even caught off guard with no makeup, tousled hair and wearing his shapeless football jersey, she'd been take-his-breath-away stunning.

Suddenly he'd been assailed by tantalizing visions of her crawling from his bed looking just like that after a night of passion. It was a rude awakening to realize any woman could still get to him like that, especially after he'd dismissed this one so thoroughly as not his type. Shallow, he reminded himself staunchly. She was bound to be shallow. Egotistical, too. Wasn't that a trait of all actors? They had to have monumental egos to survive.

He glanced at the clock, noted that ten minutes had elapsed and was about to smirk when Samantha sailed into the room, dressed as if she'd just stepped out of some fashion magazine ad for wildly expensive resort wear. Her highlighted blond hair had been swept back and caught in a clip at the nape of her neck, her makeup had been so skillfully applied it was almost impossible to tell she was wearing any, and her eyes were hidden by a pair of chic designer sunglasses that probably cost more than he'd taken in at the clinic last week. He had a feeling if he could have seen those eyes of hers, they'd be filled with mirth at winning her bet with him.

"I'm impressed," he admitted. "That's quite a transformation, and it was accomplished in record time."

"Theater training," she explained. "You get used to quick wardrobe changes. They really hate to stop the play while the actors jump into a new outfit."

Ethan chuckled as he led the way to his car, Samantha keeping up easily with her long-legged stride. Only as he was about to close her door did he hear her soft gasp. It was enough to tell him she'd seen the prosthetic, or guessed. It was impossible to tell which. He also had the distinct impression no one had warned her.

His friends said his movements looked a hundred percent normal to them, but they would say that. They were all so darned careful not to offend.

He got into the car, put the key in the ignition and glanced her way, waiting to see if she'd bring it up or sit there in embarrassed silence.

"Iraq?" she asked simply.

"Afghanistan," he responded.

"You manage very well."

"Not well enough to keep you from noticing," he commented wryly.

"I just caught a glimpse of the prosthetic," she said. "Otherwise I'd never have figured it out."

"And your sister and Boone neglected to mention it?"

"Not a word," she confirmed.

He wondered, as always, if it changed anything, but he wasn't about to ask. He'd figure that out soon enough. His radar was finely tuned these days. There'd be a pitying look or a faint expression of distaste, quickly hidden, but detectable since he'd learned to watch for the signs.

Worse, sometimes, there was the curiosity, the undue fascination that seemed to stem from a desire to figure out just what else might have been affected by the explosion that took his lower leg. Lisa's most crushing impact had been to make him so self-conscious that the prospect of intimacy was far less appealing than it had once been to someone with his healthy libido.

"Did it take a long time to adjust?" Samantha asked.

"Physically? Sure, but I was highly motivated. I worked at it," he said with a shrug, minimizing the months of painful rehab that had threatened to shatter his normal optimism more than once.

"And emotionally?"

He was surprised that she'd dared to ask that. Most people didn't risk going there.

"Still a work in progress," he admitted. "I don't want anyone pitying me."

She smiled at that. "I wouldn't think they'd dare. Not in this town, which still has a memorial wall dedicated to your extraordinary feats on the football field."

"It's not a wall," he said, flushing. "It's a couple of pictures outside the gym."

"Have you been back to the high school recently? It's a wall," she insisted, then grinned as she acknowledged, "Which is not to say you don't deserve it. Leading the team to two state championships is nothing to sneeze at. A record number of touchdown passes both years. Not too shabby, Cole."

Ethan regarded her with surprise. It wasn't just her up-to-date awareness of his football achievements and the school's embarrassing tribute, but her cut-to-the-chase insights. "You're not at all what I expected," he told her.

"Oh?" She gave him an amused look. "Something tells me you were thinking vain and shallow."

He winced at the accurate guess. "Something like that," he admitted.

"It's a common curse in my profession," she conceded. "But I try never to be predictable."

"So far you're doing a good job," he said. In fact, she was so unpredictable he wasn't quite sure what to make of her, and that really, really worried him.

A few minutes later, he pulled up in front of the new art studio being run by her sister Gabriella. He'd been to the opening a couple of months back, mostly as a favor to Boone. His knowledge of art was limited to recognizing a van Gogh when he saw one…as long as it was a painting of sunflowers. Beyond that he'd been hopeless in art appreciation classes.

"You're having your dress fitting here?" he asked, puzzled by the choice.

"Gabi can't get away. Emily's freaking out that we're running out of time. Since everyone's goal these days is to calm the bride's jittery nerves, we do whatever she asks." She grinned at him. "You might want to keep that in mind. I'm pretty sure Boone is living by the same rules. He could probably use a whole lot of moral support from his best man."

"Not a doubt in my mind about that, and I plan to do my best," Ethan said, then grinned. "I'm under strict orders from Cora Jane."

Samantha laughed. "Yes, she can strike terror into the hearts of most people I know, but she is amazing."

"No argument from me about that."

She studied him for a minute. "I know you're older than me, and that also makes you older than Boone. How'd the two of you wind up as such good friends?" Her gaze narrowed. "Or are you? Please, God, tell me that Emily didn't pressure Boone into asking you to be his best man just because of me, did she?"

Ethan laughed. "I have no idea when the diabolical plotting started, Samantha, but Boone and I have been friends for years. Our families were close. The age difference never seemed to matter much. We bonded over sports. We've been there for each other through some tough times."

"When Boone lost his wife," Samantha guessed.

Ethan gave her a long look. "And when he lost Emily before that. I was mostly away back then in med school, but I was around enough to know she broke his heart. I hope she's not going to do it again."

"Not a chance," Samantha said, not even trying to deny that her sister had made a terrible mistake years before by choosing her career over Boone. "She knows how lucky she is that they have this second chance."

"Second chances are hard to come by," Ethan said.

"Voice of experience?" she asked him.

"You could say that."

She looked as if she wanted to probe a little more deeply, but Ethan forestalled her questions by asking, "You'll have a way to get back home from here?"

Though she was clearly disconcerted by the change of topic, she merely nodded. "Sure. Emily, if I'm still speaking to her after this morning's turn of events. If not, I'm sure Grandmother will take pity on me and let me use her car."

"If that doesn't work out, give me a call. I have a light morning at the clinic, unless some big emergency crops up. I can always run you back home." Even as the offer came out of his mouth, he was mentally kicking himself for making it. Spending any more time with this woman than absolutely necessary was probably emotional suicide.

She grinned at him. "You almost made that sound like a sincere offer," she said.

"It was," he insisted.

She shook her head. "Something tells me we shouldn't be giving them any encouragement. I've seen how my family works, Ethan. One tiny little hint that their meddling is working and they won't let up. Do you really want the aggravation?"

"No, I suppose not," he said, surprised to find that a part of him was actually disappointed at the prospect of running across her only when their wedding duties required it.

"Okay, then," she said breezily. "Thanks for the lift. See you around, I'm sure."

"See you," he mumbled, and watched her go. He told himself his inability to tear his gaze away was purely masculine appreciation of a gorgeous woman, but the truth was, there was also just the tiniest twinge of regret.

Unfortunately the clinic was even quieter than Ethan had predicted, which made his determination to keep his mind off Samantha Castle much harder to achieve. If he closed his eyes for so much as a second, he could see that old football jersey of his riding up her bare backside as she stretched on tiptoe to reach into a kitchen cupboard. The fact that the image had stuck with him was troubling. Then, again, it had been a while since he'd seen a sight that provocative.

He grabbed the running clothes he kept at the clinic, changed into them in the bathroom, then stopped to let his partner, Greg Knotts, know that he was taking a break. The other Afghanistan vet gave him a knowing look.

"Something on your mind?"

"More like someone," Ethan told him.

"A woman?"

Ethan nodded.

Greg's expression lit up. "Well, hallelujah! It's about time you moved on. It was a crying shame you let an idiot like Lisa keep you from having an active social life."

Ethan grinned. Greg, along with Boone and his other friends, had been fiercely united in their dislike of his former fiancée. Unlike some of them, Greg had never been shy about expressing his opinion. That straightforward talk, while annoying at times, was one of the reasons they got along so well. Ethan knew he could trust Greg to have his back. Boone was the only other friend about whom he felt the same way.

"Lisa is old news," he told Greg. "I try not to think about her."

"But the woman's still in your head," Greg said. "I've seen you show a spark of interest in someone new a time or two, and then in a flash I can almost see the wheels in your head turning and that tape of her dumping you playing again. I think that's what I hate her for the most, not that she left, but that she ripped your soul to shreds in the process."

It was true, Ethan thought, but refused to admit. The fact that he let a woman like Lisa control his life, even a little, was crazy. Rationally, he knew that. That didn't make it any easier to burn that stupid mental tape Greg was talking about.

"No more," he insisted, more wistful than convinced that it was true.

"I hope so," Greg said. "So, who is she? The woman who's got you in a dither this morning?"

Ethan knew he wasn't going to get out of the clinic without filling Greg in. Unlike Ethan, Greg was a happily married father of three, who yearned to live vicariously through someone else's exciting social life. He'd pester Ethan until he spilled details.

"A woman named Samantha Castle," he told him.

Greg whistled.

Ethan regarded him with surprise. "You know her?"

"I used to admire all of the Castle sisters from afar. They were way out of my league. Samantha was something, even back then. I've spotted her a few times on TV, mostly commercials, but she was in an episode of

Law and Order not too long ago. Barely a walk-on, but I recognized those incredible long legs." He sighed. "What she did for a pair of high heels ought to be outlawed. It probably is in some states."

Ethan chuckled. "Yeah, I can see that. Of course, she wasn't wearing shoes when we met. Or much of anything else, for that matter."

Greg's jaw dropped. "You're kidding me!"

"I walked into the kitchen over at her grandmother's this morning and there she was, wearing nothing but an old football jersey, reaching up into a cupboard."

"How'd you know it was all she was wearing?"

"It was evident," Ethan said, unwilling to describe the glimpse he'd gotten of her delectable bottom. Some things a man didn't share, not even with his buddies.

"Holy mackerel," Greg said, his voice tinged with reverence. His expression suddenly turned speculative. "You said an old football jersey. Yours, by any chance?"

Ethan frowned. "How'd you know?"

"I remember hearing way back that she had a crush on you. A couple of guys we hung out with asked her out, but she turned them down flat. She was maybe fifteen, sixteen. You were a senior and all caught up with your adoring horde of beauties. If you ask me, not a one of them held a candle to her, but you were oblivious. I watched her stand on the fringes of a few beach parties, her heart in her eyes."

Since Boone had mentioned something similar about an old crush, Ethan couldn't dismiss the comment. "I'm surprised you didn't rush in to console her."

"Like I said, she was out of my league. And I had

enough issues living in the shadow of your popularity without risking rejection by one of your adoring fans."

Ethan knew perfectly well that Greg's ego had been healthy enough to withstand most anything back then. If Ethan had been a star on the offensive side of the football, Greg had been equally outstanding on defense. He'd even played both college and pro football briefly while studying medicine, a taxing combination that proved he had both brains and athletic skills, to say nothing of a whole lot of grit and determination.

And yet with all that potential to choose either a well-paying career in pro football or an equally successful path in medicine, he, just like Ethan, had opted for tours in the military. Unlike Ethan, though, Greg had come back in one piece, physically at least. Only a handful of people knew of the nightmares that tormented him, nightmares that left him emotionally exhausted and his wife and kids shaken.

Ethan's understanding of the toll PTSD had taken on his friend and Greg's insights into Ethan's struggles to cope with his physical disability had made them the perfect partners for this medical practice in a quiet, familiar community.

Ethan noted the signs of exhaustion on his friend's face and realized that all this focus on his social life was masking another of Greg's bad nights.

"Change and come running with me," he suggested, knowing that physical exertion could help them both. "Debra and Pam can hold the fort here and call us if there's a sudden rush of patients. It'll do you good. I might even let you beat me for a change."

Greg laughed. "Let me? Just who do you think you're

fooling? If you're brave enough to put a little money on this, I think we'll see that you're no match for me."

"You believe that?" Ethan mocked. "You're even more delusional than I thought."

"Oh, it's true. I might just give you a head start to even up your chances," Greg taunted. "Otherwise it wouldn't be fair to take your money."

Ethan scowled at that. "I'm faster these days, even on one good leg, than you are on two. You've gone soft, Knotts. Now, come on. Change those clothes and lace up your running shoes. I'll wait."

"Two minutes," Greg said, accepting the challenge as Ethan had known he would. "Loser buys lunch."

"Works for me," Ethan agreed.

"And I have a hankering for a burger at Castle's," Greg said, his expression gloating. "Just so you know what's at stake."

Ethan stared after him. Oh, he knew, all right. Lunch where there was every chance he'd catch another glimpse of Samantha? So much for clinging to whatever hard-won peace of mind he accomplished on this run.

Three

"You sent Ethan Cole to the house without warning me," Samantha said, giving her sister a swat. "How could you do that?"

"I didn't want you to tell me not to," Emily said blithely. "And to be totally accurate, Boone sent him. I didn't."

Samantha regarded her with a cynical look. "Not much of a defense, Em. Surely you can do better than that."

"Why should I?" Emily asked unrepentantly, then grinned. "How'd it go? Judging from your mood, I'm guessing it was exactly the push the two of you needed."

"We did not need a push, or a nudge or any other form of interference," Samantha retorted.

Emily merely rolled her eyes. "Resent me now, but once the two of you are as happy as Boone and me, you'll thank me."

"You think so?" Samantha said direly. "He caught me in his football jersey reaching for a mug in the kitchen cabinet. I think his eyes are still glazed over from the glimpse he probably caught of my bare bottom."

Emily burst out laughing. "Oh, that's perfect!"

"It wasn't perfect," Samantha contradicted. "It was awkward and embarrassing."

"But he's bound to be intrigued, don't you think? You do have an incredibly shapely bottom, after all. And Ethan hasn't dated a lot since his fiancée dumped him. He needs someone just like you to get him back into the game."

"Hold on," Samantha said as Emily's offhand remark sank in. "His fiancée dumped him? After he came home from Afghanistan?"

"I know. Really tacky, huh?" Emily said, her expression sobering. "I'd like to give that woman a piece of my mind."

Samantha agreed. "It was definitely a pretty shallow reaction, assuming it was about the loss of his leg," she said.

"Oh, it was all about that," Emily confirmed. "Boone says she told him she couldn't be with someone who wasn't whole or perfect or something like that."

"That's disgusting. No wonder he's so sensitive about how people are likely to react," Samantha said, seeing their conversation in a different light. "He admitted he'd expected me to be shallow and vain. Maybe it wasn't all about me being an actress, the way I took it. Maybe he feels that way about all women these days."

Emily's eyes widened. "He did not accuse you of such a thing! Of all the unmitigated gall. He hardly even knows you. There's not a shallow, vain bone in your body."

Samantha sighed at the surprisingly ardent defense. "I don't know about that. In my business I do spend a lot of time looking in the mirror and fretting over wrinkles."

"But that's just the business you're in," Emily said, loyally waving off the suggestion. "You don't judge *other* people by those standards. You'd never look down on someone who's not perfect."

"No, I wouldn't," Samantha agreed, thinking of that one moment when she'd gotten a real glimpse of vulnerability in Ethan's eyes. He'd expected to be judged or, worse, to be pitied. She couldn't imagine any man wanting pity, but for someone who'd demonstrated so much courage, it would be even more humiliating.

And Ethan, who'd once caught her attention with his charm, good looks and football prowess, was courageous. She had no doubts about that. Even in this morning's brief encounter, she'd realized the kind of strength it must have taken for him not only to survive his injury, but to move forward, to not accept limitations. In her view, that made him someone to be admired, and lifted her old secret crush to a whole new level.

Even so, she scowled at her sister. "Do not put me in that position again," she said flatly. "Ethan and I are adults. We're bound to run across each other in the next couple of weeks with all the wedding hoopla. We don't need you and Boone manufacturing excuses to throw us together. Understood?"

"Okay, fine," Emily conceded unhappily. "I was just trying to do something nice."

"The only way you could have been any more obvious would have been to send him over there with a big fat bow around his neck and a sign that said Keep Me."

Even as the words came out of her mouth, Samantha

caught the worrisome gleam in her sister's eyes. "Oh no, you don't. Your meddling days are over."

"If you say so," Emily replied dutifully. "But just so you know, I'm an amateur. The real pro, Grandmother, hasn't even gotten started."

And that, Samantha thought wearily, was scarier than just about anything else her sister could have said.

Cora Jane took one look at the sight of Ethan Cole and Greg Knotts walking into Castle's and slipped into the kitchen and called Emily.

"Have you finished with the dress fitting?" she asked, lowering her voice to a whisper.

"About five minutes ago," Emily said. "Why? And why are you whispering?"

"Because I don't want anyone to overhear me," Cora Jane said.

"Uh-oh," her granddaughter said, chuckling. "What is it you don't want Jerry to hear?" she asked pointedly, referring to Castle's longtime cook who was now courting Cora Jane. "What are you up to?"

"Stop asking so many questions," Cora Jane ordered. "Just pack up your sister and get over here to the restaurant."

"Hold on," Emily muttered. Seconds later, she was back on the line. "Does this have something to do with Ethan Cole? Is he at Castle's?"

"Just walked in," Cora Jane confirmed. "Now, will you get Samantha over here, or do I need to get Gabriella involved?"

To her annoyance, Emily laughed. "What's so funny?" Cora Jane demanded.

"Not a half hour ago I promised Samantha I'd stop meddling, but I warned her that you hadn't even gotten into the game yet."

"Well, now I see my chance," Cora Jane said. "Can you do this, or do I need to call and tell her I've slipped on the kitchen floor and think I might have broken my hip?"

"Heaven forbid!" Emily said fervently. "I'll get her over there. You just keep Ethan from getting away."

"Not a problem," Cora Jane said, "even if I have to sacrifice Castle's reputation for fast service to accomplish it. The man may not get his meal for an hour. Hurry up, honey bun. I don't want him to get too suspicious."

"Something tells me that ship has already sailed," Emily said. "But we'll be there as quickly as I can round up Samantha and get her out the door. She seems just a little obsessed with playing with the baby. I think her biological clock started ticking the second she picked up Daniella Jane. Frankly, I recognize the signs, because that kid does the same thing to me."

"All the more reason to see that Samantha and Ethan fall head over heels for each other by the time you and Boone head off on your honeymoon," Cora Jane said.

She hung up on Emily, found the server assigned to Ethan's table and warned her to take her time placing their order, then plastered a smile on her face and walked over to say hello.

"Good to see you, Greg," she said to Ethan's companion. "Ethan, I have to say I'm surprised to see you here. Did you finally come by for that meal I promised you after you took such good care of Rory Templeton and helped him get the rehab he needed so he could go back to work?"

Ethan gave her a sour look. "I'm here because I lost a bet," he admitted.

Greg grinned. "I outran him," he explained. "The man's so arrogant, he didn't think I stood a chance."

Cora Jane chuckled. "Well, whatever brings you by, I'm happy to see you, though I imagine you'll be around quite a lot over the next couple of weeks."

"That seems to be the plan," Ethan said, clearly not overjoyed about it.

"What he meant to say, Cora Jane, is that he's looking forward to the wedding," Greg interpreted. "We're still working on his manners now that he's back in polite society."

"Bite me," Ethan murmured in an undertone, though he managed a contrite look for Cora Jane's benefit. "Sorry."

"Don't apologize on my account. I've heard plenty worse. Now, tell me, has your waitress taken your order?"

"She has," Greg said cheerfully. "She told us it should be right out."

Cora Jane nodded. "Let me check on it. The kitchen's been pretty backed up today. I'll have her refresh your drinks while you're waiting."

As she was walking away, she overheard Ethan say, "She's up to something. You mark my words."

No sooner had he made the statement than he added, his tone a mix of triumph and dismay, "And there she is now!"

Cora Jane turned in time to see Samantha being nudged along by Emily, Samantha's expression just as dour as Ethan's.

"Well, look who's here!" Emily said cheerfully. "Mind if we join you, Ethan?"

Without waiting for a response, she pulled two chairs up to the table and gestured for Samantha to sit in one of them.

"I'm going to wash my hands," Samantha said, stalking off.

Cora Jane intercepted her as she headed, instead, straight for the front door. Samantha whirled on her.

"Don't think I don't know you're behind this," she said irritably. "I heard enough of that call you made to Emily to know she was up to something. What I can't figure out is why she'd take the chance of me strangling her not a half hour after I'd told her to stay out of my personal life. You must have been very persuasive."

"We just love you, honey bun," Cora Jane soothed. "We want you to be happy."

"Shoving me down the throat of a man who's not the least bit interested is not the way to accomplish that."

"Oh, posh!" Cora Jane said. "Of course he's interested. You didn't see the way his eyes lit up when you walked in the door just now. I did."

"What you saw, if anything, were sparks of anger over the meddling," Samantha told her.

"I know what I saw," Cora Jane insisted. "And you don't want to offend the best man and create tension before your sister's wedding, do you? Now, go on over there and be nice."

"Is that an order?" Samantha asked.

Cora Jane leveled a look into her eyes. "Does it need to be?" she inquired, holding her granddaughter's gaze.

Samantha finally sighed. "I'll go, but I won't like it."

Cora Jane knew it wasn't smart, but she couldn't help chuckling. "You sounded exactly like that when you were a toddler and we forced you to do something you didn't think you wanted to do."

"If you're trying to insult me by suggesting I'm behaving like a child, I don't much care."

"Actually I was just trying to remind you that in just about every one of those instances, we turned out to be right and you had yourself a good time." She touched Samantha's cheek with a soothing caress. "I'm doubting this will be an exception, unless you work hard at making it one."

"This is the one and only tiny bit of slack I'm going to cut you," Samantha warned. "I will not cave in again."

"Of course not," Cora Jane said, wisely hiding a smirk this time. "I wouldn't expect you to."

Samantha gave her a suspicious look, then headed back to the table where Ethan looked only slightly less irritated than she did. Oh well, Cora Jane thought, relationships had started with far less in common than mutual annoyance at a third party.

Satisfied, she returned to the kitchen, where Jerry turned from the stove and frowned at her. "I thought the only pot-stirring going on around here was supposed to be in the kitchen."

"You do your stirring. I'll do mine," she retorted.

"One of these days your meddling is going to blow up in your face," he warned. "Those girls of yours are independent thinkers, just the way you taught them to be."

"Well, of course they are," she said proudly. "It doesn't mean that one of them can't use a nudge from me from time to time. I don't hear Emily or Gabi complaining, now that their lives are just about settled."

"Samantha's a different kettle of fish," he warned. "So is Ethan Cole. Remember, I was with you the day you threw out the first bit of bait a few months ago. He didn't bite. In fact, he made his lack of interest pretty clear. You might need to reassess your target and your tactics."

Cora Jane shook her head. "I know what I know," she insisted. "I've known Ethan since he was a boy. Those two are perfect for each other. They just have to get out of their own way and things will fall right into place."

"I hope you're right," Jerry said, regarding her tenderly. "I know how badly you want this to work out. You're convinced if they do, you'll finally have all your girls back here in Sand Castle Bay and a dozen great-grandbabies underfoot eventually."

"And what would be wrong with that?"

"Not a thing. I just hope you haven't misjudged the situation this time."

Cora Jane heard the genuine worry in his voice, and though she'd never in a million years admit it, he gave her pause. Jerry didn't meddle, but he was a keen observer, especially of her and the granddaughters she loved. Could he have gotten it right? Were Samantha and Ethan a bad match? Or were they both so stubborn they'd fight fate just to spite her?

She thought about it, then thought some more, considering what she'd just seen with her own eyes. No, she concluded. Ethan and Samantha were every bit as destined to be together as Emily and Boone had been or Gabi and Wade. She was sure of it.

And in a lot of years of living, her gut hadn't steered her wrong on more than one or two occasions. This wasn't going to be another one of them. She'd see to it.

Samantha squirmed uncomfortably under Ethan's cool gaze. Not even Emily's steady stream of chatter or Greg's determinedly upbeat efforts to keep the conversation flowing could cut through the tension at the table. It was getting on her nerves.

When she'd finally had enough, she stood up. "Ethan, could I speak to you outside, please?"

Every single person there looked startled by the request, but Ethan rose as if she'd just offered to show him an escape route from a particularly unsavory prison.

Casting one last scowl at her sister, Samantha led the way onto the deck at the side of the restaurant and headed toward the railing where they'd have a view of the ocean across the street. Thanks to an offshore storm, the surf was churning, reflecting her own emotions. She drew in a deep breath of the refreshing, salty air and turned to face Ethan.

"I'm sorry," she said. "I should have figured out that Emily and Grandmother had hatched some kind of plot the minute Emily started insisting we come here for lunch."

Ethan's hard expression eased slightly. "Not entirely your fault. This is your family's restaurant, and I did come here, after all. I knew there was a chance you'd be around."

She regarded him curiously. "So, why did you come?"

He shrugged. "Lost a bet, to be perfectly honest."

Samantha's lips twitched at his resigned tone. "To whom?"

"Greg," he admitted sheepishly. "I'm thinking his matchmaking gene just might rival Emily's and Cora Jane's. If I'd had any idea he had such a devious, romantic streak, I'd never have opened that clinic with him."

"So, what are we going to do about this? We've been warned. We know what they're up to. Just hours ago we vowed to end the madness, and here we are again. Are we naive or just no match for their ingenuity?"

"No idea," he conceded. "I'm way out of my element here. Oh, there have been a few people who've tried to set me up ever since my engagement ended, but most of them gave up eventually. If you say no often enough and forcefully enough, people stop trying."

"So, you're dead set against ever getting involved in another relationship?" she asked, hoping there was no hint of disappointment in her voice.

"Pretty much."

"All because of a woman who, if you'll pardon me for saying so, sounds about as sensitive as a slug?"

Ethan smiled at that. "That pretty much sums up Lisa."

"Well, that's just crazy," she said. "If you can see her for the kind of woman she was, then you shouldn't let her have any influence whatsoever over the choices you make now."

He gave her a wry look. "So I've been told."

"You don't buy it?"

He hesitated, then said, "Maybe we should come at this from a different direction. You're younger than I am, but if you'll pardon me for stating the obvious, you're not a kid. Why aren't you married? Or have you been?"

Samantha winced at having the tables turned on her.

"No marriages," she conceded. "I guess I never met the right man."

"So it's not because some insensitive clod broke your heart?"

She thought about it, not sure how to explain the choices she'd made. "Amazingly, I don't have any ill will toward any of the men I've dated, not even toward the man I was pretty sure I loved."

"What happened with him?"

"He was an actor, which isn't always the smartest match for an actress, even though you both understand the demands of the business. That's the upside."

"And the downside?"

"My career took off for a time. His tanked. He couldn't handle it." It sounded so simple, but it had been the most painful period of her life. No matter how she'd fought to keep silent about her own successes to keep him from feeling like a failure, it hadn't been enough.

Ethan gave her a sympathetic look. "Pride can be a pain, can't it?"

"Masculine pride surely can," she responded agreeably. "I'm surprised you can admit that. After all, wasn't it your pride your fiancée hurt, as much as your heart?" She studied him with a worried gaze. "Or did she really break your heart?"

For a minute the look on Ethan's face suggested she'd gone too far. His jaw tensed, his eyes sparked and then, in an instant, a smile tugged at his lips.

"You don't mince words, do you?"

"I don't see a lot of point in it, no."

"That's a refreshing change," he told her. "I've spent a lot of time in recent years with people who are way too careful about speaking their minds around me. Even if what they want to say has nothing at all to do with my injury, they seem to think I'm too fragile to be challenged."

"So they think you can't take the truth?"

"Probably. And, to be honest, when I first got back and was going through rehab, I probably couldn't. If anyone even looked at me the wrong way, I'd explode. Believe me, I was impossible to get along with."

"I imagine that's just as much part of the healing process as learning to deal with the prosthetic."

He looked surprised once more by her insight. "It was. A few people, like Boone and Greg, figured that out and never gave up on me. I'd kick 'em out, but they kept right on coming back."

"Unlike your fiancée?" she said, disliking the woman intensely.

Surprisingly, he shook his head. "It wasn't my temper that pushed her away. I don't think I could have blamed her for that. No, she stuck it out until I was on my feet, so to speak. Then she bailed. She said she couldn't cope with me not being the man she'd fallen in love with, as if my leg were the most important part of my anatomy and losing it made me less of a man."

Samantha shook her head. "The woman was an idiot."

Ethan laughed. "Thanks for the ardent defense, but maybe we should get back to our immediate problem. What do we do about the meddlers?"

"Stay alert. Let them do their thing, I guess," she suggested, though she was unconvinced that the strategy would work.

"Seriously?"

"It'll make them happy to try," she said, "and there's nothing that says we have to get with the program, right?"

He held her gaze for a minute, just long enough for a spark of sexual tension to sizzle between them. "Nothing," he agreed, though he too sounded a little unsure of himself when he said it.

Samantha held out her hand. "Friends, right? We have a deal."

Ethan took her hand in his. She couldn't help noticing that his grip was strong, his fingers long and slender. It was the sure and steady hand of a surgeon.

"We have a deal," he said.

He was awfully slow to release her hand. When he did, his eyes were troubled.

"Everything okay?" she asked.

"Sure."

"Ethan, I thought being straight with each other was an implied part of our bargain," she scolded.

He gave her a rueful look. "I have this odd premonition that we've just made a fool's bargain."

"Oh?"

"I'm thinking that unless we're very, very careful, we're going to blow this whole friendship thing to smithereens," he said direly.

Samantha had to fight to hide the laugh that bubbled up at his unmistakable frustration, because the truth was, on some level, that was the best news she'd heard in a very long time.

Four

"So, when are you seeing her again?" Greg asked Ethan as they drove back to the clinic. There was no mistaking the spark of mischief in his eyes as he spoke.

Ethan frowned at him. "No idea what you're talking about," he insisted.

"You and Samantha. Don't even try to deny that something happened when the two of you were out on the deck. You came back looking like two cats that had managed to dine on some very tasty canaries."

"What a lovely analogy," Ethan commented. "You obviously have a poet's way with words."

"Not exactly the point," Greg said. "Let's stick to the accuracy of my assessment. When are the two of you getting together again?"

"Whenever circumstances dictate," Ethan said irritably.

Suddenly Greg's eyes lit up as if he'd just discovered the secrets of the universe. "And you're not happy about waiting for those circumstances to roll around, are you? Oh boy, I knew it! You've got the hots for her."

"Once more you're demonstrating your way with words," Ethan grumbled. "I do not have the hots for anybody. Turns out she's a nice woman, not at all what I expected."

"Beautiful, too. Do not try to tell me you didn't notice. Otherwise I'm going to have to check your vital signs the second we get back to the clinic."

"I noticed," Ethan said tightly. "Will you please drop this?"

"I'm thinking I probably shouldn't," Greg said cheerfully. "I'm thinking you need me to be a thorn in your side, a burr under your butt, as it were, until you finally get back in the dating game."

"Dating is *not* a game I want to play," Ethan claimed, though he was clearly not convincing his friend. He'd been happily protecting his heart for a good long time now. He saw no reason for that to change. The last time he'd taken a risk on love, it hadn't worked out so well.

"Ah, but sometimes life just comes along and gives you an unexpected chance to reach for your heart's desire, ready or not," Greg said. "A smart man seizes those moments."

Ethan scowled at him. "Heart's desire? Game? Which is it? How exactly do you see this going?"

"What I see isn't important," Greg insisted. "What do you see? And do not try to tell me you're oblivious to the possibilities."

"I see disaster waiting to happen," Ethan said with a level of frustration he hadn't felt in months, maybe not even years. Shouldn't he have a better grip on his own blasted destiny? Surely it was just a matter of willpower. If he wanted to resist Samantha, he could do it, the same way he'd avoided every other entanglement since Lisa had so unceremoniously dumped him. Of course, it didn't help that his friend refused to let the matter drop.

"Because you're not really attracted to her?" Greg persisted.

"No," he bit out.

"Because you don't think she's attracted to you?"

He recalled the look that had simmered between them more than once on the deck. Whatever she'd said about friendship, she was interested in more, no question about it. Was he insane for not taking her up on it? After all, it wasn't as if she'd be around for long. Her life was elsewhere. They could indulge in a satisfying two-week fling, no harm, no foul. Greg would certainly approve. Boone probably would, too, though he might get a little protective since Samantha was about to be his sister-in-law.

"It doesn't matter if she's attracted to me or not. We've agreed to be friends, period. We are not succumbing to the pressures of the meddlers, you included."

Greg stared at him incredulously. "Whose dumbass idea was that?"

"Hers," Ethan said. "I agreed."

Greg shook his head sorrowfully. "I always thought Lisa was the idiot. Now I'm wondering if you're one iota better."

Ethan frowned. "What's that supposed to mean?"

"This gorgeous woman, who's had a thing for you for like a million years, has been delivered practically into your arms and you're content with friendship." Greg shook his head. "It's pitiful, man. Just pitiful."

Ethan was beginning to think maybe his friend was right, but that didn't mean he intended to do a single thing to change the rules he and Samantha had just negotiated. There was safety in following those rules. There was the peace and serenity he'd claimed he wanted for years now.

And, sadly, there was total, unrelenting boredom, he admitted only to himself.

Samantha was pacing the floor with Daniella Jane, who was impatiently and loudly proclaiming that it was dinnertime. Even with the baby's cries echoing in Samantha's head, she felt this incredibly fierce tug as she held her niece.

"Come on, sweetie," she murmured soothingly. "Don't let your mommy walk in the door and get some crazy idea that I'm a terrible aunt. Settle down. Dinner is on its way, I promise."

Dinner, of course, was tied directly to Gabi's arrival. She was still nursing the baby. Normally she kept Daniella Jane with her at the gallery for that very reason, but she'd taken a visible deep breath and agreed to let her daughter come home with Samantha an hour ago. It had definitely been an act of faith. The way Samantha had heard it, the baby had barely been out of Gabi's sight since the day she was born.

Today's reluctant concession was supposed to be a win-win, giving Gabi an uninterrupted hour to get some work done while Samantha bonded with her niece. She had no idea how things were going on Gabi's end, but she wasn't exactly bonding. If anything, she felt as if she was selfishly depriving her niece of sustenance to fulfill her own maternal yearnings.

The back door of Gram's house burst open, and Gabi's guy, Wade Johnson, came in, grinning.

"That's my girl," he said, reaching for the baby, whose cries instantly changed into gurgles of delight. He winked at Gabi. "She's already learned to let the world know when she's displeased. Nobody will be walking all over this woman."

Samantha chuckled. Wade might not be Dani's biological father, but he was already a dedicated parent. "You do know that you've just given me a terrible inferiority complex, don't you?" she said. "I may give up on the whole motherhood thing after the way that child started cooing the instant I handed her off to you."

"Don't take it personally," he said, holding the baby high in the air. "Dani and I have a deal."

"A deal?" Samantha questioned, smiling.

"Yep. We work at being so good together that there's not a chance her mama will change her mind about marrying me. Right, baby girl?"

Daniella Jane giggled happily.

"So, where is Gabi?" Wade asked. "It's not like her to be late for this little one's suppertime. Did you convince her to take a nap?"

"Are you kidding me? She's using my offer to watch the baby to get some work done. You can take the workaholic out of a high-powered job, but you can't take the drive and ambition out of her. The success of that studio the two of you created is her personal mission."

"It was supposed to be a low-key alternative to that last nightmare job," Wade grumbled.

"Sorry. Gabi's not made for low-key." She studied him closely, aware of what a laid-back kind of man he was. "That's not a deal-breaker for you, is it?"

"There are no deal-breakers for me when it comes to Gabi," he said flatly. "She's it for me. If she's happy, I'm happy."

Samantha barely contained a sigh of envy at the conviction she heard in his voice. Boone sounded the same way when he talked about Emily. Was she ever going to find the same sort of devotion? Would anyone ever look at her as if she were the sun, moon and stars all rolled into one?

Gabi sailed into the house just then, her expression frantic. "Is the baby okay? I know I'm late, and I know how fussy she gets if she isn't fed right on time."

"She definitely made her feelings known," Samantha told her. "But Wade showed up with his magic touch, and she's been good as gold ever since."

Gabi bent down and gave Wade a lingering kiss. "Thanks," she murmured as she took the baby from him.

"Sit," he said, pulling her down beside him.

"But Dani needs to be fed," Gabi protested.

"And here's as good a place as any," he said, his gaze locked with hers.

When the baby settled into place, Wade grazed his knuckles gently over her cheek in a touch so tender it brought tears to Samantha's eyes. With the three of them so absorbed with this moment, she felt like a fifth wheel.

"I'll get dinner started," she murmured, though she doubted anyone heard her.

In the kitchen, she decided on pasta with a simple

marinara sauce. While the water for the pasta was boiling, she tossed a salad with fresh lettuce and tomatoes from the local farmer's stand where she'd stopped on her way home, added a bit of spring onion and blue cheese and then her own personal vinaigrette. She'd make her meal out of this, giving a token nod to her need to watch her weight.

She'd just minced some garlic into a skillet with olive oil and was preparing to add the tomato sauce when Cora Jane, Jerry and Emily came in.

"It smells fabulous in here," Emily said, sniffing the air. "I had no idea you could cook."

"All Castles need to know their way around a kitchen," Samantha recited, grinning at Cora Jane when she said it. "How many times did you say that to us when we were here in the summer?"

"Not enough, apparently, since not a one of you went into the restaurant business," Cora Jane said. She checked on the sauce, then eyed Samantha speculatively. "Of course, maybe it's not too late."

"Uh-oh," Emily teased. "Grandmother's got that look in her eye. You'd better run for your life, Samantha, or you'll be running Castle's before the summer's out. If that sauce is as delicious as it smells, there will be pasta dishes on the menu and you'll be in the kitchen making them."

Samantha handed the spoon she'd been using to stir the sauce to Cora Jane. "Not a prayer," she said at once. "This is your domain, Grandmother. I'm just an innocent bystander. I'm only in the kitchen because Gabi, Wade and the baby are having family time in the living room."

"And you let them chase you off?" Cora Jane asked.

"They didn't even know I was in the room, much less that I'd left," Samantha said. "I think we'd better get a wedding date on the calendar for those two soon."

"We're eloping," Gabi announced, arriving in the kitchen just in time to overhear the comment. "All this fuss is way too much."

"You'll do no such thing," Cora Jane said, looking horrified. "Get Wade in here right this minute, and I'll set him straight about that."

"He's putting the baby down," Gabi said. "And he and I are agreed about this. No hoopla when our time comes. Just a quiet ceremony with family."

Samantha noticed the color rising in Emily's cheeks at Gabi's words.

"Are you suggesting that my wedding is over-the-top?" Emily asked, an edge to her voice.

"No one is saying any such thing, honey bun," Cora Jane said quickly, shooting a pointed look in Gabi's direction.

"I'm just saying it's a lot of work and stress for a party," Gabi said defensively. "But I certainly don't begrudge you and Boone for having the wedding of your dreams. It's just not Wade and me."

Emily burst into tears at that and fled out the back door.

"That girl's nerves are getting to her," Cora Jane assessed. "I don't think it's all about the wedding, either. I suspect there's something else on her mind."

"Such as?" Samantha asked.

Cora Jane huffed a sigh of frustration. "No idea."

"I'd better go," Gabi said with a sigh. "I should have

kept my big mouth shut. I know she's sensitive about the wedding spinning a little out of control."

Samantha held up a hand. "I'll go. I know I'm not the traditional peacemaker around her, but I'm thinking she might not want to hear anything you have to say right now."

"Go ahead," Cora Jane said. "I'll finish up here and get dinner on the table. Don't be too long, okay?"

Samantha kicked off her shoes on the porch and walked barefoot through the grass down to the pier. Emily was sitting on the bench at the end, her shoulders hunched, her face streaked with tears.

"You probably agree with Gabi," she accused when Samantha sat next to her.

"Not the way you're thinking," Samantha said.

"See, I knew it! You always think I make lousy choices."

Samantha was saddened by yet more evidence that the two of them had a long way to go before they'd ever understand each other.

"And you always anticipate the worst from me," Samantha replied quietly. "Did you not hear what I said? I told you that though I agreed with Gabi, it was probably not in the way you were thinking."

Emily scowled at her. "You either agree or you don't."

"Does everything always have to be either black or white to you?"

"It generally is," Emily said.

"Oh, sweetie, there is an awful lot of gray in the world. Believe me, you'll figure that out eventually."

"And now you're saying I'm not that experienced or wise or something," Emily said, obviously taking offense when none had been intended.

Samantha frowned at her. "And people think I'm the drama queen in the family," she murmured dryly, knowing the comment would only add fuel to the fire. "Will you please just listen for two seconds?"

"Go ahead," Emily muttered.

"I agree with Gabi that the two of you are very different people. In fact, the three of us are very different women, despite a few similarities here and there. I think you started dreaming about the perfect wedding on the day you first laid eyes on Boone. When things fell apart and you went off to follow your career, that dream didn't die. It was just put on hold."

She took heart from the fact that Emily was still paying attention. "The minute the two of you were reunited and engaged, it's not even a tiny bit surprising that you wanted the whole fairy-tale wedding you'd always envisioned." She tucked a finger under Emily's chin. "And there is nothing wrong with that, you hear me. Nothing! None of us begrudge you this moment, Em. Not even a tiny bit. Every woman should have the wedding of her dreams."

"But Gabi said—"

Samantha interrupted. "All Gabi said was that she didn't want this same kind of hoopla. Gabi probably doesn't even want to take off a couple of hours from work to go down to the courthouse to get married."

Emily giggled at that just as Samantha had hoped she would.

"You're probably right," Emily conceded. "She's pretty focused on the studio these days, and the baby, and Wade. The ceremony is just some kind of technicality to get out of the way."

"Exactly," Samantha said. "And that's okay, too, if it suits the two of them."

"I suppose, even if I do think it's kind of sad." Emily studied her curiously. "What about you? What kind of wedding do you want?"

"I haven't looked that far ahead," Samantha said, her tone neutral. "After all, there's not even a man in my life at the moment."

"Liar," Emily taunted. "You've seen every kind of wedding imaginable on those soaps you used to do from time to time. Which one struck you as the most devastatingly romantic?"

Samantha leaned back, finally relaxing now that the crisis appeared past, and gave Emily's question some thought.

"A destination wedding," she said eventually. "On the beach, maybe, with the wind in my hair and the sand beneath my feet."

When she glanced at Emily, there was a sheen of tears in her eyes.

"It sounds perfect," Emily whispered. "And it does sound like you. It needs to be at sunset, though, with all that glorious color in the sky." She glanced over at Samantha and added, "I hope you get it."

"One of these days, if I'm lucky," Samantha said.

"Maybe it'll be even sooner than you think," Emily replied, a glint in her eyes. "And last time I looked, Sand Castle Bay was known all over as a terrific spot for a destination wedding."

Samantha frowned at her. "Do not even go there, you hear me? Or I will take back every nice thing I just said about you."

"I can take it," Emily said, grinning. "It'll be worth it to watch this thing with you and Ethan unfold. Don't forget I was right there with the two of you today when you came back inside the restaurant. Sparks were flying all over the place. It's a wonder Greg and I didn't get burned."

"Didn't it occur to you that those sparks were anger directed your way for the meddling you did to throw us together for the second time in one day?"

Emily waved off the suggestion. "Not a chance. This was all about a man and a woman who've taken a real shine to each other. Pheromones, chemistry, whatever you want to call it."

"Enough!" Samantha said, her voice rising as she tried to get the point across once and for all. "Ethan and I agreed to be friends, nothing more."

Emily merely laughed. "I know. I can just hear the two of you being all rational and determined. I had a similar conversation with Boone when I first came back to town." A grin spread. "I'll tell you now exactly what you told me then."

"What?"

"That all that denial is what's going to make this so much fun to watch."

"Enjoy yourself, but I think you're going to be disappointed," Samantha told her. "Now I have another question for you before we go back inside and you make peace with Gabi."

"What's that?" Emily asked, not arguing that it was up to her to apologize.

"Grandmother's worried that there's something else on your mind. Is there? Are you worried about the wedding? About Boone? About his nasty ex-in-laws? Anything else?"

Emily's expression immediately shut down in a way that was more revealing than words would have been.

"Emily?" she prodded.

"I don't know if Boone loves living in Los Angeles as much as I do," she admitted eventually.

Samantha had wondered when that issue was going to show up. "It's still new to him."

"But Sand Castle Bay is in his blood."

"Has he said anything about coming back?"

"No, and I thought when he moved out there to open this restaurant, it would be okay."

"Maybe it will be. Ask him what he's feeling."

"I'm half afraid to. What if he wants me to move back here, after all?"

"What if he does? What will you do?"

Emily sighed and regarded Samantha with a bleak expression. "I honestly have no idea."

"Then, sweetie, you need to talk to him now, before this wedding."

Emily shook her head. "No, absolutely not."

"But—"

"No," Emily repeated, then stood up. "We need to go back inside. I have some fence-mending to do."

She took off for the house, leaving Samantha to stare after her, far more worried now than she'd been when she'd come outside.

On Sunday evening, Cora Jane looked around the backyard with satisfaction. With the help of Jerry, Gabi, Wade and Samantha, it had been turned into a showcase of tiny lights, huge pots of colorful summer flowers and tables laden with food and gifts for Emily's bridal shower.

Samantha draped an arm around her shoulders. "You've outdone yourself, Grandmother."

Cora Jane glanced up, blinking back unexpected tears. "I can't believe the first of my girls is getting married in less than two weeks. I've waited for this for so long." She gave Samantha a pointed look. "I thought you'd be the first, you know."

"Just because I'm older?"

"No, because boys were flocking around from the time you hit your teens, and I know for a fact it was no different when you got to New York. Every time we spoke, you mentioned one man or another."

Samantha shrugged. "None of them stuck. I want to find what Em has with Boone or what Gabi's found with Wade. I guess the Castle women are all romantics at heart. We want the happily-ever-after. At least I was smart enough not to settle for less than that."

Cora Jane nodded approvingly. "You know, I think your daddy always sold you short. He thought just because you wanted to be an actress, you were flighty or something, but your mama and I always knew better. You've got a good, level head on your shoulders. You know what's important. And you'll find the right man. There's not a doubt in my mind."

Samantha gave her a hug. "Thanks for your faith in me. As for Dad, he hasn't exactly been attuned to any of us and the skills we possess."

"No, he hasn't," Cora Jane said. "I do think he's coming around, though." She glanced across the lawn to where Sam was conferring with Jerry over the grill. "Look at him. Not only is he here, but he's really trying to fit in."

"How'd you pull that off, especially for a bridal shower on a Sunday night? Tomorrow's a workday, after all. I can practically hear him making a million and one excuses for not coming."

Cora Jane chuckled. "Probably double that, but I trumped 'em all. I told him to be here. That it was an order from his mother and I'd be disappointed in him if he didn't show up for his daughter's big evening."

"Good for you. I know it means a lot to Em that he came. But aren't he and Jerry going to feel like odd men out at a party crowded with women?"

"Oh, the party isn't just for women," Cora Jane said blithely. "Emily wouldn't hear of that. There will be plenty of men around, too."

She saw the quick rise of understanding in Samantha's eyes and then the deepening of the color in her cheeks. "I imagine Ethan's on this coed guest list," she said stiffly.

"Of course," Cora Jane responded. "The entire wedding party was invited."

"Of course they were," Samantha said, shaking her head. "You and Emily don't give up, do you?"

"I have no idea what you mean," Cora Jane insisted, trying out the innocent look she'd had years to practice, but still hadn't exactly perfected. Judging from Samantha's skeptical reaction, it wasn't terribly effective this time, either.

"Do you have any idea how much you and Emily are

humiliating me?" Samantha asked. "Ethan's going to get the idea that I'm desperate or something."

"Oh, honey bun, there's no chance of that," Cora Jane assured her. "Any man looking at you is only going to wonder why no one has had the sense to snap you up. You're beautiful and, even more important, you have this huge heart. You're smart and talented and quick-witted. Any man would be lucky to have a chance with you. And a smart man wouldn't blow that chance."

Samantha looked pained by the recitation of her attributes, but by the end she was grinning. "So you're saying if Ethan doesn't take you up on this golden opportunity you're throwing his way, then he's a dolt?"

Cora Jane chuckled. "Well, I might have put it a bit more diplomatically, but yes, that's exactly what I'd conclude. Just so you know, though, I think Ethan is an awfully smart man. Now go inside and put on something pretty."

Samantha looked down at her capris and the colorful matching blouse that even Cora Jane recognized as coming from a famed New York designer's summer collection. She'd seen an ad for it in *Vogue* or one of those other fashion magazines that the girls had left lying around the house.

"Prettier than this?" Samantha inquired doubtfully.

"I'm thinking a sundress," Cora Jane said. "One that shows a little cleavage."

"Grandmother!"

Cora Jane wasn't bothered by the dismay she heard in Samantha's voice. She merely held her gaze. "Can you think of a better way to let a man know what he's missing?"

This time Samantha groaned, but she turned and headed for the house. Of course, it was anybody's guess if she'd come back wearing that sundress Cora Jane had recommended or something that covered her from head to toe. The girl did have a perverse streak that kicked in when she'd been pushed too far. Cora Jane realized that she might have tiptoed a little too close to that particular boundary, but she still had high hopes that the evening would end with one more breach in those walls of defenses those two young people had around their hearts.

Five

"Would you get a move on?" Boone called out as he paced Ethan's living room. "We're going to be late. If we are, Emily will have a cow."

"You could go on without me," Ethan called back. "I'm perfectly capable of driving myself over to Cora Jane's."

"But the question is, will you?" Boone replied. "I've been getting the distinct sense that you're not exactly getting with the program. One of my assignments for tonight is to make sure you show up and play nice."

Ethan walked out of his bedroom, a scowl firmly in place. "If, by that, you mean that I haven't tumbled straight into bed with the maid of honor, then you're right. I'm not getting with the program. Has it occurred to any of you that Samantha is no happier about this matchmaking scheme than I am? You're humiliating her."

For just an instant, Boone looked nonplused. "Seriously?"

"Seriously. My God, man, you're all but offering her up like a sacrifice in some ancient ritual. I'm surprised she hasn't packed her bags and flown back to New York."

"She'd never do that to Emily," Boone said, though he looked vaguely shaken by Ethan's assessment. "At least I don't think she would."

"You said there was some sort of issue between the two of them. Can you see any possible way that this is helping, rather than making things worse? How would you feel if I kept pushing somebody on you after you'd declared you had no interest?"

Ethan realized he'd taken the debate one step too far when amusement sparkled in Boone's eyes.

"You did your share of pushing when Emily and I were trying to put things back together and you thought we were getting offtrack."

"Entirely different," Ethan claimed. "You were meant to be together. That much was clear even to someone as antiromance as I am."

"And you and Samantha aren't meant to be?"

"We aren't," Ethan said adamantly. "As my friend, you certainly are well aware of my stance on relationships and love. I'm a nonbeliever."

"You're just scared," Boone countered.

Ethan gave him a scowl that should have shaken him to his core.

Instead, Boone looked amused. "Okay, let's say you're not terrified of taking a risk. What makes you think you know what she's thinking? Exactly how much time have you spent with her?"

"Come on, Boone. It's plain as day. We couldn't be any more different. She's a glamorous actress living in New York. I'm a small-town, one-legged doctor," he said with brutal honesty. "It just doesn't compute."

The expression in Boone's eyes turned surprisingly angry. "If I ever hear you sell yourself short like that again, I swear I will knock you off that good leg of yours and pummel some sense into you."

"Just being realistic," Ethan said, though he was admittedly a little touched by Boone's quick and vehement defense. For a guy who'd once looked up at Ethan as if he were some sort of hero, Boone didn't seem the least bit shy about calling it as he saw it now. He was the kind of friend a man needed, even if Ethan wondered whether or not he deserved it.

"Nonsense," Boone declared. "Give the woman a chance. That's all any of us are asking. What's the worst-case scenario? You'll have spent a couple of weeks in the company of a very sexy woman. No harm, no foul."

Since a similar thought had crossed Ethan's mind, he could hardly muster a believable argument against the casual interlude Boone was describing. It just felt wrong, though. Someone was bound to get hurt. No matter how innocently things started, in his experience someone *always* got hurt.

"And if one of us winds up getting hurt?" he asked Boone. "Are you going to carve out my heart if it's Samantha who gets burned?"

"I'm pretty sure Samantha can take care of herself." Boone leveled a curious look at him. "Are you thinking that could happen to you, though? Are you more attracted to Samantha than I realized?"

"Absolutely not," Ethan said, probably a little too

forcefully. "I'm just saying it could happen to either one of us. Do you and Emily and Cora Jane and whoever else is involved in this romantic conspiracy want to take responsibility for that? Because if you push and things blow up, that's on you, too."

"I think we're all looking at the upside," Boone said. "We're very big on happy endings these days."

Ethan shook his head. "Yeah, you would be, but not all of us are that lucky, pal. I speak from experience. Maybe you should leave this alone and stop tampering with fate."

Just then B.J., Boone's son, walked inside, a scowl on his face. "Are you guys ever coming? Emily just called your cell phone, Dad. I think she's getting ticked off because we're not there."

Ethan grinned at the sudden panic on the groom's face. "And maybe *that's* the relationship you should be focusing on," he advised his friend. "That's all I'm saying."

"Okay, yeah. I get it," Boone said.

But even though his words sounded sincere enough, Ethan had a hunch the meddling was far from over.

Samantha was very much aware of Ethan standing across the lawn all alone, a can of soda in his hand. He looked as if he'd rather be just about any place other than a bridal shower overrun by eager matchmakers. She could relate. Since she was probably the only one there who could, she crossed the yard to join him, taking two fresh glasses of champagne with her.

"You look as if you're in need of this," she commented.

He lifted a brow. "I don't think champagne is the answer."

"Then what is?" she asked, downing the last of her own drink. She'd discovered that two glasses was just the right amount to create a happy little buzz. Three was apparently one too many, she concluded as she wobbled slightly.

He gave her a wry look. "Keeping my mind on full alert."

"Ah, to avoid all the devious scheming going on around here tonight," she concluded.

"Exactly."

"Want to go for a walk, instead? I think I might be the tiniest bit tipsy. A walk would be good."

"It will also lend fodder to the family gossip mill," he suggested.

She airily waved off the warning. "Oh, so what? We're tougher than that."

He smiled. "If you say so."

They'd walked down the driveway and started around the block when she paused and twirled around. It made her head spin, which was unfortunate, but she managed to stay upright with Ethan's steady hand on her elbow.

"You okay?" he asked worriedly. "Any particular reason you decided to do that twirl?"

"I was showing off my dress. Do you like it? Grandmother thought you might."

She watched as Ethan's gaze dipped to the cleavage displayed by the dress's neckline. There was no mistaking the heated reaction as his gaze lingered. She giggled.

"She was right. You do like it, don't you? Especially the neckline. I've absolutely got to give that woman more credit. She is very, very wise. And sneaky." She bobbed her head. "Yep, she is definitely sneaky."

Ethan sighed. "Exactly how tipsy are you, Samantha?"

"Not tipsy," she insisted. "That's not possible. I can hold my liquor. I've only had three, or maybe four, glasses of champagne." She glanced at the empty glass in her hand. "Could be five. I just finished the one I brought for you."

"Have you eaten today?"

She thought about it. She couldn't recall having anything since the bowl of cereal and yogurt she'd had for breakfast. "Not so much."

"Then let's get you back to the party and get some food into you."

"More champagne would be lovely," she told him.

"I don't think so."

"Okay," she said compliantly, clearly startling him. Surprising him felt good. She couldn't help wondering what he thought of her, especially after all the interfering attempts to push them together. "Am I pitiful, Ethan?"

He stared at her with a shocked expression. "Absolutely not. Why would you ask something like that?"

"Because no one in my family seems to think I can find a man on my own."

"Then that would have to make me pitiful, too, since I'm the one they've targeted for you. Do you think I'm pitiful?"

She shook her head so hard it took another unfortunate spin. "You've very, very brave and sexy." She smiled at him. "I always thought so, you know. Still do."

Something in his expression seemed to soften at her words. "That's nice," he said. "But I'm not going to hold you accountable for anything you might say tonight. You're a little looped."

"Not looped," she told him. "Just unin— What's that word? *Uninhibited,* that's it. I'm uninhibited." She wobbled a little. "It's kinda nice."

"And dangerous," Ethan muttered under his breath.

"Dangerous," Samantha echoed, pleased. "I like that. Don't you?"

"Not so much," he said. "The truth is, you scare me to death."

"How come?" she asked, honestly wanting to know how she could possibly scare a man who'd been through everything Ethan had been through. Scary and dangerous sounded much better than pitiful.

"Maybe it's better if I don't tell you that," he said. "It could come back to bite me in the butt."

"How?"

"Women have been known to take advantage of a man's vulnerabilities," he said.

"And you're vulnerable to me?" she asked.

"Unfortunately, it seems I am."

She beamed at him. "That's nice," she said. "I'm glad you like me, Ethan, 'cause I really, really like you. Always have." Even as she spoke, she sank down on the grass right where she'd been standing. "I think I'll sleep now."

Ethan stood there for a heartbeat, his amusement unmistakable. But then she felt herself being scooped into his arms and carried somewhere. To his bed would be nice, she thought before falling soundly asleep.

"How's your head?" Gabi inquired even as she handed over a glass of water and a couple of aspirins to Samantha.

The sunlight streaming in through the bedroom window made her head pound. "That depends. Am I dead?"

"No, I'm pretty sure you just wish you were," her sister said, amusement threading through her voice. "Just how much did you drink last night?"

"No idea," Samantha admitted. "How big a fool did I make of myself?"

"You'll have to ask Ethan that. He was with you when you crashed."

Samantha buried her face in her hands. "Oh, sweet heaven! He must think I'm awful."

"I'm not sure what he thinks, but I don't think awful is on the list. He looked smitten and unhappy as hell about it, to be honest."

Samantha looked down and realized she was once again wearing his football jersey. "Please tell me he did not put this on me."

"Nope. I did that with a little help from Emily. You were pretty much deadweight by then. And Ethan was looking a little shell-shocked. What on earth did you say to him before you crashed?"

Samantha racked her brain, but nothing specific came to mind. Surely she hadn't said anything about how desperately she'd been hoping he'd take her to bed. Sweet heaven, what if she had?

"Oh God," she murmured, holding her head.

"What?" Gabi demanded. "Have you remembered something?"

"Not exactly. I just remember thinking it would be really nice if he carried me off to his bed, but I don't think I actually said that."

A grin spread across Gabi's face. "But you're not sure?"

"Afraid not. The man is going to think I'm a stalker, isn't he? He's going to forget all about the meddlers— Emily, Boone, Grandmother—and conclude that I'm behind everything they're doing."

"So what if he does? Liking the man and letting him know it is not so terrible."

"You don't think it's just a little bit pathetic?"

Gabi gave her an impatient look. "Let's think about this for a minute. You're gorgeous. You have a successful career as an actress and model. You're smart. I'm not seeing the downside of this for Ethan."

"He doesn't want me," Samantha replied. "He's made that abundantly clear. Chasing after him anyway just makes me look desperate." She gave Gabi a plaintive look. "I don't want him to see me as desperate. Can you think of any man on earth who wouldn't be completely turned off by that?"

"And you don't want Ethan to be turned off?" Gabi said, amusement dancing in her eyes.

"Of course not," Samantha said before she considered the implication.

"So Grandmother and Emily have been right from the beginning," she concluded. "This old crush of yours hasn't faded away."

Samantha frowned. "What's your point?"

"That you, my dear, hungover sister, are in a heap of trouble. Those two will never let up now."

"And you?" Samantha asked warily, hoping for one person who'd back her up.

"I'm on your side," Gabi confirmed, then blew it by adding, "Which puts me on their side, too."

"Traitor," Samantha accused. "Couldn't you at least be neutral, like Switzerland?"

"Were you neutral when they were pushing me and Wade together? No, you were not."

"So this is payback," Samantha concluded.

"It is, but only in the most loving, sisterly way."

Samantha frowned at Gabi's overly upbeat mood. "Bite me," she muttered.

Gabi merely chuckled. "By the way, you might want to hop in the shower and pull yourself together. Rumor has it that Ethan is due here in about twenty minutes to give you a lift over to Castle's. Believe me, I know how much pride you have. You definitely don't want him to catch you looking like this."

"Why is Ethan coming by when you're right here?"

Gabi regarded her innocently. "Do you even have to ask?"

"You could tell him to go away."

"I could, but I won't be here. My assigned duties are done and I'm off to work." She pressed a kiss to Samantha's forehead. "Love you. We all do. Try to remember that," she added as she left.

"Yeah, yeah, yeah," Samantha muttered in her wake, regretting that she couldn't crawl beneath the covers and spend the day right where she was. Of course that would risk Ethan coming upstairs in search of her. She couldn't allow him to find the disheveled mess she most likely was.

And that, she assured herself as she showered and washed her hair, was the only reason she wasn't going to defy everyone's latest attempts at meddling. Pride. Whatever impression she'd left in his head last night, she needed to imprint a totally different one today. Breezy, independent and not the least bit love-struck came to mind. Pulling off that performance was going to test her acting skills in ways no other role ever had.

Ethan still regretted answering his cell phone when it had rung at dawn. If he'd ignored it, he wouldn't be at Cora Jane's right now with two giant-size containers of steaming coffee, fresh blueberry muffins and a boatload of anxiety.

"Samantha's worried she made a fool of herself last night," Emily had told him. "You need to let her know she didn't. Otherwise, things could be really awkward between now and the wedding."

"I know what you're doing," Ethan countered.

"I'm just trying to make sure everything goes smoothly," she'd insisted in her most innocent tone. "I can't have the two key players in the wedding party not even able to look each other in the eye. Please, Ethan. I know I got things off to a bad start between you two with my meddling. Once you've settled things, I'll stay out of it. I promise."

"You are genetically incapable of staying out of it," Ethan had responded.

"I'll try. Really," she insisted. "Please do this for me."

Ethan knew he'd experienced a moment of temporary insanity when he'd agreed, but the truth was he wanted to see for himself if Samantha was okay after the way she'd practically crashed at his feet the night before. He wondered if she remembered what he'd said or, more importantly, what she'd said in response, that she was glad he liked her. That spontaneous exchange could be the spark that set off unwanted fireworks down the road, if they weren't very, very careful. Delivering coffee and muffins was not being careful.

Remembering the last time he'd arrived without notice, he knocked on the kitchen door at Cora Jane's. When no one answered, he knocked a little harder, but still got no response.

"Blast it," he muttered, wondering if this was part of the plot. Was he supposed to panic, go running upstairs, find her asleep in her bed, then jump in with her? He wouldn't put it past Emily to devise just such a scheme.

He opened the back door, then shouted, "Samantha! You awake?"

Only then did he hear the sound of the shower cutting off. It immediately sent his imagination into overdrive. All that slick bare skin, those long legs, the mane of thick hair clinging damply to her shoulders. He swallowed hard against the tide of pure lust that swept over him.

"Not doing this," he muttered, dismissing the desire to take the stairs two at a time. "No way."

He plunked himself down in a kitchen chair, opened one of the containers of coffee and took a drink, scorching his throat in the process. At least that got his mind off the naked woman upstairs. Or it should have.

"Ethan? You down there?"

"I'm here," he hollered back, his voice choked. "There's coffee."

"Oh, you wonderful man!" she called back with heartfelt emotion. "Could you bring it up?"

"Upstairs? You want me to bring the coffee to you?" he asked, trying to keep the panic out of his voice. Had she joined the plot?

She laughed as if she'd read his mind. "I promise you that you'll be safe. I wouldn't ask if I weren't in desperate need of caffeine."

He picked up the coffee and headed for the stairs. "Are you decent?"

"I can see why you'd ask," she teased. "And I suppose it's a matter of opinion, but I am clothed if that's what you really want to know."

Was that the real question? he wondered. He'd kind of liked imagining her without a stitch on. Still, this was better, he assured himself as he hit the top step.

She was waiting for him halfway down the hall, wearing jeans and a plain white T-shirt. Her feet were bare, her wet hair just starting to curl waywardly. She looked more intoxicating than the champagne she'd been drinking the night before.

"See, perfectly decent," she said, grinning.

"Too bad," he murmured before he could stop himself.

She blinked. "What?"

"Nothing," he said hurriedly. "Here's your coffee. There's a blueberry muffin in the bag." He held them out, keeping a safe distance between them. "I'll be waiting downstairs."

"It's okay if you want to stay. I just need to dry my

hair. I'm used to having men coming in and out while I get ready."

Instantly he experienced a surge of jealousy like nothing he'd ever felt before. "Is that so? Just how casually do you take relationships?"

"We're not talking relationships," she said, her amusement plain. "Dressing rooms can be crowded on soaps, especially for day players who only come in to work occasionally. And backstage in the theater, people are changing everywhere you look. Modesty pretty much disappears in a hurry."

The thought of men catching a glimpse of her half-dressed, no matter the circumstances, set his teeth on edge.

"I think I'll wait downstairs just the same," he said.

"Sure. Whatever makes you comfortable," she said agreeably.

Nothing about this situation was comfortable, he thought irritably as he went back to the kitchen and finished his coffee. Heck, he saw half-naked women all the time in his line of work. That was different, too. They were patients, and he'd trained himself to be clinical and objective when treating them.

Samantha was different. She wasn't a patient. She wasn't even a friend, despite their determination to pretend they could pull that off. She was a potential lover. He knew it. So did she. And that turned casual glimpses of bare skin and intimate little moments into something dangerous. It hadn't sounded to him as if she recognized that.

Was that because she didn't feel the sizzling chemistry the way he did? Or was she only trying to ignore it, to pretend it didn't exist?

He'd known what to do with all the meddling. It had been annoying, but too blatant to take seriously.

He'd even been able to dismiss the hints that Samantha had held a long-ago crush on him. Time faded that sort of thing, especially when they had never exchanged more than a word or two back then.

But this new twist, this need that was growing inside him? That had the potential to rip him apart.

In Afghanistan, it hadn't been possible to hide from the dangers. They were all around and part of the job. This danger was something else, something he could avoid.

And somehow he had to find a way to ignore his suddenly raging hormones and do just that.

Six

"I went downstairs and he was gone. He just took off without a word, not ten minutes after handing me a container of coffee and a muffin," Samantha told Emily later that morning when she'd finally managed to get a lift over to Castle's from a neighbor who was heading that way. "Now will you please end the plotting and scheming? It's evident that Ethan and I are not meant to be. Being pushed together constantly is just making both of us uncomfortable. If you keep trying to make something happen, one of us is likely to bail on your wedding."

To her dismay, Emily burst into tears at the warning. "Sure, you'd like nothing better than to ruin my wedding, wouldn't you? Go on and bail, if that's what you want to do. Gabi can always fill in. Maybe I should have picked her to be maid of honor in the first place."

Samantha barely resisted the desire to snap right back. Instead, she latched onto Emily's arm and drew her outside. "Okay, let's have this out right now. Do you even want me in your wedding?" She tried to temper her anger and added more gently, "Em, it's okay if you don't. Frankly, I never expected you to ask me. If you'd rather have Gabi, it would be okay."

Emily's tears flowed harder. "No, I want you in the wedding. And I wanted Ethan to fall for you. I thought it would make up for things."

"What things?"

"You know perfectly well what I mean. We've never been close."

"We've had our problems, sure, but we've been close," Samantha said. "We're sisters. We'll always have each other's backs. Nobody knows us better than we know each other."

"You and I don't get along the way you and Gabi do," Emily insisted, then added with a sniff, "Or the way you and Mom did."

Samantha stared at her incredulously. "And Gabi and I don't relate the same way the two of you do. That's nothing to be jealous about. It's just the nature of relationships. As for Mom, she absolutely adored you. You were her beautiful baby."

"No," Emily insisted, rejecting the idea. "I was the afterthought that kept her from having the life she really wanted."

The bitter words that revealed years of unexpressed pain stunned Samantha. "Sweetie, you know that's not so."

"It is so," Emily insisted. "I heard her once, you know. She was telling a friend that she'd applied for this dream job, but then found out she was pregnant with me. The same thing had happened before, when she and Dad were first married. She'd just started working and then she got pregnant with you, so she'd quit to be a full-time mother."

Samantha tried to absorb this news, or rather the implication it apparently held for her sister. Though she knew she'd been a bit of a surprise to her parents, she'd never given it another thought. And she couldn't understand why what Emily had overheard had caused this rift between her and Emily. "Okay, I knew both pregnancies were unexpected, but what does that have to do with you and me?"

"She never resented you for ruining her life," Emily said, her tone accusatory. "But she did resent me. I could hear it in her voice that day. Oh, she tried not to let it show, but I knew the truth."

"And you twisted that around to be my fault?" Samantha said, trying to follow the logic.

"Not your fault," Emily contradicted, looking slightly sheepish. "I know they were Mom's feelings."

"But you couldn't blame her, especially after she'd died, so you started taking it out on me," Samantha concluded. "Oh, sweetie, the last thing Mom would ever want would be for the two of us to be at odds over which of us she loved more. I wish you'd said something about this years ago. Maybe we could have put it to rest."

"How?" Emily asked with a sniff. "It was what it was. And Mom's not here to deny it or explain it. Not that she could."

Grateful that the outside deck at Castle's was deserted, Samantha started to reach for Emily's wind-blown hair to smooth it back from her face, then hesitated. She doubted her sister would appreciate the gesture just now.

"I wish Mom were here now, too, but you're going to have to listen to me, instead. Gabi was still young, but I was old enough to remember the look on Mom's face when she told us she was expecting you. She was over the moon, Em. She really was."

Emily still looked skeptical. "Then why did she sound so disappointed about that job?"

"I can't say for sure, since I didn't hear her, but I do believe if she'd been thinking about going to work, it was only because she didn't think another pregnancy was in the cards. She wanted the distraction of a job, not the fulfillment. Grandmother told me once that Mom was cut out for motherhood and that it was lucky for us that she was, since Dad was so caught up in his work."

Emily looked as if she was struggling to accept the truth of Samantha's words, but it was plain she was wasn't there yet.

"I know that doesn't match your perceptions, but you can ask Grandmother," Samantha told her gently. "She knew exactly how thrilled Mom was about having you." She grinned. "In fact, if anyone should have been jealous of losing Mom's affections, it should have been me or Gabi. Once you came along, you became the center of her universe. She doted on you."

"She did not," Emily denied, though she looked intrigued by the possibility.

"Did, too," Samantha retorted. "To make up for the attention Mom was giving you, I retreated into a world of make-believe, which is probably what led me to acting. Gabi became obsessed with trying to win Dad's attention, and we both know how that turned out."

"Seriously?"

"Think about it. You know it's true."

"Why didn't I see any of that back then?" Emily asked.

"Because you were the youngest. And you were the princess. That's heady stuff."

"Are you saying I was self-absorbed?" Emily asked, instantly defensive.

"No, I'm just saying that your role in the family was defined for you by Mom, just the way mine was or Gabi's. We each had a different experience growing up, even though we were in the exact same household."

Emily's expression turned thoughtful. "I heard Grandmother say something like that once. She said every sibling grows up in a different family. I had no idea what she meant."

"And now?"

"After what you've just said, I think maybe I do."

"Can we put this behind us?" Samantha pleaded. "Can you accept that I am genuinely thrilled for you and Boone, that I want to be in your wedding and that nothing is going to drive me away?"

"Not even the meddling?" Emily asked, the sparkle slowly coming back to her eyes.

"Well, you might not want to push your luck with that," Samantha warned. "I'm feeling pretty mellow and tolerant right this second, but it might not last if you decide to test it."

Emily nodded. "I'll keep that in mind."

It wasn't the airtight commitment Samantha had been hoping for, but it was a start. And with less than two weeks until the wedding and a mountain of details to attend to, perhaps the meddling would land on the bottom of Emily's list.

* * *

"You don't look so hot," Debra said when Ethan arrived at the clinic. "Late night?"

He frowned at the personal question, though he knew it wasn't in his bubbly young receptionist's DNA to censor herself. "Busy morning," he countered tightly. "What's the schedule look like here?"

"Two drop-in patients waiting, more appointments on the books and your afternoon with the kids. Greg called in. He said he'd be here before you take off."

Ethan nodded distractedly as he glanced through his messages. "Give me five minutes and have Pam send in the first patient," he said just as he noticed that one of the pink slips had a message from Marty Gray indicating that Cass wouldn't be coming on this afternoon's hike with the rest of the kids in his positive self-image group. "Hold that. I need to call Marty back. I'll let Pam know when I'm ready for the patients."

In his office, he dialed Marty's number. "Got your message," he told the harried mother, who was most likely trying to get kids off to school. "What's up with Cass?"

At seventeen, Cass was the oldest member of Project Pride. Two years ago, she'd lost her arm when it had been crushed in a riding mower accident. Though she managed well with her prosthesis, she was rebelling against everything these days. It was tough enough being a teen, he knew, without seeing herself as a damaged misfit. Cass and the others like her were precisely the kids he'd been hoping to help with his program. He wanted them to believe that their self-worth was not tied to any disabilities they might have. On occasion, he actually saw the irony of setting himself up as that particular messenger.

"Nothing new, really," Marty said with frustration. "Could be the usual teen mood swing."

"Or something happened at school," Ethan guessed.

"Always a possibility," Marty said. "But I have zero luck when it comes to getting her to open up. Teens can be notoriously tight-lipped, but Cass has raised the sullen silence to an art form."

"Which is why she needs to be here this afternoon. It's not just about going on a hike. It's a chance for these kids to open up with other kids who'll understand."

"Ethan, I know that," Marty said impatiently. "So does Cass. She says she won't go. What am I supposed to do? Get my husband to drag her over there and leave her on your doorstep? Believe me, that holds a lot of appeal for me when she's acting out, but it's not up to you to deal with her moods or to fix this."

"It may not be up to me, but I think I can help," Ethan said. "Mind if I pick her up after school? I don't think she'll be able to say no if I'm right there."

Marty hesitated. "Are you sure about this? She could be embarrassed in front of her friends. It could make things worse."

"I can be diplomatic when I need to be," he assured her. "I'm not going to toss her over my shoulder and haul her off, even if she behaves like a real brat."

"I'd actually like to see you try that," Marty said, her sense of humor kicking in. "Two stubborn wills colliding could be highly entertaining."

Ethan thought of this dance he and Samantha were performing. Stubborn wills were playing a role in that, too, he conceded before snapping his attention back to the moment.

"So, it's okay if I pick her up? If she refuses, I won't cause a scene. I'll let you know she's heading home."

"Thanks, Ethan. You really are a saint for putting up with Cass."

"I'm not just 'putting up with her.' She's a good kid. She just needs to remember that she still has a lot to offer the world."

It was a lesson that had been a long time coming for him. In fact, it was one with which he still struggled from time to time, especially when it came to opening his heart. Just look at how determined he was to keep Samantha at arm's length. It must be a hundred times harder for an insecure teen who'd just been figuring out her own identity when the accident happened.

With Debra, Pam and Greg keeping an eye on the other kids in Ethan's program until he could get back, Ethan stood outside the high school and watched for Cass to emerge. It wasn't hard to spot her.

While the other kids spilled out in chattering clusters, she exited alone, an angry expression on her face. Ethan suspected only he saw the desperate longing in her eyes as she surreptitiously glanced at her classmates.

When she spotted him, though, her frown deepened, but she didn't turn away or try to avoid him.

"What are you doing here?" she demanded, confronting him belligerently.

"Waiting for you," he said, falling into step beside her.

"I'm not going hiking, so you might as well take off."

"You know that hiking, at least the way we do it, is nothing more than going for a walk, right?"

"Which makes it a dumb way to spend the afternoon," she retorted.

"Not if you're one of the kids who has trouble walking at all," he reminded her.

"But I'm not," she countered. "My legs are perfectly fine. It's my arm that's gone, remember? Or do you not see what's right in front of you?" She waved the arm with her prosthesis to emphasize her point.

"Then today maybe you could help one of the kids who's not as lucky. It might make you feel good to do something for someone else. You could push Trevor in his wheelchair, for instance."

"Hello!" she said sarcastically. "One arm, remember?"

"And a perfectly good prosthesis on the other," he said without any hint of sympathy. "Or haven't you mastered it yet?"

She scowled at the suggestion that a lack of skill was behind her refusal to join the hike. "You know I have."

He gave her a sly glance. "Then prove it."

Cass heaved a sigh, clearly aware that she was going to lose in the end. Or maybe even wanting to participate, as long as she could do it grudgingly, as a favor to him. "Fine. I'll come on the stupid hike. And I'll push Trevor's wheelchair so fast he'll squeal like a little girl."

Ethan bit back a grin. "Thank you. I'm sure he'll appreciate your daredevil tendencies." He gestured across the street. "My car's right over there."

"I should probably call my mom and tell her I changed my mind," she told him.

"Good idea, though I told her I was going to try to convince you to come along this afternoon."

After Cass made the call, Ethan waited until they were halfway to the clinic before asking casually, "So, anything new in your life these days?"

"I go to school. I go home. It's not exactly material for a TV show."

"No after-school activities that interest you?" he prodded, knowing that at one time she'd been active in the drama club. She'd been cast in every play at the middle school and starred in one her first year at the high school. All, though, he realized now, had been before the accident.

"None," she said flatly.

Ethan glanced over and caught the tear that had leaked out, aware then that he'd hit on something. "I thought you were going to try out for the school play."

She whirled on him. "Do not mention that stupid play to me, okay? I didn't get the lead. I didn't even get a walk-on. I heard Mrs. Gentry tell another teacher it was a real shame to waste my talent, but she thought my prosthesis would be a distraction. She sounded all sad and sympathetic, but it was fake. I think she was glad to be able to give that twit Sue Ellen the lead. Like Sue Ellen will be able to remember her lines," she scoffed. "She's so busy batting her eyes at every guy in school, she can barely remember her own name."

Ethan felt a swell of fury on Cass's behalf. It was one thing for kids to be inadvertently cruel to each other, but teachers should have more sensitivity. "Sounds to me as if Mrs. Gentry needs to be replaced."

"Like that's ever going to happen," Cass said. "She's,

like, some kind of institution at the school. Her recommendations carry a lot of weight in the drama departments at some colleges, too. I guess I can't count on that anymore."

Ethan frowned at the defeat in her voice. "You don't want to act? Come on, Cass. I thought that was your passion. And I saw you a couple of years ago. You were great!"

"What's the point?" she asked with a careless shrug she couldn't quite pull off. "Nobody's going to hire me."

He regarded her with surprise. "Boy, that doesn't sound like you. I thought you were a fighter."

"I am," she said angrily, "but I know when to quit. Could we drop this, please? I'm going on your stupid hike. One victory for the day ought to be enough, even for a guy who hates losing the way you do."

With that, she climbed out of his car and went to join the other kids who were waiting to be taken to a nearby park with trails that were manageable for everyone, at least with a little assistance. She leaned down and whispered something to Trevor that had the ten-year-old grinning. For all Ethan knew, they were planning a quick getaway.

Ethan sighed as he watched her. One of the things he was still struggling to accept was that physical triumphs were sometimes a whole lot easier in the long run than emotional ones, especially with people like Mrs. Gentry feeding into doubts and insecurities. The woman might be an institution, but he thought it was time for a bit of a shake-up at the school.

Even though Emily and Boone kept their voices low, it was evident to Samantha that they were having an argument. Since they kept glancing her way, she assumed she was at the center of it. That drew her across the yard to where Boone was grilling steaks for dinner for the family.

"Hush," Emily whispered urgently as Samantha approached.

Unfortunately for her the warning came too late. Samantha heard Boone trying, apparently without success, to convince Emily that Ethan truly hadn't been available to join them.

Samantha gave her sister a resigned look. "It didn't take long for you to forget all about our conversation this morning, did it?" she asked mildly.

Boone gave her a sympathetic look. "My bride-to-be is on a mission."

"A pointless one," Samantha said. "I thought I'd made that clear."

"I'm not so sure it's pointless," Boone said, surprising them both.

Emily's eyes lit up. "Really? You think Ethan's interested?"

"I think he genuinely doesn't realize that he is," Boone said. "It's been a long time since he allowed himself to take a chance on a woman. It's not a habit that's easily broken, especially for a man as strong-willed as he is. He's focused all of his energy on getting himself as fit as possible, getting the clinic up and running and on those kids of his."

Samantha blinked at that. "Ethan has kids? Was he married at some point?" She frowned at her sister. "Don't you think you should have mentioned that?"

"They aren't *his* kids," Emily said quickly. "They're

kids with special needs. Some can't walk. Some have lost a limb. He's made it his mission to prove to them they can live a normal life. What's he call it, Boone? Project Pride?"

Boone nodded.

"I think what he's doing is wonderful," Emily added in case Samantha needed to have that pointed out.

Which she didn't, Samantha thought ruefully. In fact, it made Ethan that much more appealing. The plus column in the man's favor was literally crowded with checkmarks. The only minus, however, was huge. He wasn't interested. Or even if he was, as Boone thought, he was going to fight it. Wasn't that the same thing in the long run?

Emily's expression turned thoughtful. "You know, Samantha, I'll bet some of the girls in his group could use a woman's influence," she suggested slyly. "Remember when we used to play beauty shop? You were the one who taught Gabi and me how to put on makeup and how to fix our hair. That could go a long way to helping with their self-image, don't you think so, Boone?"

Boone held up his hands. "Out of my ballpark," he said. "You need to run that one by Ethan."

"I think I will," Emily said, nabbing Boone's cell phone from his pocket and scrolling down until she found Ethan's number.

"Not now," Samantha instructed firmly, managing to wrestle the phone away from her, just as she heard Ethan answer. She sighed, then spoke to him.

"Sorry, Ethan. Emily misdialed."

"Samantha?" he asked. "What are you doing with Boone's phone, or do I even need to ask?"

She stepped away from her sister. "You do not need

to ask. The plotting and scheming are still going on. You were wise to skip this little get-together."

"I didn't do it to avoid you," he said, surprising her by addressing her unspoken fear directly.

"Is that so?" she said skeptically.

"Honest," he said. "Though after I ran out on you this morning, I can see how you might think that."

She settled into an Adirondack chair away from the rest of the family. "Why did you leave?" she asked.

"I can't explain it."

"Can't or don't want to?" she found herself teasing, thinking of Boone's theory. "Did you have a panic attack, Ethan?"

To her surprise, Ethan laughed. "I don't think I'll answer that," he said.

"Because?" she said, not sure why she thought it was so important to push him. If Boone was right, maybe she could encourage him to take another look at the possibilities for the two of them.

"You're not going to let this drop, are you?" he asked, his frustration evident.

"I'm thinking that would be a bad idea. So?"

"I found myself a little too eager to haul you into the closest bedroom," he said with unexpected candor.

Samantha smiled at the revelation, glad he couldn't see her face.

"Are you laughing?" he asked. "Because I wouldn't blame you if you were. Here I am, a decorated war vet, and I'm admitting that you scare me to death."

"I like you all the more for being honest," she said quietly. "That takes courage, especially when there are a lot of people who might seize on that little tidbit and run with it."

"Which means it might be best if you kept it to yourself."

"I can do that," she promised, thinking it was something she could dream about tonight. "But if I'm not the reason you stayed away from dinner, what is?"

"I have a commitment on Thursday afternoons. There's a group of kids I work with."

"I just heard about that," she acknowledged. "It's a really nice thing you're doing for them."

"There are days I wonder if I'm making any inroads at all," he said. "Today was one of those. I have this one girl, she's as stubborn as anyone I've ever met, and she's determined to fight me every step of the way."

"Which makes you want to try all the harder," Samantha guessed.

"Something like that. Today she told me about something a teacher had said, something that really crushed her. I've been trying to get in touch with the teacher this evening, but so far I haven't had any luck."

"Then put it off till morning and come on over. The steaks are about to come off the grill. There's plenty of food. I'd like to hear more about these kids of yours."

"Why?" he asked.

She frowned at the skepticism she heard in his voice. "Why wouldn't I? They obviously matter to you, and what you're trying to do for them is important."

"You don't even know them."

"That doesn't mean I can't care about what you're doing." She thought of the initial impression he'd obviously had of her. "Or do you think I'm too shallow to give a thought to anybody else?"

"I never said that," Ethan said, sounding annoyed.

"It's not the first time, though, that you've suggested you thought I'd be vain and self-involved. I thought we'd put that notion behind us, but I guess we haven't." She couldn't seem to help the hurt that had crept into her voice.

"Samantha—"

She cut him off. "Come over. Don't come over. It's up to you."

She disconnected the call, then tossed the phone to a startled Boone, who managed to snag it before it landed on the grill.

"What did he say?" Emily asked, regarding her worriedly. "You didn't fight, did you?"

She thought of Ethan's admission that he was attracted to her. While that had bolstered her spirits, his underlying lack of faith in the kind of woman she was pretty much undercut all those warm and fuzzy feelings.

"There was no fight. We just clarified a few things," she told her sister.

"Did you convince him to join us?" Emily persisted.

"I doubt I could convince Ethan to stay on the curb if a Hummer was barreling toward him," Samantha said.

Emily blinked at that, glanced at Boone, who merely shrugged, then said. "What on earth did the man say to you?"

"Not important," Samantha insisted.

But it had been enough to convince her she needed to forget all those teenage fantasies that had never quite died. Ethan Cole might be a real hero, but when it came down to it, he wasn't going to be hers.

Seven

Ethan stared at his phone for at least a minute, trying to grasp that Samantha had misunderstood him so completely and, worse, that she'd actually hung up on him because of it. Wasn't that one more bit of proof that he was in dire need of a refresher course in social skills? He might want to keep his distance, but he'd never meant to offend her.

And now, he realized reluctantly, he needed to apologize. He tried to recall the last time he'd been called on to do that. He made it a practice to stay to himself precisely so he wouldn't make this kind of stupid mistake.

Though he'd removed his prosthesis and taken a shower when he'd returned from the hike, planning to settle down for a quiet evening while he tried to reach Mrs. Gentry, he strapped the leg back on, pulled on a pair of jeans and a University of North Carolina T-shirt, then headed for his car.

Five minutes later he was pulling up at Boone's. He was halfway across the lawn when B.J. spotted him and came racing his way, pulling up just in time to keep from running into him. Though Ethan's balance was pretty much rock-solid now, it would have been humiliating to have the kid knock him on his butt in front of Samantha.

"Will you play my video game with me?" B.J. pleaded. "Everybody else is talking about the wedding."

"And you're bored?" Ethan surmised.

B.J.'s head bobbed. "I want Dad and Emily to get married, but this whole wedding thing is kinda crazy. Who cares about flowers and dresses and that kind of stuff? All that matters is the cake."

Ethan laughed. "Don't let Emily hear you say that. Women care about the flowers, the dresses and all the rest. There will come a day when understanding that is real important to your peace of mind."

B.J. looked blank. "Huh?"

"Never mind. Let me take care of something, and then I'll come inside and beat your socks off at that game."

"You can't beat me," B.J. boasted. "Not even Dad beats me. I am the champion of North Carolina, maybe even the whole world."

Here was a kid who'd never have a problem with self-image, Ethan thought, smiling. Maybe he should ask B.J. to spend a little time with his group. He could teach the kids a thing or two about unbridled self-confidence. Of course, Boone was the one responsible. He was one of those dads who thought his child could accomplish anything and let him know it.

"I'll meet you inside and we'll see," Ethan told him, grinning, deciding it was way past time to stop giving the kid an edge when they played.

As B.J. scampered off, Ethan saw Boone stand up. When his friend started in his direction, Ethan waved him off and kept his gaze trained on Samantha, who was doing her best to ignore his arrival.

He walked over and stood directly in her line of vision. "Could we talk?" he asked politely. "Please."

She scowled at him, but she did stand up and excuse herself. Obviously she was no more interested in causing a scene than he was.

Ethan was fully aware of the fascinated gazes around the table as he led the way to Boone's pier, geared more toward fishing than the docking of a boat. At least they'd have a little privacy away from the rest of the family. Though he didn't doubt that the close scrutiny would continue, at least all those meddlers wouldn't hear what he had to say. That is, if he could think of something to say.

At the end of the pier, Samantha stood stiffly, her arms folded across her middle, her expression forbidding.

"I'm sorry, Samantha," he said quietly. "I never, ever meant to suggest that you're shallow or uncaring. I'm sorry you took what I said that way."

She gave him a disbelieving look. "Then what did you mean?"

"Just that you don't know these young people. You're not involved in their lives. You don't have an emotional stake in what happens to them."

"The way you do," she said, her gaze finally meeting his.

He nodded. "The way I do. I've been where they are, filled with doubts and insecurities and self-loathing.

Can you honestly tell me you've been through anything remotely like that? Can you identify with what they've experienced?"

"No," she conceded, but held his gaze. "That doesn't mean I can't feel compassion for any of you. And I have experienced pain, Ethan. It may not be physical like yours. It may not even be in the same league emotionally, but I have been hurt. I've had people tell me on a regular basis that I'm not good enough. It's the nature of my business to experience rejection. Don't you think that has the power to hurt, even when I know it's not meant personally?"

Ethan sighed. "I hadn't looked at your career that way. I just see you as this golden girl who went after what she wanted in a very competitive profession and got it."

She smiled ruefully at that. "If only it were that simple to be an actress or a model. I put my ego on the line every time I go on an audition. And every rejection chips away at my self-confidence. Worse, these days, I don't even get the auditions, which means people reject me without even hearing me read for a part. That's mostly about age, I think. And you know what? Just like these kids you're trying to help who have disabilities, my age is not something I can change. I can only change how I face it. Should I accept that roles aren't going to be there and move on, or do I keep knocking on doors and getting turned away more often than not?"

Ethan was shaken by a perspective he'd never before considered. Okay, her life wasn't all glamour. It wasn't free of pitfalls and obstacles. That made her more appealing in a way he hadn't expected. As if he needed her to be more appealing, he thought wryly.

"It seems to me you're handling it okay," he told her.

She laughed then. "You think so? You haven't looked into my freezer in New York. It's stuffed with so many containers of Ben & Jerry's, it's astonishing I'm not the size of a blimp. *That's* how I'm handling it."

He tried to imagine her with an extra ounce of weight on her and couldn't. "Why aren't you? The size of a blimp, I mean."

"I may eat more ice cream than I should, but I also go to the gym. I run. Because even when I'm at my lowest, I keep fighting to stay in shape. Tomorrow might bring the juicy role of a lifetime my way, and I need to be ready. So far, thank goodness, I haven't let the defeats steal my last shred of hope. Isn't that exactly what you want for those kids? Hope?"

He didn't want to acknowledge that she'd nailed it, that she understood things he hadn't expected her to get. Instead, he looked her over, allowing his gaze to linger on the long, shapely legs revealed by a pair of formfitting capris. "You run, huh?"

"Every day."

"Want to go running with me tomorrow?" he asked impulsively. Asking was a risk, he knew, not only because it meant spending more time with her, but because there'd be no way to disguise his prosthesis. With his running shorts, it was right there for all the world to see. It had been a long time since that had bothered him, but in front of Samantha? He was risking a lot by opening himself up to the possibility of her pity and ultimately her rejection.

She looked startled by the invitation. "You want to spend time together? Are you sure you're up for it?"

Ethan nodded. He knew it was probably foolhardy. He knew it would lead to speculation that neither of them wanted, but he hadn't been able to help himself. Seeing that one little glimpse of a woman who had her own share of vulnerabilities, rather than the out-of-reach golden girl he'd imagined her to be, had chipped away at his defenses. At the rate that was happening, he figured he was pretty much doomed. He might as well enjoy the experience.

Samantha was no slouch when it came to running. She took it seriously. She'd raced in a couple of half marathons and hadn't embarrassed herself. She doubted Ethan knew that. Even if he did, she hoped he didn't think she'd cut him any slack out of pity. Her competitive spirit wouldn't allow it. And losing must not take too bad a toll on him. Hadn't he admitted just the other day that he'd lost a bet with Greg, who'd beat him on a run? Of course that loss had been to someone he knew well and obviously respected, not to a woman. She wondered if he was the kind of man whose ego could take that.

She was waiting in the driveway when he arrived just after dawn. It was a shock to see him exit the car in running shorts that exposed his prosthesis. But then her gaze traveled to his muscular shoulders and flat abs and her mouth went dry. The artificial limb didn't detract from his masculinity in the slightest. That fiancée of his must have been a complete idiot if she'd looked on him as damaged goods.

Ethan met her gaze and she saw the hint of uncertainty in his eyes as he apparently awaited her pity or judgment. Instead, she gave him a beaming smile.

"You sure you're up to this, Cole? I run to win."

His uncertainty faded at the challenge. "So do I."

Without so much as a hint about what she intended, she took off, then called over her shoulder, "I don't fight fair, either."

They ran for the better part of an hour, Ethan guiding the way, the lead changing hands a few times. Mostly, though, they ran side by side in companionable silence.

As they turned back toward Cora Jane's however, Samantha deliberately pushed herself to another gear. Ethan regarded her with amusement, then sprinted ahead of her easily, his long-legged strides eating up the distance at a pace she couldn't have matched on her best day.

By the time she reached the driveway where they'd started, he was leaning against the hood of his car, looking as relaxed as if he'd just returned from a casual stroll. His body, slick with sweat, gleamed in the morning sunlight.

"Not bad," he commented.

She panted for breath and scowled up at him. "Next time I'll remember that you're sneaky."

"How am I sneaky? You're the one who picked up the pace and turned it into a race. I just accepted the challenge." He held out a bottle of water. "You look as if you could use this."

She accepted it without comment and took a careful sip. "Ethan, were you a runner before? I mean, before your injury?"

"If you mean did I enter marathons and that sort of thing, no, but I had to train for football, and there were plenty of long runs in the military."

"Did you enjoy it?"

"Hated it," he said succinctly. "Still do. During rehab, there was a time when I could barely stay on my feet, much less walk. Running seemed like an elusive dream."

"Which made it an irresistible challenge," she guessed. "You made up your mind to conquer it."

"Something like that."

"And if you're going to do it, you have to do it well," she concluded.

"Is there any other way?"

"That's how I feel about my career," she confessed. "If I can no longer do it well, maybe it's time to walk away."

He gave her a startled look. "Is that what you want to do?"

"No," she said. "But it might be the only choice. Living in New York is crazy expensive. Emily's suggested I come to Los Angeles and stay with them. She has great contacts in the movie and TV business."

"Sounds like something worth trying," he said, his tone neutral.

"I don't know. Maybe a few years ago, I'd have been up for it, but now? I'm not sure I have the drive left to start over. Acting is not something you can do half-heartedly. It takes a huge amount of determination and drive. I had that when I first went to New York. I'm not sure I do anymore."

"What are the alternatives?" he asked, sounding genuinely interested.

Since this was the first time she'd honestly confronted the situation, unfortunately she didn't have good answers for him. "I don't know," she admitted. "That's the scary part." She met his gaze. "You were a surgeon, right? That's incredibly demanding. You had to be a hundred percent dedicated to the job at some point. How did you know that opening an emergency clinic in Sand Castle Bay would work for you, that you wouldn't be bored?"

He smiled, though his expression was tinged by a surprising weariness. "Iraq and Afghanistan," he said simply. "I'd had about as much excitement as I could handle. So had Greg. When I was in rehab, we started talking it over. He didn't want to go back into trauma medicine. It seemed as if we were in the same place. And his family was anxious to have him back home. I loved growing up here, so even though my folks had moved away, this felt like home to me, too. It just felt right."

"Any regrets?"

He shook his head. "I don't believe in regrets. If it hadn't worked out, I'd have made a change by now, but it has worked. This is a great place with terrific people. Summers with all the tourists are a little frantic. I like it best when the pace slows down."

He studied her. "Are you thinking it would be dull as dirt after living in New York?"

Samantha grinned. "Something like that."

"Hey, life is what you make it, wherever you are. You can be alone and bored in a big city or invigorated and busy in a small town. It's up to you."

"I actually think Gabi's come to realize that," she

said. "My sister was the ultimate workaholic in Raleigh, but she had no personal life. Here she's not only found the balance her life was missing, she's started a whole new demanding career that suits her need to be challenged professionally."

"There you go," Ethan said. "Proof positive that it can be done."

But while the examples set by Ethan and even her sister were inspirational, Samantha couldn't quite envision what sort of satisfying niche she could carve out for herself.

Since she had no answers, she announced, "I'm ready for food. How about you? I don't have Grandmother's skill in the kitchen, but I am capable of whipping up omelets and toast. Do you have time, or do you need to get to the clinic?"

"Sounds good, and I have time. Greg opens today. I go in around eleven and stay to cover the evening hours."

She lifted a brow. "Was that a deliberate choice?"

"What do you mean?"

"A noble way to avoid dating on a Friday night?"

Ethan chuckled. "I honestly hadn't considered that particular benefit. Besides, we rotate, so I'm not always there on Friday nights. Sometimes I cover Saturdays instead."

"Sounds like a win-win for a man who openly declares he doesn't want to date."

"Or I can just be straightforward and say no when people try to set me up on a blind date," he suggested. "That's worked reasonably well, too, at least until your family got involved."

Samantha thought about that as she led the way into

the house. As she pulled eggs, cheese and ham from the refrigerator, she wondered what might have happened had she and Ethan crossed paths under different circumstances, without all the pressures of being participants in a wedding, without all the well-meant matchmaking.

As she whisked the eggs, she glanced his way. "Ethan, do you think things might have been different if all these people hadn't been meddling in our relationship?"

"What do you mean?"

"Well, you have to admit with everyone caught up in wedding fever, it adds an element of stress to the situation."

"You mean because it's so clear that some people would like to see us be the next couple to walk down the aisle?"

"Exactly, though I do think they're counting on Wade and Gabi being next. But you get the idea."

"Possibly," he conceded, "but the truth is our paths might not even have crossed if it weren't for the wedding. You might not have been pulled back to Sand Castle Bay. You could be packing your bags for Los Angeles or fighting tooth and nail for some Broadway role. The wedding has brought you here and given you a time-out to think about the future. It's all good, Samantha."

He took a deep breath, then met her gaze. "Despite the meddling, I don't regret that we're getting to know each other."

"I don't, either," she said softly, hoping that her heart wasn't in her eyes. Because the better she got to know Ethan, the stronger her infatuation became. And given his adverse reaction to any kind of involvement, that was a surefire path to heartbreak.

Ethan might have told Samantha that he didn't believe in regrets, but right this second he was deeply regretting that he didn't have time for another run to drive all thoughts of the tantalizing woman straight out of his head.

Discovering that she had hidden depths and her own share of uncertainties tapped into a long-buried desire to be somebody's knight in shining armor. He'd thought that working with his group of special-needs kids would satisfy that urge, but apparently that couldn't compensate for the far more personal role he wanted to play in a woman's life. At least this woman's.

"This is bad, Cole," he lectured himself as he drove home, showered and changed clothes. Since he wanted to stop by the high school en route to the clinic, he wore khakis and a dress shirt, rather than the scrubs he often wore to work.

At the high school, he went to the office and asked to speak to Regina Gentry. "I'm Ethan Cole," he added.

The teen working at the desk regarded him with awe. "There are pictures of you on the wall outside the gym," she said, giving him an adoring look. "And you're, like, a real war hero. Hold on a sec. I'll page Mrs. Gentry."

When she'd made the call to the drama teacher, she came back and stared at him as if she were absorbing every detail. Ethan squirmed under the intense scrutiny.

"I'm Sue Ellen, by the way," she said. "I'm a senior. I just work in here during my study period. My grades are great. I don't need the extra study time."

"Good for you," Ethan said, wondering if this happened to be Sue Ellen the twit, who'd gotten the part in the play over Cass. She certainly had the eye-batting thing down pat.

Thankfully, Mrs. Gentry arrived within minutes, looking flustered. "Ethan, I couldn't believe it when Sue Ellen told me you were here. It's been a long time."

"A very long time," he agreed, recalling the English class that had nearly destroyed his grade average. He'd never quite grasped all the fuss over Shakespeare, which had deeply offended the woman whose passion was not only for the written word, but for drama.

"What brings you by?" she asked.

"Could we speak privately?" he suggested, noticing Sue Ellen's avid interest in their exchange.

"Of course," she said, leading the way into the hall. "I'm afraid there are students in my classroom, so it will have to be right here."

"This is fine," he said. "I wanted to speak to you about Cass Gray."

Her expression immediately turned somber. "What a sad, sad situation," she said, her voice laced with pity. "She had such a promising future ahead of her."

"And you no longer think that's the case?" he asked, annoyed by her condescending tone.

"How could it be? No one wants to see someone without an arm onstage. It's uncomfortable. The audience will be so focused on that, it will ruin the production."

She said it with such pious certainty that Ethan nearly lost it. He made himself tamp down his anger.

Yelling wouldn't accomplish a thing. He needed to educate her, instead.

"Do you think when I'm sewing up a bad gash in my clinic, my patients care that I have no leg?" he inquired.

She blinked at the softly spoken query. "It's not the same thing. They come to you for medical care, not to be entertained."

"Let's go at this from a different direction," he suggested. "Is Cass a good actress?"

"Of course. I had such high hopes for her before she was injured."

"Isn't a good actress supposed to be capable of engaging the audience in the play, making them forget all about reality?"

"Yes, but it's hard to ignore that the child has no arm, Ethan. It would be cruel to put her in front of an audience and allow people to feel sorry for her."

"I think it's just as cruel to rip her dream into shreds without even giving her a chance." He leveled a hard look into her eyes. "You crushed her spirit."

"Well, I never intended to do any such thing," she said indignantly. "I just did what I thought was best for her and for the production. I didn't want her subjected to ridicule."

"Is the person you cast a better actress?"

She hesitated at that. "Sue Ellen's a beautiful girl. You met her just now. I'm sure you saw that for yourself."

"That isn't what I asked. Is she as talented as Cass?"

She looked flustered by the question. "She's quite competent," she said eventually.

"And you're not the least bit worried that she'll blow her lines and be subjected to ridicule, as you put it?"

"I intend to work closely with her," she insisted. "She won't blow her lines. Sue Ellen has the lead. I can't very well take it away from her now."

Ethan sighed. "Look, I didn't come here to get you to change your decision. I was just hoping to give you another perspective on some possibly unintended consequences of what you did when you kept Cass out of the lead and even out of the cast."

"She needed a reality check," Mrs. Gentry insisted. "Better that it come now, rather than down the road from someone who won't care about her as people here do."

"I disagree. If she has no talent, a time will come when she needs to face that," Ethan told her. "I don't think it was up to a high school drama teacher to destroy something she's worked toward for years, and certainly not based on whether or not she has an infirmity." He held her gaze, his expression unrelenting. "Just something to think about."

He turned and walked away, then stopped and faced her again. She was still standing exactly where he'd left her, obviously shaken. "By the way, I have to ask," he said. "Were you focused on my missing leg while I was delivering *my* lines, Mrs. Gentry? Or did my message come through loud and clear?"

She looked vaguely chagrined by the question. "You made your point, Ethan. I'll think about what you've said. I'm not so old I can't learn from my mistakes."

He gave a nod of satisfaction. "All I'm asking."

Ethan was sitting behind the desk in his office catching up on patient notes when the door burst open and

Cass came bouncing in, the color in her cheeks high, her eyes sparkling.

"What did you say to Mrs. Gentry?" she demanded. Though she tried to sound indignant, it was evident she was thrilled by the outcome.

Ethan feigned innocence. "What makes you think I said anything?"

"Sue Ellen was all gaga because you were in the office. She couldn't stop talking about it. She told everybody you came to see Mrs. Gentry. The next thing I know Mrs. Gentry apologized to me. *She* apologized to *me!* It was crazy. I never thought she'd do that."

"Are you going to be in the play, after all?"

"No, but she promised she'd consider me for the next one. I'm going to work with her on this one as, like, an assistant or something. She wants me to run lines with Sue Ellen, as her understudy, which totally sucks, but hey, somebody definitely needs to do it."

"You can live with that?" Ethan asked, though it was evident that she was eager to put her previous disappointment behind her.

"Come on," she scoffed. "I deserved to get the lead, but Mrs. Gentry told me she was wrong. That's huge. Teachers usually don't admit stuff like that, not to their students, anyway. I guess I can cut her some slack."

"Then I'm glad it worked out for you," Ethan said. "I have to say, though, I was looking forward to seeing you onstage, knocking everyone dead with your performance."

"You'll probably get to," she said with a hint of laughter in her eyes. "Sue Ellen is so not going to learn those lines. Mrs. Gentry will freak. Sue Ellen will puke. And, *bingo,* I'll go on."

Ethan couldn't help laughing at the welcome return of her self-confidence. "That's the spirit. You might want to temper it around Sue Ellen, though."

She gave him an impatient look. "I'm not stupid," she said. "Gotta go. I need to memorize those lines."

"I still expect to see you here on Thursday."

"I'll be here," she promised. "I figure I'm going to owe you from now till forever because of this."

"You don't owe me a thing," he said. Just seeing a smile back on her face and a spark of excitement back in her eyes was reward enough.

Eight

"I am going completely stir-crazy," Gabi told Samantha on Friday night. "Do you realize I have not been anywhere or done anything without Dani since she was born? Other than that day you gave me a break to get some work done at the office, that is."

Samantha regarded her sister with amusement. "I'm pretty sure that was your choice," she reminded her. "Wade's offered to stay home with your daughter. Grandmother's offered. So have I, for that matter. You've turned us all down, with some very inventive excuses, I might add."

Gabi regarded her with annoyance. "Are you making fun of me because I'm behaving like every other new mom in the universe by being overly protective of my baby?"

"Something like that, especially since Wade and Grandmother both have more experience with babies than you do."

"Okay, so I wasn't ready then," Gabi conceded.

"But you are now?"

"I am so ready," Gabi said fervently. "I want to eat an entire meal, uninterrupted. I want to get a manicure and maybe even a pedicure. I need to get my hair done. I need to shop."

Samantha chuckled. "Okay, it's not sounding as if you're looking for a date night with Wade. I was going to suggest I keep Dani tonight so the two of you could have an evening to yourselves."

"Wade has already claimed Dani for the night. He's taking her over to his sister's so the kids can dote on her. Now the question is, will you go on a girls' night out with me and keep me from calling him every ten minutes to check on the baby? Despite what you think, I do recognize that I need to chill out."

"I can do that," Samantha said readily. "What about Emily? Is she coming along?"

"She's having another of her powwows with Grandmother and Boone over wedding details. What they could possibly have left to plan is beyond me, but checking things off her list, then double-checking them, seems to make her happy. Who am I to question that?"

"Says the master list-maker," Samantha teased. "I'm betting you already have a timetable for tonight written down in your day planner."

"It's on my smartphone, but yes," Gabi admitted without a hint of apology. "Those organizational skills of mine are being put to good use these days." She gave Samantha a sly look. "I can spare some time to work on a new PR campaign for you, though."

Samantha stilled. "Is that what tonight is about? Is this your sneaky way of trying to fix up my career again?"

"No, tonight is about manis and pedis and pampering," Gabi insisted. "The rest is just mental doodling, something to think about while we're getting pretty."

"If you say so," Samantha said, but her enthusiasm for the evening ahead had dwindled just a little. "What makes you think my career needs another boost? I haven't said a word about work."

"Precisely," Gabi said. "And since you're usually brimming over with excitement when things are going well, I find that silence pretty deafening. So do Grandmother and Emily."

"But you're the designated interrogator?"

"No interrogation," she promised. "Just an offer to pitch in if you want my help."

"Let's just stick to the makeovers, dinner and girl talk, okay? Talking about my career will just depress me. I have a lot of things to figure out."

"Talking it through might help," Gabi said.

"Actually I did talk a few things through with Ethan."

Gabi didn't even attempt to hide her surprise. "When did you and Ethan have this little heart-to-heart? Last night when he showed up at Boone's and dragged you off?"

"Then, and again this morning," Samantha revealed.

Gabi's eyes widened. "Hold on. Did you go home with Ethan last night? I could have sworn you slept in your own bed at Grandmother's." Her mouth dropped open. "Or did Ethan stay at the house?"

"Wipe that mental image right out of your head," Samantha scolded. "I'm not likely to bring a man I hardly know into my bed under Cora Jane's roof. She'd tan my hide and load up her shotgun to ensure a wedding."

Gabi laughed. "Yeah, I think that's why Wade refuses to stay over, too. And we're already committed to walking down the aisle once Emily's big shindig is behind us. So, when did you and Ethan continue your conversation?"

"We went for a run together this morning," Samantha said casually as if it were an everyday occurrence. "The coastline is especially pretty just after sunrise. In fact, everything has this lovely golden glow. I'm thinking I'd like to check out Sea Glass Island if we go running again. All those beautiful bits of colored glass that wash ashore must look amazing in that light."

"And how does Ethan look at daybreak? Amazing?" Gabi teased.

"Oh yeah!" Samantha replied with a heartfelt sigh before she could stop herself. "The man is a god!"

"So much for any attempt to claim that you're past that old high school crush," Gabi said. Her expression turned worried. "Samantha, be careful."

The genuine concern in her sister's voice was troubling. "What do you mean? I know what I'm up against. Ethan doesn't do relationships."

"But you do," Gabi reminded her. "Just not for the long term. Add in the distance, and I see a rocky road ahead. Ethan had his heart ripped out once. I'd hate to see it happen again."

Samantha didn't even try to hide her surprise. Why hadn't it occurred to anyone to worry about Ethan *before* they started throwing them together at every opportunity?

"So you're worried about him, not me?" she said, trying to clarify.

"I'm worried for both of you."

"Well, you can stop worrying. We both understand the situation. I'm here for another ten days or so. We're not going to do anything crazy in such a short time. We're having fun. That's it."

"Bedroom fun?"

"That hasn't come up," Samantha admitted, then thought of the undeniable attraction always simmering just below the surface whenever they crossed paths. "At least not yet."

"Sweetie, some men might enjoy casual sex without giving it a second thought. I don't think Ethan is one of those guys."

"And I'm not one of those women," Samantha retorted heatedly. "Come on, Gabi, give me a little credit here. I don't go around seducing men, then deliberately set out to break their hearts."

"I'm just saying—" Gabi began, but Samantha cut her off.

"I know what you're saying. I'll be careful." She gave her sister a plaintive look. "It's just that being around him, after all those years of fantasizing about him…" She smiled. "It's better than I ever imagined."

Gabi regarded her with dismay. "This has gone way beyond fantasizing, hasn't it? You're falling in love with him, aren't you? I'm not sure any of us really anticipated that before we stuck our noses into this. I know I just wanted a little payback for the way you all pushed Wade and me together."

"I'm not sure I know what real love even feels like," Samantha replied. "But, yes, maybe."

"What do you see happening next?"

Samantha sighed at that. "I have no idea, but since

Ethan is pretty adamant about not ever getting involved with anyone, it's probably a moot point."

"Samantha, that's his brain talking, not his heart. If his heart and his libido get involved, the man will fall like a ton of bricks no matter what his head is telling him."

"I think we're a long way from that happening," Samantha said realistically. But, that said, she couldn't help hoping just a little that Gabi was right and she was wrong.

"Samantha, is that you?"

Samantha heard the familiar voice as she waited for Gabi to come out of a dressing room in the boutique and whirled around. "Mrs. Gentry!" she exclaimed with genuine delight. She'd worked with Regina Gentry on two summer productions years ago right here in Sand Castle Bay. She'd learned a lot from her, more than she'd learned from the teachers at her own school. "How are you?"

"I'm just fine," the drama teacher said. "And I don't need to ask how you're doing. I see you on TV all the time. You've done us proud."

"Hardly," Samantha replied. "But thanks for saying that."

"You must be home for the wedding. It's the talk of the entire town. Everyone here is so happy for Boone and Emily. Theirs has been quite a romance. It's nice to see someone finally get their fairy-tale ending."

"*Finally* being the operative word," Samantha said. "It hasn't been easy for either of them."

"No. It was a tragedy what happened to Jenny

Farmer, but at least she and Boone had their son before she died. I know that boy is the light of his dad's life."

Samantha smiled. "B.J.'s great." Wanting to change the subject and thinking of what Ethan had told her about one of his teens, she asked, "How's the high school drama department these days? Are you working on a production?"

"Indeed, we are." Her eyes lit up. "In fact, why don't you stop by rehearsal one afternoon and talk to the students? I know they'd love the chance to speak to someone who's made a career of acting. Not that most of these young people will ever travel down that path, but I have a few who want to give it a try."

"My time's pretty booked up with wedding details," Samantha told her, not sure if she wanted to try to put on an optimistic front when her career was currently in such turmoil.

"An hour," Mrs. Gentry pressed. "Surely you can spare an hour to inspire some young people."

"When you put it that way, how can I refuse?" Samantha conceded reluctantly. Maybe she'd get a chance to meet this young woman Ethan had told her about, too.

"Monday afternoon at three-thirty in the auditorium?"

"I'll be there," Samantha promised, giving her a wry look. "It's nice to see you haven't lost your powers of persuasion."

"I certainly hope not. I'll see you then."

She scurried off, obviously fearful that Samantha might change her mind if given half a chance to reconsider.

Samantha watched her go. Maybe talking about her

career—the struggles and the triumphs—would be good for her, too. It might help to put things in perspective, maybe even remind her why it had once mattered to her more than anything.

"Was that Mrs. Gentry who just took off?" Gabi asked when she stepped out of the dressing room, her arms loaded with the clothes she'd been trying on. "I thought I recognized her voice."

"It was," Samantha confirmed. "And she just convinced me to talk to the kids in her next production on Monday afternoon."

"Next thing you know she'll have you directing the play," Gabi predicted. "I've heard all about how she doesn't give up when she wants something."

"Well, that's one thing I can guarantee she won't get," Samantha said flatly. "I've never harbored a secret desire to direct."

"I thought a lot of actors wanted to get behind the camera at some point in their career, tell other people how a scene should be done."

"Some do," Samantha said. "I'm not one of them." She glanced at the assortment of skirts, blouses, slacks and dresses Gabi was holding. "Nothing fit?"

Gabi grinned. "It all did," she said triumphantly. "So I couldn't decide. I'm so excited to be back to my old size I'm buying all of it."

Samantha laughed. "Good for you. I guess that ice cream sundae I've been craving isn't in the cards when we leave here."

"Who says? I deserve a celebration after fighting for months to lose that baby weight. And I have room to spare in these clothes, so one sundae isn't going to ruin what I've achieved."

"So, how's our checklist for the night coming?"

"Hair's done. We've had out manis and pedis," Gabi said. "Dinner at Boone's Harbor was fantastic, though I wish he'd let us pay for the meal. I'm all shopped out. If I weren't nursing, I'd suggest a drink, but ice cream sounds much better, anyway. I can't tell you the last time I allowed myself to indulge in a sundae. The only treats I've had the past couple of months are the warm doughnuts Wade brings me with coffee in the morning. I refused to give up those."

"What you didn't want to give up was having Wade drop by for a morning kiss," Samantha accused.

Gabi blushed. "Well, that was a perk."

Unexpected tears filled Samantha's eyes at the talk of such tender intimacy between her sister and the man she loved.

"Sammi?" Gabi said worriedly, using an old childhood nickname. "What's wrong? Why are you crying?"

"I don't know," Samantha said, swiping impatiently at the tears.

"You must have some idea," Gabi said, pulling a package of baby wipes from her purse. "No tissues, but I have these."

Samantha grinned through the tears. "You are such a mom."

Gabi looked startled for an instant, then chuckled. "Yeah, I am. Now tell me what's going on."

Samantha didn't even have to think about it. She wanted what Emily and Gabi had found—the love of her life, a family, a place to call home.

She'd always thought of New York as home. She loved the vibrancy, the lights, the nonstop bustle. When she'd been onstage, she'd felt invigorated. The sound of applause washing over her had been like music to her ears.

But then, more often than not, she'd gone home to an empty bed, or, if not empty, then one occupied by a man who'd been important, but not her destiny. Never her destiny the way Boone had been Emily's or Wade had been Gabi's. At least, she'd been wise enough to understand that there was a difference.

"I think I'm jealous," she said, embarrassed by the admission.

"Of me?"

"You and Emily both. You have it all. You have careers you love, especially now that Emily's working on those safe houses for victims of domestic violence and you have the artist's studio here that you and Wade created together. You have men you adore and who love you just as deeply. And you…" She smiled. "You have Daniella Jane, this perfect little baby."

"You can have all that, too, if it's what you decide you want," Gabi said fiercely. "Samantha, there's nothing to stop you from making whatever changes you want to make professionally. As for the man of your dreams, you just have to open your heart. I think you've kept too many men at arm's length because you weren't ready or you knew they weren't the right ones. Is it because of Ethan you're thinking like this?"

"He's part of it. He's this solid, stable guy who knows exactly who he is. Those traits aren't exactly commonplace among the actors I've met."

"But you've dated men who weren't actors. Some were pretty high-ranking businessmen, as I recall."

"They were just as absorbed with ambition, though, as the actors. Maybe that's one of the things I admire in Ethan. He gave up the fast track in surgery and is thoroughly at peace with the decision. That says a lot about who he is." She allowed herself a smile. "Maybe I just want to *be* Ethan."

"Content with a slower pace?" Gabi suggested. "You can do that. I'm here to testify it can be a very rewarding transformation. This has been a huge change for me."

"It has been, hasn't it?" Samantha said. "No regrets?"

"Not a one," Gabi said. "It's not always easy, though. I still find myself compulsively addicted to work from time to time, but then Dani cries or Wade pokes his head into my office and my priorities immediately shift. I get that much-needed sense of balance back."

"Balance," Samantha echoed. "That's it! That's what I want."

Gabi leveled a look at her. "Do you want it here?"

Samantha knew what her sister was really asking, that she wanted to know if Samantha was ready to let go of one dream in exchange for another that was even less certain.

"I don't know," she replied quietly.

"Well, until you do, I'll say what I said earlier, be careful with Ethan."

"Not a problem," Samantha said. "I don't think he's going to allow anything else."

Ethan was feeling surprisingly edgy as he left the clinic. Normally after a busy day, he went home feeling a sense of fulfillment. He was ready for a good meal, maybe a glass of wine and a game of some kind on TV. Though the baseball season was down to the wire and the Braves weren't in the pennant race, he still loved to watch.

Tonight, though, none of that held any appeal, which was one reason he'd stayed late at the clinic. When his cell phone rang, he answered eagerly.

"Why are the lights still on at the clinic?" Greg asked. "Please tell me you're not still working."

"On my way out now," he told him. "And how do you know the lights are on?"

"I'm taking the kids for ice cream to get them out of Lindsey's hair for an hour. Want to meet us?" He named the ice cream parlor the locals frequented only a mile or so from the clinic. "We're pulling into the lot now."

"Sure," Ethan said impulsively. At least it would drive Samantha out of his head for a little while. Greg's kids always seemed to cheer him up…and leave him more than a little envious.

"Good. Maybe you can corral them. They listen to their uncle Ethan a whole lot better than they listen to me."

Ethan smiled at the frustration he heard in Greg's voice. "You're a doctor. Hasn't it occurred to you that if they're out of control, feeding them ice cream at this hour might not be wise?"

"I'm desperate," Greg admitted. "And I was not up for a round of miniature golf, which seemed to be the preferred alternative. See you in a few."

"On my way," Ethan said.

Five minutes later, he walked into the ice cream

shop and immediately spotted Greg and his kids. To his dismay, Gabi and Samantha Castle were setting their purses on the same table and heading to the counter to order. He regarded his friend suspiciously.

"Scheming?" he inquired in an undertone.

Greg gave him an innocent look he didn't entirely trust.

"They just walked in the door," Greg swore to him. "I told them you were on the way and asked them to join us. Seemed like the polite thing to do. Are you going to run off?"

"Of course not," Ethan said, though that was precisely what he wanted to do...or what he thought he *ought* to do. "I'd better go up and order."

He stepped into line behind Samantha and Gabi. "This is a surprise," he said.

"We're having a girls' night out," Gabi said cheerfully. "We've been pampered and buffed and fed. I've bought out most of the clothes at my favorite boutique and now we're having dessert."

"And did you shop, too?" he asked Samantha.

"She didn't buy a single thing," Gabi said, her frustration plain. "I think she's deliberately trying to make me feel guilty for splurging the way I did."

Samantha shrugged. "I have a closetful of clothes I never wear. Why buy more?"

Gabi put her hand over her heart in an exaggerated gesture of dismay. "What sort of woman says a thing like that? You're going to ruin shopping for the rest of us."

Ethan laughed, though he wondered if Samantha's restraint had less to do with an aversion to shopping than with finances. He had no idea how well an acting career might pay, especially one that was faltering the way she claimed hers was.

"All I can say is that Samantha's attitude is music to a man's ears," he said. "And since you always look beautiful, I can't see why you'd need a new wardrobe every few weeks, anyway."

"Thank you," Samantha said with a surprising blush on her cheeks.

As they reached the counter, Ethan said, "The ice cream is on me. Go crazy."

"You might not want to say that," Samantha warned. "Gabi's been on a diet and I've already told you about my addiction. Between the two of us, we could blow your ice cream budget to smithereens."

"I'll take my chances," Ethan said.

"Okay, then, you asked for it," Gabi said, ordering a banana split that was big enough for two or three people. It was a favorite with teens double-dating.

Samantha showed only a little more restraint, ordering a double hot fudge sundae with extra hot fudge.

"I'll have what she's having," Ethan said, pointing to the sundae. He grinned at her. "Of course, for me this is dinner."

"And for me, it's God's gift to the dessert menu," Samantha retorted. "You are not going to make me feel guilty."

He laughed. "Never my intention." He'd just wanted to see that quick rise of becoming color in her cheeks again. She hadn't disappointed him.

Back at the table, Greg's kids outdid themselves trying to get Ethan's attention. He had one settled in his lap, another leaning into his side, when he spotted the look of envy on Samantha's face. Easily identifying with it and knowing the ache of emptiness that usually accompanied those feelings, he leaned toward her. "You okay?"

"Just thinking how good you are with them," she said. "And I've seen you with B.J., too. You're a natural."

"It's a good thing, given the number of kids I see in the clinic every day."

"Doesn't it make you want to be a dad?"

"Sometimes, yes," he said candidly. "I just know it's not in the cards. How about you?"

"I wasn't sure I had any maternal instincts until the first time I held Gabi's baby. Now…" She sighed. "But why wish for something I'm not likely to have?"

"It's not too late for motherhood. You're only in your thirties, right?"

"Without a relationship in sight," she reminded him. A grin teased at her lips. "Unless you're volunteering."

Now it was Ethan's turn to blush. He could feel the heat climb into his cheeks as he considered the idea for just a heartbeat. Him. Samantha. A baby. It was a picture, all right, he thought, recalling Boone's comment a while back.

"I'm sure if you let it be known that you want a baby, you'll have plenty of volunteers," he said, all but choking on the words. He hated the idea of anyone other than him touching her, but he had no right to feel such intense jealousy.

"Just anyone won't do," she said with a resigned expression.

Ethan was relieved to hear it, but he couldn't let her see that.

Thankfully, Greg stood up just then. "Okay, Cameron and Lily, say good-night. I need to get you home and into bed."

"But we want to stay with Uncle Ethan," Lily said, holding tight to Ethan's arm.

"Little girls need to get plenty of sleep so they'll be beautiful when they grow up," Ethan told her emphatically.

Lily turned a shy look on Samantha. "Like her?"

Ethan smiled. "Exactly like her."

"Is she your girlfriend?" Lily asked.

Greg chuckled at Ethan's choked reaction, but he did scoop his daughter up. "Enough with the personal questions, kiddo. It's not polite."

"But you always say if I want to know something, I should ask," Lily said, obviously confused by the contradiction.

"One of these days we'll have a long talk about which questions are acceptable and which ones aren't," Greg said. "I think I'll let your mother handle that. Tell your uncle Ethan good-night."

Both kids gave him fierce hugs, then ran to the door. Greg gave him a wink. "Enjoy the rest of your evening."

Ethan had a hunch his was going to be a whole lot less stressful than Greg's, given that he was heading home with two kids on a sugar high.

Nine

No sooner had Greg left with his children than Gabi gave a dramatic yawn and stood up. "I think I'm about to crash, too. It's the curse of motherhood. I have no stamina anymore. Ethan, would you mind giving Samantha a lift home? I know she's not ready for the night to end."

Before Samantha could protest or Ethan could reply, she took his acceptance for granted and sailed out of the ice cream parlor.

"That was subtle," Samantha said, embarrassed by the obvious ploy. She stood up. "I can still catch her."

Ethan reached for her hand and shook his head. "No, it's fine. You're not finished with your ice cream and neither am I. Stay."

"Are you sure?" she asked, surprised by his easy acceptance of the situation.

"Given that I just saw your sister peel out of the parking lot like she has a curfew, I'd say I have to be," he said wryly. "She wasn't taking any chances you'd bolt after her."

"I actually thought for a time she was immune to

the meddling gene, or at least averse to it, given what we all put her through with Wade, but I guess not," Samantha said with a resigned shrug. She pushed the remains of her sundae away. "As for this, my eyes were bigger than my stomach. Hard to imagine, but I can't eat another bite of ice cream."

"Want to go for a walk?" Ethan asked, surprising her yet again. "We could drive down by the town pier and walk either along the sand or out to the end of the pier. Of course, if it's overrun with fishermen, we might be taking our lives in our hands."

"Still, a walk definitely sounds good. It's a beautiful night." A romantic night with a full moon predicted, she thought to herself. Would that put Ethan in the same mood she was in? Or was he immune to such things?

By the time they reached the waterfront, the sky had darkened and the huge moon was casting its light across the water, bringing silver-tipped waves to shore. They walked down to the water's edge. Samantha kicked off her shoes and let the waves lap over her feet. She was going to suggest Ethan do the same before it dawned on her that walking in sand might be difficult with his prosthesis and that water might not do it any favors, either. Since he'd suggested the walk, though, she wasn't about to hint she thought he might not be up to it. He knew his own capabilities better than anyone, and obviously prided himself on having mastered the use of his artificial limb.

Instead, she focused on the tranquil scene before them. "It's beautiful, isn't it?" she said, unable to keep a note of awe from her voice. "I never see such clear skies in New York."

"It is beautiful," Ethan said, his voice oddly ragged.

When she glanced up, she saw he was looking at her, his gaze intense. "Samantha…" His voice trailed off, leaving an opening.

She seized it and stepped closer. "Don't say anything," she whispered, putting a hand on his cheek. The sandpapery texture was all male. So was the heat.

"Bad idea," he murmured, though he defied his own warning and leaned down, touching his lips to hers.

To the contrary, Samantha thought it was an excellent idea as she lost herself in the kiss. It was sweet and tender and restrained, but there was an unmistakable sense of urgency just below the surface. She wanted desperately to tap into that, to shake Ethan up, to make him let go and kiss her the way he had done a thousand times in her teen fantasies.

Though she'd been seduced far more than she'd been the aggressor, she dared to touch her tongue to the seam of his lips, earning a moan of pleasure. Even so, he put his hands on her shoulders and took a step back, exhibiting that same exasperating restraint that had marked all their encounters. How would they ever get past that, she wondered, when on some very deep level, he didn't want to?

"I still think we're playing with fire here," he said.

She smiled at the worry in his voice. "I hope so," she retorted, eager for the fulfillment of all those long-ago daydreams and not caring for the moment that she was putting her heart on the line.

His eyes widened at her bold response. "You really are going to be the death of me, aren't you?"

"I hope not. I just want to tempt you."

"You accomplish that by walking into a room," he said with unexpected candor. "This goes way beyond temptation, Samantha."

"Not if we're still standing here instead of racing to your place," she said.

Ethan smiled at that, then took yet another step back. "Which we are not going to do," he said firmly. "One of us needs to think clearly. I can't give you what you need, Samantha. I don't believe in forever or happily-ever-after. Even if it does exist, I know I'm not cut out for it. And you're only here for another week or so. Why start something that could only end badly?"

If Samantha hadn't seen the struggle underlying his words, she might have pressed her advantage, but how could she, knowing that Ethan—the man who never had regrets—would be filled with them in the morning? So would she, more than likely. She might not agree with the limits he'd put on his life, but how could she not respect them?

"Could we just sit on the pier, enjoy the night?" she asked, not ready for the evening to end, not if it wasn't going to have the ending she'd hoped for. "Maybe have a little friendly conversation?"

"Sure. We can do that," he said, taking her hand for the walk back. He glanced at her. "And just so you know, Samantha, that may have been the hardest thing I've ever done in my life."

"Telling me no?" she said, startled by the admission. He nodded.

"Then why did you do it?"

"Because it was the right thing to do. You deserve so much more than I have to offer."

She frowned at the suggestion that he couldn't possibly be enough for her. "Can I ask you something?"

"Of course."

"One of the reasons you're spending time with these kids is to bolster their self-confidence, right?"

Though he must have felt the question came out of left field, he didn't even hesitate. "Absolutely."

"How can you possibly be any good at helping them when your own self-image is lousy?"

A frown flitted across his face. "My self-confidence is just fine," he contradicted.

"And yet you can stand there and say that you don't have enough to offer me or presumably any other woman. If you ask me, that's your former fiancée talking and we've already agreed that she was a jerk."

Ethan looked startled by the straight talk.

"I'm just being realistic," he insisted. "For all the things we've discovered we have in common, there are still plenty of things that make us a bad match, not the least of which is you needing to figure out what you really want out of life."

She wanted to tell him that she had figured it out, that she wanted him and a family and a home right here, but how could she? The idea was still too new to her, too far from certain. She let her silence speak for itself, let him think he'd gotten it right because she couldn't honestly deny that he had.

As they sat on a bench in the glow of the moonlight, he faced her, longing in his eyes. He caressed her cheek, his hand charmingly unsteady. Samantha wanted to capture it, press a kiss to his palm, but she held back.

"You figure things out," he said quietly. "Then we'll talk."

Though the comment offered more hope than anything he'd said before, she wasn't satisfied with the concession. "Just so you know, in my opinion, talking is highly overrated."

"And yet you get onstage and deliver lines for a living," he teased in an obvious attempt to lighten the mood.

"Those are somebody else's words, someone else's emotions," she said. "In the real world, I'm just saying there may be better ways to communicate."

He draped his arm around her shoulder, warming her when she shivered in the breeze off the ocean. "A topic for another day," he said. "Let's just focus on the here and now. You. Me. The moonlight. The sound of the waves. What's not to love?"

It was more than he'd ever offered before, so she took him up on it. She leaned in to all that solid strength and heat and sighed. "It's a perfect moment," she agreed, her voice shaky.

Though there was a very good chance that all this sweet proximity with no payoff just might make her a little crazy.

Ethan felt as if he'd brushed up against danger and emerged with little more than battle scars as he drove over to Cora Jane's. He'd wanted everything Samantha had been offering at the beach, wanted it with a level of desire he hadn't felt even when he'd been engaged. He liked that she challenged his assumptions, liked that she deliberately tempted him, putting her own emotions on the line. The attraction he felt for her had spiked by several heated degrees tonight. But attraction didn't always last. His engagement had been proof of that. And when it wore off, hearts could get broken. He didn't want it to be hers any more than he wanted to go through that pain again himself.

He knew he'd spend the lonely hours in his cold bed kicking himself for not giving in, but he also knew he'd still be able to look in the mirror in the morning. Sex would have been easy. Doing the right thing took a toll.

As he parked in Cora Jane's driveway, he turned to face Samantha. "Any idea what's on tomorrow's agenda? Do we have wedding-related duties?"

"Boone's folks are flying in with their respective spouses. He's expecting all of us for dinner at the restaurant in the private dining room. Personally, I think we should have eaten in the main dining room with everyone else."

"Why is that?"

"Have you ever been around both of his parents at the same time? Now that his mom is on her third or fourth husband, they're barely civil. She always has some snarky comment about his dad's trophy wife that gets things started. He replies in kind and it pretty much goes downhill from there."

Ethan winced. "I haven't crossed paths with them since the divorce years ago, but it sounds like a barrel of laughs. Maybe he should include the Farmers, too, and complete the circle of warring factions."

"Are you kidding? Emily told me that Boone insisted they be invited to the wedding as a courtesy. He thought maybe they'd finally accept the situation for B.J.'s sake."

"I assume they didn't," Ethan said.

"Hardly. Jodie shredded the invitation. She even crossed out the preprinted address on the envelope because it was Emily's and sent the bits of paper directly to Boone."

Ethan sighed at the woman's all-too-typical response, her deliberate attempt to inflict pain on Boone. "I hope one of these days she'll be able to let go of her grief and anger, if only for B.J.," he said. "He doesn't need to feel as if he's torn between his grandparents and his stepmother. He loves them all."

"And needs them," Samantha agreed. "I just don't understand why Jodie can't see that she's his tie to his mom. There are *so* many stories she can share with him, stories B.J. needs to hear. He was so young when Jenny died. I know he doesn't want to forget about his mom. Instead, if Jodie keeps this up, she'll only alienate him."

"I hate it when children get caught up in adult warfare," Ethan said. "Usually it happens after a divorce. Even Boone, one of the most stable guys around, has baggage from his parents' split. Of course, in his case, it's turned out to be a positive thing. He works twice as hard to protect B.J. and to keep the peace with the Farmers, even when Jodie makes it all but impossible."

"What about your family?" Samantha asked. "I just remember seeing your mom and dad at football games on the few times we came over here in the fall to visit Grandmother. They were certainly united in their support of you."

"They're happily united, period. They've retired and moved over to Asheville. They sit on their porch in the evening, holding hands and watching the sun set in the mountains. I feel like a fifth wheel every time I visit."

"You can see that level of contentment and not believe in happily-ever-after?" Samantha asked, studying him incredulously.

Ethan understood the contradiction. He'd wrestled with it a time or two, though not lately. Something told him, though, that Samantha was going to make him re-examine everything he'd believed about love.

"They're the exception, not the rule," he said finally. "And sure, there was a time when I wanted what they'd found."

"And then came What's-her-face," Samantha said sarcastically.

"Lisa," he supplied.

"My point is that you let one bad apple ruin a lifetime of apparently good memories. She doesn't deserve to have that much power over you."

"Intellectually, I know that," he agreed. "And I think we've been down this road enough for one night."

"Maybe so, since I'm obviously making no inroads in changing your mind," she said, her frustration plain.

"Want to try again tomorrow?" he asked. "I could pick you up for this dinner thing."

Her lips twitched. "As a courtesy or as a date?"

He'd be more comfortable calling it a courtesy, but they both knew better. "Do we have to define it?"

"I think we should."

Ethan thought about it. He recognized the sensible answer. He also recognized that it wouldn't delude either one of them. "Might as well call it a date," he said, hoping he sounded casual. "Throw a bone to the meddlers."

She patted his cheek. "Said with so much enthusiasm," she teased. "I'll look forward to it." She opened her door, slipped from the car, then leaned back in the open window. "Just so you know, since it's a date, I'll be looking forward to a kiss at the end of the evening."

With that, she sashayed off, leaving Ethan with his heart in his throat and a whole passel of anticipation.

"Rumor has it you were out with Samantha last night," Boone said when he dropped by Ethan's on Saturday morning, two large containers of coffee and a box of warm doughnuts in hand.

Ethan regarded the offerings with suspicion. "No need to ask why you're here," he commented dryly. "Who sent you? Emily or Cora Jane? And what makes any of you think that information can be bought with coffee and doughnuts?"

Boone grinned. "Experience has taught me you're much more amenable after coffee. The doughnuts were Gabi's idea. I gather Wade started making solid inroads with her when he showed up with them. I figured it was worth a shot. Besides, I never miss a chance to grab a box of these whenever I can."

He proved his point by opening the box and nabbing an old-fashioned glazed doughnut, which he finished in three bites before reaching for one iced in chocolate.

Ethan leaned against his kitchen counter, sipped his coffee and shook his head as he watched Boone devour three doughnuts in a row.

"Care to explain why you're so nervous?" Ethan asked eventually, moving the box out of reach before his friend made himself sick.

"I'm not nervous," Boone insisted. "What do I have

to be nervous about? I'm marrying the love of my life a week from today."

"So you're not having second thoughts about Emily?"

"Not a chance," Boone said emphatically.

"What, then?"

Boone hesitated, then asked, "You swear to God you won't say a word about this, not to a single person?"

"As your best man and your friend, my lips are sealed," Ethan promised.

"It's this whole Los Angeles thing," Boone admitted, his voice low as if he feared being overheard. "The restaurant's doing great. Emily's all caught up in these safe houses she's designing and refurbishing. B.J.'s in a good school."

"But," Ethan prodded.

"I hate it," Boone admitted. "I wish I could explain why, but I don't have an answer. How am I supposed to talk Emily into getting out of there if I can't explain why the place makes me crazy?"

"My hunch is it's not about Los Angeles at all," Ethan said, empathizing with him.

"What, then?" Boone asked, obviously eager for an outside viewpoint.

"It's not home," Ethan suggested. "You grew up here. You have roots here. You're close to Cora Jane and think of her as family, even though she's Emily's grandmother. Now even Gabi and Wade are settling here, so more family ties. Your business started here. Even Jodie and Frank are here, for whatever that matters. This is home, simple as that."

Boone's eyes lit with understanding. "That's it, exactly. And I feel guilty as sin, because I can see that

Emily's thrilled to pieces. Home's supposed to be where the heart is, right? And Emily is my heart."

"But Sand Castle Bay and the ocean breezes are in your blood, same as me," Ethan suggested.

"It's a coastal community," Boone countered. "Lots of water. Los Angeles has a great big ocean, too."

"Not the same," Ethan said. "It's on the wrong side, for one thing."

Boone laughed, just as Ethan had intended. "True, but I can't see Emily buying that as an argument. So, how do I tell her? Or do I? Maybe I just need to suck it up and make peace with being there."

Ethan regarded him worriedly. "You haven't had this conversation with her at all?"

Boone shook his head, his expression miserable. "How can I? She's so ecstatic about her work, so grateful that I came out there. I guess she just assumed I was making a permanent move."

"And you never so much as hinted that you saw it as a temporary compromise?"

"No. I didn't want some endless long-distance relationship, so I came up with a solution. Open a restaurant out there, give her some time to take advantage of this incredible opportunity she'd been given and then we'd come back here. I figured it was understood."

"But she assumed it was permanent?"

"Yes, and she's already looking at some jobs that will extend into next year or even the year after," Boone said. "As soon as she told me about them, I realized we were not on the same page at all."

"Then you have to tell her," Ethan said.

"A week before our wedding?" Boone protested. "How can I do that?"

"Because if you wait until after the wedding, it'll blow up in your face. Resolve this now, pal. That's my advice."

Boone sighed. "I know you're right." He glanced at his watch and groaned, muttering an expletive. "Dear old Dad and his perky young wife are due any minute now. Mother's due to arrive pretty soon, too. I'd better get home before warfare breaks out." He gave Ethan an exhausted look. "You are coming to this dinner thing tonight, right?"

"Looking forward to it," Ethan said wryly.

"Yeah, I'll bet," Boone retorted. His gaze narrowed. "Or is it true that you're bringing Samantha? In that case, I can almost believe you are looking forward to it."

"I'm picking her up," Ethan conceded. "Don't make too much of it, though. In fact, you might want to consider the possibility that we're simply conspiring to play all sorts of nefarious tricks on the happy couple before your big day. I hear that's something that the best man and maid of honor are almost duty-bound to do. Try messing with my life, and I can make yours hell." He beamed at his friend. "I'm just saying."

Boone laughed. "Message received. I'll back off. Unfortunately, I can't speak for my bride-to-be, her grandmother or her sister."

And that, of course, was where the real danger lay.

Gabi pinned Samantha with an eager look. "What happened after I left you and Ethan alone last night? Spill. I want details."

"Not a thing," Samantha told her discreetly. "And thanks for that, by the way. You embarrassed me."

"Oh, fiddlesticks!" Gabi replied. "You don't embarrass that easily. Besides, you need to keep the goal in mind. You want Ethan. We're all doing our part to see that you get him."

"How am I supposed to know if I really want him when I spend most of our time together trying to defend my crazy family?"

"If you're not taking advantage of these little opportunities," Gabi said, "then you're not the sister I looked up to for dating inspiration."

Samantha shook her head. "Here's the problem with your theory. I was great at dating. I was the queen of dating…in high school, Gabi. Not lately. And dating is not exactly the goal here, is it?"

"And what might the real goal be?" her sister inquired, a twinkle in her eyes. "Sex? A short-term fling? A genuine relationship? Marriage? We'd all be a whole lot more effective if we knew exactly what you're after."

"It is not my goal to ensure your effectiveness. I want you to butt out," Samantha declared, knowing full well it wasn't going to happen.

In fact, Gabi merely waited her out with the patience of a woman who understood that the tactic of silence always worked. Cora Jane had always been notorious for getting them to reveal their secrets simply by sipping tea and waiting.

"I've been down here a week," Samantha finally retorted with exasperation. "That's not exactly long enough to formulate a plan for the future with a man I barely know. I do know that an old crush years ago for a man I idolized from afar is not a solid foundation for forever."

Gabi nodded. "Fair enough. Which way are you leaning, though? You think he's hot, right?"

"Of course he's hot," Samantha said impatiently. "Last time I checked, that wasn't a good basis for a lasting relationship."

"But it is a fascinating place to start," Gabi countered.

"So says the woman who managed to ignore the very steamy Wade for months."

Gabi frowned at the comparison. "When you all plunked him down in front of me like some decadent dessert, I was already involved, remember?"

"No, you weren't," Samantha said. "You were deluding yourself."

"True, but be that as it may, I *thought* I was in a committed relationship."

"And then you knew you weren't. You still resisted."

"I was pregnant!"

Samantha shrugged that off, too. "Yeah, well, it didn't seem to bother Wade. He fell for you, anyway."

"Why are we getting sidetracked?" Gabi demanded, her frustration plain. "This is about you and Ethan."

"I thought it was a conversation about sexual attraction versus a meaningful relationship."

"Same thing," Gabi insisted. "One can lead to the other. A real relationship has to start somehow. Hopping into bed could definitely kick-start it."

"Ethan doesn't just hop into bed," Samantha said. "I admire that about him."

"How do you know? Is that what he says or have you actually tried to seduce him?"

"Enough!" Samantha said, unwilling to reveal such intimate details about her relationship with Ethan. "This is ridiculous."

Gabi's eyes widened. "You have, haven't you?" she gloated. "You tried to get him to sleep with you and he wouldn't."

"Not discussing this," Samantha said, grabbing her coffee and heading back upstairs. She'd suddenly remembered the downside of being surrounded by sisters. They could be totally intrusive pests. For once she regretted that baby Daniella wasn't screaming her head off to distract Gabi from her morning mission.

Instead, Gabi was right on her heels as she climbed the stairs. When Samantha shut her bedroom door in her sister's face, Gabi merely opened it and followed her inside. Sadly, while the doors might have locks, the keys had vanished long ago. Samantha regretted not having dealt with that on an earlier visit.

"Go away," she ordered. "I'm about ten seconds from tossing you down the stairs."

Gabi openly laughed at that. "Not worried. One of these days you're going to admit you don't have a clue how to get what you want with Ethan and you're going to beg Emily and me for tips. Cora Jane, too."

Right now Samantha was thinking she was more likely to be asking for tips on where she could dump the bodies.

Ten

The tension in the air in the Boone's Harbor private dining room that night was so thick it could have been cut with a knife, Ethan decided. Some of that could be attributed to the uncensored barbs being tossed around between Boone's parents, but Samantha seemed to be at odds with Gabi, and Boone and Emily were outside on the deck, obviously exchanging heated words. He had a terrible feeling he knew the topic under discussion.

"What's with those two?" Samantha asked, gesturing toward the supposedly happy couple as she joined him.

"A difference of opinion, I'd say," Ethan said. "How about you and Gabi? Did something happen between the two of you?"

"Just the usual sisterly disagreement," she said, obviously minimizing it.

"Granted, I've never had a sister, but it seems more serious than that to me," Ethan said. "You didn't fight because she bailed on you last night, did you? I told you it wasn't a big deal."

"Nothing like that," she insisted, but offered no further explanation.

"If you say so," he said, just in time for the door to the deck to burst open. Emily stormed inside, grabbed her purse off a table and sailed through the dining room, ignoring everyone who called out to her, including her grandmother.

"Oh, no. This can't be good," Samantha murmured, and ran after her, as did Gabi and Cora Jane.

Boone entered more slowly, his expression shell-shocked. "Sorry about that," he said, though his voice was barely loud enough to be heard by those close by. He headed directly to the bar, ordered a drink, then faced everyone. He tried for an upbeat expression, but it fell flat.

"I hope you'll all stay and enjoy dinner," he said stiffly. "Emily's not feeling well. She had to leave."

B.J. ran to his dad's side, his expression filled with worry. "Daddy, Emily looked mad. Did you have a fight?"

Boone ruffled his son's hair with a halfhearted gesture. "Just a little disagreement, son."

Ethan thought otherwise. He also thought Boone was maybe a split second from shattering. Ethan didn't want that happening in front of B.J. Keeping a concerned eye on his friend, he approached Boone's mother. "Could you keep an eye on B.J. for a bit? I need to speak to Boone privately."

She blinked at the request, obviously not used to playing the role of doting grandmother, then nodded. "Sure, I can do that. You don't think there's real trouble in paradise, do you?"

"Hard to say," Ethan replied tersely.

The other party attendees, sensing a real crisis, were wise enough to give Boone a wide berth. Ethan crossed over to the bar, ordered his own drink, then waited.

Boone finished the drink in front of him, then ordered another.

"Can I assume you just filled Emily in on your thoughts about Los Angeles?" Ethan inquired eventually.

Boone responded with a wry expression. "Oh, yeah. Bad idea, Ethan. Ironically, I actually think she'd been expecting it, but she didn't take it well, just the same."

"Better now than later," Ethan said, sticking to his guns.

"You saw her. Did she look as if she might forgive me any time this century?"

"Forgive you for what? Being open and honest with her?"

"That's not exactly how she sees it. She said, well, she said a lot of stuff, not the least of which being that I'd deceived her. I believe the word *betrayal* was thrown around quite a bit, as well."

Ethan winced. "Okay, I suppose you can't entirely blame her for feeling like that," he said, then added quickly, "Not that you intended to do that, of course."

Boone gave him a bleak look. "It's over."

Ethan regarded him incredulously. "Don't be ridiculous. It is not over," he said with confidence, then studied him worriedly. "Did she say it was over?"

"She didn't throw the ring in my face, if that's what you're asking, but she might as well have. She says she doesn't want to see me again, that she wants me out of the house in Los Angeles before she gets back since I hate it there so much. I'd say that's pretty clear."

"Heat of the moment," Ethan said, even as he wondered if it could really be more than that.

"I can see the handwriting on the wall," Boone contradicted despondently.

"You're not a fortune-teller, Boone," Ethan said with a touch of impatience. He was fully aware of the irony of him, of all people, giving a pep talk about lasting love. Still, he continued. "Stop anticipating disaster. It's a bump in the road. You'll work this out. You caught her off guard. Give her time to cool down and think this through."

"Not this time," Boone said. "Time's not going to change anything."

Ethan wasn't used to being in the position of defending relationships, but he found himself advising Boone to trust in what he and Emily had. "You hurt her. She's striking back. Please do not tell me you're the kind of man who walks away at the first sign of trouble. I thought this woman was the love of your life. You let her go once. If you do it again, you'll never forgive yourself."

"She's the one who walked out," Boone grumbled. "Both times."

"Meaning it's up to her to fix this so your pride can remain intact? That'll be cold comfort to you when you're all alone in your bed. Don't you remember how that felt?"

Boone sighed. "All too well," he admitted.

"Then what are you going to do?"

"I wish I knew."

"Well, talking to me isn't the answer, I can tell you that."

"And you think I'm going to get within a hundred yards of her tonight once Gabi, Samantha and Cora Jane turn that house into a fortress against the enemy?"

"A very dramatic description, but last time I checked, every one of those women adores you and wants you and Emily to live happily ever after. I suspect you can talk your way past them. Now, go."

"I need to check on B.J.," Boone protested.

"Your son is with his grandmother. She'll make sure he gets home. I'll check in on him, too. Stop delaying. Get over there and grovel, if you need to."

"Groveling's one thing," Boone said. "I can do that. It still won't solve the core problem."

"And that's what compromise is all about. You give a little. She gives a little. And voilà! A solution materializes and the wedding's back on."

Boone listened to what he had to say, then chuckled. "It's no wonder you're not married. Forget the infamous Lisa. You live in some sort of delusional world when it comes to women. I'm going to pay for this. I'll be living in Los Angeles till I'm ninety just to prove how much I love her."

"Then you're not the man I thought you were," Ethan told him. "Rumor has it you have excellent negotiating skills. Seems to me it's never been more critical that you put them to good use."

Boone didn't seem to buy the pep talk, but he did head out.

Ethan pulled his cell phone from his pocket and called Samantha. "How are things where you are?"

"Ugly," she said in an undertone. "Hold on."

He waited while she apparently sought some privacy. "Ethan?"

"I'm here. Boone just left. He's on his way over to make peace."

"Seriously? Is he delusional? He can't turn up here with flowers and champagne and make this right. He led Emily to believe that he understood her need to live in Los Angeles. She thought they had an agreement." She sighed, then added, "Okay, to be honest, she *hoped* he'd adapted."

"And he thought it was a temporary compromise," Ethan responded. "Till this job was wrapped up."

"He talked to you about this?" Samantha asked incredulously. "You knew he wanted to move back to Sand Castle Bay?"

"We discussed it this morning," he confessed, "but I've had a pretty strong hunch all along that's what he was thinking. Boone's roots are here. This is home to him, the same as it is for me."

"And that's it? You're the men, so you win?"

"Why are you getting annoyed with me?" he asked, bemused by her attitude. "It's not a matter of winning or losing. Mature couples compromise all the time. They can split their time between coasts. Or Emily might find that she can have an equally fulfilling career here. Boone's given Los Angeles a try. Maybe she could give Sand Castle Bay a try. I don't know what the answer is for them. I do know they're the only ones who can figure it out."

"Emily thought they had."

"Then she wasn't really listening, was she?"

"I can't talk to you right now," Samantha snapped. "My sister needs me."

And that, Ethan thought as he heard the sound of the call being disconnected, was precisely why he didn't believe in happily-ever-after. If Boone and Emily, who'd loved each other practically forever, couldn't even make it through the vows, what chance did the rest of them stand?

"Who was that?" Emily asked suspiciously when Samantha returned to the bedroom where Emily had been crying her eyes out for the past hour.

"Ethan," her sister admitted. "He says Boone is on his way over."

"I don't want to see him," Emily said, even though her expression was filled with longing.

"Do you really think avoiding him is the answer?" Gabi asked gently.

"She knows it's not," Cora Jane chided. "Honey bun, the two of you need to talk this through. Don't let it turn into some mountain that can't be climbed."

"You mean rather than the molehill you consider it to be?" Emily asked wearily. "I know you'd love it if I'd just cave in and agree to move here."

Cora Jane regarded her patiently. "Where you live isn't up to me, now, is it? Boone saw how important this job in Los Angeles was to you, and he uprooted himself and B.J. to accommodate that. He even opened a restaurant out there. That shows the lengths he was willing to go to just to make you happy."

"And now it's my turn?" Emily asked miserably. "There's nothing for me here."

"Except family, history and potential," Cora Jane reminded her. "And there was nothing in Los Angeles for Boone except you. He made it work."

"You wouldn't be the first couple to take turns following each other's career choices," Gabi suggested.

"I saw it all the time. One partner would get a fantastic offer someplace and the couple would move. Next time, they'd go where the other one landed a dream job."

"I've seen that, too," Samantha chimed in. "One actor has a movie role on location and his wife and kids go along. Next time the wife lands a part in a sitcom and they settle in Los Angeles while that's taping. You work things out."

"If you say anything about it being the mature way to handle things, I may have to smother you with a pillow," Emily warned.

"Then I won't use that word," Samantha said. "Even if it does apply."

Emily sighed. "You all make it sound so blasted reasonable. It didn't feel reasonable when Boone dropped this bombshell on me earlier."

"Did he demand that you come home to North Carolina immediately after the honeymoon?" Samantha asked.

"No. He just said that he hoped it was something I'd consider once this safe house project was completed."

"That sounds pretty reasonable to me," Cora Jane said.

Emily frowned at her. "It probably is. It just felt like a betrayal. And it was even worse, because I'd been half expecting it all along. I'd just hoped I was wrong about how miserable he was out there. I don't understand why he had to bring this up now, a few days before our wedding."

"Maybe he understood that you'd gotten the wrong idea and thought it was important to get these particular cards on the table before the wedding," Samantha suggested. "Perhaps you should give him points for trying to be honest and up front with you. How would you have felt if he'd waited and hit you with this in a few months?"

"I don't want to give him points for anything," Emily grumbled, then sighed when there was a knock on the door downstairs.

"You going down?" Samantha asked. "Or do we send him away?"

Emily glanced around at the expectant expressions everyone was wearing and sighed. "Of course I'm going down there," she grumbled. "But he's not off the hook yet."

"Wouldn't expect him to be," Gabi acknowledged with a grin.

As Emily started from the room, Cora Jane called out to her.

"What?" Emily asked.

"Just keep in mind how much you love this man and how much he loves you. Do that and everything will turn out all right," Cora Jane told her.

Samantha wrapped her arms around her grandmother. "And *that's* where we all get our romantic optimism."

She couldn't quite decide if that was a blessing or a curse.

Cora Jane turned to Samantha as soon as Emily had left the bedroom. "Now let's talk about you," she said, an unrelenting note in her voice.

Samantha regarded her with surprise. "Me? Why?"

"Did you or did you not fight with Ethan when he

called just now to let you know Boone was on his way? I could see it in your eyes when you walked back in here that you were furious."

"Okay, yes, I was annoyed that he knew what was on Boone's mind and hadn't warned any of us," Samantha said.

"It wasn't his place," Cora Jane said firmly. "And if you were being fair, you'd know that. Are you just looking for an excuse to keep him at arm's length?"

"Oh, she wants him a lot closer than that," Gabi said, her voice threaded with laughter.

"Gabriella!" Samantha protested.

Cora Jane chuckled, satisfied with the revelation. "Okay, then. I'm happy to be wrong about that. Call the man and make peace. One couple fighting is all this family can handle right now."

"I'll call him in the morning," Samantha said. "Or see him at that brunch you're planning. I imagine you'll figure out some way to be sure we're seated together."

Cora Jane gave her an impatient look. "Allowing bad feelings to simmer overnight is never a good thing. Haven't I told all you girls that good marriages mean going to bed with a kiss, not a frown?"

Samantha shook her head. "I can't help believing that an occasional night of someone being banished to sleep on the couch can get a point across."

Cora Jane shook her head. "Okay, let's look at it another way. When is it easier to apologize, the second you know you've done something wrong or after you've allowed the misdeed to grow and grow in the other person's mind and in your own?"

Samantha scowled at her. "You're talking about me

waiting to tell you I was sorry when I broke the antique silver mirror that had belonged to your grandmother, aren't you?"

"How many days did you suffer before you finally told the truth and apologized? Was that any fun? Was it any easier after waiting all that time?"

"No," Samantha said grudgingly. "And I didn't sleep a wink for two nights. Maybe, though, that was the punishment I deserved."

"So this is about punishing Ethan for being loyal to his friend rather than to you?" Cora Jane asked.

She could tell from Samantha's resigned expression that she'd nailed her feelings on the very first try.

"Something like that," Samantha conceded with unmistakable reluctance.

Gabi had been listening intently, and now a grin broke across her face. "Here comes the lecture on maturity, right, Grandmother?"

"Save it," Samantha pleaded. "I get it. I will call Ethan. I hope you won't mind, though, if I take a little delight in waking him out of a sound sleep."

"Something tells me he's going to be every bit as wide awake as you are," Cora Jane said. "Nobody sleeps well when things between them and a person they care about are unresolved." She stood up. "Now, if you don't mind, I'm going to give Jerry a call. I all but abandoned him at that dinner party. He's owed an apology, too."

Samantha turned to Gabi. "What about you? Anyone you need to mend fences with tonight?"

"Nope. Wade and I are good. In fact, he's in Daniella's room right now, rocking her to sleep."

"Well, for once, just tell the man to stay put and

spend the night here," Cora Jane said. "Sending him out the door at midnight isn't fooling anyone."

That said, she walked out of the bedroom, leaving Samantha and Gabi staring after her. Nothing pleased her more than surprising her granddaughters and leaving them with a little something to think about. She'd done a good night's work just now, hopefully given them a push to get their lives back on an even keel. She could hardly wait to tell Jerry all about it.

Ethan had been stewing ever since Samantha had hung up on him. He would have gone barging in over there to set the record straight, but he figured with Boone trying to work things out with Emily, there was enough drama going on.

He'd taken a shower, crawled into bed and was staring at the ceiling when his phone rang. He glanced at caller ID and saw that it was Samantha.

"Hello," he said, his tone chilly.

"You're furious," she said at once.

"Not furious," he contradicted. "I am a little confused about how this thing between Boone and Emily got to be about you and me."

"Because I made it about us," she admitted. "And I shouldn't have. I'm sure Boone talked to you in confidence."

"He did."

"And I would have thought less of you if you'd betrayed his trust," she admitted.

"Sort of a catch-22 for me, wouldn't you say?"

She laughed. "Pretty much. I'm sorry."

"Are you? Or did Cora Jane insist you apologize?"

"She might have mentioned she thought I was in the wrong and owed you an apology. Still, I really am sorry."

Ethan relented. "Me, too. How are things over there?"

"Boone's here. Emily went downstairs to talk to him. So far there's been no yelling. No doors have slammed. And Boone's car is still outside."

"Then it's possible they're working things out?" he said, relieved.

"You afraid you weren't going to get to dress up in your tuxedo?"

"Believe me, that was not even on my list of worries," he said. "If Boone weren't counting on me, I'd have happily skipped that part."

"I'll bet you're going to look sexy as anything in a tux," she said in a low, sultry voice. "Maybe a little James Bond with a hint of George Clooney thrown in."

"It'd take more than a fancy suit to put me in their league," he said. "You're just trying to get back on my good side by tossing all these compliments my way."

"Nope. That's how I see you. Very sexy. Very sophisticated."

"I'm a small-town doctor," he reminded her. "I might look like I'd fit in, but I'd never be truly comfortable in a city like New York."

"Fair warning?" she asked.

Ethan hadn't thought of it that way when he'd said it, but she was right. "As a matter of fact, yes. Just so there are no misunderstandings between us the way there were between Boone and Emily."

"So, unlike Boone, you flat-out won't compromise at all?" she asked.

Ethan heard the challenge in her voice. "Uh-oh. We're back to us again. Sweetheart, you and I have issues that have nothing to do with locale."

"You sure about that? Didn't you once tell me that one of the things standing in our way was that you live here and I live in New York?"

Ethan sighed. "I suppose I did. Distance is hard on a relationship, no question about it. But it is not the real issue. The real issue for you and me is that you believe in love and I don't."

"Then why'd you push so hard for Boone and Emily to work things out?"

"Because they *are* in love. Even I can see it's the real deal. Me? I'm not cut out for it."

"Too selfish? Too cynical? Low self-esteem?" she prodded.

Ethan saw exactly what she was doing. She was trying to push his buttons by suggesting negative traits he didn't want to envision that he possessed. Still, he couldn't deny there was some truth in all of those things.

"Could be," he said candidly.

Her gasp suggested she was shocked that he'd acknowledged it. "Ethan, you don't mean that! I've been around you enough to see how kind and generous you are, how caring. You may want to be cynical, but I saw the expression on your face when you talked about how in love your parents are. And we've beat that low-self-esteem horse to death already."

"What's your point?"

"I think you want to be antilove because you're scared," she told him. "Burned once, twice shy. Isn't that the expression? You were badly burned. It's little wonder you might not want to take another chance on putting yourself out there, on making yourself vulnerable. Love can rip your heart out. There's no denying that. Why risk it? Isn't that really your philosophy? Isn't that what keeps you sitting on the sidelines?"

What she was suggesting sounded an awful lot like saying he was a coward. That grated. And yet he could hardly tell her she was wrong when she'd hit so close to the mark. He never again wanted to feel the way he'd felt when Lisa had walked out on him. It wasn't the rejection per se. He liked to think he was tough enough to get past a woman leaving him. It was Lisa's view of him as damaged goods that he simply couldn't get out of his head.

Of course, there was a case to be made that they hadn't really been in love, not the kind of love that Samantha obviously believed in. That deep and abiding love didn't bail at the first sign of trouble…or at the loss of a limb.

"Do you have the qualifications to try to pinpoint what makes me tick?" he asked irritably.

"I pay close attention to human nature. It helps with acting," she responded, clearly not offended by his remark. "Am I wrong?"

"Not entirely," he conceded.

"Can I ask you something else? Will you answer honestly?"

"If I can," he said.

"Am I anything at all like your ex-fiancée?"

"Heavens no!" he said fervently. Oh, he'd wanted her to be shallow and vain, but mostly so he could dismiss the undeniable attraction between them. Instead, he'd seen time and again that she had substance, that she cared about her family, even when they got on her last nerve. That's what made resisting her so blasted difficult.

She laughed at his emphatic response. "Well, thank goodness for that. How'd you fall for a woman like that, anyway?"

He had to think about it. His impression of Lisa now was seriously jaded by all that had happened. What had he seen in her at the beginning?

"She was beautiful and smart," he said eventually. "She made me laugh. I was a pretty serious guy back then. I was working hard, first in med school, then through my internship and residency. She made me lighten up."

"Those sound like good things," Samantha suggested.

"Seemed that way to me, too," he said. "But there wasn't a lot to laugh about when I got back from Afghanistan. And it made me realize that the things she'd loved about me were, ironically, the way I looked in a tux and the future she'd envisioned as the wife of a well-respected, big-city trauma surgeon."

"And then you decided to open a clinic in Sand Castle Bay," Samantha concluded.

"Sure. I think that was one of the deal-breakers for her, but not the only one."

"What else?"

"Last time she saw me, I was not exactly looking like a model for Armani. I'd let my hair and beard grow, because I couldn't be bothered. I could barely walk down the hall, much less hit the dance floor at the country club. And I was treating everyone as if I were a bear with a thorn stuck in its paw, lashing out at the most innocent remarks."

"All understandable," Samantha insisted. "Couldn't she see that?"

"She tolerated my lousy mood surprisingly well, even coaxed me into laughing a time or two. But she clearly couldn't envision a future with a man who couldn't keep up with her or take her to the places she wanted to go."

"And yet you kept going," Samantha said. "You didn't let any of it defeat you. Do you know how re-markable that makes you?"

"Not remarkable. In an ironic twist, I have her to thank for my recovery. When she took off, it made me more determined than ever not to let my life be over because I'd lost my lower leg."

"Then don't let it be over," Samantha said. "Unless you open your heart, you'll be living a half-life, Ethan. Take a chance. If not with me, with someone."

Ethan sighed as she once again disconnected the call. He wanted to do as she asked, wanted to take that kind of emotional risk. More and more, though, he realized that if he dared to do that, then it would have to be with her. And none of the issues he'd just mentioned to her were going away. Nor would they be easily resolved.

Maybe that's why love was best left to the very young, he thought with a touch of well-honed cyni-cism. The older people were, the more their lives had been shaped exactly as they wanted them to be. Com-promise came less easily.

And yet he couldn't help thinking that maybe the reward would be worth it.

Eleven

After speaking to Ethan, Samantha stood at the top of the steps listening to see if she could still hear Boone and Emily. She wanted to go out on the porch and think about her conversation with Ethan, but she didn't want to interrupt the couple if they were working things out.

There wasn't a sound from the living room, though. She tiptoed down until she could peek into the room. She saw her sister wrapped securely in Boone's arms, her head on his shoulder. Both of them were asleep, or so it seemed.

She tried to ease her way past them, but Boone's eyes immediately snapped open.

"Sorry," she whispered. "Everything okay?"

"Getting there, I think," he said. "You going out?"

"Just to the porch," she said. "I'm not ready for bed yet. Close your eyes. I'll just grab the afghan from the back of the sofa and sleep outside tonight. I won't be wandering back through."

Boone frowned. "No need to do that."

She grinned. "You never know. Emily could wake up and things could take a turn toward interesting."

Boone chuckled. "Not likely. She's still working on forgiving me. Interesting's a ways down the road."

"Well, good luck with that," Samantha told him, and left them alone. At least this time, they were working at communicating, rather than going to their separate corners to let wounds fester and destroy them. Maybe maturity would save them yet.

On the porch, Samantha settled on the chaise longue, the afghan wrapped securely around her, and let her mind wander. She couldn't seem to help dissecting her call with Ethan. Would he ever get past the way Lisa had hurt him and allow himself to love someone again? Committing fully to a relationship was scary enough under the best of circumstances. She was cautious enough, and she'd never been seriously burned. Maybe when someone loved deeply and lost, they never got over it. In the case of Ethan—a man with so much to offer—going through life alone would be a real tragedy.

She was considering that and whether she had the fortitude to wait him out while he wrestled with old demons, when a car pulled into the driveway. To her shock, her father got out and headed toward the house.

"Dad!"

He stopped in his tracks and stared into the shadows. "Sammi? Is that you?"

"It is. What on earth are you doing turning up here this late?"

"Command performance," he said succinctly. "Your grandmother informed me that I was behaving badly by not being here for every wedding-related event. She said if I missed her brunch for Emily and Boone tomorrow, I might as well not bother showing up at all. She said I didn't have to be here to pay the bills. She'd send 'em over to Raleigh and add a ten percent surcharge to cover her consulting work. I got the impression she was ready to step in and walk Emily down the aisle in my place, as well."

Samantha chuckled. "Blackmail, huh?"

He nodded, his expression sheepish. "I'm probably lucky she wasn't planning to add thirty percent." He sat down in a rocker beside her. "What are you doing out here at this hour? It's going on midnight."

"Things to ponder," she admitted.

"Such as?"

She hesitated, uncertain how much insight her father could really have to offer. He'd never been around before to give advice. That had been her mom's domain. Still, he was here now and she could use a friendly ear... and a male perspective.

"Have you ever wondered what you'd have done if the whole biomedical research thing hadn't worked out?" she asked.

She could see his blank expression in the moonlight and knew that she was asking for something beyond his frame of reference.

"Never mind," she said, resigned to muddling through on her own. "I guess you never had any doubts about what you wanted, did you? You were driven, dedicated and determined from the get-go."

"Sure I was," he replied, then startled her by adding, "But what I truly wanted was to be the finest pediatric oncologist in the country."

Samantha regarded him with shock. "Are you serious? I never knew that. What happened?"

"Are you sure you want to hear all this? It's old news."

"I definitely want to know." Not only might it help her now, but it would give her a rare insight into this man who'd been an enigma to his family for so long.

"The minute I went through my pediatric rotation in med school, I realized I'd never be able to look into those sweet little faces and know that I couldn't save them. It would have torn me apart. I was lucky that I recognized that about myself in time to choose a new direction." He shrugged. "So I dedicated myself to the research side of medicine. No tricky emotions to face. No losses. I have some regrets about that even now, but it was the healthier decision."

"Why didn't any of us know this?"

"The decision was made long before you came along."

"And Mom supported you? She didn't think any less of you for giving up?"

He smiled. "She told me once that she admired me for admitting I was on the wrong path. See, that's the thing about unconditional love. You always want what's best for the other person, even if you have to shift your own needs to accommodate it."

She tried to reconcile that with her grandmother's emphasis on compromise. Surely he'd grown up with the same reminders about its importance.

"What about compromise?" she asked.

He laughed. "Ah, that's the thing. If you truly love the other person, you won't let him make all the sacrifices. And, yes, I know you girls think your mother did make all the sacrifices, but it's not entirely true. We worked through every decision together. We were in

Raleigh, rather than New York or another Northeast city, because she felt more at home down here and insisted we be close to your grandmother. She wasn't that close to her own family, and she liked the ties to mine that being just a couple of hours away from here gave us."

"I never knew that. Of course, I knew she didn't talk too much about her parents, but I had no idea you'd ever thought about living in New York or some other big East Coast city."

"There was no reason you should have known. That's another decision that was made before we even discussed having children. We were both content with it."

"You didn't feel as if she'd tied your hands, kept you away from making huge breakthroughs that might have come if you'd been working with researchers at Sloan-Kettering or Johns Hopkins or Harvard?"

"Teamwork?" He gave her a wry look. "I'm sure you've noticed I'm not so good at dealing with people."

"But you run a major biomedical research company."

He laughed. "Other people run it. I'm smart enough to let them. My name may be on the big office, but mostly I stick with what I do best—research."

"But Mom was such a people person," she remembered. "You must have driven her crazy."

"At times," he agreed readily. "Especially when I'd miss a party because I was caught up in something at work. How your mother managed to look beyond all those times I let her down and love me anyway is a mystery. I'm thankful every day of my life that she did, though. Not many women would have put up with me, no question about it. I keep hoping that I'll figure out how to get it right with you girls after all this time, too."

"You've made a great start," Samantha acknowledged. "Stepping up to pay for Emily's wedding, at least pretending to be interested in the details."

He gave her a wry look. "Never knew I could fake anything the way I have listening to her and your grandmother go on and on about flowers and food, though."

"It's been an admirable performance, all right. And the way you stood by Gabi when you found out she was pregnant," she added. "You were a great dad then."

He gave her a long, sad look. "Haven't done so well by you, though, have I?"

"I haven't hit any major roadblocks, thank goodness."

"Not even with your career?" he asked carefully. "Isn't that why you were asking me about whether I'd ever had doubts about mine?"

She regarded him with surprise. "Who knew you were so insightful? I never expected you to get that."

"My goal is to keep surprising all of you," he said, a rare teasing note in his voice. "So, is everything going the way you want it to? I have a clipping service, you know. They send me any items about you that appear in the New York papers. Seems as if there haven't been too many recently."

"You hired a clipping service?" she asked, stunned.

"Your mom kept up with any reviews or mentions, but after she died, it seemed like the best way to see for myself what you were up to. I probably haven't said it nearly often enough, but I'm proud of you, Samantha."

He'd nearly left her speechless. "Thank you," she murmured, fighting tears.

"So, how are things?"

"Not so great, as a matter of fact. I just can't figure out if it's time to throw in the towel."

"The time to quit anything is when you no longer feel the same passion for it," he said. "There are people who work because they know they need the money, and there are people whose very soul depends on doing the kind of work they've chosen."

"That's how I felt about acting," Samantha said.

"Past tense," he noted.

She drew in a deep breath, then nodded. "Past tense. I want more. I just don't know exactly what."

"You'll figure it out," he said with confidence. "You know how I know that? Because of the way you made the decision to go to New York. Everyone thinks that Gabi and Emily are the orderly, focused, ambitious ones in the family, but you set the example."

"I did?"

"You bet. When your mother and I challenged how you were going to make it in such a risky profession, especially since you were determined to choose it in lieu of college, you organized facts and figures. You came to us with a plan, a timetable, financial prospects. You left us without a single doubt that you'd be okay if we'd just back you for one year."

Samantha had forgotten how sure she'd been of herself back then. She'd known she was talented. She'd believed she'd make it, despite all the odds stacked against her in a tough, competitive world. Now she no longer had that faith or that drive. It was time, she concluded, to quit.

Could she come back here, though, without an equally solid plan? She couldn't base such a decision on things working out with Ethan. They might not. This decision had to be about her, what she wanted for her future.

"Thanks, Dad."

He regarded her with surprise. "I helped?" he asked, sounding astonished.

"You did."

"Be sure to tell your grandmother about that. I could use a few brownie points with her."

"Will do," she promised.

"I'd better get up to bed," he said. "You're okay out here?"

"I'm fine. Be careful going through the house, though. Emily and Boone fell asleep in the living room in the middle of an argument."

"Oh, boy," he muttered. "Do I want to know what's going on?"

"Probably not. I think they're working it out, but stay tuned. Who knows what morning might bring?"

She wasn't even certain what might lie ahead for her, much less for her sister.

Ethan didn't show up for Sunday brunch. Though there were a couple of dozen people gathered in clusters all over the backyard, enjoying Jerry's improvised omelet station, pecan waffles and homemade grits, the absence of one person was giving Samantha heartburn.

"I pushed him too hard last night," she grumbled to Gabi.

"Pushed him how?"

"I told him he needed to open his heart, take a chance

on love. I should have known he'd decide I had an ulterior motive. I scared him off."

Gabi laughed. "I don't think Ethan scares that easily. I'm sure there's another explanation."

"Has he spoken to Grandmother? Sent his regrets to Boone or Emily?"

"Sweetie, you're asking the wrong person," Gabi said. "Just ask one of them if they've spoken to him."

"Asking would only make me look pathetic," Samantha said.

"Okay, I'm officially confused," Gabi said, a twinkle in her eyes. "Is this about you having hurt Ethan's feelings with something you said last night, or is it about him hurting yours by not showing up today?"

"Oh, bite me," Samantha said irritably. "I know I'm not making a lot of sense."

"Sense rarely has much to do with falling in love," Gabi said.

"I am not falling in love with Ethan," Samantha said hurriedly, because she felt she needed to. Maybe if she could convince everyone else of that, she'd believe it herself. It was absolutely the worst possible time for her to fall in love with anyone, much less Ethan, who had complication written all over him.

"How about a big glass of orange juice?" Gabi said.

"What? I don't think OJ, for all of its nutrients, is the answer."

"Oh, come on," Gabi urged. "It'll make you feel better, especially if you lace it with enough champagne. I hear Jerry makes a really potent mimosa."

"You're drinking mimosas? What about nursing the baby?"

Gabi gave her a chiding look. "I never said I'd tried one. That's just the rumor that's going around, that his are excellent. I'm almost regretting that I haven't weaned Daniella."

"You do know that sooner or later that baby is going to day care, right? To the one you handpicked after consulting with Wade's sister about every child care facility in the entire region?"

Gabi looked flustered. "Truthfully, I've been thinking about that. It's working out okay taking her with me to the gallery."

Samantha stared at her incredulously. "You can't be serious! I hear a half dozen artists have complained about the noise."

Gabi waved her off. "Artists are notoriously temperamental. It doesn't mean a thing."

"Not even if one of them happens to be your soon-to-be husband? Wade says he hasn't been able to concentrate on his carvings for weeks now. The only time he gets any work done is at home in his old studio."

"Oh, phooey. That's because every time that child so much as whimpers, he has to run and check on her," Gabi said. "That's on him."

Samantha backed off. "Your decision," she told her sister. "I'm just reporting what I'm hearing."

Gabi frowned. "Wade really said that to you?"

"He did."

"Why hasn't he said it to me?"

Samantha smiled. "He seems to think you'd get a little defensive. Judging from your reaction just now, I'd have to say he knows you pretty well."

Gabi drew in a deep breath, then sighed. "I'd better

find him and talk about this. I thought he liked having the baby close by as much as I do."

"Sweetie, he adores that child. Make no mistake about that. He's just not a huge admirer of her lung capacity when he's trying to be creative. And those other artists? They're not even half as addicted to that sweet baby as Wade is."

"How'd you wind up in the middle of this?" Gabi inquired curiously.

"I wasn't. Grandmother caught wind of it. She mentioned it to me and said she was reluctant to tell you. I had a chat with Wade myself, heard the frustration in his voice and decided you needed to know."

"I needed to know," Gabi confirmed. "I'll call the day care tomorrow, see if I can get Dani in there tomorrow or the next day. With everything going on this week for the wedding, it's good timing, anyway."

"If you make the arrangements, I'll be there on her first day to offer tissues and moral support," Samantha promised.

"That's all well and good," Gabi said. "But Wade needs to show up with at least two dozen of those doughnuts he uses to bribe me to get his way."

"I'm sure he'll be happy to oblige."

"Yeah, he will," Gabi said, smiling, though there were tears in her eyes. "How'd I get to be so lucky?"

"By being a fabulous, incredible Castle woman," Samantha told her.

"In that case, you deserve one of the good guys, too. And, for the record, I hope it's Ethan."

"Too soon to tell," Samantha said. But she couldn't deny that she hoped so, too.

* * *

By the time Ethan was able to get away from the clinic and over to Cora Jane's, most of the guests had left. Only Boone's car and one other remained parked in the driveway along with the family vehicles. Though he'd made a quick call to Boone earlier to explain that he'd had to deal with an emergency, he doubted if that message had been passed along to the one person likely to be offended by his absence. Why hadn't he thought to insist that Boone spread the word?

As he crossed the lawn, he was aware that all eyes seemed to be on him. He was also very aware of the frown spreading across Samantha's face. Rather than going straight to her, though, he approached Cora Jane, bent down and kissed her cheek.

"I apologize for not getting here earlier," he told her.

"Not a problem," Cora Jane said, patting his hand. "I heard about the emergency. Is the boy okay?"

Ethan nodded, his gaze on Samantha, who was looking slightly less annoyed now. "He will be. He was scared more than anything. He took in a lot of water when he got caught up in that rip current. And no matter how often people are told to just let the current carry them, rather than fighting it, they panic. The natural tendency is to swim against it. That's a sure way to wear yourself out. He could easily have drowned if the lifeguard hadn't gotten to him when he did. I give the lifeguard a lot of credit. He did a good job on the scene and had the presence of mind to have someone call me, as well as 911."

"You were close by?" Samantha asked.

Ethan nodded. "Fortunately I happened to be just up

the street at the clinic and got there even before the paramedics. I stayed with the boy at the emergency room until his family could get there. They thought he was at a friend's house. I imagine once nerves settle down, he'll be grounded for a good long time."

"He's not the first kid who went surfing when he was supposed to be safely on dry land," Boone commented pointedly.

Ethan laughed. "And we always got grounded, too."

"When we got caught," Boone replied, then glanced at B.J., who was taking in the exchange with interest. Boone frowned at his son. "Just so you know, young man, my spies are everywhere. You will *always* get caught."

"I don't even know how to surf," B.J. said in obvious frustration. Then with a naive innocence he asked, "Can you teach me?"

Ethan chuckled. "Kid, you need to learn about timing. This could be the wrong moment to suggest that."

"Got that right," Boone said.

Samantha stood up and walked to Ethan's side. "Have you eaten? There's plenty of food inside. I can make you a plate."

"Thanks. I'll come with you."

Inside, she busied herself spooning fruit and salad onto a plate while Ethan stood back and watched her nervous movements.

"Everything okay?" he asked eventually.

"I'm trying to decide if I need to apologize to you."

"For?"

"Misjudging you," she admitted, lifting her gaze to meet his. "I thought you'd bailed today just to avoid me."

"I thought maybe that was on your mind," he admitted. "First, I'm not the kind of man who skips out just to avoid someone. Second, if I'm being honest, I should have called you, rather than Boone. So, maybe the truth is, I'm more of a coward than I'd like to think."

"You didn't owe me an explanation. It's not my party."

"Technically true, but I do think common courtesy is in order. I wonder if I wanted to see if you'd miss me."

She stared at him, then shook her head. "Boy, we're a real pair, aren't we? Even when we swear we're not going to get involved, we keep playing crazy games. Is it just the nature of the male-female dynamic?"

"I certainly hope not, though I wouldn't doubt it. Men and women have been messing up for eons."

"And here I thought we were special," she teased, setting the plate on the table, then gesturing for him to sit. "Want an omelet? Or a waffle?"

He shook his head. "Just some company."

"How about a mimosa? Word is they're lethal."

"I'm on call at the clinic, so no," he said. "You haven't tried the mimosas?"

"Nope. I'm starting to realize I need to keep a clear head these days, especially after that little performance I put on the other night, collapsing at your feet on the front lawn."

"All that told me is that you're not a heavy drinker under normal circumstances. Otherwise a few glasses of champagne wouldn't have knocked you on your butt."

"I'm not much of a drinker," she confirmed. "I never really saw the point. And after the other day when I woke up feeling as if there was a full-blown orchestra of kettledrummers in my head, I don't think that's going to change."

"Yeah, there's not much to love about a hangover," he agreed.

"Did you ever turn to alcohol when things were tough during your therapy?" she asked.

"Nope. It wouldn't have mixed well with the drugs I needed for the pain. I didn't even like taking those, but they did allow me to work harder at rehab, so I put up with the side effects for a few weeks, then tossed those, too. I like being in control."

Her eyes lit up. "Aha!"

"What?"

"That's the piece of the puzzle I was missing. You're a control freak," she said triumphantly. "And people who like control have lots of trouble with emotions, which are usually messy and unmanageable."

Ethan could hardly deny the truth of that. "Okay, sure. I do like things to be orderly."

"How'd you reconcile that with emergency medicine? From what I gather, there's nothing nice and neat about working in a trauma unit."

"Ah, but you're wrong," he insisted. "The cases may be unique and the scene totally chaotic, but the doctor's job is to bring order to it, to focus on the details that will lead to a positive outcome for the patient. We cut through the chaos, because we know how to tackle anything that's likely to happen."

"Even the unexpected?" she inquired doubtfully.

"Even that," he said. "We train to expect the unexpected, just so we can control the situation. Lives depend on us being calm and in control."

It was ironic, really, because in that most stressful of environments, he'd never felt the kind of uncertainty he felt when dealing with the woman seated across from him right now. She was trying so hard to figure him out, to pin a label on him that could make sense of his reluctance to get involved.

The truth was actually quite simple. She represented something he'd once wanted with all his heart. Now, though, life had taught him that a man couldn't always have what he most desired. As soon as he dared to reach for it, there was every likelihood it would be snatched away.

And though he'd coped with an injury that could have destroyed a weaker man and a loss that had torn him up inside, something told him that he might not be strong enough to deal with losing Samantha.

Twelve

Samantha slipped into the back of the high school auditorium and was suddenly assailed by a hundred memories. Even the way the room smelled—some sort of mix of greasepaint, wood shavings from the set design and the mustiness of old costumes—seemed familiar. So did the giddy sense of anticipation and nerves she could feel emanating from the stage.

It was in an auditorium much like this one where she'd honed her skill and developed her love of live theater. TV, modeling and all the rest took a backseat in her heart compared to the immediacy of being onstage in front of an audience.

She smiled as the girl onstage succumbed to a bad case of nerves, her mind obviously going blank as she stared into the darkened auditorium with a hint of panic in her expression. Samantha could relate. At that age, she'd suffered her share of memory lapses.

An impatient voice from the wings fed the girl the right line. Even with that help, the teen looked vaguely lost, then stumbled over her next line, as well.

"Let's take a minute," Mrs. Gentry called out, then stood up and turned away from the stage, probably to keep herself from saying something she'd regret to the obviously unprepared student.

She must have spotted Samantha standing in the shadows, because a smile broke across her face and she immediately headed up the aisle.

"There you are," she said excitedly. "I didn't mention to the students that you might be stopping by because I was afraid something would come up and you wouldn't make it."

"You mean I had a choice?" Samantha said lightly. "It didn't sound that way when I saw you."

"Sometimes my command performance approach works. Sometimes it lets me down," the drama teacher replied. "Anyway, I'm delighted you're here. If you've been here long, you know it's been a tough afternoon. The kids could use a pep talk."

"Your lead seems to be having trouble with her lines."

Mrs. Gentry shook her head. "She tries. She really does, but the truth is, Sue Ellen's not cut out for the pressure. I'm not even sure why she tries out for every play, except for the accolades that might come her way or this competitive thing she has with one of the other girls." She sighed heavily, then confided, "I probably made a mistake casting her."

Samantha regarded her with surprise. "Then why did you?"

"Long story and one that doesn't show me in a very good light," the long-time drama teacher said. "Ethan Cole certainly took me to task for it."

Ah, Samantha thought. This was the situation he'd

been so worked up over a few days ago. "Is Ethan involved with the school?"

"No, not officially. That didn't stop him from coming by to tell me just how terrible my casting decision had been. He was quite passionate about it."

"He thought someone else deserved the role?" Samantha asked, trying to fit the pieces together.

Before Mrs. Gentry could answer, a girl hesitantly approached them. "Mrs. Gentry, Sue Ellen's in the restroom throwing up. Do you want to cancel the rest of the rehearsal?" She gave Samantha a curious look, then asked with surprising directness, "Do I know you?"

"Samantha used to spend her summers in Sand Castle Bay," Mrs. Gentry explained. "Now she works in New York."

The teen's eyes lit up. "On TV!" she said excitedly. "You were on one of my mom's soaps that she used to tape before it went off the air."

"I had a couple of small soap parts," Samantha confirmed.

"You got killed off. My mom hated that."

"I wasn't thrilled about it, either," Samantha said.

"Cass, this is Samantha Castle," Mrs. Gentry said. "Samantha, this is Cass Gray. She's working as my assistant and Sue Ellen's understudy in this production."

Samantha didn't miss the grimace that passed over the girl's face at the mention of her role as an understudy. She held out her hand. "Nice to meet you, Cass."

Only when Cass didn't grasp her hand did she notice the prosthesis she was wearing. Samantha pulled her hand back, embarrassed.

Instantly the pieces of the puzzle fell into place. This

girl was one of Ethan's protégés. She had to be. And he'd apparently felt she'd been robbed of the lead role, most likely because of her arm, Samantha concluded. If that was the case, no wonder he'd taken Regina Gentry to task.

"So, are we canceling rehearsal or what?" Cass asked, her cheeks flushed after that momentary awkwardness when Samantha had held out her hand.

"We'll put it on hold, but gather everybody down front," the teacher instructed. "Samantha's going to give a little talk about her experiences to the group. You all can ask questions about what it's like to be a working actress."

"Really?" Cass said, her expression animated. "Gimme five minutes. I'll corral everyone, even Sue Ellen."

Mrs. Gentry nodded. "Perfect. Thank you."

Samantha kept her gaze on Cass as she hurried away. "Is she any good?" she asked Mrs. Gentry. "Cass, I mean."

"She's excellent," the teacher admitted. "And, yes, that was the mistake I made, leaving her out of the production because of her arm. I should have been more open-minded. Ethan made sure I saw that. Of course, I couldn't very well take the part away from Sue Ellen at that point. Cass has been a surprisingly good sport about being her understudy, even though we all know she's the better actress. I'm ashamed to say I lost sight of that."

"At least you're able to admit you made a mistake," Samantha said.

"I'm not sure that's much comfort to Cass."

"Perhaps not, but learning that adults do make mistakes and that they need to own up to them isn't a bad lesson."

But even as she let the teacher off the hook for what she'd done to that vulnerable girl, Samantha's mind was sorting through ways she could maybe reach out and make things better.

After leaving the high school, Samantha stopped by the gallery to see Gabi. Though her sister was in her office, tears were streaming unabashedly down her face and Wade was trying to soothe her.

"Uh-oh, did I come at a bad time?" Samantha asked as she hesitated in the doorway.

"Separation anxiety," Wade said succinctly. "I took Dani over to day care after lunch."

"Oh, boy," Samantha murmured, crossing the room to give her sister's shoulder a comforting pat. "Sweetie, it's okay. She's in good hands."

"I know that," Gabi said, her voice choked. She sniffed and blotted at her face with a fistful of tissues. "I just don't like it. I miss her."

"Well, of course you do," Samantha said. "But just think of the work you'll be able to get done with all this peace and quiet."

Gabi burst into tears again. "I *hate* peace and quiet."

Samantha smothered a smile. "But you *love* work," she reminded her. "And look at that desk of yours. I've never seen such a disorganized mess in my life."

Gabi glanced at her desk, her eyes widening in obvious dismay as she took in the sorry sight. "What has happened to me?"

"You became a mom," Wade said. "And despite the way your desk looks, you have this place running like clockwork. No one could have done a better job, especially with juggling the demands of a baby."

Gabi looked from Wade to Samantha, then managed a watery grin. "Are you two double-teaming me?"

"Something like that," Samantha said. "We both want you to see this change as a positive thing. It'll even be good for Dani to socialize a bit."

"She's an infant," Gabi scoffed. "How much socializing is she likely to do? She already gets passed around like a football when you and Emily are around. Even Jerry likes to take a turn holding her up in the air till she giggles. Grandmother swears the baby is the real draw for him these days, not her at all."

"Then Dani will get to rest up from all that undue attention while she's at day care," Wade countered.

Gabi rolled her eyes. "Okay, I can see you're going to manage to put a positive spin on any concern I express, so I give up. No more tears. I will be brave." She gave Wade a defiant look. "But I am going to pick her up early today just to be sure she isn't traumatized by the separation."

"If anyone's been traumatized, it's you," Samantha suggested.

"Do you really want to toy with my emotions right now?" Gabi challenged. "I'm on edge and trying to make the best of things, but it won't take much for me to snap."

"Got it," Wade said, pressing a kiss to her forehead. "I told the day care people you'd be by in an hour."

Gabi gave him a startled look, then laughed. "No wonder we're such a good match. You know me so well."

Wade turned to Samantha. "Try to keep her from

leaving before the hour's up, okay? I already consider it a coup that she didn't follow me over there and retrieve the baby the second my back was turned."

"Will do," Samantha promised, settling into a chair.

Gabi sighed when Wade had left them alone. "This is killing me," she said unnecessarily.

"I can see that," Samantha said. "It will get easier, or so they say."

Gabi didn't look convinced. "If I'm going to last a whole hour, I'm going to need a distraction. Why are you here? You obviously didn't know about Dani going to day care, because I just arranged that this morning."

"Actually I have a little crisis of my own," Samantha told her.

Gabi instantly looked alarmed. "What? Is it Ethan? Work?"

"My life," Samantha replied.

"Ah, the easy stuff," her sister said. "Tell me."

Samantha drew in a deep breath. "You already know that work hasn't been going that well. I had a talk with Dad the other night and he helped me to see things more clearly."

"Dad did that?" Gabi said incredulously. "Our dad?"

"One and the same," Samantha said, smiling at Gabi's stunned reaction. "You should have been there. He was surprisingly insightful. I actually got a hint about the man Mom fell for all those years ago."

"Astonishing."

"It was, actually. Anyway, he said the time to quit something is when you no longer feel the passion and drive that brought you to it in the first place."

Gabi's expression turned thoughtful. "I think he's

right about that," she said slowly. "That's exactly how I knew it was time to forget about fighting for my job in Raleigh or even going back there to look for something else."

"I hadn't drawn the parallels, but I can see that now," Samantha said. "So you get where I am."

"I think so. Months ago you were getting tired of battling for bit parts and being ignored by your agent." She studied Samantha. "But I thought that had changed."

"It did for a little while, thanks to all that PR buzz you stirred up. The new agent seemed to be energized. Now, though, I think he's hit a wall, too."

"We can do the PR again," Gabi said eagerly. "It was fun."

"You have enough on your plate," Samantha argued. "Besides, it'll be a never-ending battle. I can't let you bail me out every time my career hits a snag."

"Are you sure about that? Because I don't mind. I really don't. I'm happy to do whatever I can for you. If I can't put my skills to use for family, then what good are they?"

"You need to stay focused on this place," Samantha countered. "It should be more than enough professional challenge for you. And with Wade and Daniella, you have the balance in your life you always needed. I'm not going to be the one who shifts that balance till it's out of whack again."

"Sweetie, making a few calls and sending out some press releases is not that demanding."

Samantha laughed. "Don't minimize what you do. I know just how hard you worked to get that buzz going last time."

"Okay, okay, your mind is made up," Gabi concluded, relenting. "So, what's next?"

"I was thinking about something earlier when I stopped by the high school."

"Oh, that's right, you were going to talk to Mrs. Gentry's students. How'd that go?"

"About like you'd expect. Lots of questions about which celebrities I've met through the years, a few about how hard the work is and a handful of really insightful questions about the business from two or three kids who seemed seriously interested."

"And those two or three caught your attention," Gabi guessed.

Samantha nodded, thinking particularly of Cass, who'd been both eager and knowledgeable. "I didn't get to see any of them perform, so I don't have a clue if they're truly talented, but what if someone with experience coached them? I know Mrs. Gentry has a great reputation as a drama teacher, but she's teaching in a high school where most of the kids are more interested in having fun than in serious acting."

Gabi's eyes lit up. "You want to open an acting school? Here?" she asked excitedly. "Oh, do it, Samantha! I'd love it if you were living here. That would make life just about perfect. I think even Emily will cave eventually and she and Boone will settle here, at least part-time. Can you imagine all of us living in this fantastic place, raising our families together, sitting at Grandmother's while all the cousins run around the yard? What could be more idyllic?"

Samantha gave her a wry look. "Since you're the only one with a child and Emily's the only one so far who's got a date set for her wedding, I'd say you're getting a little ahead of yourself. Let's stick to my career move for the moment. What do you think?"

To her dismay, Gabi didn't jump all over the idea with enthusiasm. She sat back, clearly weighing it, letting her businesswoman's mind sort through the pros and cons. Since Samantha had come to her precisely for her business acumen, she waited patiently for the verdict.

"I think with your résumé, you could open an acting school anywhere and draw students," Gabi said slowly. "The right PR could ensure that."

"So you think it's a good idea," Samantha said, relieved.

"Hold on. It's not a bad idea," Gabi contradicted, then grinned. "I just think it could be better."

"How?"

"Open a playhouse. Do a few productions every year, especially in summer, maybe one during the holidays geared more toward the locals. Use your contacts to bring in an artist-in-residence every so often to teach and star in the next production. Let the kids learn not just from you, but from the best. You'll be buried under applications from all over the state. And with tourism booming, your theater will be packed every night."

Samantha regarded her sister with awe. "You came up with that whole concept in five minutes? You're amazing. I've been thinking about this since I left the school and only came up with the idea to teach a couple of acting classes."

"You were thinking too small. I say if you're going to do it, make it big. Just like this place. I could have opened a small gallery, brought in an artist now and then for a show, but by turning it into a working studio with several artists actually working on-site, it's become a real tourist draw."

She beamed at Samantha. "And you know what? It's working. We've been getting a lot of press regionally, and people are making this one of the places they want to see when they come to the North Carolina coast. I have a waiting list of interested artists who'd like to rent one of the studio spaces. And art collectors and gallery owners from major cities are popping in to see whose works are being displayed, looking for the next big talent."

"It's fantastic that it's working so well," Samantha said. "But could I really do anything on such a large scale? It's not as if I have piles of savings to invest the way you did."

Gabi waved off the problem as if it were of no consequence. "Get a few investors. Use the school auditorium for productions, if you have to at first. Then build your playhouse a couple of years down the road when you've become a huge success. Or buy a fixer-upper now and let Wade and the guys he and Boone know convert it into a showplace for you. You know they'll do it for a good price, the same way they did this gallery for me. This building was a shambles till they got started on it. Look at it now."

"It's beautiful," Samantha agreed, infected by her sister's enthusiasm. "It would be amazing to create a playhouse from scratch, even perform from time to time." Then her excitement was overrun by worry.

"What if I'm no good at any of this? I've never taught. I've never run a business."

"Take on one or two students for a few weeks and see how it feels," Gabi advised. "As for the business stuff, you have me, you have Emily and you have Grandmother, who's no slouch when it comes to making a success of a business in this community. She, by the way, will be absolutely over-the-moon about this idea."

"Don't say anything yet, okay?" Samantha cautioned. "I need to think some more. Maybe find a couple of interested kids and test the idea with them."

"Do whatever you have to do to be comfortable with this whole thing," Gabi said. "But I know it's going to work. I can feel it in my bones."

Suddenly Samantha was every bit as excited as her sister was. She just wished she shared Gabi's unbridled confidence.

Ethan was finishing up making patient notes for the day when Cass came barreling into his office, a beaming smile on her face. The smile was so rare, he didn't have the heart to remind her that she was supposed to have permission before coming into the back part of the clinic.

"Before you yell at me for busting in here, Debra said it was okay and to tell you she was leaving."

So, it was the receptionist who needed a reminder about office protocol, he concluded. No surprise there. Debra liked pulling the occasional stunt like this, especially when she was annoyed with him, which she apparently was today. He had no idea why. If she weren't generally good at her job, he'd have given up on her long ago. Amazingly, Greg didn't seem to have the same problems with her.

Debra, however, could wait for another day. He focused on Cass.

"You look happy," he commented. "What's going on? Don't tell me Sue Ellen quit the play."

"No," Cass said, a note of disgust in her voice. "Even after forgetting almost every single one of her lines today, she doesn't have sense enough to call it quits. The play's going to be a disaster."

"Is that what has you looking so cheerful?" he inquired worriedly. Gloating wasn't an especially attractive trait. It certainly wasn't one he intended to encourage.

"No. We had a speaker today, a real actress who's been in commercials and TV shows and on Broadway. It was soooo awesome!"

There was little question in Ethan's mind who that actress was, but he asked, anyway. "Anyone I'd have heard of?"

"Maybe. She's from around here, or spent summers here or something like that. Samantha Castle. Her grandmother owns that restaurant across from the beach, Castle's-by-the-Sea. She's probably younger than you, so you probably never met her."

"I know her," Ethan said. "I'm the best man in her sister's wedding on Saturday. She's the maid of honor."

Cass's eyes widened. "Wow! How cool is that? Do you think you could introduce me to her?"

He regarded her with confusion. "You just met her."

"That was at school. She met a lot of kids. She might not even remember me."

"I doubt that," Ethan said. Cass was not easily for-

gettable and not just because of her prosthesis. "Why
do you want to spend more time with her?"

"Because she's an honest-to-goodness working actress," Cass said impatiently. "Maybe she'd give me
tips or something." Her expression filled with worry as
she glanced at her arm. "Or maybe she'd be like Mrs.
Gentry and tell me to forget trying to be an actress. I
guess if she told me that, I'd have to believe her. She
sees casting people all the time. She probably knows
exactly what it takes to get chosen for a part, that it's
not always about the acting."

Oh, boy, Ethan thought. There was a mine field Samantha would want no part of. She wasn't the kind of
woman who'd ever knowingly crush a kid's dream, but
she was honest. What if she happened to agree with Regina Gentry? Could Cass handle that?

The only way to protect Cass was to have a long conversation with Samantha before ever bringing them together. For now, he was making no promises.

"This week is real busy with wedding activities," he
told Cass. "I doubt she'll have any time. I'm not sure
when she's planning to go back to New York, but if she
does stick around, I'll see what I can do," he promised,
hoping that was vague enough that Cass wouldn't hold
it against him if he failed to deliver.

Cass gave him a penetrating look. "You don't want
me to see her, do you? How come?"

Ethan hated that she'd read him so easily. "I never
said that," he replied.

"Is it because you think she'll tell me I don't stand
a chance?" Cass persisted. "I swear I can take it if she
does. I'm not some baby who can't deal with bad news.

I've already had to deal with more than my share, you know?"

"I know how strong you are, Cass. I honestly have no idea what Samantha would tell you," Ethan replied. "I really don't know her schedule. It's as simple as that."

"If you say so," Cass said doubtfully.

"I say so."

She stood up and started for the door, then turned back. "I pushed Trevor to school today in his wheelchair," she said. "Not that I'm looking for brownie points or anything. He said it was embarrassing having his mom take him all the time. He might be just a kid, but he doesn't need that aggravation."

Ethan bit back a smile. "That was very thoughtful of you."

She shrugged. "No big deal. I just thought you should know. I figure since we're all about self-esteem around here, I'm doing my part to help with his."

"I know Trevor appreciates that."

"He's not such a bad kid," she admitted. "And he's way too smart for the classes he's taking. He's going to help me with my math, if you can believe that. I think he may know more than the teacher, and he's still in elementary school. He must be some kind of genius or something."

"When it comes to math, I think he is. His mother told me they're thinking of letting him take a class at the junior college next semester."

Cass frowned at the news. "But he'll be like this social misfit," she said worriedly. "Are you sure that's a good idea? He might get bummed out."

"I don't think you or I get to decide that, but maybe you could talk to him, see how he feels about it."

Her expression brightened. "And if he's scared or something, I could take him sometimes," she offered. "Nobody would mess with him on my watch."

Ethan smiled at her fierce protectiveness. "I like seeing this side of you, Cass."

She looked confused by the compliment. "What side?"

"You're thinking about other people's feelings. That's a really good thing."

"Trevor's okay," she said with a shrug. "It's no big deal."

"It *is* a big deal," Ethan corrected. "Don't ever try to hide that big heart of yours."

She rolled her eyes. "Whatever. See ya, Doc."

"See you," he responded. Only after she'd gone did he allow a full-blown grin to spread across his face. She was going to be a success story, a kid who'd once again discovered that life had no limits.

At least as long as Samantha didn't inadvertently slip up and take that away from her.

Thirteen

After dinner, Samantha retreated to her room, relieved that for once there were no wedding duties tonight. She had a lot to think about. With a pad of paper in front of her, she intended to make one of those lists her sisters insisted kept their lives on track.

Unfortunately after a half hour of staring at the blank page, she hadn't come up with even a first step to take to see if this new career path might be viable. Why did Gabi and Emily think this was such a great process? It just made her realize how little she knew, not even the kind of questions she needed to be asking.

When there was a tap on her bedroom door, she welcomed the interruption. "Come in."

It was her grandmother who looked in. "Ethan's downstairs."

Samantha glanced down at her old jeans and his football jersey and sighed. Of course he was.

"Tell him I'll be down in a minute," she said, already stripping off the jersey.

Cora Jane winked. "Good decision. That jersey's a

dead giveaway about your feelings for him, and he's already seen you in it once."

"I'm aware of that," Samantha said tightly, rummaging in a drawer for something not only prettier, but less of a red flag emotionally.

She found a blouse with three-quarter sleeves and a few ruffles on the front. With a couple of buttons left undone, it was very feminine. She considered changing to capris and putting on shoes, then shrugged. He'd dropped by unannounced. This was as good as he was getting, she decided, padding to the stairs in her bare feet.

Downstairs, she found him in the kitchen with Cora Jane, Jerry and Gabi all studying him expectantly.

"Feel like going for a walk?" he asked, an almost desperate note in his voice.

Samantha might have enjoyed his discomfort if she hadn't been so eager to get away from their speculative looks herself. "Sure. I'll grab a sweater and my shoes."

His gaze immediately landed on her bare feet with the fire-engine-red polish she'd chosen for her pedicure on Friday night. She intended to exchange the sexy shade for a more sedate pink for the wedding, but the red was obviously a very good choice the next time she had seduction on her mind. Ethan looked a little dazed.

As soon as she'd grabbed her things, they left the house. Only when they were heading toward town did he seem to draw a deep breath.

"Does my family make you nervous?" she asked, smiling.

"They didn't until they started plotting. And I have to admit, Jerry scares the daylights out of me. He's a big guy and he's clearly very protective of you, Gabi and Emily."

"Jerry's harmless," she insisted. "Unless Grandmother or one of us asks for his help. Just so you know, I haven't felt the need to do that in a long time."

"But you did?"

"Sure. When I worked at the restaurant, there were guys who came on to me. Most of them I could handle, but if I had any doubts, one glance in Jerry's direction and he'd have my back."

"A good man to have in your corner, I'm sure." He studied her. "Were there a lot of jerks?"

"Sure. I was a teenage girl and there were always guys who wanted to prove what big men they were. I still run across a few even in the very fancy New York restaurant where I work as a hostess between acting gigs. Some men are genetically incapable of accepting rejection. Add in a few drinks and it can get ugly."

Ethan frowned. "Does your boss there back you up?"

"You bet she does," Samantha said. "I swear she had to have been a bouncer in a previous life. She can't be much more than five foot five, but I've seen her escort men who had at least fifty to seventy-five pounds on her to the door so fast their heads must have been swimming. I think she has taxi drivers on the payroll or something, because there's always one right outside, ready for whoever she's ejecting. It's actually awesome to watch."

She grinned. "And the few she can't handle are dealt with by the bartender, who's six foot three and two hundred pounds of solid muscle."

Ethan nodded, looking relieved. "That's good, then." He hesitated before asking, "Do you work there much?"

"More than I'd prefer in recent months," she confessed. "It's not a bad place and the people are great, but being there is always a reminder that things aren't going so well with my so-called real job."

"Ever thought of giving up?"

"Sometimes," she said. "Especially recently."

"What's stopped you?"

"Stubbornness, mostly. I'm not a quitter by nature. I'm an optimist. I always think the next big thing could be just around the corner. Enough little things pop up to keep that hope alive." She paused, then added, "Or at least they did."

"Not so much anymore?"

She shook her head.

"That must be tough."

"I can't deny that it is," she said.

"I guess I always thought of that world as being glamorous and exciting. I never stopped to think about the constant stress of not knowing what's coming next."

"It takes a toll," she said, not really sure why she didn't want to reveal just how powerful a toll it had taken recently and that quitting was more and more on her mind.

They walked to downtown Sand Castle Bay in silence, but as he led the way toward a small bar on the waterfront, she glanced up at him. "Were you just lonely tonight or is there something on your mind?"

"I need to talk to you," he said. He gestured toward an available table with a view of the water and the bar's host nodded. Ethan led the way, then held her chair.

Only after they were seated and their drink orders had been taken did he continue. "Something happened today and it has me worried."

Samantha heard the real anxiety in his voice. "What happened?"

"Cass Gray stopped by my office."

"Ah, I see," she said, immediately grasping the problem. He wanted to warn her not to tamper with the girl's emotions. "She told you we'd met at the high school."

"She did. And I think it's great that you took the time to speak to the cast. Cass was obviously thrilled. Whatever you said inspired her."

"Isn't that a good thing?"

"It should be," he conceded. "What I'm worried about is that she wants to get to know you better. I think she has some idea that you hold the key to her entire future. When she found out we know each other, she asked me to set up something."

"Why is that a problem?" she asked, though she thought she knew the answer. He still didn't entirely trust her not to be insensitive.

"It isn't necessarily a problem," he said quickly. "I just know how crushed she was by Mrs. Gentry's failure to cast her in the play. I'm afraid if you tell her she's wasting her time pursuing an acting career, it will be the last straw. I know she talks tough, but Cass is fragile. What she needs more than anything these days is to hang on to hope."

"Even if it's false hope?" Samantha asked, although she did understand his concern.

He regarded her with immediate dismay. "Do you think it will be?"

She put her hand over his. "Ethan, I have no way of knowing. I didn't see her act or even read a single line. Mrs. Gentry says she's good, and I trust her judgment."

"But that didn't stop her from rejecting Cass for a part in the play."

"She knows now that she made a mistake, that she based her decision on appearances, not on Cass's talent," Samantha told him. "She says you made her see that, by the way. Good for you!" She held his gaze. "I can promise you this, if I do get to know Cass, if I do have the chance to hear her read for a part, I won't judge her the same way."

Ethan didn't look as relieved by that as she'd thought he would be. "Not good enough?" she asked defensively, hurt by his lack of faith in her.

"I know it's perfectly reasonable. I'm just scared for her. She's finally making some progress with her self-esteem and her self-image. I don't want her to go backward."

"You can't protect her from life," Samantha warned him. "If you were listening to me earlier, you know that this business she's chosen isn't easy. It takes a tough hide to handle the rejections that are a natural part of it, or the bad reviews, or sniping from actresses who thought they should have gotten the part you were given."

"Maybe it's not possible to protect her from that forever," he agreed. "But for now, I only want her to experience the most positive things possible."

"And you don't think you can trust me to be real with her without crushing her spirit?" she concluded.

"I trust you," he insisted. "I'm just worried for her."

"So, what's the bottom line? Will you get us together or not?" She held his gaze. "You do know if she wants this badly enough, she'll find another way to get to me. Even with all the tourists, Sand Castle Bay is essentially a small town. She'll know where to look if she wants to cross paths with me."

He gave her a wry look. "No question about it," he acknowledged. "So, if you're still around after the wedding, we'll work something out."

"Not this week?" she asked, disappointed. Cass was one of the people she'd envisioned as a test case for this acting school idea.

He frowned. "I get the sense that you're almost as eager to see her again as she is to spend some time with you. Is there a reason for that?"

Samantha wasn't ready to reveal her plan just yet. For one thing, she didn't begin to have everything worked out in her head. For another, ironically just like Cass, she wasn't sure she was strong enough to hear from any naysayers. It was possible Ethan would be a big booster, but she wasn't quite ready to find out.

"Just an idea I wanted to run past her," she said eventually. "I'm still working out the details."

He didn't look overjoyed about being left in the dark. "When you have them all worked out, fill me in," he replied. "Then we'll move forward."

"You're a tough negotiator," she said.

"Thank you."

"I'm not so sure I meant it as a compliment," she grumbled.

In fact, right this second, it seemed as if he was standing in the way of *her* dream.

* * *

Something was going on with Samantha. Ethan had seen it in her eyes when he'd insisted on knowing more before he brought her and Cass together. He couldn't imagine, though, what she felt the need to hide from him. He did know it hurt that she wouldn't confide in him. However, since he was the one who'd put the brakes on getting too close, he supposed this was fair turnabout. But he didn't have to like it.

"You look cheery," Greg noted when he walked into Ethan's office. "Somebody steal your morning coffee?"

"Nobody *made* my morning coffee, come to think of it," Ethan said. "Where is Debra?"

"She took the day off," Greg revealed. "Didn't she mention it to you?"

"Apparently she's not speaking to me. Any idea why?"

Greg settled into a chair across from him, shook his head and gave him a pitying look. "No wonder my wife thinks men are oblivious."

"Oblivious to what?"

"Our receptionist has a serious crush on you."

"She's a kid!" Ethan protested.

"She's twenty-three, which makes her a woman and old enough to have a serious, if unrequited, crush on her boss."

Ethan frowned. "This isn't good."

"Well, it's not exactly great, but it's not a calamity," Greg said. "The good news is that she knows nothing is ever going to happen, not only because of the age difference, but because you're not the kind of guy who hits on an employee."

"You're sure she's clear about that?" Ethan asked worriedly.

"A hundred percent. We've talked about it. Just yesterday I told her she needs to move on, find someone her own age and fall crazy in love."

"Well, that answers one question," Ethan concluded. "I wondered why she was barely looking me in the eye yesterday afternoon and bolted without saying goodnight."

"Yeah, she wasn't real happy about the wake-up call I delivered in my most fatherly, compassionate way."

"Did she come to you, or did you take it upon yourself to step in?"

Greg grimaced. "Do I look like the kind of guy who wants to get all tangled up in some woman's emotional stuff? She came to me, of course. As soon as she opened her mouth, I regretted not having had a drink with lunch."

Ethan chuckled. "Sorry she put you on the spot."

"Better me than you," Greg replied. "At least I have a reputation for diplomacy. You'd probably have ticked her off so bad she'd have quit."

"Probably," Ethan agreed.

The door to Ethan's office opened, and Pam stuck her head in. "Anyone in here planning to see patients today?"

"He will," Greg said, then grinned at him. "You owe me. I think I'll go surfing."

"Surfing? Since when?"

"I thought I'd take it up. I hear you get to see lots of girls in bikinis that way."

Ethan knew better. Greg's wife would kill him for looking, much less acting on any wayward impulses.

"You're going home to crawl back into bed with your wife, aren't you?" he said, surprisingly envious.

Greg winked. "Could be. I'll be back to take over by one. Or two."

"Take your time. Enjoy yourself."

"Thanks."

"No, thank you for having my back on the Debra thing."

"Just trying to keep the peace around here," Greg said.

Ethan laughed. Who knew such a simple thing would turn out to be so tricky?

Samantha had barely walked in the door at Castle's-by-the-Sea, where she planned to meet Emily and Gabi to discuss what they were going to do for Emily's prewedding girls-night celebration, when Cora Jane stopped her and handed her an order book.

"Wait on tables seven and twelve," she said. "One of the waitresses called in sick. Her replacement's due in an hour, but we're already swamped."

"Sure," Samantha said. She'd pitched in enough since the hurricane when she and her sisters had first started coming home more regularly to remember the drill. "Any specials?"

"On the chalkboard, like always," Cora Jane said, clearly harried by the unexpected disruption in her typically smooth-running operation.

Samantha took drink orders for the assigned tables, then headed into the kitchen, where Jerry saw her and lifted a brow.

"Drafted into service?" he asked.

She nodded. "What's up with Grandmother? Usually having a waitress call in sick doesn't faze her."

"Wedding frenzy," he said succinctly. "She has a thousand things on her mind. I told her to stay home and focus on those, but she told me the day she can't juggle a few details will be the day she retires. Since I'm all for her realizing she needs to retire, I clamped my mouth shut."

Samantha nodded. "I'm with you on the retirement thing, but we both know she'll never do it. In the meantime, though, I will try to get her to head home to concentrate on the wedding. I can stick around for the rest of the lunch rush."

"Bless you," he said, and went back to flipping burgers with one hand and giving an occasional stir to a pot of soup with the other.

Samantha placed the food orders for her assigned tables, seated guests at three other tables, then all but dragged Cora Jane aside.

"Go home," she said quietly. "You're always the first one to remind us that family takes precedence over everything else. That means Emily's wedding needs to be your priority, especially since you flatly refused to let her hire a wedding planner and insisted you could handle it. Go home and do that."

Cora Jane scowled at her. "Jerry put you up to this, didn't he? He thinks I'm too old to keep so many things straight." She waved a fistful of papers. "That's why I keep lists."

Samantha bit back a smile. "Nobody is saying you're old. We wouldn't dare. We just want you to relax and enjoy this wedding. We don't want you so worn out you sleep through it. Besides, you ordered Dad to get over here. He's here. Put him to work."

"What does your father know about planning a wedding?" she scoffed.

"Absolutely nothing," Samantha said. "Which means you get to boss him around. You'll love that."

Cora Jane chuckled at that. "You're right. That could be fun. Okay, I'll go if you're sure you can handle things around here."

"What I can't figure out, I'll ask Jerry or one of the waitresses about. Emily and Gabi are due any minute. I'll put them to work, too. It's all good."

Even with that reassurance, Cora Jane hesitated. "Maybe I should call in another waitress."

"I'll be insulted if you do. Now go!"

Cora Jane eyed her suspiciously. "You planning a takeover?"

Samantha laughed. "You wish."

"Call me if you need me."

It took another five minutes to coax Cora Jane out the door. By then Samantha was more exhausted than she would have been waiting on a dozen tables.

"Good grief, she's stubborn," she muttered to Jerry in passing.

"Part of her charm," he said, then winked. "Just so you know, all three of you girls got a fair share of that from her. It helps when you're going after something you want."

He almost sounded as if he knew that Samantha had something big in mind, but how could he? Gabi wouldn't have blabbed, and no one else knew.

"I'll keep that in mind," she said as she picked up

an armload of orders and headed back into the dining room.

She knew she had the professional expertise to execute her dream. Now Jerry had reminded her that she more than likely had the grit it would take to make it happen.

But until she'd put a real plan down on paper, she didn't intend to say a word to anyone. She needed to see the concept laid out in black-and-white, maybe even with a few financial figures attached, before she'd allow herself to believe.

"You left Samantha in charge at Castle's," Sam Castle said incredulously to Cora Jane. "Ma, what are you up to?"

"Up to? She practically kicked me out," she told him, mustering up a suitable amount of indignation.

"Which was exactly what you wanted," her son concluded. "You are not thinking that Samantha is your last, best hope to take over the restaurant, are you?"

"Well, why not? Anyone can see she's at loose ends. On top of that, she's falling for Ethan Cole. She needs a reason to stay here."

"And you need to let her find her own reason," Sam said. "Don't trick her into this. You'll just make her miserable and live to regret it."

"Well, what would you have me do? You're the one who said you thought she didn't want to be an actress anymore. I'm giving her an alternative."

"One she's repeatedly made it plain she doesn't want," he told her. "Let her work this out for herself. Samantha has a very good head on her shoulders."

"Oh, what do you know? How much time have you spent with her in recent years?"

He frowned at that, but he didn't try to deny it. "Maybe that's exactly why I can see things more clearly," he said. "And I can recall how carefully she planned out the whole New York thing. She was every bit as thoughtful and meticulous with the details as Gabi and Emily were with their careers. Samantha will do that again as soon as she's figured out what she wants next."

"Will you object if she says she wants to take over Castle's?"

"Of course not. But the restaurant was Father's dream. You've kept it going. Maybe it's time to let go."

Cora Jane felt tears well up at the suggestion. "How can I do that? That's our family's legacy."

"Then find the perfect caretaker, someone you trust to take it over, keep it the way you would."

"You're talking about Boone," she said.

"You trust him, don't you?"

"Of course. And he knows how important Castle's is to this community. He wouldn't turn it into something it was never meant to be," she conceded.

Still, she waved off the idea. "That's not something that needs to be decided right now. Did you make all those calls on the list I gave you?"

He grinned at her. "Of course. And every person confirmed that every little detail is handled and on schedule. This wedding is going to come off without a single hitch. You can stop worrying."

"Maybe so, but checking and double-checking is the best way to be sure of that," she told him. "And I don't care if you do make fun of me, that's exactly what I intend to do."

He laughed. "Never doubted it."

"And you're going to help me," she told him emphatically.

"Never doubted that, either," he said, looking resigned.

She studied this man she'd borne but sometimes felt she barely knew. "You're enjoying being a part of all this, aren't you?"

"Surprisingly, yes," he admitted. "So I suppose I should thank you for seeing to it that I do more than write checks."

"No thanks necessary," Cora Jane told him. "Just remember that it's never too late to get things right."

He bent down and kissed her cheek. "And thank you for seeing to it that I'm aware of that, too. I'll head out and take care of those errands you wanted run now."

Cora Jane watched him go, then smiled. Though she'd despaired about his relationship with his daughters for a long time, she thought those days were finally behind them. She'd keep a watchful eye, though, just in case.

Fourteen

After what Ethan had told her the night before, Samantha was not the least bit surprised when Cass Gray walked into Castle's just after the restaurant's three o'clock closing. She approached Samantha hesitantly.

"I'm not sure if you remember me from school yesterday. I'm Cass Gray," she said in a rush. "I was wondering if you might have some time." She glanced around the empty restaurant worriedly. "Is it even okay that I'm here? I saw the sign said Closed, but the door was unlocked."

Cass's gaze went to Gabi and Emily without waiting for an answer. They were seated in a booth with Samantha. She immediately turned pale. "I guess I'm interrupting. I'm sorry." She turned to go.

Samantha stood up and touched her shoulder. "Cass, it's okay. We hadn't locked up yet. These are my sisters," she explained, making the introductions. "And you're not interrupting anything important. We were just talking about Emily's wedding. It's Saturday."

Cass's eyes lit up. "Come on. That *is* important! I

heard about the wedding from Dr. Cole. He says he's the best man."

"Well, I actually think my husband-to-be is the *best* man," Emily joked, "but Ethan's a close second."

Cass grinned. "You're funny."

"Oh, she's a real stand-up comedian, all right," Gabi commented. "I need to get her out of here." She glanced at Samantha. "So we're agreed about the whole girls-gone-wild thing for tonight?"

"I am," Emily affirmed. "I can hardly wait to have one last crazy fling before I tie the knot."

"You will not be having any flings," Gabi chided. "Samantha and I have to answer to Boone."

As Gabi led Emily away, Samantha turned to Cass and gestured to the booth they'd vacated. "What brings you by?"

Cass squirmed uncomfortably. "I wanted to ask you some more questions about how hard it is to be a working actress. That is, if I'm not being a bother."

"It's no bother," Samantha assured her. Keeping Ethan's concerns in mind, she still felt compelled to say, "It's not easy, Cass. Only a very, very few become huge stars overnight. Most of us struggle to keep working. It takes real drive and determination to stick with it. And there are big differences between starting in New York on the stage and in Hollywood in films or in TV. Some people do commercials when they're starting out. I still do."

"As long as it's acting, I don't care what I do," Cass said. "I like being somebody else for a little while."

Samantha wondered if that had always been true or if

she'd developed that interest after her accident. "When did you first know this was something you wanted to do?"

"In second grade when I got to sing a solo in the holiday pageant at school." Cass beamed. "People clapped and cheered."

"The applause is addictive," Samantha confirmed. "Ever been jeered?"

Cass looked horrified. "Never. Have you?"

Samantha nodded, recalling an off-Broadway production that had been an all-around disaster. "It wasn't nearly as much fun."

"Well, whoever did that was just plain rude," Cass said indignantly.

"True, but critics can be cruel, too. Their reviews can amount to the same thing as jeering and in a much more public forum. Think you're tough enough to handle that?"

"Sure," Cass said with bravado, then hesitated. "I guess I couldn't go punch them, could I?"

Samantha laughed. "It's frowned on, but I imagine it's happened once or twice."

"When you started, were you scared?"

"Sometimes," Samantha admitted, "but mostly of letting my family down."

"Did you go to college?"

"I didn't, but it's a good choice, a place to keep learning the craft and get some more experience. In the right drama program, you'll be seen by directors and producers who will be able to help your career along if you have the talent."

"Why didn't you go?"

"I thought about it, but college can be expensive. I

thought some of that money would be better spent by my folks if I went to New York for a year to try to prove myself. In a way, I thought of college as my backup plan, the thing to do if I couldn't find work. I'm not sure it was the smartest plan, but it worked out okay for me. I wasn't afraid of hard work, so I juggled a couple of part-time jobs, took some serious acting classes and tried to find an agent. I won't lie to you, it was a tough year. I thought about giving up more than once."

"But you stayed and it was worth it, I'll bet," Cass said eagerly. "I'm a hard worker. I can handle a tough schedule. I'd do anything to make this happen." Her expression fell. "But I know there are some people who think I'd be wasting my time."

"What people?"

"Mrs. Gentry mostly." She held up her prosthetic arm. "This is why she didn't cast me in the play at school. She said it would be a distraction, that people would just feel sorry for me."

Samantha felt the same surge of annoyance that Ethan must have felt. "Sweetie, I can't deny that your injury could keep you out of some parts, but there are lots of other roles where it wouldn't matter at all. It might even be a help, something that could be worked into a script. Do you recall the actor who was severely injured while serving in the military, then went on to become a big hit on *All My Children,* despite his very visible scars? The show worked those into his story line. He even won on *Dancing with the Stars* because he made people look beyond his burns to see the wonderful, funny, inspirational, talented man he is."

"That's J. R. Martinez," Cass said at once. "He's awesome. Sexy, too."

"He really is," Samantha agreed.

"So you're saying it's not impossible for me to succeed?" Cass asked hopefully.

"I'm a big believer that nothing is impossible if you want it badly enough," Samantha told her. "But you do need the talent to back up that dream."

"I have that," Cass said with an unabashed confidence that would have made Ethan proud.

"Want to show me?" Samantha asked.

Cass blinked at that. "What do you mean?"

"We could read a couple of scenes together, maybe try a few with another actor or actress and see how it goes. I know you know Sue Ellen's role by heart. We could start with that."

"Really?" Cass asked excitedly. "I wouldn't be imposing?"

"Not in the least," Samantha assured her. "But it will need to be one day next week. This wedding is going to be all-consuming for the rest of this week."

"Next week works for me," Cass said. "Any time you say." She hesitated, making a face. "Well, not when we have rehearsals. Sue Ellen's lost if I'm not there to feed her the lines. It would be irresponsible of me not to show up."

Samantha nodded approvingly. "It shows a lot of character that you're willing to put the play first, even though you must have been hurt not to be in the cast."

Cass shrugged. "Somebody has to try to keep it from being a disaster. Just so you know, though, I'm not as much of a Goody Two-shoes as that probably makes me sound. I figure I'll end up on stage when Sue Ellen passes out from stage fright or something. I want to be sure I'm ready."

Samantha laughed. "I love your attitude, actually. Does Dr. Cole know what a natural optimist you are?"

"Nah, because mostly he's seen me at my worst," Cass admitted. "Since the accident, not every day has been such a good day. I didn't show a lot of love for anybody or anything there for a while. He had to really push me to see that maybe my life didn't totally suck."

"Understandable," Samantha said. "The key to living a good life, I think, is to wind up with more good days than bad ones. And you know what? I really do believe we have some control over that."

"That's what Dr. Cole says, too," Cass told her. Her expression turned thoughtful. "Maybe you two should get together sometime. You might hit it off."

Great, Samantha thought. Just what she needed, yet another meddler! And she could only imagine what Ethan would have to say if he heard about Cass's theory.

"Maybe you should steer clear of the matchmaking and stick to preparing those readings for me," Samantha said. She gave Cass a piece of paper. "Write down your phone number and I'll give you a call on Monday. We'll set something up."

Cass gave her the number, then gave her an impulsive hug. "This is so great! Thank you so much."

"Don't thank me just yet," Samantha said. As much as she liked Cass's eagerness and admired her determination, she still didn't have the first clue about whether the teen had what it would take to overcome the natural biases she was likely to face from some casting directors. And if she didn't, letting her down was going to require diplomatic skills Samantha wasn't entirely certain she possessed, no matter how confidently she'd assured Ethan that she would protect Cass's feelings.

Ethan had arranged to move his regular session with the kids to Tuesday this week since he'd scheduled Boone's bachelor party for Thursday night on the outside deck at Castle's, which would be long closed by the party's starting time.

Today he planned to take them to a pool where he'd arranged for them to have swimming lessons. Most kids who lived in the coastal communities were in the water practically from infancy, but for some whose injuries had affected their mobility, the ocean had become the enemy. He wanted them to rediscover the joy of swimming. For many of them, exercising would even be easier with the water's natural buoyancy. He'd assembled several volunteer instructors who had experience working with people under these conditions, enough that the kids would have close to one-on-one instruction.

When it was time to leave for the pool, he kept glancing at the clock, then looking for Cass. When he could wait no longer, he told the driver to take them on to the pool. En route, he dialed Cass's cell phone.

"Where are you?" he asked without preamble when she answered. "You know you were supposed to be at the clinic ten minutes ago."

"Oops," she said, though she sounded more excited than apologetic. "I've been with Samantha Castle. I forgot we'd switched the day for our outing."

Ethan felt his heart sink. He'd worried about exactly

this, and Samantha herself had warned him that Cass would seek her out on her own, if she wanted her advice badly enough. At least Cass sounded upbeat.

"You had a good conversation?" he asked.

"The best," she assured him. "I'm going to read some scenes with her next week. Can you believe it? I get to read with somebody who's been on TV and in plays on Broadway."

"That's great," he said, forcing himself to sound enthusiastic. At least that meant Samantha would be sticking around a little longer. He couldn't help wondering what that meant, if anything. "Do you want to meet us at the pool? You can tell me all about it."

"Is it okay if I miss today? I really didn't remember about the switch, so I don't have my bathing suit with me, and by the time I get home to get it and make it to the pool, you'll be finishing."

"Fine," Ethan said, relenting at her logic. "But I do want to hear more about your meeting with Samantha next time I see you."

"Promise," she said at once. "I'll probably talk till you're sick of hearing about it. She is sooo amazing."

Yeah, Ethan said to himself. He thought so, too. And more and more he was wondering if he was a fool not to do something to try to keep her right here in Sand Castle Bay.

As soon as Samantha got home, her grandmother took one look at her and smiled. "You look like the cat that swallowed the canary. Something happen after I left Castle's today?"

"Cass Gray stopped by," Samantha told her.

"I see," Cora Jane said. "She wanted your advice about acting, I'm guessing."

Her comment startled Samantha. "You know her?"

"Of course. I've made it my business to attend all the productions at the schools to lend my support to the kids. Cass was always a real standout. What did you tell her?"

"I asked her to read with me next week. I want to see if she truly has what it takes before I say anything about her prospects. It could be tough enough for her even if she's loaded with talent. If she's borderline, she needs to know that now." She sighed. "Of course, Ethan doesn't agree."

"Oh?"

"He's made it clear how strongly he feels about her being surrounded by positive vibes these days."

Cora Jane nodded. "I suppose he has a point. She's traveled a rough road the past couple of years. Adjusting to an injury like hers would be tough enough, but with her longing to be in a profession that relies so heavily on looks, it's been particular devastating."

"I understand that, but what am I supposed to do? Should I lie to her?" Samantha asked in frustration.

"Well, hopefully, you won't have to do that. As I said just now, I've seen her in several plays. Of course the ones in elementary school hardly count, but the spring play she did in middle school and the first one she did at the high school were quite good. And she had unmistakable star qualities, or at least it seemed that way to me. She has a lovely singing voice, too. That high school play was a musical, and she was the lead. I've heard enough kids butcher the melodies of some beautiful songs to recognize one with talent when she comes along."

Samantha's mood brightened. "That's definitely encouraging. I'm still not looking forward to telling Ethan about this, though. He wanted to control the situation, set up when and where we met. Cass settled that by showing up at Castle's on her own."

"Not your fault," Cora Jane said, waving off the issue. "But I have to say, you seem awfully eager to check out this girl's capabilities. Any particular reason for that?"

Samantha hesitated, then admitted, "After stopping by the high school rehearsal the other day, I've been giving some thought to maybe teaching a few acting classes here."

Cora Jane's eyes immediately lit up. "You'd stay?"

"At least long enough to give it a try. What do you think?"

"I think it's an incredible idea, but would it provide the fulfillment and lifestyle you're looking for? You wouldn't make much, I imagine."

"Gabi thinks I'm thinking too small. She wants me to go big and open a playhouse."

Cora Jane clapped her hands together at that. "What a wonderful idea! It would be an incredible addition to the community."

Samantha studied her closely. "You're not just saying that because you want me to stick around?"

"Well, that's certainly a consideration, but it's not the only one. I can see all sorts of potential for a playhouse, especially with you in charge. You have all those amazing contacts you've made over the years. It would be a real contribution to our cultural landscape."

"That sounds a little grander than it's likely to be," Samantha said wryly. "But it could be fun."

"What can I do to help?"

"Nothing just yet. I have a lot of details to iron out before I even know if it's feasible. For one thing, I'd have to figure out an affordable location, determine if there are enough people interested in acting in this region, probably a million other things I haven't even thought of. I was going to make a list, but I don't seem to have Gabi's or Emily's gift for that."

"You'll work it out. As for that location, talk to your father. He has some land with a little house on it. Your grandfather left it to him. It's in an area that's been zoned residential/commercial now, so it would be easy enough to get the zoning approved. I have no idea what condition the house is in, but there's enough land around it for parking, I think. And Tommy Cahill and Wade could tell you if it would cost a fortune to convert it."

Stunned by the news, Samantha threw her arms around her grandmother. "You've just given me exactly the boost I need to move on to the next step. You actually make it all sound feasible."

"It *is* feasible," Cora Jane said emphatically. "Castles can make even the impossible happen. Remember that!"

Samantha laughed. With an energetic, positive woman like Cora Jane as a role model, how could she possibly forget?

Rather than three sisters on the town on their own for Emily's night out, they'd decided to include a few of the friends Gabi had made since moving here. Wade's sister Louise, Meg, who owned a stunning gift shop in town, and Sally, who'd tried to mentor Gabi in making glass wind chimes, had been asked to join them at a casual local bar that had a country band playing.

"I can't tell you the last time I was out like this with the girls," Louise, a mother of five, said. "Thank you for including me."

"We're counting on you not only to be the sensible one, but to help us wriggle out of any trouble we get into," Gabi told the woman, who also had a busy career as an attorney.

Louise frowned. "Does that make me the designated driver, too? I really don't want to be the designated driver," she said, looking longingly at the frozen margarita that had just been placed in front of her.

"No designated driver," Samantha said. "Boone, Wade and Ethan are coming by later to pick us up and carry us home."

"My brother is coming?" Louise said, looking shaken. "I'll never hear the end of it." Then she shrugged. "Oh, well," she said, taking a long, slow drink of her margarita. She sighed with pleasure. "This is definitely worth a little aggravation."

Emily didn't look much happier about the arrangements than Louise did. "My fiancé isn't supposed to see me tonight," she protested.

"He's not supposed to see you on the day of the wedding," Gabi corrected. "Tonight, though? He practically begged to get in on this. So did Ethan, by the way," she added with a pointed look at Samantha. "He seemed especially anxious to spend a little time with my sister, in fact."

Samantha slugged back a healthy amount of her margarita. "He might be just the teensiest bit annoyed with me," she admitted. "He told me to stay away from Cass Gray."

"Who's Cass Gray?" Sally asked. A relative newcomer to the area, she wasn't as familiar with the locals. Nor, apparently, had she been around when Cass's accident had made the news.

Samantha explained about the teen's disability and her desire to act. "So, of course, Ethan's worried I'm going to kill her dream. He has no faith in my diplomatic skills at all. I don't want to see Cass hurt any more than he does."

"Sweetie, if you keep going through drinks the way you're going through that one, he won't be able to have an intelligent conversation with you tonight, anyway," Emily teased.

Samantha grinned. "An excellent point," she said, and ordered another one.

"Oh, dear," Gabi said worriedly. "If she's the only one who's totally sloshed, we are going to have some explaining to do."

"To Ethan?" Samantha asked. "He's not the boss of me."

Emily chuckled. "Something tells me it's too late for second thoughts. Our sister is a lightweight when it comes to alcohol."

"Maybe it'll help if we dance," Meg said, checking out the dance floor enviously. "I've always wanted to learn the two-step."

"Let's go, then," Sally said, pulling her up. "Nothing says we can't corral a couple of the men in here to teach us. Who looks as if they know what they're doing?"

"That one," Meg said, her expression brightening as she pointed toward a lanky guy who looked especially good in a pair of faded jeans and a tight T-shirt.

"That's Tommy Cahill," Gabi said, following the direction of her gesture. She caught Meg's hand. "Come on. He works with Wade, or Wade works for him. Doesn't matter. He's a sweet guy."

With the possibility of an actual introduction squarely in front of her, Meg held back. "Married?"

"Nope," Gabi assured her. "Not even dating as far as I know. He's a contractor with an excellent reputation for building and remodeling high-end beach houses."

Now Sally frowned. "Gay?"

Gabi smiled. "Not a chance. Just shy, I think. Now come on. He's with friends. I imagine we can get them all on the dance floor. It won't be like I'm trying to set you up," she assured her friend.

"Oh, what the heck? I wanted to dance, not to get married," Meg said, following Gabi across the wide-planked wooden floor.

Samantha hung back.

"You're not going to dance?" Emily asked her. "You used to love dancing. You taught both me and Gabi."

"That was when I could stand up without falling right back down," Samantha said.

Emily laughed. "Your head's already swimming?"

"Uh-huh," she admitted. "You were right. I am a lightweight. And since I do not want to make a fool of myself in front of Ethan again because I've had too much to drink, I'm switching to coffee."

"Do you think Boone will be furious if he comes in and catches me dancing with another man?" Emily asked, looking enviously at the other couples who were stumbling their way through the two-step by now.

"I think he'd want you to enjoy your bachelorette party," Samantha told her. "Just skip the slow dances." She looked across the room. "Looks to me as if there's someone over there without a partner. Go for it."

Emily started to cross the room, then turned back, her eyes wide. "It's Boone," she said, her voice hushed. "He's not supposed to be here yet."

Samantha chuckled. "I guess he couldn't stay away."

"Maybe he doesn't trust me," Emily whispered.

"That glint I can see in his eyes suggests something else entirely," Samantha told her. "He's on his way over here, so put on your prettiest smile and go dance till you drop. He's always been the only man for you, so why pretend otherwise, even for a night?"

"He is pretty gorgeous, isn't he?" Emily said, a slow smile spreading across her face. She put a little extra sway in her hips and headed in Boone's direction. "Hey, sailor, want to give a girl a turn on the dance floor?"

Boone grinned. "I was looking at that beauty sitting over there behind you. Is she available?"

Emily punched him in the arm. "Not even remotely funny. You stay away from my sister."

Boone looked down at her, his expression filled with adoration. "She doesn't hold a candle to you," he assured his bride-to-be.

That was the last Samantha heard as he pulled Emily into his arms. She sighed. She wanted that. She really did.

"Care to dance?"

Startled, she glanced up to find Ethan standing beside her. "You're here!"

He smiled. "So it seems. I'm not so sure what sort of moves I have left, but I'm willing to try if you are."

"Sure," she said, eager to feel his arms around her.

She stumbled on the way to an empty space on the floor. Ethan's eyebrow went up. "Tipsy already?"

She sighed. "Afraid so."

He laughed. "This should be fun, then."

But when he drew her into his embrace, she could feel all that solid muscle and taut control and knew with absolute certainty that she was in safe hands.

"Ethan, are you mad at me for talking to Cass?" she found herself asking.

"Not now," he said, his breath feathering across her cheek. "Let's just live in the moment."

"But you aren't happy with me, are you?" she persisted.

He looked down into her eyes. "I'm still worried, that's all. And we're not going to resolve this tonight, so let's leave it for another time. Why don't you just enjoy tormenting me?"

"Tormenting you?" she asked, intrigued.

"Sure. Don't you know that holding you this close and knowing that this is where it's going to end is pure torture for me?"

"A lesser man might conclude it didn't have to end here," she whispered.

She felt his smile against her cheek.

"Then it's a good thing I'm not a lesser man," he said.

"You could reconsider," she suggested. "Go a little wild."

He laughed. "Believe me, darlin', that idea holds a lot of appeal."

"But you're not going to give in to temptation, are you?"

"Afraid not."

She sighed and rested her head against his chest, listened to the steady beat of his heart, wondered what it would take to scramble his pulse so badly he'd have to give in.

One of these days, she decided, she was going to do everything in her power to find out.

Fifteen

"Do you think Ethan will hire a stripper for Boone's bachelor party?" Emily asked plaintively over breakfast on the morning after her bachelorette party. "I don't think I'd like that, especially after the guys crashed my party and kept me from having my last fling as a single woman."

"There was never going to be any fling," Gabi said sternly. "You're all talk, little sister. You'd never do that to Boone."

Emily smiled, her expression dreamy. "You're probably right. Why would I want to cheat on perfection?"

"Oh, gag me," Gabi said.

"I think it's sweet that she's all caught up in the romance," Samantha said. "That's the way it should be. Watching you and Wade being all sensible and practical, well, it's a little scary. What happened to being crazy in love?"

"We *are* crazy in love," Gabi insisted. "We're just mature."

"Uh-oh," Samantha said, catching the glint of an-

noyance in Emily's eyes. "She doesn't mean you're immature, Em. Just that all couples are different, right,
Gabi?"

"Absolutely right," Gabi said hurriedly.

"Whatever," Emily said, taking another sip of her
coffee. "Let's get back to the bachelor party. What if
Ethan does invite a stripper?"

Samantha chuckled at her sister's genuinely worried
expression. "That doesn't strike me as Ethan's style,"
she reassured her sister, then thought about it. "But I
don't think I'd be all that thrilled about it, either, now
that you mention it. I wouldn't want my man ogling a
naked woman right before our wedding."

"Exactly," Emily said.

Gabi listened to them and shook her head. "You
could order a cake and jump out of it just to see what's
going on," she suggested mildly.

Emily's expression immediately brightened, taking
her ludicrous comment seriously. "Great idea! Samantha, you do it. I don't want Boone to think I don't trust
him."

Samantha frowned at the pair of them, Gabi for coming up with such a ridiculous idea and Emily for seizing it like a lifeline. She knew her younger sister well
enough to know that Emily was unlikely now to let
go of it.

"I am not jumping out of a cake," Samantha told her
flatly, though she'd taken on more embarrassing jobs to
pay the bills in her early days in New York.

"It would dazzle Ethan," Gabi suggested, getting into
the spirit of things, or maybe trying to pacify Emily by
siding with her for once. "You told us yourself he seems

to respond to the unpredictable side of your nature, to say nothing of the glazed over, gaga looks he gives you every time you walk into a room. And that's without ever seeing you naked."

"Exactly," Emily enthused. "And you wouldn't have to be naked. In fact, that would be tacky, but you'd look fantastic in a bikini. I'll even pay for you to get a spray tan."

Samantha studied her sisters incredulously. "You're really serious about this? You want me to jump out of a cake at Boone's bachelor party just so I can make sure there are no strippers there?"

"And to stir up a few fantasies for Ethan," Emily said. "He needs to live a little. Oh, he's doing everything he has to do for the wedding, but he's way too somber these days. This is practically your patriotic duty, to say nothing of the favor you'd be doing me. And we all know you want to get him into bed, even if you intend to deny it with your dying breath."

Samantha could see that her sister's heart was set on this absurd idea. Since she'd made a promise to herself to do nothing to spoil these next few days for Emily, she sighed.

"If you can arrange for the cake, I'll do it, but I'm taking one quick look around and then I'm out of there. I can bear only so much humiliation, even for you."

Gabi grinned and slapped Emily's outstretched hand. "Told you she'd go for it. Mentioning how staid and uptight Ethan is these days was a nice touch. She came home last night all hot and bothered because he's still holding out on her."

Samantha frowned at the on-the-mark but annoying observation. "Watch it. I can still back out."

"But you won't," Emily said, throwing her arms around her. "Because you love me too much. And you're at least half in love with Ethan. This could push that along nicely."

"Whatever relationship I have with Ethan—and I'm not saying there is one—it does not need to be pushed along by the likes of you," she declared, though it was obviously a wasted argument.

"If not us, who?" Emily inquired. "Grandmother's good, but she's not half as inventive as Gabi and I are."

"Maybe because Grandmother has the good sense to know when to leave well enough alone," Samantha retorted.

Gabi chuckled. "Nah, that's not it. She's just biding her time. I'm pretty sure she still has a few tricks up her sleeve in case you and Ethan don't get with the program. But she's not likely to push the boundaries of good taste the way Emily and I will."

Samantha suspected her sister was exactly right. The thought of Cora Jane kicking her matchmaking skills into high gear scared her to death. Hopefully she was so preoccupied with wedding details that Samantha and Ethan weren't on her radar just yet.

Ethan glanced up when the door to the deck at Castle's opened to allow a huge cake to be pushed through on a trolley. There wasn't enough icing in the universe to disguise that the cake was fake. Since he hadn't ordered a cake of any size, its arrival was definitely a surprise, and a suspicious one at that.

Suddenly there was music, too. Boone and the dozen or so men who had gathered for the bachelor party ceased talking and stared. Boone turned to Ethan with a questioning look. Ethan shrugged.

Boone backed away from the cake. "Please tell me Emily is not going to jump out of that cake," he said, his eyes glued to the lavishly decorated cardboard monstrosity. "And if she is, please, please don't let her be naked. That view is meant for me alone. I am not sharing."

"No idea," Ethan said tersely.

"And it's not a stripper?" Boone asked.

"If it is, then someone else called for one," Ethan assured him. "Sorry, but the thought didn't cross my mind, since I thought all the men here tonight were more mature than that."

Boone grinned at the stuffy remark. "Then, again, it is a bachelor party. Who knows if I'll ever again get to see a naked woman who isn't my wife? I'm starting to hope it *is* a stripper."

"If you're too eager for the sight of naked women, you might want to reconsider getting married," Ethan suggested wryly, even as the top layer of the cake began to sway dramatically. That was accompanied by a few grunts and a pounding noise, then a yelp of dismay. That yelp sounded oddly—distressingly—familiar.

"Maybe we should do something," Boone suggested, his gaze glued to the cake.

Ethan grinned, discovering that he was oddly fascinated by the prospect of seeing just what Boone's bride-to-be had cooked up...with a little help from her sisters, no doubt. "Allow me."

He walked closer to the cake and tapped on the top layer. "Having problems?" he inquired.

"Get me out of here," an imperious voice commanded.

"Won't that spoil the effect?" he asked, his suspicions confirmed about who was inside the cake. Samantha! Who else would Emily be able to talk into pulling a stunt like this? Why she'd done it hardly even mattered.

"Ethan, if you don't help me right this second, when I do get out of here, I swear I'll…" Words seemed to fail her.

"What?" he asked curiously.

"I'm not exactly sure, but you won't like it."

"We could wait and see."

"Ethan, I'm hot and I'm annoyed."

"Okay, okay. How were you supposed to get out?"

"The top is supposed to pop right open, but it's stuck or something. I think all that fake icing turned into glue."

He searched for some sort of hinge, then realized that when that final layer had been set on, the paint had probably still been a little wet, or maybe the icing had turned to concrete. It was hard to say. Either way, the sections were stuck together, as was the lid. He pulled a Swiss Army knife from his pocket and went to work on the edges, unsealing the paint and chipping away at the icing.

"Try it now," he said. "It should pop right open, and you'll be able to make your grand entrance. Want a little stripper music? I think the tape ran out. You probably need to hit Rewind and start over."

He was pretty sure her reply was anatomically impossible.

Apparently she gave the lid a good hard push, because it toppled off and Samantha stood up looking a lot like a magnificent, harried goddess who'd just tangled with an entire Greek army. She might have emerged a winner, but she definitely wasn't happy, not even after cheers and masculine catcalls erupted around the deck. As the men stomped and whistled at the sight of her bikini-clad body, Ethan's mood deteriorated as quickly as hers had.

"Okay, that's it," he muttered. "You've had your show. Let's go."

Samantha merely lifted a brow. "I'm supposed to sing."

"I think you can be forgiven if you don't."

She regarded him stubbornly. "I rehearsed Boone's favorite song. It's the only part I was looking forward to."

"Really? You wanted to stand in the middle of a tacky cake being ogled by a bunch of drunks while you sing?"

"Well, not when you put it that way," she said, trying to climb out of the cake and nearly tumbling off the trolley and onto the floor. Fortunately she landed directly in his arms.

Ethan looked into her eyes, shook his head and aimed for the door. "I knew the first day I laid eyes on you that you were going to be a handful."

"According to a few people we both know, that's just what you need," she said, as if she'd made it her assigned mission to rectify the situation.

"No, what I need is to get through this wedding without losing the rings, and then go back to my nice, peaceful existence," he assured her.

She studied him doubtfully. "You were happy being bored?"

"I'm never bored."

"Lonely?"

Now, that, he thought, was another kettle of fish. "Not lonely, either," he lied.

She sighed at that. "Lucky you," she murmured, in a way that took him once again by surprise.

Ethan thought it was probably something they should talk about, this glamorous life he'd envisioned her leading, and what was, perhaps, a very different reality. These admissions of hers that her life wasn't rosy kept surprising him. Tonight, though, with a nearly naked Samantha snuggled in his arms, talk was pretty much the last thing on his mind.

Only the sheer grit that had gotten him through two wars kept him from giving in to temptation, hauling her into some private corner of Castle's away from prying eyes and checking out whether she really intended to go through with what she was so blatantly offering.

Being carried unceremoniously out of Castle's, Samantha sensed that she'd gotten on Ethan's last nerve. But underneath his disapproval, she'd seen something else, a man on the edge of giving in to temptation. Wasn't that interesting?

"You can put me down now. My car's right over there," she said, gesturing toward the far side of the parking lot.

"And mine is right here," he countered, opening the passenger door and depositing her unceremoniously inside.

"You can't leave your own party," she said, though her pulse was starting to scramble at the tight line of his jaw.

"I'll be back soon enough," he said. "They'll hardly miss me."

"Ethan, I'm not drunk," she said, even though the thought of having a drink or two before climbing into that awful cake had been very appealing. "You don't have to drive me home."

"Who says I am?"

"Are we going to your place?" she asked, knowing she probably sounded a little too eager.

Despite his frown, there was no mistaking the quick tug of a smile at the corners of his lips. "You'd love that, wouldn't you?"

"I wouldn't say no," she said agreeably.

He shook his head. "I was afraid of that."

"The idea of sleeping with me makes you afraid?"

"Not the act of making love," he assured her. "The implications." He shook his head. "No, scratch that. The *complications*."

"There don't have to be complications," she argued. "We're a couple of consenting adults. We both want this. Why would it be so wrong?"

"Because you deserve forever, Castle women are all about forever, and that's not on my agenda."

"Maybe we should test your theory. You could be wrong about what you want." Even as she spoke, she buried her face in her hands. "God, I sound pathetic. Or desperate. I'm sorry. I don't know why I'm pushing so hard when you're so obviously not into me."

He regarded her with dismay. "You don't sound desperate. Don't you dare think of yourself that way. It's not what this is about."

"Oh, please," she protested. "I'm all but begging you to take me to bed. That sounds pretty desperate to me."

To her surprise, he pulled off the coastal road and into the parking lot at his clinic, then cut the engine. When he turned to face her, he looked as miserable as she felt.

"I'm trying to do the right thing, Samantha. I've been honest about where I stand on relationships. Yet here you are."

She allowed herself a smile. "Not scared off," she guessed. "That must be making you crazy."

"It really is. I'm only human. I'm only so strong. And God knows I want you."

Her heart leaped at the reluctantly spoken admission. "Thank goodness for that. I was beginning to think I was out on this limb all by myself."

"Well, you're not, okay? I don't know what to do with you."

"Take me home. Maybe I can remind you."

"Samantha!" Her name emerged on a tortured moan.

She reached across the console of his sports car and rested her hand against his cheek. The tiny muscle tensed under her touch.

"I'm not going to beg, Ethan. I'm sitting here in a bikini, for heaven's sake. There's not a lot left to your imagination and yet you're still resisting. I get the message."

He captured her hand in his and pressed a kiss to her palm. "I don't think you do, not if the message is that I'm rejecting you."

"Isn't that the bottom line?"

"I'm *protecting* you," he insisted.

She shook her head. "You can keep right on telling yourself that if you want to, but I know better, Ethan. You're protecting yourself."

He looked momentarily startled, then sat back. He closed his eyes and fell silent. Samantha waited.

"Maybe I am," he conceded eventually.

"You've taken a lot of risks in your life, Ethan. You put your life on the line when you served in Iraq and Afghanistan. Let me know when you're ready to take one more, okay?" She opened the door and got out of the car.

"Where are you going?" he asked, clearly caught off guard. "Get in here. I'll take you home or back to your car, wherever you say."

"No, thanks." She pulled out her cell phone, which had barely squeezed into her bikini bottom. "Emily's waiting for my call. She'll come to get me. Go back to the party, Ethan."

"I'm not leaving you here, all alone in the dark," he said stubbornly. "Just let me take you back."

Samantha had already dialed her sister, though. "Em, I'm in the parking lot at Ethan's clinic. Come get me, okay?"

"Ten minutes," Emily said tersely. "And if that man has done anything to upset you, I'm going to personally rip his heart out."

Samantha grinned at the fierce declaration. "I might let you," she said softly, trying to keep the tears that had gathered in her eyes from falling.

She disconnected the call. With her back to Ethan, she said, "She's on her way. You can go."

"I'll leave when she gets here," he countered, his tone unrelenting.

"She says she's going to rip your heart out," she said, glancing his way to judge his reaction. He merely smiled.

"Probably deserve it," he said. "I'm still not leaving."

Since it was clear he was going nowhere until her ride showed up, Samantha leaned against the car with her back to him to wait. Only when she saw the headlights of her sister's car turning into the lot did she walk around to the driver's side. Ethan rolled down his window, and before he could guess her intention, she leaned in and kissed him the way she'd been longing to since she'd first set eyes on him that day in her grandmother's kitchen.

"Just a little something to remember tonight by," she said breezily, walking away quickly and getting into Emily's car.

Gabi was fanning her face in the front passenger seat. "That was not the sort of goodbye I was envisioning all the way over here," she said.

"Me, either," Emily concurred.

Samantha grinned. "Ethan wasn't expecting it, either. You know what they say in show business? Always leave 'em wanting more. I imagine Ethan's going to spend the rest of tonight wanting a whole lot more than that kiss."

"Oh, boy," Gabi said.

"What the devil went on tonight?" Emily asked.

"Not what you're probably imagining," Samantha told her. "No strippers at the party. No wild passion in the clinic parking lot. Just another standoff between two immovable objects."

She had a hunch, though, that one of them was about to crumble. Her last glimpse of Ethan's face as she'd walked away had revealed a man who was almost as fed up with being stoic as she was with trying fruitlessly to tempt him.

Ethan walked back onto the deck at Castle's and poured himself a stiff drink. He turned to Greg, who was sipping club soda.

"You're seeing to it that I get home," he told his friend.

"Happy to oblige," Greg said readily. "Especially if you'll tell me what went on between you and the delectable Samantha. Speculation went wild around here till Boone reminded everyone they were talking about his future sister-in-law. That shut everyone down."

"We fought," Ethan told him. "Same as usual. And that is all I intend to say about that."

"But you got her home?"

"Actually I got as far as the parking lot at the clinic, where I parked to have things out with her. Then she called her sister to pick her up."

Greg stared at him incredulously. "Man, you are seriously out of practice at this whole dating thing."

"I hadn't planned on ever being adept at it again," Ethan reminded him.

Greg studied him closely. "But you want to be, don't you? Against all that better judgment you claim to possess, you want this woman."

"Of course I want her. What man wouldn't want Samantha? It hurts to breathe when I'm around her."

"I'm talking about more than sex," Greg said.

Ethan sighed. "So am I, if I'm being honest. She says I'm scared of taking a risk."

"No question about it," Greg said without hesitation.

"Thanks for being on my side."

"I'm always on your side, but the truth is the truth. Until you get that stupid former fiancée out of your head, it will always be this way. You'll edge right up to the dance floor, but you won't step onto it."

"I was on the dance floor just last night."

Greg regarded him impatiently. "It was a metaphor."

Ethan sighed. "I know that. I just hate admitting that anyone could possibly be right about me being a coward. I'm a decorated war hero. No one should be able to mention cowardice in the same breath with my name. Yet you're the second person in the past half hour who's made the comparison."

"I don't think anyone's questioning your credentials in the hero department," Greg said. "You aren't the first man who'd rather face a bullet than put his heart on the line. I think it was easier falling in love the way I did, back when I was young and stupid and didn't know enough to be scared out of my wits. Now I'm scared every damn day that my wife will get tired of all my PTSD drama and walk out the door with my kids."

"That will never happen," Ethan replied with certainty, relieved to have the focus shift away from his issues. "That woman is so crazy about you she'd walk through fire for you. You're not going to chase her off as long as you let her in. Lindsey just needs to know you trust her enough to do that."

Greg's gaze narrowed. "You two have talked about this?"

"You know we have. She doesn't have anyone else to talk to about it, so don't get your knickers in a knot. Neither one of us is betraying you. We love you."

His friend sighed. "I get that. And nobody gets this better than you do. I just hate that I'm putting her through this. It's not what she signed on for."

"She signed on to love you no matter what," Ethan corrected. "And she's definitely strong enough to get through this. So are you, by the way."

They fell silent and sipped their drinks. The Scotch no longer held any appeal for Ethan, so he put it aside and ordered his own club soda.

"Nice job of deflecting the conversation away from Samantha, by the way," Greg said, his good mood restored.

"Dodge and weave," Ethan commented. "The first defensive maneuver we learned."

"I don't think it was meant to apply to a conversation between two buddies," Greg said.

"Probably not," Ethan agreed. "But I am done talking about Samantha, my love life or the entire freaking topic of romance for tonight." He glanced across the deck to see Boone weaving a bit. "In fact, given my cynical mood, I think I'd better make a toast to the happy groom now, before I'm tempted say something that will be a real buzz-kill on the party."

"You sure it's not already too late?" Greg asked worriedly.

"Nah. I know my lines. Emily's the best. The future's bright. You're a lucky, lucky man. Yada yada."

Greg laughed. "Try saying that with a little more feeling, okay?"

"Do my best," Ethan promised. Unfortunately, he shared none of Samantha's acting skills, so it was odds-on that he'd miss the mark.

Sixteen

Samantha's headache in the morning was only marginally better than the hangover she'd endured the week before. She, Gabi and Emily had stayed up past midnight talking after they'd rescued her from the clinic parking lot. Samantha had practiced her little-used bartending skills to make strawberry daiquiris. A lot of daiquiris, apparently, judging from the pounding in her head. She'd lost count after the third batch.

She stood in a hot shower for a long time, hoping to clear away the cobwebs. Overnight one thought had echoed again and again—that the only way to grab the future she wanted was to stay here in Sand Castle Bay and fight for it. That meant letting go of New York and everything it had once represented. She needed to wholeheartedly embrace a new plan for her life, then throw herself into it with total passion.

And, she told herself firmly, it couldn't be about Ethan. It had to be what she wanted. She had to keep reminding herself of that. If he eventually fit in, all the better.

When she finally made her way downstairs, she found both of her sisters already at the kitchen table. The coffee had been made, but she noticed that neither of them appeared to have the stomach for food this morning.

"You look surprisingly good for a woman who staggered upstairs after midnight," Gabi said cheerfully. "Is that due to great recovery powers or excellent makeup?"

"Bite me," Samantha suggested cheerfully, pouring steaming coffee into the largest mug she could find before joining them.

Emily chuckled. "I love seeing you like this."

"Like what?"

"Off your game," Emily said. "I've always known you had vulnerabilities. You wouldn't be human if you didn't, but you always covered them so well. Along with everything else, that made me a little crazy."

"Happy to give you the gift of my insecurities," Samantha responded. "Consider it a wedding present."

"I'd be content with that and nothing else," Emily claimed, then grinned. "But the crystal wine goblets you sent are gorgeous and way too extravagant."

Gabi looked thoroughly amused by the claim. "I didn't think there was anything you'd consider to be too extravagant. Your bridal registry choices were evidence of that."

"Since I'm only doing this once, I wanted things that would last a lifetime," Emily told her without the slightest hint of remorse. "I imagine you're not even bothering to register, since you don't want all the wedding commotion."

"As a matter of fact, we're not," Gabi responded.

"But from you we expect presents. Lots and lots of them. I'm thinking Waterford crystal, French china and antique sterling silver place settings. To make up for the guests we're not inviting," she added with a grin.

"So you can use them for barbecues in the backyard?" Emily taunted right back.

"There's no reason not to set a lovely table, no matter where it is," Gabi retorted, sounding a lot like Cora Jane.

"Enough," Samantha said, trying not to laugh at the silly argument. She lifted her mug. "Here's to each of us having the wedding of our dreams, period. And happily-ever-afters, et cetera."

"I can drink to that," Emily said.

"Me, too," Gabi agreed.

For a moment, they sipped their coffee in companionable silence, until Emily regarded Samantha with real concern. "Are you going to give up on Ethan? That's how it sounded last night. For the record, I think it would be a crying shame if you do."

"I agree," Gabi said. "Even after what happened last night, here you are in that football jersey of his. It's like your personal comfort blanket, your way of being close to him. I know you're not immune, no matter how badly you want us to believe you are. I don't care if you do think he's the one protecting himself from the risk of being hurt again. I think you're only marginally better. Maybe he needs to see that this isn't some game to you, that you're not going to walk away. It might reassure him."

"He knows I'm not immune to him," Samantha said. "Why isn't that enough?"

"Because he's Ethan and he's terrified of another rejection," Emily responded.

"Blast it all, I'm not Lisa!" Samantha said.

"We know that," Gabi soothed. "On some level, he knows that, too. Still, after what he's been through, it's bound to be scary to put his pride on the line again, to say nothing of his heart."

"I know all that," Samantha said. "So does he, if he's being honest with himself. That doesn't mean we can resolve things between us."

"Well, you sure won't resolve them if you go running back to New York right after the wedding," Emily said. "I can give testimony on how difficult it is to work things out long distance. Even with the best intentions in the world, Boone and I almost didn't make it."

Samantha drew in a deep breath, then told them what she'd decided. "I'm not going back, at least not to stay. Eventually I'll go back to pack up my things and sublet my apartment, but I'm staying here."

Gabi's eyes lit up at once. "And opening that playhouse?"

"I'll have to see about that," Samantha said cautiously. "But if Grandmother doesn't mind me hanging around here with her, I'll at least start those acting classes and see where that leads."

"That's fantastic," Gabi said with real enthusiasm.

Samantha glanced at Emily, whose expression wasn't nearly as thrilled. "You disagree?"

Emily shook her head. "No, I think the classes and the playhouse sound great, just perfect for you. I'm just thinking about me. Selfish, I know, but it's going to add to the pressure for me to give in and move back, too."

Tears filled her eyes. "Not that I wouldn't love to be right here with you guys so our kids can all grow up together, but I'm so afraid I'll lose myself and everything I've accomplished if I'm here. It'll be so easy to forget about everything I wanted to do."

Gabi gave her a sympathetic look. "You know that I totally get that kind of concern, but I'm here to tell you that you can reinvent your life to be anything you want it to be right here in Sand Castle Bay."

"And if you need to do the occasional job in Los Angeles, I imagine Boone will be supportive of that," Samantha added.

Gabi's expression brightened. "And if you want to make a contribution by designing safe houses for women who need them, then start an organization in North Carolina that does that, if one doesn't already exist. I'd be willing to bet that Sophia would give you all the help you ask for. Being here will only limit you as much as you allow it to."

Samantha nodded. "I totally agree, Em. You've proven yourself, maybe even exceeded your wildest expectations. Now take all that experience and talent and run with it. Do something that really matters to you, just do it here."

"I'm living proof it can happen," Gabi reminded her.

A smile broke across Emily's face at last. "I can do that, can't I? Especially with you guys as cheerleaders."

"Of course you can do it," Gabi said. "Castle women can do anything they set their minds to. We have Cora Jane's word on that."

"As soon as Boone and I get back from our honeymoon, I'm going to speak to Sophia, see what she thinks," Emily said with resolve.

"Why wait?" Samantha asked. "She'll be here later today for the rehearsal dinner, won't she? Sit down with her this afternoon. You'll go into the wedding with a lighter heart if you have her ideas and her blessing. I know you think of her as a role model and mentor."

"I'll do it," Emily said, jumping up to hug them both. "I love you guys. You're amazing."

"We're Castles," Gabi repeated. "According to Grandmother, it's in our DNA." She turned to Samantha. "Now that we've got Em pointed in the right direction, what's your next step? Are you just going to put up flyers? Announce you're teaching classes? Find a storefront space and open a school?"

"I'm still working out the details," Samantha said.

"Well, if your focus is on teaching acting, why not start by talking to Regina Gentry?" Gabi suggested. "I imagine she'd have plenty of ideas about what she'd like to see available in the area. She might even have a long list of potential students she'd share with you. And it might even be wise to get her more involved."

Samantha frowned. "More involved? How? Why?"

"She's been the respected drama teacher around here for years," Gabi reminded her. "You don't want to give her the sense that you're trying to take over from her. It could cause a rivalry you don't need. Ask her to direct scenes for you for a showcase. Have her teach some specific technique. I don't know. Just get her invested in your plans beyond giving advice."

Though Samantha worried a little about what Ethan would think of her working with a woman he'd so recently called out for her insensitivity, she immediately seized on the idea. "You're absolutely right. I'll head over to the high school later this morning, see if she's available. I need to kick-start this plan so Ethan knows I'm serious about it."

Emily and Gabi exchanged a look.

"Despite your denials, I knew Ethan was the real reason behind this," Emily said, obviously delighted. "Am I good at this matchmaking stuff or what?"

"As soon as you've finished congratulating yourself, how about butting out?" Samantha pleaded. "I can take it from here."

"That remains to be seen," Emily said. "If I don't see progress, I'm butting right back in."

Samantha sighed. "Of course you are."

"It's nothing any loving sister wouldn't do, right, Gabi?" Emily said, grinning.

Gabi chuckled and once more lifted her mug. "Count me in."

Samantha frowned at them. "You do realize I'm not the holdout, right?"

"She's right," Gabi said, her expression turning thoughtful. "We need to get Wade and Boone working on Ethan."

"Please don't," Samantha begged. "He'll pack up and move to Alaska or something."

"Where you could hunt him down and make love in front of a roaring fire," Emily said dreamily.

Samantha rolled her eyes. "I thought I was the one who'd made a career out of make-believe."

"Fairy-tale endings aren't make-believe," Emily protested. "I have mine, Gabi has hers and yours is just around the corner."

Samantha laughed. Nothing like a healthy dose of pie-eyed optimism to get the morning off to a good start.

When Samantha dropped into the high school office, she was greeted by a wide-eyed girl who looked vaguely familiar.

"Hi, I'm Sue Ellen," the teen said. "And you're Samantha Castle. I can't tell you how inspired I was by your talk after rehearsal the other day. It just made me want to work all the harder to become a huge star."

Samantha smiled, remembering now that this was the play's lead, the girl with the almost terminal case of stage fright. "You're serious about acting?" she asked carefully.

"Sure," Sue Ellen said, then flushed. "I mean I know I suck in front of an audience. All those people scare me to death, but I can act. And movies and TV aren't as hard, right? Just learn a few lines at a time, then play to the camera."

"It's not quite that simple," Samantha told her, but Sue Ellen didn't seem to be swayed by her gentle wake-up call. "I came to see Mrs. Gentry. Is she available?"

"She has study hall right now, but I'll bet she wouldn't mind if you stopped by." She wrote down the room number and drew a map of the hallways. "Just go on in. You're supposed to have an official pass, but nobody's going to care."

Clearly Sue Ellen was a rule-breaker, Samantha thought, hiding a smile. Maybe that would be enough to give her an edge in Hollywood.

A few minutes later, she found the room, tapped on the door, then poked her head in. Mrs. Gentry's eyes lit up. She hurried over to the door.

"Samantha, what brings you by? Isn't the wedding tomorrow? I thought you'd be swamped with last-minute details."

"Cora Jane's had everything under control for a month," Samantha said. "She swears all we need to do is to show up for tonight's rehearsal dinner and the ceremony tomorrow."

"Lucky you. I remember how chaotic it was when my daughter got married, but then I don't have your grandmother's organizational skills."

"Few of us do," Samantha agreed.

"So, what can I do for you? Can I persuade you to stop by another rehearsal next week? Maybe give the students some pointers?"

"I'd be happy to do that, but I'm sure they don't need my suggestions," Samantha said. "You've always been an excellent director. I remember how much I enjoyed working with you. I learned a lot that summer."

"A good student takes something away from every experience," Mrs. Gentry said. "I'd love it if you came by Monday afternoon."

"Then I'll do that," Samantha promised. "In the meantime, I wanted to run an idea by you."

"Oh?"

"I'm thinking of staying here in Sand Castle Bay and offering a few acting classes," she told the teacher. "Maybe starting a school and, down the line, even a playhouse. If I do all that, I'd love it if you'd get involved with me. What do you think?"

The teacher hesitated for a long time before replying. "If I'm being totally honest, I have mixed feelings," she said. "And I hope you won't take this the wrong way. It's absolutely not because I'm jealous or afraid that you'll steal my most promising students. As I said just a moment ago, I think the most dedicated students could learn a tremendous amount from you."

"But you're not enthusiastic," Samantha concluded, her spirits sinking. "Why?"

"Some people in this community are fairly conservative," Mrs. Gentry explained. "They think of the acting profession the way they think of Hollywood, as if it's a bunch of wildly liberal people who aren't in touch with reality. While they'd never say such a thing to Cora Jane, there are some who'd be suspicious of anyone in that field. You'd have to be completely above reproach for them to entrust their children to you."

Samantha wavered between indignation and the realization that Regina Gentry could well be right, that her background, rather than being an asset, could be a liability in some circles.

"I haven't exactly lived a life in the tabloid headlines," she responded. "And Cora Jane is a respected member of this community. So are you, which is one reason your participation could be so beneficial."

"Those things are definitely a plus," the teacher agreed. "But there wouldn't be a lot of room for missteps."

"If you feel this way, why would you have invited me to speak to your students?"

"A guest lecturer with your credentials is one thing," she replied easily. "Letting a child attend classes with you on a regular basis, where you could influence him or her in unwanted ways…" She shrugged. "That's something else."

Samantha fought to cover her shock at the unexpected reaction. "Thank you for being candid with me," she said, keeping her tone neutral. "I'll have to give this some more thought."

She was about to walk away when the teacher stopped her with a touch. Her expression sympathetic, she said, "If you do decide to stay, I just wanted you to know what you might be up against, Samantha. That said, I hope you stay. In my opinion, anything that encourages these children to follow a dream and gives them additional resources to do it is a good thing. And I would be happy to get involved, if you still want me after this."

"I'll be in touch," Samantha said, unwilling to commit to anything more.

Samantha tried not to feel discouraged as she left the high school. Despite her final words, it was clear that Regina Gentry wouldn't be offering a rousing endorsement. She might not even steer students in Samantha's direction if she thought it might damage her own sterling reputation.

But, Samantha reminded herself, those like Cass Gray who were dedicated and determined might find their way to her on their own.

She tried to imagine any scenario from her past that could be twisted into a negative that would influence parents to keep their kids away. Nothing came to mind. And since she was well past her rebellious, daredevil days, it seemed unlikely that anything would crop up now.

* * *

Ethan wasn't sure what to expect when he walked into the church for the rehearsal on Friday night. He knew the role he was there to play, but no one had fed him any directions for dealing with Samantha after the previous night's disaster in the clinic parking lot. He reminded himself sternly that they were two adults here to be supportive of Boone and Emily. He vowed to do nothing to make the evening awkward or uncomfortable.

Samantha had apparently made a similar vow, because she gave him a hesitant smile as he walked to the front of the church. Drawn to that smile as he would have been to sunlight, he slipped into the pew beside her.

"You got home okay, I see."

Her smile widened at that. "And I didn't send Emily and Gabi back to rip your heart out. All in all, a good night for both of us."

Ethan chuckled. "I suppose so." He nodded toward Emily, who was flitting around the sanctuary like a hummingbird. "Is she okay?"

"She's on an adrenaline high," Samantha said. "Even though she's been over Cora Jane's lists a thousand times herself, she's convinced something critical has escaped their notice. How's Boone doing?"

"Calmer than I would be," Ethan told her. "He's eager to put the ceremony behind them and get on with married bliss."

"You sound skeptical."

Ethan merely lifted a brow. "I think I'd best table my cynicism for the next couple of days."

"Probably a good idea."

He stood up. "I'd better check in with Boone. He's over there trying to pacify his parents, and he's starting to look a little desperate."

Samantha followed his gaze. "Go. I don't envy you."

"Just part of my duties, or so I'm told," he said, and crossed to the groom's side of the sanctuary. "Everything okay?"

Boone's scowl was response enough.

"What's the problem?" Ethan asked.

"My mother seems to object to my father being allowed to sit in the same row for the service," Boone explained, directing a frown at his mother. "Of course, what she really hates is that he'll be accompanied by his wife."

"I'm just saying, she's not family," the former Mrs. Dorsett said.

"Neither is your husband," Boone's father retorted. "Are we banishing him, too?"

Ethan held up a hand, deciding to test his peacemaking skills. "It's a big pew. Couldn't you all share it for Boone's sake? The ceremony will take, what? An hour? Surely you can remain civilized for that long."

"I will not sit in the same row with that bimbo," Felicity retorted at once.

"Do not refer to my wife as a bimbo," her ex-husband snapped. "Or I'll call that man you married exactly what he is."

She got up in his face. "Which is? Say it, Martin. What is it you think he is?"

"He's a gigolo," Martin said heatedly. "And everyone here knows it."

"Well, Sheila is a money-grasping fortune-hunter," she replied. "Why else would a twenty-three-year-old marry you?"

Boone lifted his eyes heavenward. Ethan got between the two warring exes. "Enough!" he said emphatically. "This is not about either of you or about your opinion of each other's marriage. Tomorrow is all about Boone and Emily, and if you can't behave like reasonably civilized adults, then maybe you both should stay away."

Boone's mother stared at him in shock. "You want me to miss my only son's wedding?"

"I don't want you to miss anything," Ethan replied, hanging on to his patience by a thread. "I just don't want you to ruin it with this childish game you're playing."

She burst into tears and ran up the aisle. Boone's father turned on Boone. "And you agree? That's what you want? For us to stay away?"

"I want you here," Boone contradicted. "But Ethan's right. Not if you're going to cause a scene."

Martin Dorsett looked taken aback by his son's response, then slowly nodded. "That woman could always get on my last nerve, but you're right. I'll deal with this." He glanced at Ethan. "Thanks for trying to be a voice of reason. I know it's a thankless task when it comes to Felicity and me."

Ethan nodded. "It was worth a shot, just the same."

As he left, Boone held up his hand for a bump. "Thanks for having my back. I was about at my wit's end with the two of them. You'd think after all these years apart, the old anger and resentment would be dead and buried."

"You treat children with authority," Ethan said, then grinned. "Even if they are in their fifties."

Boone nodded. "I'll have to remember that if I'm ever insane enough to get them into the same room again." He sighed. "I'd better see if Emily's ready to start. For all I know, this little scene has scared her off."

"I think it'll take more than a spat between your parents to scare her off," Ethan said.

Boone started away, then came back, his expression worried. "You and Samantha okay? I know something went down between the two of you last night. When I spoke to Emily last night, they were in the kitchen at Cora Jane's getting soused."

"Samantha and I are fine," Ethan assured him. At least he hoped they were. And if they weren't, they'd just have to fake it for the next twenty-four hours or so.

Samantha had watched with amazement the scene unfolding across the church as Ethan clearly fought to get the situation under control. Better him than her, she'd concluded. Though she hadn't been able to hear the words being exchanged, it was apparent that Boone's parents were behaving badly.

Once the situation had calmed down, the rest of the rehearsal went by without a snag, and an hour later they were all in the private dining room at Boone's Harbor for the rehearsal dinner. Several of Emily's Los Angeles friends had been invited to join the family for the occasion, so their presence masked whatever ongoing differences there were between Boone's parents. She noted, though, that Ethan had apparently made it his mission for the night to keep the two apart.

In the lull before dessert, Samantha glanced across the room and noted that both of Boone's parents were missing. She scanned the crowd, but couldn't spot them.

"Uh-oh," she murmured and went looking for Ethan. When she found him, she leaned in close to whisper, "Your charges seem to have escaped."

He glanced down at her, his eyes filling with alarm. "What?"

"Boone's mother and father are AWOL."

Ethan muttered an expletive. "Help me look, okay? Any sign of their spouses?"

She nodded in the direction of the table where one of the couples had been seated earlier. Now the step-parents were huddled together there, minus their mates. Neither looked especially happy. It did not bode well, she decided.

"That can't be good," Ethan said, expressing her own impression.

"Just what I was thinking. Any thoughts on where Mom and Pop might be?"

"Hopefully far, far apart," he replied. "You check the ladies' room and any other nooks and crannies in here. I'll check the men's room, then scout around outside."

Samantha tried to open the door to the ladies' room, but found it to be locked from the inside. Since she knew it was a large restroom with many stalls, she also knew that locking the door was unnecessary unless someone had sought out privacy. Her stomach sank.

"No, please, no," she whispered, waiting for Ethan to come back before she did anything else. She pressed her ear to the door, then groaned, a sound that seemed to be reflective of the passionate noises coming from inside the restroom.

Ethan appeared within minutes, took one look at her and asked, "What?"

"I can't be sure, but I think they've locked themselves in there," she told him.

Ethan stared at her. "But why?" he asked, then gasped as understanding dawned. "Are you sure?"

"Take a listen," she said, stepping out of his way.

He put his ear against the door, turned pale and jumped back. A smile tugged at his lips and before Samantha could react to that shocking sight, he was laughing. He grabbed her hand and tugged. "Let's get away from here."

"But shouldn't we do something?"

"I'm not breaking down that door," Ethan said. "How about you?"

"They could be killing each other," Samantha said, casting a last worried look in the direction of the restroom.

"Did you hear any screaming?"

She shook her head. What she'd heard definitely wasn't screaming, at least not the shouts of someone in trouble.

"Then let's hope for the best," he said.

"Which is what exactly?" she wondered. "That Boone's long-divorced-and-now-remarried-to-others parents are in there getting it on?"

"Not a scenario I especially want to lock in my head," Ethan said, "but yes. That's the one that makes it none of our business."

Samantha was outside before her own laughter started. "We can never tell Boone and Emily about this, can we?"

"Maybe someday," Ethan said. "When we're all very,

very old and sitting on a porch somewhere with very strong beverages."

Samantha gave him a wistful look. "Do you think we'll know each other then?"

Ethan held her gaze, then caressed her cheek with a tender gesture. "I'm starting to think we can count on it."

When he draped an arm around her shoulders as they walked along the marina, she snuggled into all that strength and heat and took comfort in his words. It was far from a commitment, but on the eve of her sister's wedding, it gave her hope that he might be opening his heart.

Seventeen

Samantha stood in the back of the church and watched as her father nervously ran a finger under his shirt collar. Sam Castle in a tuxedo with that bit of distinguished gray in his hair was an impressive sight.

"Dad, you look incredible," she told him. "You were made to wear a tuxedo."

Rather than looking reassured as she'd hoped, he frowned. "Do you know one of the things I regret the most?" he asked. Then, without waiting for a reply, he answered his own question, "That I wore one so seldom with your mother."

"The two of you weren't exactly big partygoers."

"Precisely my point. She loved getting dressed up for fancy parties, and I couldn't be bothered. She stopped showing me the invitations after a while. I inadvertently cast her in this role as dutiful corporate wife, then wouldn't cooperate with any of the things she considered to be important, no dinner parties, no charity balls. Worse, I neglected her."

"I'm sorry." She wanted to tell him it wasn't true, but

she couldn't. Obsessed with his work, he'd emotionally abandoned all of them.

"Let it be a lesson to you, Samantha. Life is short. I always thought there'd be time to do the things your mother wanted to do sometime down the road. There wasn't."

"Mom understood your priorities," Samantha reminded him. "She was proud of you and your work."

"She shouldn't have had to understand or to take a backseat to my priorities, not a hundred percent of the time, anyway," Sam Castle replied. "She should have been my priority. She and you girls." He glanced inside the church. "She should have been here for this."

"I think she is," Samantha said softly. "And she would be very happy that you're putting us first now."

"Too little, too late." He waved off the comment. "Not the time to be dwelling on my mistakes. From here on out, actions will speak louder than words. I will be here for all of you. I owe it to your mother, to you and to myself. Maybe I'll do better by my grandchildren than I did by you girls."

He studied her for a minute. "You assigned to keep my nerves from getting the better of me?" he asked.

She chuckled. "Something like that. And Gabi does better at keeping Emily calm than I do."

He frowned. "Why is that?"

"The usual sibling dissension," she said, minimizing it. "It's mostly all worked out. Nothing for you to worry about. Today's all about happiness."

He nodded. "Today we'll focus totally on your sister," he agreed, "but tomorrow you and I will talk. I want to know why you haven't asked me about that land my father left me."

Samantha gave him a startled look. "Grandmother told you about how I might be able to use that?"

"You know how she likes to ensure a certain outcome," he said, his eyes twinkling. "She wanted me to be in a receptive mood when you asked. Since I've never been interested in claiming that land, I don't know what she was worried about. It's yours if you want it."

"Just like that?" she asked, wide-eyed.

He smiled at her shock. "Even I am capable of the magnanimous gesture from time to time, especially if it will make one of my daughters' dreams come true."

"I'm not sure if it is my dream," she admitted. "Or how ready I am for such a huge step."

"Then we'll talk about that, too," he promised. "I think I can convince you that you are."

Samantha laughed, despite his perfectly serious tone. "Boy, when you get into this whole fatherhood thing, you jump in with both feet, don't you?"

"Only way I know to do things," he agreed. "You might keep that in mind," he added with a wink.

Ethan was so worried about getting Boone to the altar on time, not losing track of the rings and keeping an eye on the wayward parents that the ceremony pretty much passed in a blur. When it was over, he breathed a sigh of relief.

That feeling that his duty was done only lasted until the photographer rounded them up for pictures. It seemed an endless number of them were required. The only saving grace was being positioned by Samantha's side for most of them.

When they'd been at it for what seemed like an eternity, he bent down and whispered in her ear, "Want to make a run for it? I know a restroom where we can lock the door and hide out."

She laughed. "As intriguing as that offer sounds, I'm afraid we'd be missed," she told him, though there was obvious regret in her voice.

"Not by Boone and Emily," he countered. "Those two haven't taken their eyes off each other since she appeared at the back of the church to walk down the aisle."

"As it should be," Samantha said. "If couples are ever visibly crazy in love, it ought to be on their wedding day."

"Isn't that part of the problem?" Ethan asked, unable to stop his cynicism from showing. "After that day of nerves and high romance, reality sets in. There are arguments over picking socks up off the floor, or putting the dishes in the dishwasher."

"Those things are pretty petty compared to the big picture," Samantha argued.

"But they eat away, just like a tiny drip of water eventually erodes the cliff beneath."

"Hey, you two," Emily suddenly interrupted. "You're spoiling the pictures. Whatever has you looking so somber can wait."

Ethan nodded. "Got it," he said, forcing a smile.

Samantha's was only marginally more sincere.

"You know," she said, when the photographer finally released them, "just yesterday I was thinking your attitude toward love was improving."

"Afraid not," he said.

She stopped him from walking away and held his gaze. "You sure about that?"

"Of course I'm sure," he said firmly.

"Want to know what I think? I'd lay money that you say those things automatically because cynicism is second nature to you. It's your defense mechanism, the way you avoid getting involved. It probably makes most women run for the hills, at least the few you allow to get close in the first place."

Ethan wasn't sure how to respond to the accuracy of her assessment. Being cynical had become easy over the years. It had kept women at bay, leaving his emotions untouched and his life uncomplicated. No one had ever called him on it before. Well, no woman, anyway. Greg and Boone called him on it all the time. It was easy to ignore their well-meant opinions. They were great guys, the best of friends, but insightful? Nah.

Discovering that Samantha knew him well enough not only to figure this out but to call him on it made him think of her a little differently. He saw a new depth to her, an almost irresistible degree of sensitivity. He'd seen hints of it in her understanding of Cass, too. She was quite a woman, he concluded. She understood the things that mattered.

"You figured this out all by yourself?" he asked suspiciously, hopeful that one of his friends had filled her in on their theories. He was in deep enough without discovering yet another reason to stop holding her at arm's length.

"Yes, Ethan, all by myself," she responded with amusement. "You're not that complicated."

"So you believe the cynicism is an act," he said.

"Not an act so much as a convenient way to get out of sticky emotional situations. I think on some level you do believe every word, but it's starting to sound hollow, even to you."

"Are you thinking I've undergone some huge transformation because of you?"

"Heavens no! I'm not taking credit for this. I just think the cynicism has outlived its usefulness. Sooner or later, I'll bet even porcupines take a chance on love."

He laughed despite himself. "I'm the porcupine here?"

She smiled. "If the shoe fits…"

"Why haven't you long since given up on me?"

"You mean the way other women did?"

He nodded. "Not that there have been many other women, mind you. I could count my repeat dates on one hand since the breakup of my engagement."

"Maybe I'm just stubborn," she said lightly. She held his gaze, then added quietly, "Or maybe it's because I think you're worth fighting for." She touched a hand to his cheek. "Something to think about, Ethan. I'll see you inside. Save a dance for me."

He tried to understand the feelings that washed over him as he watched her go. Desire, never far from the surface, was there, for sure. But there was also longing. For the first time in recent memory, he wanted something that he was almost convinced was just within reach: a woman who would love him unconditionally. Could he trust his heart? Or maybe, more important, did he dare trust Samantha, a woman destined to leave and return to a far more glamorous life?

The reception was being held outside at Boone's home. A tent had been erected near the water and filled with tables. A band was playing in a temporary gazebo with a dance floor set up in front. Flowers were everywhere, a mix of white roses and blue hydrangeas. Small arrangements of the same flowers served as centerpieces, set on periwinkle-blue tablecloths. Candles were ready to be lit as soon as dusk fell. Twinkling white lights in the shrubbery and trees would add a fairy-tale element as the guests danced under the stars. Boone and Emily were clearly expecting the party to go on forever.

Samantha sought out her grandmother. "It's absolutely beautiful," she told Cora Jane, giving her a huge hug. "You outdid yourself with everything. You gave Emily her dream wedding."

Cora Jane smiled with pleasure at the compliment. "I think she's happy with the way it all turned out."

"Of course she is. Who wouldn't be?"

"Even when she didn't say it, I knew your sister thought some fancy Hollywood wedding planner would make it better."

"No way could this have been any better," Samantha reassured her, just as Emily's friend Sophia Grayson joined them.

Apparently she'd overheard Cora Jane's lament, because she beamed at her and said, "I've done my share of elegant Hollywood parties, Mrs. Castle. None have ever been more elegant than this."

Cora Jane gave her a startled look. "You sound as if you mean that."

Sophia laughed. "I may be from Los Angeles, but I'm not an actress. When I say something, it's sincere."

"Thank you," Cora Jane said.

"Now tell me how much longer I'm going to be able

to claim Emily's time before you all lure her back here permanently," Sophia said.

"That's up to her," Cora Jane replied, "but I can't deny I'd like to see her and Boone raise their family here."

"She told me just yesterday that she'd like to do the same work she's doing in Los Angeles but closer to home," Sophia said. "She's meant to do something meaningful with her life. Where she does it hardly matters. I promised her I'd help in any way I can." She glanced around. "I might even spend a little time on this coast myself to help her get things off the ground."

"What a generous offer," Cora Jane said. "I know that will mean the world to my granddaughter. She admires you."

"As I do her," Sophia said. "Something tells me she takes after you. I look forward to getting to know you better. Now I'd better circulate a bit. I saw a very handsome man earlier who caught my eye."

To Samantha's shock, when she walked away, she gravitated directly toward Sam Castle.

"Well, I'll be," Cora Jane said, her eyes round. "You don't suppose...?"

Samantha laughed. "Well, it is a magical night. And something tells me if Dad is in Sophia's sights, he'll never know what hit him."

Cora Jane nodded, clearly pleased. "Just exactly what he needs. She's the kind of woman who could make him think about something other than work." She faced Samantha. "Where's your young man?"

"Ethan's avoiding me, more than likely. I cut a little too close to the truth earlier, and it scared him. He doesn't like thinking he's not that big a mystery."

"Men never do. Find him, honey bun. Keep him on his toes. If anyone ever needed to have his life shaken up, it's Ethan. It's pained me to see him keeping to himself since that awful woman broke their engagement." She leveled a look at Samantha. "Wouldn't hurt for you to take a few risks, either."

Since staying out of Ethan's path wasn't nearly as much fun as butting heads with him, Samantha took her grandmother's advice and went looking for him. If nothing else, he owed her a dance.

Ethan stayed on the move during the reception, convinced that he'd be less of a target for the Castle meddlers if he always appeared to be on a mission. Samantha's comments earlier had shaken him more than he wanted to admit. She'd seen through him, something few others had taken the time to do. In fact, she'd seen something he hadn't wanted to admit, even to himself, that he wanted someone in his life, after all. Maybe even Samantha.

Unfortunately, letting go of the stubborn posture he'd taken since the breakup was going to provide entertainment for a lot of people. Greg and Boone, for two, would laugh themselves silly if they found out they'd been right all along.

"You can't avoid me forever," a voice filled with amusement whispered in his ear just then.

He whirled around to find that the very woman in question had slipped up behind him. She'd kicked off the high heels she'd worn for the ceremony and was barefoot in the grass. Her dress, which was an utterly feminine shade of peach, brought out the color in her cheeks and made her eyes sparkle. Or maybe that was the mischief he thought he detected.

"I wasn't trying to avoid you," he claimed. "I've been busy. You know what they say, a best man's duties are never done."

She looked skeptical. "Then shouldn't it also be true that neither are the maid of honor's? Nobody's given me any duties, other than the toast I'll have to make in a bit."

"Ah, but your side of the equation doesn't include Felicity and Martin," he reminded her. "Boone wants me on high alert, and that's even without his knowing about last night's turn of events."

Samantha glanced around. "Come to think of it, I haven't spotted the oh-so-happy exes. Where are they?"

"Settled with their respective spouses at the moment," Ethan assured her. "At separate tables. I switched a few place cards around to make sure they were nowhere near each other."

"Cora Jane may kill you if she finds out about that," she told him. "It took her weeks to settle on the seating arrangement."

"I'll take my chances. Better a lecture from Cora Jane than a debacle at the groom's family table."

She laughed. "You have a point." She gazed at him expectantly.

"What?" he asked, pretending not to know why she'd sought him out.

"I was hoping for that dance you were supposed to save for me," she said.

"Now?" he said warily, scrambling for a believable delaying tactic. "We should probably do the toasts, get our official duties over with before we start enjoying ourselves."

She grabbed his hand. "Then let's do that," she said, leading the way to the front of the tent where the bridal party had been seated, at least until some of them had wandered away to evade prying eyes.

To Ethan's dismay, she picked up a crystal champagne glass, beckoned for the waiter and had it filled to the brim before tapping on it to get the guests' attention.

She turned and winked at her sister. "You know, when I was a little girl and Emily came along, I was just old enough to read her fairy tales. In the ones she liked the best, the handsome prince always came along to capture the heart of the beautiful princess. I think those stories shaped the woman she became, because when her prince came along, he stole her heart forever. Emily and Boone didn't fall into each other's arms and live happily ever after at first glance—they were only fourteen, for heaven's sake—but I think that's what makes their story so incredible. Their love never died, and when they got a second chance, they grabbed it."

She lifted her glass. "To my sister and her prince. May your future be as joyous as you dreamed. To Emily and Boone!"

"To Emily and Boone!" The toast echoed around the room.

Ethan smiled down at the woman beside him. "And now I have to try to top that," he said, drawing laughs. "I've known Boone for most of my life, from the first time his parents came over to visit mine with this scrawny little bundle in their arms. I have to admit, I wasn't impressed."

"Thanks, pal," Boone said, lifting his glass in a mocking salute.

"Just wait," Ethan scolded. "It didn't take long for me to discover that this kid who was soon shadowing me everywhere was a talented athlete and a good friend, and he grew up to become an amazing man. He became the kid brother I never had, and now he's one of my best friends, one of those who never shies away from the truth, even when it hurts."

He lifted his glass in Emily's direction. "At the very core of who he is, at his soul, there is Emily. From the moment they met, it was evident that they were meant to be together. Now, just about everyone in this room knows I'm not a big believer in love everlasting, but I can't deny this truth. Theirs has lasted. And I can only stand here today in awe and respect and wish them years and years of the same emotions they're feeling right at this moment."

To his surprise, he actually felt the sting of tears in his eyes as he held his glass high. "To Boone and Emily. May you find all the happiness you deserve."

"Already found it, pal," Boone shouted. "Now it's your turn." He glanced pointedly toward Samantha, then grinned at Ethan's discomfort. "Just saying."

A cheer erupted from the guests, or maybe it was just from the Castles, but all Ethan heard was people chanting, "Kiss her, kiss her."

Maybe it was meant for Boone and Emily. Maybe it was directed at him, but he couldn't seem to draw his gaze away from Samantha's upturned face, her expectant expression. What the heck? he thought, giving in to long-overdue temptation.

He pulled her into his arms and captured her lips, aware of nothing else but the way her mouth opened for him, of the way she molded her body to his, the heat and desire that were suddenly all-consuming. She was everything he'd anticipated, and then some.

He'd known it would be like this. He must have. That's probably why he'd fought against his feelings for so long. He'd known that once he let her in, even a little bit, he'd be lost.

And right now, with both of them pouring heart and soul into that kiss, he knew his fight was over. He'd done the one thing he'd vowed never to do. He'd fallen hopelessly in love.

Samantha regarded Ethan with a dazed expression as he eventually released her. "Boy, when you fall off the wagon, you really take a tumble, don't you?" she whispered, her voice breathless.

He smiled. "If you're going to do something, you'd better give it your best shot," he confirmed. "That's always been my motto."

"Want to go somewhere less public and do it again?" she asked hopefully. "You did say that once our official duties were complete, we were free to enjoy ourselves."

She saw him waver for just a heartbeat, clearly tempted, but then that stoic resolve of his kicked in one more time.

"Maybe we'd better have that dance now, instead. If you and I get caught making out, speculation will run rampant. We'll steal Emily's thunder. She'll never forgive us."

"Or she could cheer," Samantha told him. "This is what she wanted."

"True, but probably not in the middle of her wedding reception." He held out his hand. "Let's dance. It's a slow song. I can hold you close."

"If that's your best offer, I suppose I have no choice but to accept," she said, following him to the dance floor. When she was settled in his arms, she whispered, "But fair warning. Don't think I'm going to stop trying to seduce you tonight."

"Duly noted," he said.

She could feel his smile against her cheek.

They moved around the dance floor with surprising grace, Ethan's firm hand guiding her.

"Okay, what's up with the dance moves?" she asked. "You were great the other night, too. Have you been practicing for all the wedding festivities?"

He flushed under her scrutiny. "Not really."

Samantha frowned. "But you have had dance lessons since your injury," she persisted. "You must have. Your moves are totally fluid."

"Okay, yes, I had a few lessons," he admitted, clearly uncomfortable.

"Because?"

"Lisa insisted," he said. "The people in charge of my rehab suggested it would help with balance and coordination. Since I thought it might convince her that I wasn't going to trample her feet, I went along with it. I think we both knew by then that it was over, but I couldn't make myself throw in the towel. I kept trying to prove to her I was the same man."

Samantha regarded him with dismay, indignant on

his behalf. "You aren't the same man, though. You're a thousand times better. You're courageous and brave. You've overcome a serious injury that could have destroyed you."

"I haven't overcome anything that thousands of other soldiers haven't had to face."

"And you're all heroes, Ethan. You're worth more than a hundred self-involved, shallow women like Lisa."

He looked a little startled by her fierce defense, even though she'd said much the same in the past. "You sound so sure of that."

"I am sure of that."

"What have I done to earn that kind of support?" he asked, sounding bewildered. "I've done nothing but give you a rough time since we met. Never mind years ago, when I apparently didn't even notice you were alive."

She shrugged off the past. "You were a big-shot football hero back then. I was just a kid. It's little wonder I wasn't on your radar, so you're forgiven for that," she told him. "As for everything that's happened since our paths crossed this time, I get it." She held his gaze. "I really do, Ethan. Sometimes I have a little trouble believing this is real myself, and I'm a big believer in love."

"You've never let your doubts show," he said.

"I figure one of us sitting on the fence was tricky enough. One of us needed to be all in."

He looked startled by her choice of words. "And you're all in?"

She nodded. "And don't you dare let that terrify you. You'll get there when you get there." She shrugged, trying for a nonchalance she was far from feeling. "Or you won't."

"And you're okay with that?"

"I'm not okay with it," she said. "Of course not. But I can't change it, can I? Your feelings are your feelings. I just want you to be sure you really know what those feelings are before you throw away this chance we have."

He shook his head. "You scare me to death," he said.

"How so?"

"You make it sound so easy."

"I never said it was easy. Look at Boone and Emily, or Wade and Gabi. Nothing about their journeys was easy. I just believe love is worth all the hard work that goes into it."

She glanced around the reception, then looked up into his eyes. "Looks like this party's breaking up."

He followed the direction of her gaze. "Looks that way."

"What happens next, Ethan?"

He hesitated for so long, she thought she'd lost to-night's battle, if not the war.

"You come home with me," he said with just the faintest hint of anxiety behind the words.

She could read the vulnerability in his eyes, hear it in his voice. Even now, it was evident he feared rejection, if not in this moment, then later, when it could be even more devastating. She nodded at once, hoping that her eagerness would reassure him.

"Best offer I've had in ages," she told him, meaning it.

"Maybe you ought to wait and see about that," he said.

"Don't," she said emphatically. "Don't you dare sell yourself short, Ethan."

"Just giving you fair warning that I'm pretty rusty at this."

Her heart swelled at the trust he was placing in her. "No matter what, you are man enough for me, okay? Nothing that happens tonight is going to change that."

She was willing to guarantee it, but the relief in his eyes told her he was taking her at her word. She intended to see that she didn't let him down.

Eighteen

Ethan had never been more terrified in his life, not even in Afghanistan and Iraq. There he'd put his life on the line. Tonight he was testing his heart and soul. Samantha had demonstrated a level of blind faith in him that stunned him. That alone would have made him love her, but so many other reasons had already convinced him that he couldn't let her go. Tonight, he knew he couldn't let her—or himself—down.

He'd made love since he'd been out of rehab, even once with Lisa, though that had been a disaster best forgotten. She hadn't cut him even the tiniest bit of slack or done anything to put him at ease. As always, it had been all about her, and he hadn't been able to satisfy her, not the way he once had. She clearly hadn't been patient enough to see if his awkwardness would change.

Other encounters had been more successful but hadn't involved emotion, just physical satisfaction. At least they'd been reassuring on that level.

Now here was a smoldering-hot woman who wanted to put him first, who believed in him completely. And whether he liked it or not, his heart was engaged. To-night wasn't about sex. It was about forging something lasting, something with the potential to endure. That raised the stakes to a previously unimaginable level.

When he pulled into the driveway at his place, he cut the engine and turned to Samantha. "Still time to bail," he said, injecting a light note into his voice as he made the offer.

She blinked at the suggestion. "Why would I do that?"

He shrugged. "Second thoughts."

"I don't have any." A frown knit her brow. "Do you?"

"A whole boatload of them," he admitted, then caressed her cheek. "But I want this, Samantha. I want to have this night with you. More than I ever wanted anything."

She gave a pleased little nod of satisfaction. "Then we need to get out of this car before you change your mind."

Inside, he paused in the kitchen. "Wine? I think I can even find a bottle of champagne, if you'd prefer that."

She shook her head. "I want a clear head," she said. "Or as clear as it can be after drinking all those toasts earlier."

Feeling out of practice and out of sorts, he stood a second longer, then admitted sheepishly, "I have no idea what to do next."

She laughed. "You can't possibly be that rusty."

"I warned you," he reminded her. "Sex? I can do that. Making love? Not so sure. I feel as if I should have scattered rose petals all over, set the stage with candles. You know, given you the romance, but I refused to let myself even hope that tonight would turn out this way."

He gave her a wry look. "I was still deep in denial about where we were headed."

She stepped closer and rested her hands against his chest, right above his thundering heart. "That's very sweet, but you're the romance, Ethan. Just you. That's all I need."

Encouraged, he scooped her into his arms, drawing a startled look.

"Seriously?" she said, though there was a smile spreading across her face.

"Scared I'm going to drop you?" he said, more light-hearted and confident than he could remember being for ages.

She snuggled closer, obviously putting her trust in him. "Not for a second," she told him.

When he reached his room, he regretted again the lack of ambiance. The decor hadn't much mattered to him. It was clean and the bed was big and comfortable. Right now it happened to be bathed in moonlight, so that, at least, was something. He settled her on the chocolate-brown comforter, loving the way her dress hiked up to reveal those long, shapely legs of hers. He'd been captivated by those legs for a while now.

"You're ogling my legs," she teased.

"I am," he said unrepentantly. "Haven't been able to get them out of my head since the day I walked into Cora Jane's kitchen and found you there in nothing but my old football jersey. It's not an image a man forgets."

"How do you know that was all I was wearing?"

He grinned. "I knew," he said, opting not to reveal the glimpse of bare bottom he'd caught. "A weaker man would have hauled you upstairs right that second."

"And you've held out for a whole two weeks," she said. "I'm awed by your strength of character."

"Well, it's been shot to blazes now," he said, taking off his jacket, then loosening the collar of his shirt before settling on the bed beside her.

"Come here," he said, rolling her on top of him, loving the weight of her, the way her curves fit his body.

He cupped her face in his hands, studying the way her eyes darkened with anticipation, the way the tip of her tongue moistened her lips. "How could any man resist you?" he murmured.

"It would take a saint," she remarked, the teasing note back in her voice.

"Then you've got the wrong guy," he said, giving himself over to sensations he hadn't experienced for far too long.

And even as he rediscovered passion, he found something unexpected, the pure joy of abandoning all pretenses and falling head over heels in love. Amazingly, it felt nothing at all the way it had when he'd been involved with Lisa. As good as that had been in the beginning, this was a thousand times better, and not just because he felt this soul-deep connection, but because it felt easy, as if he'd spent a lifetime waiting for exactly the right woman and had finally found her.

Knowing what was at stake—Ethan's unmistakably fragile self-esteem—Samantha had worried herself sick on the ride to his house. She had to get this right, had to prove to him that he had everything to offer.

In the end she discovered that her worries had been for nothing. They came together as if they'd been made to connect in this way, with surprising abandon and loss of inhibitions. Making love with him was magical, surpassing every fantasy she'd ever had. Even the potentially awkward moment when he'd removed his pants and revealed his prosthesis had passed in a comfortable blur, overshadowed by the sensations he was able to stir in her with a simple caress here, a long, slow stroke there.

"Oh, sweet heaven," she said breathlessly, falling back against a stack of pillows. "That was…" Words failed her.

"Amazing?" Ethan supplied from his position on his back beside her. He lifted himself onto his elbow and studied her. "Or am I wrong?"

"Oh, no," she said. "You are definitely not wrong. *Amazing* sums it up. So does *incredible*. Maybe *mind-blowing*."

"Don't go overboard," he said, though he was smiling.

"Not going overboard," she assured him. "I promise."

There was a flicker of relief in his eyes. "I thought it was pretty darn good, too."

"Pretty darn good?" she said indignantly. "I'll accept magnificent, nothing less."

He laughed. "Magnificent, then. I guess we can scratch one worry off that very long list of mine."

"Oh?"

"Sex is not going to be a problem for us."

"Oh, no," she said fervently, then regarded him curiously. "What else is on that list of yours? I thought the fact that I'm here in your bed meant you'd crumpled it up and tossed it away."

He hesitated.

"Come on, Ethan. Let's get it all out there."

"Even if it ruins the moment?"

"Nothing is going to ruin this moment," she assured him. "Unless you're planning to get out of this bed, put on your clothes and take me home."

"Not on my agenda," he assured her. "At least not before morning." He paused, his expression thoughtful. "Or maybe afternoon."

"Now you're talking!" she enthused. "So, what else is on that list?"

"Distance," he said. "I know New York isn't the other side of the country, but it's too far to suit me."

She smiled. "Then isn't it a good thing that I have a plan that will relieve your mind?"

He frowned. "It doesn't involve me coming to New York, does it? The city makes me claustrophobic. Too many people crowded into one place."

"Who knew you were such a small-town guy?" she said, shaking her head as if in despair. "One day you'll come to New York, and I'll change your mind. The key is choosing the right neighborhood, finding the small-town atmosphere within the big, impersonal city."

"Not buying it," he said. "It can't be done."

"Okay, skeptic, that's just one more challenge for me to deal with," she said. "But you can cross the worry off your list. New York is not a requirement for the future."

"Oh?"

"Nope. You're safe." She hesitated, letting the moment build before her big announcement, or perhaps stalling for time in case it didn't go over as well as she was hoping it would.

"Samantha," he prodded. "Why isn't New York an issue?"

"Because I'm coming back here. I've already started making the arrangements." In fact, she'd called her landlord earlier this morning and told him to start looking for someone to sublet. Since apartments in her neighborhood were in high demand, it shouldn't take long.

Ethan looked startled, then worried. "Not because of me, I hope."

"No, you're just a plus, at least if you want to be," she told him candidly. "I want to open an acting school, teach a few classes, maybe eventually open a playhouse."

She allowed her announcement to sink in, watched as he considered it.

"And that's why you were so eager to meet Cass?" he guessed eventually. "You think she's a potential student."

"Maybe. We'll have to see if she's interested. I won't waste her time or her money, though. I can't do that to her, Ethan."

He frowned. "So if these tryouts or whatever the two of you have planned for this next week don't go well, you're going to break her heart?"

"Not if I can help it," she said, then added impatiently, "Give me a little credit. Cass matters to you, so she matters to me. And even if that weren't the case, I know how tender young feelings are. My goal is to encourage these kids as much as possible, even if I refuse to give them false hope."

He sighed. "You're right. I'm sorry. Besides, Cass isn't the issue right now. This is about you. Is this school something you really want? It's the first time you've mentioned it."

Samantha nodded. "Actually things started coming together for me the day I went to the high school for that rehearsal. I found myself wanting to jump in to help Mrs. Gentry, to find some way to cure Sue Ellen's stage fright, to get young people excited about performing onstage the way I used to be."

He smiled at her enthusiasm. "It's a good goal."

"I think so, and potentially a really rewarding one, but it's not all about that. I want to be around family again. New York has been an amazing experience for me. I don't regret a single second of it, but I'm ready to come home. And I made this decision before what just happened, so don't get all paranoid and weird on me, okay?"

"I do not get paranoid and weird," he protested.

"Oh, please."

"Well, maybe a little. This is a scary change for me, letting somebody into my life. It was difficult enough when I thought you were leaving. Now that I know you might stay, it's even more terrifying."

"How so?" she asked.

"No easy out."

His candor was surprising, but welcome in a way. "I'm only going to be in your life as much as you want me to be," she assured him. "I'll just be in the vicinity in case you decide you can no longer resist me."

"I thought we'd just settled the fact that I have no resistance left where you're concerned."

She beamed at him. "So we did. Want to see if that's still the case?"

"Why not?" he said eagerly. "As long as you're right here in my bed, anyway."

"Just what I was thinking."

"We really didn't think this through," Samantha said as Ethan drove her back to Cora Jane's at midday on Sunday. She glanced down at her maid of honor dress and the strappy, high-heeled sandals she was holding in her lap. The dress was a little the worse for wear, and hardly suitable daytime attire anywhere other than a wedding. The shoes, pretty as they were, weren't made for comfort.

"Afraid everyone's going to wonder what you've been up to?" Ethan inquired, his eyes sparkling with amusement.

"Oh, they're going to know exactly what we've been up to," she lamented. "They're likely to give us a rousing cheer."

"Think Cora Jane has a shotgun lying around?" he asked, suddenly sounding a tiny bit more nervous.

"If you're lucky, it's still locked in the closet," she told him.

"And your father? What's his reaction going to be?"

She frowned at the question. "You know, I have no idea. He was never one of those dads who waited up for us to get home from dates. I don't think he's especially protective. Then, again, he's done a lot the past few days that's taken me by surprise."

"So he's the wild card," Ethan said, nodding. "I'll do a preemptive strike."

Samantha laughed despite the awkward situation. "Exactly how do you intend to pull that off?"

"I'll tell him my intentions are honorable," he said.

She shook her head at once. "Oh, no. Bad idea. Honorable intentions tend to lead straight to the altar, at least in their view. We do not want to set them up for a huge disappointment just to save your hide today."

"It's something to consider," he argued.

Samantha stared at him incredulously. "What is? Marriage? This from a man who didn't even want to have sex with me this time yesterday?"

To her annoyance, Ethan laughed. "Oh, I wanted to have sex with you," he said. "I just didn't want any messy, emotional complications."

"What do you think marriage is?" she asked. "A few hours ago, weren't you still thinking of that as the messiest emotional complication of all?"

"Can't deny it," he said. "I've given it some more thought. Maybe we should just go for broke."

"Boy, I must be much better in bed than I thought," she muttered under her breath.

"You're amazing in bed," he confirmed. "But it's not about that."

"Then it's about a transformation worthy of some sci-fi film," she said. "Nobody changes their entire belief system that quickly."

"I don't know that it was that quick," he argued, sounding perfectly sincere. "I think it's been coming on since the instant I realized that I was attracted to you. I fought it tooth and nail, but here we are. Maybe it's time to stop fighting."

"It's the *maybe* I find worrisome," she said. "I know you're the kind of man who wants to do the right thing, but I'm not some starry-eyed teenager whose virtue you've stolen. We were equals in that bed last night. There are no expectations today, not from me, and definitely not from my family."

"Well, since there are a half dozen people peering out of various windows in the house, maybe we should table this conversation till later," he suggested, nodding toward Cora Jane's.

Sure enough, Gabi was positioned in an upstairs window overlooking the driveway, Wade right behind her, a smirk on his face. Cora Jane and Jerry were the fascinated observers from the kitchen. And standing together at the French doors in the living room, to Samantha's shock, her father and Sophia Grayson, of all people, seemed to be regarding them with amusement.

She kept her focus on that unlikely duo. "I think I've just spotted the answer to our prayers," she said. "My father and Sophia. If we walk inside and I go on the offensive about what they're up to, we can forestall the inquisition about us."

She was about to step out of the car when Ethan stilled her with a touch. She turned back to him. "What?"

"Do you really want to throw the spotlight on them? Your dad's been alone since your mom died. This thing with Sophia—if there even is a thing—could be the best thing that's happened to him. Why stir up trouble just to take the heat off us?"

She knew he was right, but his thoughtfulness was certainly inconvenient for the two of them. "Do you have a better idea? Other than avowing your undying love, that is?"

He smiled. "Let's just go in there, face the music and

see what's for lunch. You know Cora Jane won't be able to resist the opportunity to feed us."

"I doubt she'll be placated by the opportunity to whip up sandwiches," Samantha said.

"Southern hospitality is ingrained in her," Ethan insisted.

"Okay, but it's your neck on the line."

"I'll take my chances," he said, coming around to help her from the car. He leaned in close and pressed a kiss to the hollow behind her ear. "And in case things go terribly wrong in there, I just want you to know, it's all been worth it. I'll take the memory of last night to my grave."

He said it with an exaggerated sincerity that made her laugh.

"What on earth am I supposed to do with you?" she murmured.

He grinned. "I'll try to come up with a list."

"Just concentrate on surviving long enough so we can get to it," she said direly, then winked. "Just in case, though, I thought it was worth it, too."

Ethan was not the least bit surprised to find that everyone had gathered in the kitchen by the time they made their way inside. Everyone was making a determined effort to look busy and thoroughly disinterested in the new arrivals.

Cora Jane glanced up from the pot of soup she was stirring, her expression innocent. "There you are," she said. "Hungry? You're just in time for lunch."

Ethan shot a triumphant look toward Samantha, who merely shook her head.

"Starving," he said. "What can I do to help?"

"Are you kidding?" Gabi said. "With Grandmother and Jerry in charge, you'd only be getting in the way." She turned her attention to her sister. "I think there's time if you want to get out of that dress." A feigned expression of shock registered on her face. "Are those grass stains I see on the back?"

Ethan saw embarrassed color flood Samantha's cheeks before it dawned on her that there were no grass stains. There couldn't possibly be, since they'd been safely inside Ethan's bedroom before they'd started tumbling around in each other's arms.

"Stop it!" she told Gabi. "You're just trying to stir up trouble!"

Gabi grinned. "I know, but the look on your face was priceless. Something definitely went on last night."

"Stop teasing your sister," Sam Castle said, his tone surprisingly firm even though his eyes were sparkling with amusement.

Gabi and Samantha both stared at him with shock.

"Dad? Where'd that come from?"

He laughed. "Just trying out a little used disciplinary technique I learned from your mother."

"Very forceful," Sophia said, regarding him with evident fascination. "You girls are lucky to have a father who's so involved in your lives."

Gabi started to choke. Samantha wavered between wanting to set her straight and allowing the charade to go on. In the end it was Sam himself who corrected her impression.

"I'm afraid the whole involvement thing is very new to me," he told her. "It was their mother who brought them up to be the amazing women they've become. She did it with very little help from me, I'm sorry to say."

Sophia looked momentarily taken aback by his candor, but then she smiled. "I'm not sure I've ever known a man who so readily admitted his mistakes." She turned to Cora Jane. "I imagine that comes from you."

"I believe in being straightforward and honest, yes," Cora Jane said. "Until right this minute, though, I wasn't sure my son had seen the value in that."

"Even an old dog can still learn a trick or two," he replied.

Ethan noted that Samantha appeared to be marveling at the scene. He leaned down. "Good time to make your escape, don't you think? Once you've changed out of that dress, maybe they'll forget all about you showing up here still wearing it."

"Oh, you sweet dreamer," she whispered back. "But I will change. If they turn on you, my bedroom's the second one on the right at the top of the stairs. I'll protect you."

"Oh no, you don't," he said. "You are not luring me up to your room."

"But…" she sputtered. "I wasn't trying to…"

"I think I'd better take my chances by staying right here. The second I head for those stairs, I'm afraid there will be a posse after me."

"Your choice," she said, then winked. "But it would be a lot more interesting upstairs."

Ethan shook his head. "You really do like to live on the wild side, don't you? How'd I miss that?"

"You were too busy trying to figure out how to evade my devious trap," she told him.

"Too late now," he said. "Now my focus has to be on keeping your addiction to danger from getting us into more trouble than we'll know how to handle. Now scoot. I'm going to stay right here and do some damage control."

She frowned at that. "How?"

"Never mind. I've got it."

"Do not go that whole honorable-thing route," she warned. "Remember what I told you."

"Duly noted," he agreed, but committing to nothing. He'd do whatever it took to keep her family from thinking any less of him, while assuring them that her heart was in good hands.

Nineteen

Cora Jane looked around her kitchen with satisfaction. Wade and Gabi were hovering over the baby. Ethan was gazing at Samantha with stars in his eyes. And her son—she bit back a smile—well, Sam looked a little dazed by the very determined woman at his side. Sophia Grayson obviously was a woman who went after what she wanted, and for whatever reason she'd apparently decided she wanted Sam. It was an unexpected twist, but not an unwelcome one.

"What's on your mind?" Jerry asked, pulling his chair a little closer. "You're looking awfully pleased with yourself."

"I'm feeling more optimistic than I have in years," she told him. "I saw my granddaughters achieving great things in their professional lives, but I couldn't help worrying that they were going to miss out on the best thing life has to offer."

"Falling in love," Jerry guessed.

She nodded. "Just look at them. Gabi's a devoted mother with a man who adores her and that baby of hers.

Samantha's found not only a new dream right here in Sand Castle Bay, but the right man to share it with her."

"And your son? Is he part of this contentment you're feeling?"

"I have to say, I never anticipated that," she admitted. "But look at him. His expression's more animated than I've seen in years. Sophia is openly disagreeing with him, something his wonderful wife never did, and he's clearly loving it. Maybe they're just caught up in all the romance that usually surrounds a wedding, but I can't help thinking she could be good for him. She's not the sort of woman who'll sit back and let him get away with hiding in his work. She'll draw him out, ensure that he has a life. It could be downright interesting to watch."

Jerry laughed. "What on earth will you do when you have your family happily settled?"

"Enjoy it," she said at once. "Especially if it turns out that so many of them are underfoot right here."

"Are you including your workaholic son and the globe-trotting Sophia in that image? I find that a stretch."

She smiled. "Stranger things have happened. Sam could retire tomorrow and live comfortably for the rest of his life. Sophia obviously has the means to do whatever she wants, as well. And she has committed to helping Emily start a safe house project in this part of North Carolina. It makes sense for them to settle here."

"And you?" Jerry asked, regarding her intently. "What are your plans, beyond basking in everyone else's contentment?"

"I'm living exactly the life I want to live," she told him, only to see a frown crease his brow. "What's wrong with that?"

"I was hoping you'd find time to think about putting some of that balance you espouse back into your own life."

Startled by the exasperation in his tone, Cora Jane stared into his eyes. "Are you losing patience with me, Jeremiah?"

"I've had years and years to practice being patient," he responded. "I can hold on a little longer, but I have to wonder why you're so set on wasting any more of the precious little time we might have left on this earth."

Cora Jane thought of Caleb, the man she'd fallen in love with as a young girl, the man with whom she'd raised a family, the man she'd lost so many years ago. Why was she clinging to the past with such a determined grip when the man beside her now was everything she could hope for? Jerry had loved her in silence for years, respecting her marriage. He loved her still now, when there were no more obstacles, other than her own stubbornness and nostalgia.

"Do you want to move in here?" she asked, her heart in her throat at the daring suggestion.

He smiled. "Only on one condition," he replied. "That we're husband and wife. I won't settle for less, Cora Jane, but I can wait some more, if you're not there yet. I just think with all this love around us, it's time for us to claim some for ourselves."

She hesitated, terrified to take the leap and shatter the way things were for something far less certain. At her age shaking up the status quo seemed like a particularly risky business.

Then she once more gazed around her kitchen at the people she loved, people whose lives were changing in front of her eyes. Surely she was capable of taking the same risks with her heart that she was encouraging them to take with theirs. Wasn't she the one who'd tried to teach them all that love was something to be seized and cherished?

"Okay," she whispered, her gaze locked with Jerry's. His was steady, filled with certainty. She clung to the reassurance she saw there.

He blinked then. "Okay?" His voice climbed, catching the attention of everyone in the kitchen. "Did you just say okay? You agreed to marry me?"

Cora Jane nodded, aware of the heat climbing into her cheeks as startled gazes turned to the two of them. "I did."

"Well, I'll be," her son said, delight breaking across his face, when she'd been anticipating disapproval. He jumped up and came over to pump Jerry's hand. "Congratulations!"

Gabi and Samantha were next, showering Jerry with kisses and her with hugs.

"It's about darn time," Gabi said. "Now I'll have something to tell Emily when she calls. What about a date? Have you thought of a wedding date?"

Cora Jane held up a hand. "Not until after you and Wade are married," she said firmly.

Gabi looked so taken aback that Samantha laughed.

"Way to go, Grandmother!" Samantha said approvingly. "That's just the pressure she needs to get the show on the road."

"Amen to that," Wade concurred.

Cora Jane held Samantha's gaze with another unrelenting look. "You, too, young lady." She shifted her eyes to Ethan. "Am I clear?"

"Grandmother!" Samantha protested.

"That's my plan, and I'm sticking to it," Cora Jane told them all.

Jerry sighed heavily. "I guess that puts my fate in your hands." He looked at Wade. "You, I'm not so worried about." He turned to Ethan. "Try to remember I'm not getting any younger, okay?"

Ethan laughed.

"I'm not kidding," Jerry said sternly.

Cora Jane leaned in and kissed him. "And that is exactly why I love you. We're always on the same page."

It should keep whatever time they had left lively.

On Monday morning Ethan waited for panic to set in, now that the wedding was behind him and the reality of Samantha's staying was starting to sink in. Instead he felt more optimistic than he had in a long time. Even Jerry's added pressure wasn't as weighty as it would have been even a week ago.

"You look cheery," Greg said, eying him suspiciously. "Something happen this weekend to put you in a particularly good mood? Given how you feel about love and marriage, I thought you'd be impossible to live with today. Isn't that what usually happens with cynics, they go overboard to prove they didn't buy into all that romantic nonsense that weddings entail?"

"If you were hoping for me to be especially grouchy, keep pushing. I'll happily accommodate you," Ethan told him.

Greg grinned. "That's more like it."

"Don't you have patients or something to do besides pestering me?"

"Nope. It's quiet in the reception area. I checked. No walk-ins and the first appointment isn't for a half hour." He hesitated. "Of course, Debra seems to have a lot to say, but I left Pam out there trying to talk her down."

"What's she carrying on about today? Please tell me I'm not at the center of it."

"Apparently she took my advice and went on a date. It didn't go all that well. I believe she's discussing the sorry state of the male population. I have to admit I ran before I got the whole tirade. Pam, however, seemed genuinely enthused about it. She and her husband must have had another fight over the weekend."

Ethan shook his head. "And you wonder why I have so little faith in love and marriage."

"You pick and choose your examples," Greg countered. "What about me and Lindsey? Or Boone and Emily? Wade and Gabi?" His expression turned sly. "You and Samantha?"

Ethan gave him a hard look. "Me and Samantha?"

Greg chuckled. "She is the reason for this bright and sunny mood of yours, isn't she?"

"Okay, maybe a little," he conceded. "Hanging out with the Castles yesterday made it hard to be a skeptic. Love was definitely in the air. Cora Jane finally agreed to marry Jerry. Even Sam Castle looked to be caught up in a little post-wedding romance with one of Emily's Hollywood friends."

"That must have been the elegant woman wearing a diamond that could have paid off all our med-school loans," Greg said. "She was working the crowd like a pro, and I say that with awe. It's no wonder she's been able to raise all that money out there. I've never before met anyone who could look a stranger in the eye and know his life story in less than two minutes. She's scary charming."

"You find that admirable?"

"In certain circumstances, absolutely. I like people who know how to get things done. I can see why that would appeal to Sam Castle. I don't really know him, but I know his reputation, and I've followed the research going on at his company. They've been ahead of the curve with a lot of things. Just think what they could do with an infusion of cash to add even more top-notch researchers."

"You think he's after her money?" Ethan asked, not liking that particular spin, even though it made an awful kind of sense.

"Absolutely not," Greg said, looking shocked by the suggestion. "I think he's interested in her powers of persuasion." He hesitated, his expression thoughtful before he added with a smirk, "Or maybe he's just after her body. She's pretty hot for a woman her age."

"I'm sure she'd be thrilled by the compliment," Ethan said dryly.

Greg merely shrugged. "Let's get back to you and Samantha."

"Let's not."

"You know, I suffered through the whole Lisa fiasco with you. I think it's only fair that I get to share in the good times, too."

"Stop trying to live vicariously through me," Ethan

chided. "You have a lovely wife at home. It's slow here. Take an hour and go home to Lindsey."

"She's room mother at school this week," Greg lamented. "She left the house with enough cupcakes to send the entire class on a sugar high for a week. And do you know the worst part of that?"

"She wouldn't let you have one," Ethan guessed.

"Exactly. How is that fair?"

Ethan hid a chuckle at his friend's indignation. "Maybe she was being protective. She probably knows you're no more in need of all that sugar than the kids."

"But they're getting the cupcakes," he protested. "They looked good, too. Chocolate with swirls of icing on top and sprinkles."

Ethan laughed aloud now. "How old are you? Shouldn't you be beyond the pouting stage? If you're that starved for cupcakes, go to the store and buy a dozen."

"It's the principle," Greg argued. "I paid for these. My wife baked them."

Apparently the words pouring out of his mouth finally registered with Greg, because his expression turned chagrined. "I'm losing it, aren't I?"

Ethan nodded. "I'd say so."

"And that is why you should distract me with tales of your weekend adventures with Samantha," Greg concluded.

"Nice try," Ethan commended him, "but no. Go rearrange the supply cabinet. Not only will that distract you, it will be productive."

Greg was shaking his head before the words were out of Ethan's mouth. "No way, man. Last time I did that, Pam almost took a strip out of my hide. She has it exactly the way she wants it."

Just then Pam stuck her head in. "Either of you care to actually do some work this morning? Mitzi Rogers is out here bleeding all over the reception area from a tiny cut on her forehead and her mom is hysterical."

"All yours," Ethan told Greg.

"But you usually see Mitzi," Pam protested.

"And today Greg will."

"He's a little worried that Mitzi's mom has designs on him," Greg explained. "And his heart belongs to another."

Pam's eyes lit up. "Is that so?"

"Would you two care to focus on the patient and leave my love life alone?" Ethan pleaded. "I have things to do."

"What things?" Pam asked suspiciously.

"I'm coming up with a list," Ethan told her. "And they will all require me to be far, far away from here."

Samantha made good on her promise to show up for rehearsal at the high school on Monday. As soon as Regina Gentry spotted her, she clapped for attention. When she had it, she once again introduced Samantha to the students.

"I've asked her to watch rehearsal today and give you all some pointers," the teacher said. "Before we get started, Samantha, perhaps you could take Sue Ellen aside and give her a few tips on overcoming stage fright."

Samantha thought it was going to take more than a

quick chat to rid Sue Ellen of her fears, but she nodded and took the girl to the back of the auditorium.

"I wish she wouldn't call attention to my stage fright," Sue Ellen said, her expression distraught. "It just makes me more self-conscious."

"You know what really makes it worse?" Samantha asked gently. "Not knowing your lines. Do you think it's possible that's part of your problem?"

Sue Ellen blinked at that. "That's like one of those chicken-egg questions," she said. "Do I panic because I don't know my lines, or does the stage fright make me forget my lines?"

"Could you run them with me right now?" Samantha asked. "Just you and me, right here?"

"Sure," Sue Ellen said with confidence. "I nailed 'em at home last night."

Samantha wondered about that. Had she really nailed them, or had a helpful family member conveniently fed them to her? Only one way she knew of to find out. She glanced at the script Mrs. Gentry had handed her and told Sue Ellen which scene they were going to do, then read the opening line.

Sue Ellen responded, not just with accuracy, but with the right emotional intensity.

As the scene went on, she faltered only once or twice, which wasn't bad considering that they'd only been in rehearsals a couple of weeks.

"I'm impressed," Samantha admitted at the end of the scene.

Sue Ellen beamed. "I told you, it's because I get too nervous in front of all those people."

"If you're going to do theater, you have to do it in front of an audience," Samantha reminded her.

"Which is why I want to do anything else but theater," Sue Ellen said with feeling. "Around here, though, this is all there is." She hesitated. "There's something else throwing me off, too."

"What's that?"

"I know everybody thinks Cass deserved this part. It doesn't help that she's my understudy. I can see her waiting in the wings for me to blow it. Then when I do, she gloats."

Samantha couldn't imagine Cass gloating, at least not publicly, but her presence certainly could throw an inexperienced, uncertain actress off stride. "Would you rather someone else be in the wings to feed you your lines if you need prompting?"

"That would be awesome," Sue Ellen admitted. "But I don't want Cass to get mad at me, at least not any madder than she already is. And it's okay that she's my understudy. That shouldn't change."

Samantha nodded. "I'll talk to Mrs. Gentry and Cass and see what can be worked out. Now go on up there and deliver those lines as convincingly as you did for me just now."

"Thanks, Ms. Castle!" she said before running back to the stage.

Samantha was slower to return to the front of the auditorium. She told Mrs. Gentry about Sue Ellen's feelings and suggested that somebody other than Cass help out. "It may be all in Sue Ellen's head, but Cass seems to intimidate her. That could be part of her problem."

Mrs. Gentry nodded, quickly assigned another student to do the job, then called for the scene to be read. Cass joined them in the auditorium, a frown on her face. Samantha gave her hand a squeeze. "I'll explain later," she promised.

To everyone's apparent shock, Sue Ellen performed the scene without a single mistake or hesitation. Mrs. Gentry applauded, then walked to the stage to give the actors her notes.

"Holy smokes!" Cass said when she was alone with Samantha. "She was actually good."

Samantha grinned. "You were scaring her."

Cass's eyes lit up. "No kidding!"

"I wouldn't look so pleased about that," Samantha scolded.

Mrs. Gentry returned. "I'm impressed, Samantha."

"No big deal."

"Well, it is to me," Mrs. Gentry told her, then clapped for attention. "Everyone, I have an announcement. Ms. Castle has told me that she's going to be offering some acting classes here in Sand Castle Bay in the near future. You've seen what a difference she was able to make with Sue Ellen today. If any of you are interested in learning more about those classes, I'll have a sign-up sheet here for you at the end of rehearsal. Then she'll be in touch with you with the details." She glanced at Samantha. "Will that work for you?"

"That's amazing," Samantha said, taken aback by the unexpected show of support. "Thank you."

Mrs. Gentry lowered her voice. "Just remember what I told you. You need to be above reproach."

Samantha nodded.

Cass regarded her eagerly. "Can I sign up now?"

"You can sign up as soon as there's something specific to sign up for," Samantha told her. "In the meantime, if you're free tomorrow afternoon, why don't you come by Castle's after school and read a couple of scenes with me?"

"Awesome! I know you're impressed with the way Sue Ellen got her act together just now, but wait till you hear me," Cass said. "I'm going to knock your socks off."

Samantha grinned at her confidence, wishing Ethan were around to hear it. He'd done his job well.

"I'm counting on that," she told the girl. Because Cass was going to have to be head and shoulders above the other actresses competing for parts if she was going to overcome the undeniable obstacles ahead.

And for more reasons than she cared to examine, Samantha wanted her to have the talent to surprise the most jaded of Broadway directors.

Twenty

When Samantha walked in the door at home after her eventful afternoon at the high school, Cora Jane nodded in the direction of the backyard, her eyes twinkling.

Samantha frowned. "What?"

"You have company."

Samantha glanced toward the water. Ethan was sitting on the end of the pier, his pants legs rolled up, his good foot dangling in the water. He'd seemingly locked the prosthesis in a position that would keep it dry, rather than removing it. In his work clothes, he looked very much like a man who'd played hooky.

"Is he fishing?"

"Not the way you mean. He came by trolling for information on your whereabouts. Since I had no idea where you were, I suggested he wait. I figured you'd call or turn up sooner or later. Let me know if he's staying for dinner."

Samantha nodded, kicked off her own shoes and walked barefoot through the grass to join him. He glanced up as she started along the wooden pier, then held out his hand to help her drop down beside him.

"I wasn't expecting you," she said.

"You should have been. You should have known you'd be on my mind all day."

"Really?" she said, pleased. "All day?"

"Every livelong minute," he confirmed, not sounding entirely happy about it. "And when I managed to distract myself for a minute, Greg was there to pester me for details about my weekend. He seemed convinced you were responsible for my mood."

She slanted a look at him. "Were you cranky?"

He smiled. "Quite the opposite, in fact."

"That's good, then."

"No, it is very, very bad. It makes people who know me suspicious. When they get suspicious, they ask questions I don't know how to answer."

Samantha knew the whole concept of a relationship was new to him or, if not exactly new, a painful reminder of all that could go wrong. It was clear he was struggling with it. She opted to let him off the hook.

"You know," she began, "nothing's really changed."

He stared at her incredulously. "You can't be serious. Everything's changed." He frowned. "At least for me. Are you saying nothing that happened this weekend matters to you?"

"Of course it matters. I'm definitely hoping it wasn't a one-night stand, but if it was, then so be it. It was remarkable just the same."

His frown deepened. "It was not a damn one-night stand!" he told her emphatically.

She smiled at his fierce declaration. "Good to know. Any other definition come to mind?"

His gaze narrowed. "You want me to define what happened between us?"

"It might help to clarify things for both of us," she said. "You seem a little lost."

"I'm not lost. I'm annoyed."

"At me?"

"No, at all the people who expect us to pin labels on what happened."

"But that includes me," she reminded him.

"Yeah, but you're only trying to help. They're just nosy."

She laughed at the likely accuracy of that. "Ethan, you don't owe them an explanation. You do owe yourself one, and I wouldn't mind knowing what you've come up with. No rush, though. There's plenty on my plate without worrying about exactly where we stand."

Just to change the topic and give him some breathing room, she filled him in on what had happened at the high school with Sue Ellen, Cass and Mrs. Gentry.

"I couldn't believe Mrs. Gentry gave me her blessing and started a sign-up sheet. Last week she sounded pretty skeptical. She seemed to be afraid all sorts of skeletons were going to come tumbling out of the closet and I'd ruin her reputation if we were too closely aligned."

Ethan looked intrigued. "Skeletons? Do you have some?"

Was that a hopeful note in his voice? she wondered. Surely not. Or was he hoping for something that would give him grounds to walk away?

She returned his curious gaze with a steady look of her own, then shrugged. "Not that I know of, but heaven knows what might get people's tongues wagging around here. I suppose with a bad spin most of us could stir up controversy with things we've done in the past."

"So you're moving forward with teaching classes?" he asked.

"I thought I'd start with two or three," she said. "See

what the demand is. I need to sit down and figure out the focus of each class. I suppose I could do beginners and advanced, or maybe something devoted to comedy and something else to drama."

"No musicals?"

She smiled. "Not my forte. If you'd let me get away with singing when I showed up at Boone's bachelor party in that cake, you'd know that. My problem is, I love to sing. I just can't carry a tune. I had big hopes for that night. A captive audience. Drunk, too, so more likely to be appreciative."

Ethan laughed. "Think of it this way, I saved you from embarrassing yourself."

"Hardly," she said, laughing with him. "It was way too late for that." She sobered and glanced over at him. The tension in his shoulders seemed to have eased. "You staying for dinner? Cora Jane says you're invited."

"Only if we can go to my place for dessert," he said.

"Sounds like a deal to me," she said, leaning in to his side. "Panic attack over with?"

"I was not having a panic attack," he protested. "In case you haven't heard, until you came along, my life was all orderly and predictable. Now not so much. Just trying to get those doggone ducks back in their rows."

There was no mistaking the frustration in his voice. She managed, though, to hide a smile. "Are they lined up now?" she asked.

He shrugged. "Not really," he said, a smile now playing on his lips. "But I'm suddenly starting not to care."

It was just past noon on Wednesday when Samantha got a call from Gabi.

"Anything on your agenda for today at four?" her sister asked.

"No. I've been helping out at Castle's this morning, but I'll be free by then. What's up?"

"Could you go home, put on something pretty and meet Wade and me at the courthouse?"

Understanding dawned immediately, followed quickly by dismay. "You're getting married? Today? Does Grandmother know? Oh, my gosh, she's going to have a fit, Gabi. She wants you to have a dream wedding just the way Emily did."

"No, she wants me to marry Wade. I don't think the fancy details matters to her, any more than they do to us."

"But you can't get married when Emily and Boone aren't even in town," Samantha protested. "They'll never forgive you."

"I already have their blessing. They're going to throw a reception for us when they come back. Nothing pacifies our sister like offering her the chance to throw a big party. And it'll guarantee she stays on the coast for a couple of extra weeks, which will make Grandmother ecstatic. It's one of those win-wins everybody loves."

"But it's so fast," Samantha found herself protesting. "What about Dad? Are you at least inviting him?"

"He hasn't even left town yet. He's holed up in some hotel on the ocean with Sophia. I think he'll be thrilled with any ceremony that doesn't cost an arm and a leg. He's my next call. First I had to be sure I had my maid of honor."

"You've got her," Samantha assured her.

"You can bring Ethan," Gabi told her. "I'm telling Dad he can invite Sophia, and of course, Jerry will be there with Grandmother. Louise, her husband and all Wade's nieces and nephews will be there, along with

Meg and Sally. Tommy Cahill is Wade's best man. I think that's as much for Meg's benefit as Wade's. They hit it off at that bachelorette party we threw for Emily. That's it for the guest list. Then we're having a barbecue in the backyard. Jerry's cooking. Louise is finding some kind of cake at the bakery and dressing it up with wedding bells or something appropriate."

"I don't believe this," Samantha murmured. "What can I do?"

"If you can get home by three, you can keep me from falling apart. Otherwise, just get to the courthouse on time."

"I'll be at the house," Samantha promised. "You want a bouquet? I can pick something up, just a single flower with some ribbons if that's all you want, but you should carry something. It's a shame most of the flowers at Grandmother's are past their prime."

"Fine, fine. Whatever," Gabi said, clearly uninterested. "I'll leave that to you. Now I have calls to make. You're in charge of getting Ethan there."

"Got it," Samantha said. "Sweetie, I am so happy for you and Wade. I hope today is everything you want it to be."

"As long as he and Daniella are there, it will be," Gabi said with conviction.

"I'm buying a bunch of disposable cameras, too," Samantha told her. "You need pictures, and nobody prints out the ones they take with their cell phones."

"Thanks. I don't intend to forget a second of this, but pictures would be nice."

As soon as she'd hung up from speaking to Gabi, Samantha called Ethan.

"Hold on to your hat," she told him. "We have an impromptu wedding today at four."

He laughed. "It's not ours, is it?"

"Nope, not even I am that spontaneous. It's Gabi and Wade. I guess they caught wedding fever or something. Can you meet us at the courthouse?"

"I'll make it happen," he promised.

"And don't worry," she told him. "I'm not getting any ideas."

"Then you may be the only one who isn't," he murmured, then hung up.

She didn't have time to ponder what on earth he meant by that, because Cora Jane came bustling across Castle's just then, a huge smile on her face. "You heard?"

"I heard," Samantha confirmed. "You're not upset that they're doing this in such a rush?"

"They're getting married. How they do it hardly matters."

Samantha gave her grandmother a fierce hug. "That's the spirit."

Cora Jane winked at her. "Two down, one to go."

"Do not get started on me," she warned her. "Or on Ethan."

"Oh, come on. The man's sitting on the edge. One quick shove and he'll tumble straight into your arms."

"I'm not so sure about that," Samantha said, though she desperately wanted to believe her grandmother was right. "Just make sure you're not the one doing the shoving."

Louise's children were running around the judge's chambers creating even more chaos in an already unruly situation. Ethan was tempted to snag them, but since no one else seemed to be fazed, including the judge, he let them be.

Sophia slipped up beside him. "I'm starting to fall in love with this family," she told him. "When I flew here from Los Angeles for Emily's wedding, I had no idea I'd be getting two for the price of one."

"Much less a new man in your life?" Ethan asked.

A blush tinted her cheeks a shade of pink that couldn't be manufactured. "Definitely a bonus," she said, glancing toward Sam with an unmistakable sparkle in her eyes. "So, where do you stand on the whole romance thing? Will you and Samantha be next? Obviously Cora Jane is counting on that."

"A worrisome situation," Ethan said.

She laughed. "I imagine so. Cora Jane seems like the kind of woman who gets what she wants."

"So do you," he commented.

"Absolutely true, which is why I understand what you're up against."

In an attempt to deflect the conversation away from himself, Ethan asked, "Mind if I ask something personal?"

"Have I not just been butting into your life?" she asked, clearly amused by his hesitation. "And you don't even need to ask. Yes, I find Sam fascinating. It's been a long time since I met a man with substance and values and a great sense of humor."

"Do you plan on sticking around?"

"For a while."

"Until the novelty wears off?" he inquired, worried that Sam might be in way over his head. That might not be his problem, but it would be a concern for Samantha and her sisters.

"I'm not looking at it that way," she chided. "When

you get to be my age, you learn to seize the good things that come your way and treasure them for as long as they last."

Ethan found himself in the uncomfortable position of defending happily-ever-after. "That sounds a little fatalistic. I thought good relationships were something you were supposed to nurture, that if you worked at it, they could last forever."

She lifted a brow. "Voice of experience?"

He shook his head. "To the contrary, I've never believed in love-everlasting, at least until recently. Much to my own surprise, I find myself coming around."

"It must be something about the Castles," Sophia said. "After several divorces, I'm starting to think Sam could make a believer out of me, too."

Again, her gaze sought out Sam Castle, who was leaning down to whisper something in Gabi's ear. He glanced up, caught her eye and winked. To Ethan's amusement, this polished, sophisticated woman suddenly looked as flustered as a schoolgirl.

"Go on over there," he encouraged her.

"I don't want to intrude," she protested.

"Judging by that gleam in his eye, he won't consider it an intrusion."

He watched her walk across the room, every bit the confident, powerful woman they all thought her to be. He liked knowing that there was a hint of vulnerability just below the surface. He could relate. That's how Samantha made him feel, too.

Samantha smiled as Judge Masters, an old family friend, performed the brief civil ceremony. Gabi and

Wade looked as if they were unaware of another single soul in the room. The only time they glanced away from each other was when Daniella whimpered in Samantha's arms.

"She's fine," Samantha reassured them, rocking the baby to quiet her.

The judge gave a nod of satisfaction. "In that case, Gabriella, do you take Wade to be your lawful wedded husband?"

"I do," Gabi said, a smile on her lips.

"And, Wade, do you—"

"Oh, yes," Wade said, jumping in.

The judge gave him a scolding look. "Hey, I don't have that many lines. You could at least let me finish the ones I do have."

"I knew where you were going," Wade countered. "I was anxious to get there."

Judge Masters chuckled. "In that case, let's wrap this up. I now pronounce you husband and wife."

Daniella chose that moment to wave her little fist in the air and let out a full-throated cry. Wade immediately turned and reached for her.

"Is that you approving of me and your mom getting married?" he asked the baby, who immediately gurgled happily.

Gabi shook her head. "I swear that girl has him wrapped around her little finger."

"Looks the other way around to me," Samantha said. "It's kind of wonderful to see how they've bonded. As far as Wade's concerned, biology be damned. That little sweetheart is his."

"It's pretty amazing," Gabi agreed. "We're so lucky, me and Dani. We've got the perfect guy in our lives."

Samantha hugged her sister. "I'm so happy for you."

"Me, too," Ethan said, joining them and slipping an arm around Samantha's waist. "And I have to say there's a lot to be said for this whole impromptu wedding thing. Much less stressful."

"Don't get any ideas," Gabi warned. "This is what Wade and I wanted. Samantha has her own ideas."

"Not the time," Samantha protested as Ethan turned a little pale. She patted his hand. "It's okay. This little run of Castle weddings has nothing to do with you and me."

"You have to admit, they're going to be hard acts to live up to," he said.

Samantha shook her head. "No, they're not. The whole extravaganza thing suited Emily. This simple ceremony was exactly right for Gabi."

He regarded her with apparent interest, no hint of panic evident. "And for you? What's your dream wedding?"

"Sunset on the beach," she told him. "Maybe in Hawaii or the Caribbean."

"Even here?" he asked. "I understand we have a fairly long stretch of ocean nearby. Couples come from all over to take advantage of the setting. Weddings are a big industry in this area."

"True, but we did a location wedding in Hawaii once on a soap opera I was on. I got to go for the filming. My heart's kind of set on a destination wedding."

He nodded. "I'll keep that in mind."

Gabi's eyes lit up. "Interesting. He said that without

the slightest hint of hysteria in his voice. Could it be he's resigned to his fate? Even eager?"

"Could we drop this, please?" Samantha said. No matter how calm Ethan seemed, she knew he was nowhere near ready for that kind of leap forward in their relationship. Neither was she.

"Even more interesting," Gabi noted. "You're the one who looks a little shaken, Samantha."

"I just think we're all getting way ahead of ourselves. You and Wade have been together for ages. Boone and Emily, well, they've been in love for years. Ethan and I have only been acquainted for a couple of weeks."

Ethan's eyebrow shot up. "Acquainted? That's how you see things?"

She elbowed him in the ribs. "I'm trying to get you off the hook. You need to cooperate."

Gabi was openly laughing at the squabble. "I must say you've given a new definition to getting acquainted in my book, too. I think I'll do a quick survey of the crowd here to see what they think."

"You do and you won't live to have a honeymoon," Samantha warned.

"You don't scare me," Gabi retorted. She grinned at Ethan. "She used to utter all these dire big-sister threats when Emily and I were annoying her. She never followed through on any of them."

"Times change," Samantha said. "I learned a few secrets about committing the perfect crime when I was hanging around all those soap operas."

"Okay, you two, stop fussing at each other," Cora Jane said as she joined them. "This is a happy occasion."

Gabi beamed at the reminder. "Yes, it is." She met Samantha's gaze. "I forgive you."

"For what?" Samantha asked indignantly.

"Threatening me on the happiest day of my life."

"Obviously I'm supposed to give you a pass for meddling, since it's your wedding day," Samantha grumbled.

"That would be nice," Gabi agreed. "Especially since I only have your best interests at heart."

"There," Cora Jane said with satisfaction. "That's the way it's supposed to be. Now let's go home and celebrate. Jerry's already left to get the barbecue going." She gave Gabi a stern look. "Your father has gotten you the bridal suite at his hotel on the beach. You and Wade will stay there tonight. Samantha and I will look after Daniella. No arguments, is that understood? And tomorrow Wade will move in, at least until you decide if you're going to live in his house or find a new place of your own."

Gabi enveloped her in a hug. "I'm glad one of us has this all figured out. I have to admit, I only got as far as picking today for the wedding."

"The most important piece of the puzzle," Cora Jane assured her. "And you can always count on family to have your back for anything else."

Samantha knew that was true. And lately she'd come to count on it more and more.

The party for Gabi and Wade had wound up early, partly because Wade had been openly eager to get his new bride off to himself and partly out of respect for the early hours demanded of Cora Jane and Jerry to have Castle's open just after dawn. Ethan took off, too.

"Do you think he looked awfully relieved to be getting away from here?" she asked her grandmother.

"Absolutely not," Cora Jane told her. "He just saw that you're going to have your hands full with Daniella since I need to get some sleep."

"Sophia and I will stick around in case Samantha needs a hand," Sam Castle volunteered. "At least until the baby's down for the night."

Samantha regarded him with surprise. "That's not necessary, Dad."

"We want to do it," Sophia said, beckoning for the baby, then cuddling her in her arms. "It's been a long time since I've had a chance to pamper a little one this size. Even the youngest of my grandchildren are in elementary school by now. The oldest is a senior in high school."

Sam looked startled. "You must have been a child bride."

"I was, and unfortunately my oldest daughter followed in my footsteps. When people lead with their hearts, some mistakes just can't be avoided, it seems."

Samantha had a feeling it was a topic Sophia and her father ought to be exploring in private, but she wasn't about to leave them stuck with her job as babysitter. Instead, she turned to her father. "Maybe we could talk about that property," she suggested.

To her surprise, Sophia's eyes lit up. "Your father says you're thinking of opening a playhouse. What a wonderful idea! You must be so excited."

"Right now I'm more terrified than excited. I keep wondering if I'm biting off more than I can chew."

"Don't you dare think like that," her father scolded. "If this is something you believe in, then you can make it happen. Sophia and I drove by the property earlier today. I think the location would work, but the house is in bad shape. Maybe we should get Tommy Cahill over there tomorrow to see if it can be salvaged. I can give him a call."

Samantha nodded. It was the logical next step, even if she felt as if things were starting to move way too quickly.

"It's too bad Emily's not here," Sophia said. "She's an absolute genius when it comes to doing renovations on a tight budget. I wish you could see the miracles she's performed with these safe houses."

"She'll be back next week," Samantha said. "She can take a look then. I'll definitely want her input."

"But this is your project," her father reminded her. "You need to be sold on the idea. Could be you'll want to tear it down and start from scratch."

"I don't think I'll have the budget for that," Samantha said.

"You will," her father contradicted. "It may make more financial sense in the long run. We'll work it out."

"Listen to him," Sophia encouraged. "He's very smart about these things."

Samantha hid a smile at the faith Sophia clearly had in a man who'd been unreliable in so many ways for his family. Either she was starry-eyed, or this new leaf Sam had turned over ran even deeper than Samantha had realized.

Sophia glanced down at the baby in her arms. "I think she's down for the count," she whispered.

"I'll take her up to bed," Samantha said, reaching for her. "Thanks for sticking around."

"We'll see you in the morning," her father said. "How's ten o'clock?"

"I'll meet you there," Samantha said. "If Gabi and Wade haven't turned up to take over with the baby, I'll call to postpone."

"They'll be here," Sam predicted. "I'm surprised Gabi hasn't called a dozen times already to check on her."

"She has," Samantha told him, laughing. "Grandmother fielded the first half dozen, Ethan took a couple and I spoke to her at least twice before I told her I wasn't answering the phone again."

Sophia laughed. "I remember that stage. We all survive it. I'll have to tell her that."

"Please do," Samantha said, turning for the stairs. "Good night," she called back softly, but when she glanced their way, she noted they were gazing at each other in a way that suggested no one else mattered.

What, she wondered, was in this ocean air? The most unexpected love stories seemed to be unfolding all around.

Twenty-One

As anticipated, Gabi and Wade arrived at Cora Jane's just as Samantha was getting the baby fed.

"Some honeymoon," Samantha commented when they walked into the kitchen.

"We'll take a proper honeymoon later," Gabi said, already reaching for the baby.

"When Daniella is in college, I imagine," Wade commented, though his own gaze was on the baby, too.

"You do realize if this protective phase doesn't wear off, your child is going to stage a teenage rebellion the likes of which this family's never seen," Samantha told them.

"This little angel?" Gabi said skeptically. "No way."

"Just remember how you felt when Mom hovered," Samantha said. "I fielded bitter complaints from you and Emily daily."

Gabi stared at her and shuddered. "True, but I realize now that she was just making up for Dad being absent," she said, the defense more automatic than heartfelt.

"It doesn't change the fact that the hovering made

you a little nuts," Samantha said. "I'm just saying that even babies probably need their space."

"Wait till you have one, then tell me that," Gabi countered.

Samantha laughed. "Okay, you've got me there. I'll probably be worse than you've even dreamed of being."

"What's on your agenda for today?" Gabi asked. "Do you have plans with Ethan?"

"No, but I am supposed to meet Dad and Sophia over at that property he owns to see if I could convert it into a theater. Dad was going to arrange for Tommy to meet us there."

Wade's eyes lit up at the mention of a renovation. Though he was making more money these days with his wood carvings that were shown in their new gallery, he still loved doing restorations and custom cabinetry. "What time?" he asked.

"Ten o'clock."

"I'll come, too," he offered. "Won't hurt to have another pair of expert eyes."

"Great idea," Gabi enthused. "I was going to take Dani to day care, then stop by the office for a couple of hours. We could all meet later for lunch at Castle's. I can't wait to hear what you think about that property. I'm so anxious to know that you're moving forward and staying right here, Samantha. It's going to be so great."

"It will be," Samantha agreed, finally allowing herself to get totally caught up in all the positives about making this move. "And meeting for lunch sounds like a plan. Wade, are you taking your own car, or do you want to ride over with me?"

"I'd better take my own car," he said. "We'll probably be heading in different directions at some point. I might even try to persuade my bride to play hooky from work after lunch."

"There you go!" Samantha said approvingly. "The honeymoon phase lives on, after all. I'm so relieved."

She caught the look between her sister and Wade and concluded she was intruding into that phase at this very moment. "I'm off to get dressed," she said, but no one appeared to be listening. It was getting to be a pattern around here.

Ethan was relieved to find that he had a jam-packed schedule at the clinic Thursday morning. The afternoon would be taken up with a Project Pride field trip to Corolla to see the wild horses on the beach. With luck, there wouldn't be a spare second in there for his mind to wander to thoughts of Samantha and that dream wedding she'd described.

As she'd talked, he'd found himself wanting to give her that. He wanted to be the man at her side when the sun slid over the horizon in a brilliant orange glow. He wanted to be the one starting a future with her.

And that had scared him to death. How on earth had he come so far so fast? Was this some kind of crazy Castle spell? Had he forgotten he didn't believe in love? Had his memories of the pain it could cause faded, after all? He needed to figure all of that out, and he needed time and space to do it.

Not too much time, though. In his heart, he knew he couldn't leave Samantha in suspense for long. Her own doubts would creep in, and what they'd found could be tainted, maybe even destroyed, if she thought he'd never make the necessary leap into the future she so clearly envisioned.

So, today, he'd have his space. Maybe tomorrow, too. And then he'd know, though how he expected to find certainty amid his own doubts was beyond him.

"You okay?" Pam asked, regarding him worriedly from the doorway to his office.

"Great," he said, standing up. "Who's next?"

Pam hesitated, then said, "Before you see your next patient, you probably need to see this. It may come up." She handed him the local weekly. "Front page."

He stared at the image of Samantha in his arms at Boone's bachelor party, that awful cake behind her, then read the caption describing her as a stripper. He muttered a colorful expletive.

"I've already had a couple of people call to ask about that," Pam said. "I thought you should know there could be repercussions. You know how some people are, always eager to spread a little dirt."

Ethan didn't want to believe his nurse could possibly be right, but he knew better. And if not for him, this kind of publicity could be very bad for Samantha's plans to establish a new career here in Sand Castle Bay. He wondered how long it would take her to decide that this wasn't the place for her after all.

"I can't deal with this now," he muttered.

"It'll blow over," Pam said in an attempt to reassure him. She regarded him worriedly. "Maybe I shouldn't have shown it to you."

"No. I needed to see it," he told her, then added briskly, "Now let's get started. We have a busy morning."

"You don't want to give Samantha a call?"

"Later," he said tersely.

Pam looked as if she wanted to argue, but instead she sighed, handed him a file, then rattled off the information on the patient's vitals that she'd gathered already. Ethan nodded, then plastered a smile on his face as he opened the examining room door.

From that moment on, his morning went exactly according to plan, with not a spare moment to be found. Only one problem. Samantha managed to creep into his head just the same, along with this new complication that seemed likely to doom their relationship. He'd always been a local golden boy, thanks first to his high school sports success and later to his war hero status. But he'd seen the flip side. He knew the damage negative press could do in a small town. Samantha, despite her relationship to Cora Jane, wasn't a local. Folks wouldn't cut her the same kind of slack they might cut him. And if that killed her plans for a new professional future, where would that leave the two of them?

Maybe it was time to admit defeat after all, cling to his last shred of pride and set her free to go back to New York where she belonged, where a story like this would barely register on anyone's radar.

That was definitely the smart thing to do, the safe thing, he concluded.

But his heart didn't seem all that happy about the decision.

Samantha showed up at the emergency clinic at lunchtime with a picnic basket filled with all the things her grandmother assured her were Ethan's favorites. She'd begged off from the lunch at Castle's, eager to share her news about her father's property with Ethan. Her head was reeling, filled with exciting possibilities for the renovations.

When she walked in the door, she was greeted with a smirk by the receptionist at the front desk.

"You must be Samantha," the twentysomething woman said. A name tag indicated she was Debra. "You don't look like a stripper."

Samantha paled. "I'm not a stripper. Where did you get that idea?"

"That's what the paper said."

Samantha felt a cold chill spread through her body. There was only one reason anyone would label her a stripper, the incident at Boone's bachelor party. What on earth had made her think no one would ever learn the humiliating details of that night? While she doubted anyone had brought a camera to record the night's events, every single person there had probably had his cell phone out seconds after Ethan had pried open that catastrophe of a cake, and she'd popped out in her revealing bikini.

"The paper?" she echoed with dread.

"Sure thing," Debra said happily, clearly delighted to be the bearer of bad news. "Boone's a big deal around here, and this wedding of his is getting wall-to-wall local coverage. If you ask me, though, that picture doesn't do you justice. You're much prettier. I think they caught you at a bad angle. And the lighting was all wrong." She beamed. "I'd have done a much better job with that."

Samantha's knees felt as if they might give way. Though it was pretty clear what had happened, she kept trying to make sense of it. "There's a picture in the paper?" she asked to be sure.

"Uh-huh. Haven't you seen it?" Debra grabbed her copy and shoved it in Samantha's direction.

It struck Samantha that Debra seemed a little too pleased to show Samantha the humiliating photo. In fact, her attitude bore all the traits of a jealous woman eager to get revenge on the competition. That, however, was something Samantha would have to explore another time, not in the middle of a very real crisis.

Samantha stared at her image. On the front page, no less. At least it was a local weekly. The bachelor party must have squeaked in right under their deadline. It was probably much more titillating than the wedding itself would have been.

"Oh, sweet heaven," she murmured as she saw herself being scooped out of that ridiculous cake by Ethan, who looked as if he had all sorts of preferably dire fates in store for her. This was not a hero rushing to the rescue. It was a man operating on his last frayed nerve. He had been awfully testy, now that she thought about it.

Panic set in. Ethan had wondered about skeletons in her closet. Apparently he was going to be caught smack in the middle of this particular one. That night might have been totally innocent, but the newspaper's spin sure made it sound otherwise.

"Where's Ethan? I need to see him."

"He's off this afternoon. He's always off on Thursday afternoon. It's his day with the kids."

Samantha stared at her blankly before it dawned on her that Debra was referring to the kids he worked with.

She just hadn't realized which day he'd designated for the outings.

"Of course. I should have remembered," she mumbled.

It was clear, though, that Debra wasn't buying her quick attempt at recovery. The girl gave her a pitying look that said she couldn't possibly mean much to him if she didn't know about his schedule.

"Surely he's mentioned Project Pride," Debra said, though the gloating in her voice suggested a level of superiority that she knew things that Samantha did not. "Today they've gone to see the wild horses up at Corolla."

"I see," Samantha said, though she didn't see anything. She gestured toward the picnic basket. "Just give him that when he comes in and tell him I stopped by. Tell him we need to talk."

The receptionist suddenly looked vaguely guilty for having given her such a hard time. "Won't the food spoil? Maybe you should drop it off at his place later. Or you can meet the van when they come back from Corolla. That's probably better. It should be here about five."

"Sure," Samantha said, eager to get away. "I'll come back."

Or not. Maybe today wasn't the best time to see Ethan, after all, not with everyone in town probably ragging on him about that newspaper photo. She'd be lucky if he ever spoke to her again.

Another thought suddenly struck her. This was exactly the sort of thing that Regina Gentry had worried about when she'd warned Samantha that her behavior needed to be above reproach. That blasted picture and its implications could be just enough to sabotage all the plans she'd been starting to make for her future.

And if they were ruined because she'd done a stupid favor for her sister, Emily was going to be overcome with guilt when she found out. Just one more wrinkle in an already strained relationship that had finally started to heal.

Though she told herself at least a dozen times to stay away, at five o'clock Samantha was sitting in her car in the parking lot outside the emergency clinic when a large van pulled in. A half dozen parents milled around nearby, obviously awaiting its arrival, but none of them paid the least bit of attention to her.

As soon as the bright red van adorned with a Project Pride logo pulled to a stop, double doors on the side opened and a ramp was lowered to accommodate two wheelchairs and their passengers, who looked to be no more than ten or twelve. Next, three boys scampered down, one wearing a heavy leg brace, one on crutches and one walking with an awkward, stiff gait. What really distinguished them, though, and made Samantha's breath catch in her throat, were the beaming smiles on their faces and their exuberant shouts as they caught sight of their parents. Words tumbled out in a rush as they tried to top each other with stories of the day's adventure.

Ethan stepped out of the van next, a cherubic girl with a halo of curls in his arms. Samantha bit back a gasp when she saw that the younger girl was missing the lower part of her right leg.

Samantha got it all then. Sure, she'd heard about the kids he was determined to inspire, but she hadn't really understood the depth of his passion. *This* was everything that mattered to him. It was what he'd meant by saying he cared about far more than the healing powers of medicine. This was the way in which he wanted to make his life matter, showing these kids that nothing could stop them from achieving their dreams.

It made her own worries and fears over a few wrinkles seem petty and inconsequential. And it made the stunt she'd pulled at Boone's bachelor party seem silly and immature, even though she'd done it simply to please her sister and maybe just a little to annoy Ethan.

She was so shaken by her discovery that she sat right where she was, slumped down behind the wheel of her car, praying he wouldn't notice her as he chatted with the parents and sent the kids on their way.

Still, she wasn't surprised when he walked over to her car after the last family had driven off. He opened the passenger door without asking and slid in. The jovial attitude he'd had only moments before had vanished. Instead, he looked worn out. That tore at her as much as what she'd just discovered about him.

"It must be hard," she said quietly.

He glanced her way. "What?"

"Giving them what they need." She tried to find the right words to prove she got it. "Showing them what their lives can be like, especially when some of them aren't ready to hear it."

There was a flicker of surprise in his eyes. "You saw all that in a couple of minutes?"

"The only way to be a decent actress is to know how to observe people, to try to get inside their heads."

"And you think you're inside mine?"

She smiled at that. "Not just yet, but I'm getting there."

He studied her for what seemed like an eternity. When he spoke, he shocked her. "Do you know how badly I want to kiss you? For a man who thought he was immune to love a few short days ago, I seem to be obsessed with you."

Would he say that if he knew about the photo? She doubted it. She swallowed hard at his unexpected admission, tried to focus on that. "I'm afraid I missed the signs of this obsession of yours."

He sighed. "Probably because I didn't want you to know. Heck, I didn't even want to admit it to myself. And now? It's pretty ironic really."

"What?" she asked, regarding him in confusion.

"I don't think we can pull this off, after all," he said.

She sighed heavily. "You did see the paper," she said, deflated. "For a minute there I thought you hadn't."

"Everyone I know saw the paper," he said. "Every parent here just now had a comment."

"It's not really any of their business," she suggested tentatively, hoping he would see it that way.

He gave her an incredulous look. "I know you're not that naive, Samantha. They entrust their kids to me. Are they going to do that if they think I'm behaving inappropriately in such a public way?"

She winced at that. "Is that what they actually said? Did they threaten to take their kids out of the program?"

"Not yet," he admitted. "I think I was able to convince them that crazy things sometimes happen at bachelor parties. I think they'll give me a pass this once." He glanced her way. "What really worries me, though, is that you won't be so lucky."

"What does that mean?"

"You know what Regina Gentry told you about skeletons," he said. "This incident isn't even dead. It's very much front and center."

"And you want me to give up without a fight? You expect me to walk away?" she asked.

"Maybe it would be for the best," he said, though he didn't sound happy about it. "Why put yourself through a battle?"

"Are you kidding me?" she asked indignantly. "I'll put myself through it because it's worth fighting. You know exactly what happened at that party. You know it was totally innocent. Now suddenly, what? A little local weekly describes me as a stripper—which I could sue them for, by the way—and what? You figure the world will see me as a slut?"

He looked genuinely shocked by her description. "Of course not. You are a free spirit, though."

"Ethan, that's not exactly a crime."

"I just don't want to see you hurt by a bunch of small-minded people," he claimed.

"Is it me you're worried about?" she asked. "Or you? Are you afraid this will damage your reputation?"

"I've already said I can weather this," he insisted, though he didn't meet her gaze. Instead, he stared straight ahead.

Samantha got it then. "This is it, isn't it? The excuse you've been hoping for to call this whole thing off?"

He frowned at that, but he didn't deny it.

"Oh, Ethan," she whispered. "When are you going to stop waiting for this to blow up? You're convinced I'm going to turn tail and run, so you're already cutting your losses."

She reached over and rested her hand against his check, felt his jaw clench. "I'm not going anywhere."

He still didn't look as if he believed her.

"Do you honestly believe this stupid picture is some kind of proof that I'll never fit in here? Well, Ethan, no matter what you think, I *intend* to fit in right here in Sand Castle Bay."

Samantha looked in his eyes as she spoke, thought she even saw just the faintest flicker of wistfulness, but she couldn't be sure.

Could she go through with her plans if Ethan insisted on cutting himself out of her life? She'd told herself her plans to stay and a future with Ethan weren't linked together, but in reality, was that true?

Only a few hours ago, she'd thought everything was settled. She'd been excited about the prospects for opening a playhouse, thrilled by the possibility of finding and nurturing new talent and eager to explore the growing feelings between Ethan and her. She'd even started to think she was close to figuring out who she really was and discovering a purpose much bigger than herself, just as Ethan had done.

Now, thanks in part to the fallout from that ridiculous picture in the paper and in part to Ethan seizing on it as an excuse to push her away, nothing made any kind of sense anymore.

"I have to go," she told him. "I came over here today

to share news with you. Then your receptionist showed me the paper, so I came back to apologize. I can see, though, that nothing I have to say matters to you. You've made a decision—for me, no less—with no input from me required."

She waited for a comment, a reaction, anything. Instead, he sat beside her, staring stoically straight ahead.

"Fine," she said, when she'd had all she could take of his silence. "It's really too bad, though, because unlike you, I think we were on the verge of something amazing."

His grip on the door handle tightened, but he didn't open it. "Samantha," he said finally, his voice ragged. He glanced over, then sighed. "Goodbye."

She stared at him in shock as he left the car and walked away. He didn't even look back as he went inside the clinic.

She imagined Debra waiting there, eager to console him, and wanted to go inside and throttle them both. Instead, though, she started the car and drove to Cora Jane's, stopping twice to wipe away the blinding tears she couldn't seem to keep from falling.

She'd barely made it to the driveway when her cell phone rang, announcing a call from Regina Gentry. She knew what the teacher was going to say before she even answered. Still, she sat and listened with no comment, not even attempting a defense.

It's over, she thought as she disconnected. *It's all over.*

Cora Jane took one look at Samantha's swollen eyes and distraught expression and guessed exactly what had happened.

"You saw the paper," she said angrily. "Honey bun, I am so sorry, but this will fade away. Nobody takes that seriously. It was a bachelor party prank."

"It might have been a stupid prank, but Ethan just broke up with me because of it."

Cora Jane didn't even try to hide her shock. "He did not! Why would he do that?"

"He seems to think it's going to be the catalyst for my whole playhouse project to be a failure, that I'll be forced to leave town and abandon him. I get that he's protecting his heart, that he may even think he's saving me from being hurt, but the bottom line is, we're done."

"Nonsense!" Cora Jane said.

Samantha gave her a rueful look. "Well, he was right about one thing. There are already repercussions. I had a call from Regina Gentry just as I pulled up outside. She's withdrawing her support for my acting classes. She told me she can't in good conscience recommend me to impressionable teenagers."

"Well, she's wrong," Cora Jane said, then studied her worriedly. "I know this is a setback, but you're not going to change your mind and leave, are you? It would be a crime if a silly thing like this drove you away."

To her dismay, Samantha didn't vow to stay and fight. In fact, she looked utterly defeated.

"Samantha, don't you dare let someone as narrow-minded as Regina chase you off," she said. "Just this morning you were bubbling over with enthusiasm. You couldn't stop talking about how excited you were when you came by Castle's to pick up that lunch to take to Ethan. Nothing's changed, not really."

"Except that my key backer withdrew her endorsement and the man I care about dumped me," she responded.

"You can overcome Regina Gentry's disapproval. My word carries as much weight as hers in this region. You'll have more students than you ever imagined. I can call in a few favors with some movers and shakers, and your playhouse will be welcomed like the genuine boon it will be to this community."

Samantha smiled at that. "You've never lacked confidence, have you?"

"Sure I have," Cora Jane said, needing her to see that everyone faced setbacks in life. "When your grandfather died, I was terrified of taking on Castle's on my own. I thought seriously about closing it down or selling it to Jerry. I even approached him about it."

"He turned you down?" Samantha said, clearly surprised.

Cora Jane smiled. "He did. He said that restaurant belonged with me, that it would lose something without me. He said a bunch of nonsense about me being the heart and soul of the place."

"It wasn't nonsense," Samantha contradicted.

Cora Jane shrugged. "Be that as it may, he convinced me he'd be right there every step of the way, that we'd be a team. So I took a deep breath and stuck with it. That's what you need to do, take a deep breath before you make any decisions."

"I don't think I'll change my mind about this," Samantha said. "Maybe Ethan's right. Maybe I belong in New York, after all."

"I'm not going to push too hard one way or the other," Cora Jane told her. "It's your decision. I do have one question for you, though. Right now, New York seems safe and familiar, but were you truly happy there? Not back in the beginning when it was fresh and exciting, but recently? I think if you answer that honestly, you'll know what you need to do."

Now all Cora Jane could do was sit back and pray that Samantha would find her way through the pain she was experiencing right this second and focus on the bright possibilities ahead.

"You've been happy. I know I behaved badly today, but maybe you should reconsider. It's about time you got a life."

Greg frowned then. "You did break up with her, right? Samantha didn't dump you? She'd have every right to, I think. It's because you're who you are and Boone's who he is that the picture ever made it into the paper. And that speculation about her being a stripper? That had to be somebody's idea of a joke. What was Ken Jones thinking that he'd print something like that? Did he owe somebody a huge favor?"

Ethan dragged himself out of his own misery long enough to consider what Greg was saying. He'd done the right thing for Samantha by pointing out what she'd be up against in this town, but he didn't feel all that good about it.

"Now that you mention it, I can't help wondering who gave that picture to the paper," he admitted, his ire starting to stir at the person who'd started this chain of events. "It had to be somebody at the party, right? I seriously doubt there were paparazzi lurking around outside at a bachelor party in Sand Castle Bay."

Greg's expression turned thoughtful. "You sure about that?" he asked slowly. "Not paparazzi, but how about somebody sent by Boone's former in-laws? Maybe they intended to catch him doing something stupid. That whole custody issue supposedly died down, but maybe that was only wishful thinking on Boone's part. Jenny's folks could have taken one last stab at discrediting him, hoping to stake their claim on B.J."

Ethan considered the possibility. It was something the deeply embittered Farmers might have done. "But that photo doesn't incriminate Boone. I'm the one holding a supposed stripper in my arms."

"Maybe they figured the whole atmosphere was toxic enough to help their cause," Pam suggested. "And it was Boone's sister-in-law-to-be you were holding. I'm sure they'd love to create the impression that the Castles are going to be a bad influence on B.J. Everyone knows they blame Emily for anything and everything that went wrong in their daughter's life. No one agrees with them, by the way. We all know Boone did the best he could by Jenny. She was happy with him. That doesn't keep the Farmers from hating Boone, Emily and anyone connected to them."

"That's just plain twisted," Ethan said, even though he knew it was a hundred percent true.

"But it's not out of the realm of possibility that they'd do this," Greg countered. "Bottom line, you and Samantha were both innocent bystanders in this plot."

Ethan had to give him credit for a good spin. "Nice try, but Samantha did show up in a cake wearing a bikini. The Farmers didn't plot that."

"And you're going to hold that against her?" Greg chided. "Come on. She was doing a favor for her sister. You know how persuasive Emily can be, and everybody was jumping through hoops to give her everything she asked for leading up to the wedding, even you."

"Samantha's motive doesn't change anything," Ethan insisted, holding tight to his stance, even when he could see he was on remarkably shaky ground. "It was a bad decision on her part. If she's going to be a successful businesswoman in this town, she has to think things through."

Greg scowled at him. "When did you become such a stuffed shirt?"

Ethan knew that's how he sounded, but he'd made his decision. He had to defend it. "Do you know how quickly I had to tap-dance around the whole issue just now with the parents of the kids in Project Pride? A couple of the moms were eager to pull their kids out of the program, but I persuaded them that this was just a crazy misunderstanding. I tossed Cora Jane's name around quite a bit, since there's nobody around here who doesn't respect her, no matter how much mudslinging goes on."

Pam regarded him incredulously. "So you used Samantha's grandmother to get yourself out of hot water? Nice going, boss."

"I was getting Samantha out of it at the same time," he protested. "I told them Samantha had every bit as much integrity and trustworthiness as her grandmother, that they shouldn't be judging her based on a prank. I defended her."

"A pretty convincing argument," Greg agreed. "Too bad it didn't persuade *you* to overlook this newspaper fiasco." He shook his head. "I hate to say it, but I wouldn't blame Samantha if she never forgave you for not going to bat for her, maybe raising a ruckus with the paper. Did you even consider doing that? You've known Ken forever, same as me. Of course, he always was a little weasel."

Ethan's own scowl deepened. He hadn't gone to Ken because this whole mess, unfair as it was, had worked for him. It had given him a cowardly way out of a relationship that terrified him. What did that say about him? Nothing good that he could think of.

"Of course you didn't, because it didn't suit your purposes," Greg said, answering for him and hitting the nail smack on the head. "Geez, man. What has gotten into you?"

"I don't get it, either," Pam said, regarding him with unmistakable disappointment.

Debra looked indecisive, then winced. "I'm with them," she admitted. "You blew it."

He probably had, Ethan conceded to himself. But he'd felt a thousand times safer once he'd sent Samantha away.

He couldn't help wondering, though, if safe was the way he wanted to live anymore. He had a hunch it was going to get awfully lonely.

Samantha hadn't been able to shake her conversation with Cora Jane the night before. Truthfully, she hadn't been happy in New York for a long time. And while being in Sand Castle Bay still felt new to her, it also filled her with hope. She liked being around her family. She was hooked on being an aunt. She didn't even mind so much the shifts she put in at Castle's to fill her spare time. The customers were friendly, and the locals made her feel welcome.

And if this summer was supposed to be about some big transformation, she imagined that it ought to be about more than changing career directions. There hadn't been much about acting that was within her control. Now, though, she had a chance to take charge of her own destiny. She needed to do it.

She was winding up another shift at Castle's when her father and Sophia arrived and settled into the family booth. Her father was wearing casual sports clothes she knew with absolute certainty weren't part of his wardrobe in Raleigh. Sophia looked as if she'd stepped out of an ad for expensive designer resort wear. Despite that, they looked perfectly at home in the restaurant's casual seaside atmosphere, where other patrons were mostly wearing bathing suits with coverups and flip-flops.

"I saw the paper," her father said without preamble.

Sophia gave her hand a squeeze. "You must have wanted to go over there and rip into them, but believe me, it serves no useful purpose. Just have a little patience. This will blow over by next week's edition."

"Unfortunately, there have already been repercussions," Samantha told them, explaining about Regina Gentry's withdrawal of her support, and then, after taking a deep breath, about Ethan's reaction.

Her father regarded her with indignation. "Nobody cares what Regina Gentry thinks," he said with certainty. "But I'm shocked by Ethan. I thought he was a stand-up guy."

"So am I," Sophia said. "He's being totally unreasonable."

"He's not really judging me. He's just retreating into his shell," Samantha said in his defense. "We all dragged him out kicking and screaming. This gave him the excuse to go back to his nice, staid lifestyle."

"That's a crying shame," Sophia said. "I like him."

Tears welled up in Samantha's eyes. "So do I, but it was probably bound to happen."

"Forget about Ethan," her father advised. "None of this changes the bottom line where your future is concerned. I've worked out a budget with Tommy. He's ready to start on those renovations as soon as you say the word."

"No," she said, not quite ready to take the leap, after all. She had to think about this, determine how badly she wanted it. Was it enough to fight for it?

"I don't know if I want to go forward," she told them. This whole incident had shaken her more than she'd realized.

"Of course you're going forward," Sophia said firmly. "Backward is never a good option in life. Remember that we were with you yesterday. Your father and I both saw how much this whole project means to you. You were bubbling over with ideas and enthusiasm. If you walk away because of a spat with Ethan or because of a commotion in some silly little local weekly, you'll never forgive yourself."

"It's not a spat," she told Sophia. "And the commotion isn't silly, not to some people around here."

"Ethan will come to his senses," Sophia argued. "If he doesn't, he's not the man any of us think he is, and you'll move on without him."

"You sound so sure of that," Samantha said.

"Oh, there are plenty of things in life to keep me guessing, but this isn't one of them. I'm pretty good at reading people. He loves you, Samantha. He may still be struggling with that, but love always triumphs, even when it's least expected." She glanced at Sam when she said it, a whole world of meaning in her eyes.

"Listen to her," he told Samantha. "She's a smart woman."

"That doesn't mean other people will be able to look past this," Samantha said.

Sophia gave her a long look. "Has one single person in here brought it up today?"

"Well, no," Samantha conceded, "but they're mostly tourists."

"Not so," her father said, taking a look around. "I recognize a half dozen locals in here right now."

Samantha knew he was right, knew that it was possible she was as guilty of seizing on this excuse to run as Ethan was. "Okay, maybe it will blow over eventually," she agreed.

"It will," her father said with confidence. "Now, shall I tell Tommy to get started?"

Just as her father and Sophia recalled her excitement the day before, Samantha tried to recapture that feeling. She thought about Cass and even Sue Ellen, who might benefit from what she had to offer. Even the community might be enriched by what she could bring to town with her classes and this playhouse.

She drew in a deep breath, seized on her one last shred of confidence, then nodded. "If you're sure you don't mind loaning me the money, go for it," she told her father.

He gave her an approving look. "That's my girl!"

"You won't regret this," Sophia told her. "I just know everything is going to work out exactly the way you want it to."

Samantha wished she were half as sure about that as Sophia seemed to be, but she was going to fight like crazy to make it so.

"How about going for a run?" Ethan asked Greg at the end of the day a couple of days after the impromptu intervention by the clinic's staff. He'd forgiven them all for butting in, since it was so evident how much they cared.

"Sure," Greg agreed readily. "But only if you understand that I'm going to bug you incessantly about being too stubborn for your own good."

"Didn't expect anything less," Ethan said. "You need to know, though, that you're wasting your breath. Things turned out for the best."

"I doubt Samantha would agree. Down deep, I suspect, neither do you."

"I said it, didn't I?" Ethan replied with a trace of impatience.

Greg shrugged. "Just expressing my opinion. You don't have to listen to me."

"I'm not going to," Ethan replied flatly.

Greg shook his head. "I'll get changed and meet you out front."

Twenty minutes later, they were running along the coastal road. There wasn't much of a shoulder and the sidewalk was crowded, so they had to be careful to accommodate the nearly bumper-to-bumper traffic. At least it moved at a snail's pace, unlike the much faster clip on the highway just two blocks west.

They ran past the town pier, curved around to the main highway and started back north on the sidewalk. Ethan deliberately set a pace that made conversation difficult. Add in the traffic noise, and talk was impossible.

When they came to the shuttered property that he knew belonged to Sam Castle, he paused and stared. The driveway was packed with pickups, and the grounds were bustling with activity. He spotted Tommy Cahill in the middle of it.

"Hold on," he told Greg, pulling up and waiting for him. He nodded toward the activity. "I need to check this out."

Tommy caught sight of him and walked over. "Nice evening for a run."

"What are you doing here?" Ethan asked. "Has Sam Castle decided he wants to renovate and move in here?" He made the latter inquiry with a hopeful note in his voice. He wasn't happy about the more obvious answer, that Samantha was sticking around and moving forward with her plans despite all the obstacles he'd predicted.

Tommy shook his head. "We're gutting the house and turning it into a playhouse, at least that's the plan as soon as Samantha and I can get all the designs drawn up and the permits pulled. She's not wasting any time. The woman knows exactly what she wants," he said.

Tommy's admiring tone set Ethan's nerves on edge. "I thought you were seeing Meg," he said testily. "Didn't the two of you hit it off?"

Tommy regarded him with bewilderment. "We've been out a couple of times. What does that have to do with anything?"

Greg shook his head. "Man, you are pitiful," he told Ethan, then turned to Tommy. "Don't mind him. He broke up with Samantha, but apparently doesn't want another single male within a hundred yards of her."

A grin broke across Tommy's face. "You're jealous? Of me and Samantha Castle?"

"I am not jealous," Ethan said, grinding his teeth.

He scowled at Greg. "He has no idea what he's talking about."

"Sounded to me as if he hit the nail on the head," Tommy replied, clearly amused. "You've got nothing to worry about. Samantha is way, way out of my league. Besides, I thought things between the two of you were all but settled. It's against my code to poach on a friend's woman."

"She is not my woman," Ethan reiterated, imagining Samantha's reaction if she heard him trying to claim otherwise. He doubted she'd like the idea of being anyone's possession, and at the moment, since he'd let her go rather than publicly jumping to her defense, she probably wanted no connection to him at all.

"We need to go," he said abruptly. "See you, Tommy."

Greg gave Tommy a sympathetic look. "Don't mind him. He's a little stressed."

As they took off, Ethan frowned at him. "You might want to remember that," he warned Greg.

"What?"

"That I'm stressed. Shouldn't you be trying to settle me down, rather than adding to it?"

Greg clapped a hand down on his shoulder. "Nah. My mission is to help you to see the error of your ways. We're not there yet."

Ethan gave him a resigned look, then upped his pace. He might not be able to stop Greg from sharing his annoying insights, but it was entirely possible that he could outrun him.

Only thing he couldn't get away from, though, was his own conscience. A good man, the one everyone around here believed to be a hero, should have been in Samantha's corner from the start of this debacle.

Samantha had been spending a lot of time with her father and Sophia, finalizing the design for the playhouse. He'd taken on the assignment of getting the plans approved at City Hall.

"I have a secret weapon," he told her, gesturing to Sophia. "She's charmed every single person in the place. It's astounding to watch her in action."

"Lots of practice," Sophia said modestly, but pleasure sparkled in her eyes.

They'd been getting together every afternoon at Castle's, spending an hour or so going over everything from budgets to promotional plans. Gabi sat in on those sessions, eager to help with the launch when the time came.

They were just winding up today, when Cass Gray came in looking for Samantha. Judging from her sullen expression, she wasn't happy.

"Are we finished here?" Samantha asked her father. "I need to spend some time with Cass."

"Go ahead," he said. "We're all set. We're coming over for dinner, so we'll see you later."

When they'd left, Samantha gestured to the seat they'd vacated. "Join me."

Cass tossed her book bag into the booth, then slid in after it.

"No rehearsal today?" Samantha asked her.

"I skipped it," Cass said.

Uh-oh, Samantha thought. That was definitely a bad sign. "Why would you do that?"

"Because Mrs. Gentry said some stuff. I came to see if it's true."

Samantha's heart sank. "What stuff?"

"That you were probably leaving town."

It wasn't the response Samantha had been expecting. "Did she say why she believed that?"

"She said there was some scandal, and you'd never live it down." She stared at Samantha miserably. "It's because of that stupid picture in the paper, isn't it?"

"There was a bit of a fuss over that," Samantha admitted. "You do know it's not true, right? I've never been a stripper."

"Oh, who cares if you were!" Cass said impatiently. "You've done all this other cool stuff. That's what counts. I'll bet Dr. Cole told you the same thing. How can you leave him? He was starting to have a life, you know what I mean? I saw him yesterday, and he was acting like a grumpy bear. That's because you're leaving, I'll bet."

Samantha thought the dynamics of her relationship with Ethan should remain between the two of them. "Let's leave Ethan out of this. The bottom line is that I'm not going anywhere."

Cass's eyes lit up. "You're not? Seriously?"

"Seriously," Samantha confirmed.

"But you haven't called about classes."

"I had some things to take care of before I could think about those," Samantha told her.

"Like what?"

"Like drawing up plans for a playhouse and getting the work started," she said.

"Holy cow!" Cass said, clearly astonished. "You're going to produce plays here? In a real playhouse?"

"That's the plan."

"Can I be in one?"

Samantha laughed at her eagerness. "If you can handle any of the parts, you definitely can be. And before you ask, I have no idea what the first production is likely to be. I'm sure it won't be before next summer, though. There's a lot that needs to happen before we get to that point."

"But you're not leaving, for sure?"

"For sure," she promised.

Cass beamed at her. "That is the best news ever!"

Samantha could only pray that everyone would see it that way. She smiled at Cass. "Now tell me how the rehearsals are going."

"Well, to everyone's shock, Sue Ellen's gotten her act together. She's not half bad."

"Glowing praise, coming from you. I guess that means you're not likely to get onstage. How are you feeling about that?"

Cass shrugged. "What can I say? I hate it, but things like this are going to happen. I have to learn to deal with it, right?"

"Then maybe this lesson wasn't such a bad thing, after all," Samantha suggested. "Because you're right. There will be rejections, Cass, and disappointments. It's the nature of the business."

"Have you been rejected?"

"More times than I can count," Samantha admitted.

"What do you do?"

"Eat a lot of ice cream," Samantha said ruefully.

"And then I go out on another audition, and then another, till something clicks."

Even as she spoke, she realized it was a practice she'd almost forgotten. She'd let the situation with Ethan throw her so badly she'd been ready to leave town rather than dealing with it. Hadn't she learned anything from all those times she'd had to bolster her spirits and face another casting director or producer?

Thankfully her father, Sophia and Cora Jane had kept her from making a terrible mistake, but she needed to remember her own philosophy and the fighting spirit that had kept her working when others might have given up.

"Thank you, Cass."

The teen blinked. "For what?"

"Reminding me how important it is to keep trying when something matters enough."

"Isn't that what you've been telling me all along?" Cass asked, her expression puzzled.

"Yes, but apparently I hadn't been listening to my own advice."

"Am I supposed to know what you're talking about?"

Samantha laughed. "No, not really."

"But I helped?"

"You did."

Cass beamed. "Cool."

"We'll talk soon," Samantha promised her. "I hope to announce those classes in the next week or so."

"Great. And don't worry about Mrs. Gentry. I'll spread the word. I know Sue Ellen wants to come. She thinks you're some kind of goddess because you cured her of stage fright and got me out of her hair. Some of the other kids are really interested, too. And when they hear about this theater thing, they're going to go crazy. Can I tell them?"

"Of course," Samantha said.

Maybe if word got around town that Samantha was here to stay, a certain gun-shy physician would have second thoughts about walking away from what they had. And if not, well, she intended to take one last stab at showing him how wrong it would be to throw their future away.

Once Greg had planted that seed about Boone's former in-laws being behind that photo in the paper, Ethan had given it a lot of thought. On the one hand, he'd told himself to let it go, that what was done was done. On the other, he knew he owed it to Samantha to set the record straight.

He drove over to the newspaper's office, determined to get to the bottom of it. He also intended to do what he should have done when he'd first seen the paper, demand that a retraction of that bit about Samantha being a stripper. Maybe that was her fight if she wanted to pursue it, but as Greg had reminded him, he had a history with Ken Jones and he intended to use his clout to force the issue.

Ken looked up when Ethan crossed the newsroom, removed his glasses and stood up. "I was expecting a visit from you a lot sooner," he admitted, his expression somber and maybe just the slightest bit guilt-ridden. "Look, I know that picture was probably upsetting, but you and Boone are news around here. It was too good an opportunity to pass up."

"Sure, if you're more worried about selling papers

than destroying reputations," Ethan countered. "Is that it, Ken? Is this little rag of yours in financial trouble?"

Ken blinked at the attack and put his glasses back on. Ethan wondered if the little weasel subscribed to the idea that no one would hit a man wearing glasses.

"It was news," Ken repeated, though he sounded a little more nervous than he had.

"And describing Samantha as a stripper? Where'd that idea come from? You know it's not true."

"Yeah," he said, wincing. "I got an earful about that from Cora Jane and from my mother."

Ethan allowed himself a smile. "Good for them. I should have been here sooner to add my two cents. You do know it probably rises to the level of libel if Samantha wants to pursue it?"

"So I've heard from my lawyer, who's no happier about it than you are."

"Where'd you get the idea that she was a stripper in the first place?"

"The photographer," he admitted.

"Who is? I noticed there was no credit line under the photo."

Ken winced. "The picture came to me via email with no request for credit or payment. Since cameras don't lie, I printed it."

"But people who send anonymous emails do lie, and they do leave a trail. You're not stupid, Ken. You were the biggest computer geek in our class. And somewhere buried deep inside are the remains of a real journalist. Where'd the picture come from? I'm sure you know."

Ken hesitated, probably trying on several arguments about confidentiality for size. Then he caved. "Jodie

Farmer," he admitted. "And I know she has an axe to grind against the Castles, or against Emily, anyway. I should have used better judgment, okay? No question about it."

"Then I imagine you won't have a bit of trouble using all that temporarily forgotten integrity to correct the situation," Ethan said, his tone mild but unyielding.

"I don't know what good it would do now."

Ethan regarded him incredulously. "You describe someone as a stripper, which you know could hurt her reputation, and you don't see why it's necessary to fix that? Let me help you. If clearing your conscience and the record aren't good enough reasons, how about this? I will encourage Samantha to sue you for every penny she can get from this sleazy rag of yours and from you personally for knowing you made a mistake and not fixing it in the next edition. How's that for motivation?"

Ken heaved a sigh. "Okay, you're ticked off. I get that, Ethan. Want to tell me what your stake is in this? Are the rumors true? Are the two of you a hot item?"

"My relationship with Samantha is none of your concern. This is about righting a wrong." He held the other man's gaze. "On the front page in type big enough that the world can see it from across the street, the same way they could spot that photo."

"Come on, now," Ken protested.

"Do it," Ethan repeated. "Or I will see that Samantha nails your sorry hide."

He felt a thousand percent better when he walked away, but he wondered if he'd done enough to make things right. Or was this one of those situations he'd be regretting for a lifetime, berating himself for doing too little too late?

Twenty-Three

Samantha was walking through the gutted building that would eventually become a small theater seating a few hundred patrons when Gabi came running in, waving the local weekly. Samantha regarded her warily.

"Not again," she muttered. "What did they print this time?"

"Wait till you see," her sister gloated. "It's an apology, on the front page, no less."

Samantha stared at the large front-page display in shock. "What on earth brought this on? Retractions usually appear in teeny-tiny type buried somewhere inside the paper."

"According to the editor, the fact that there was no evidence that you were or ever had been a stripper was brought to his attention by none other than local hero Ethan Cole!"

"What?" Samantha said incredulously. "Let me see that."

Gabi held the paper away from her. "Wait, it gets even better. He also conceded that the initial report was given to him by someone who might have had an axe to grind against the Castle family."

"Who on earth?" Samantha asked.

"Jodie Farmer, that's who," Gabi said. She jabbed a finger at the front page. "It says that right here. Boone is going to have a conniption."

Samantha sank down on a convenient sawhorse. "Oh, brother! I never saw that coming."

"Well, apparently Ethan forced the information out of the editor, some guy named Ken Jones. Wade was so indignant when he saw this he charged over to the paper himself and had a little come-to-Jesus chat with Ken. I guess Ken spilled his guts about the way Ethan stormed into the office, demanded answers, threatened lawsuits and who knows what else. Wade added his two cents. It'll be a long, long time before this Ken Jones takes on any of the Castles again."

Samantha was more stunned by Ethan's late display of loyalty than Wade's. "Ethan did all that?" she murmured, bemused. "Why?"

"Because he loves you, you idiot. He was standing up for you."

"But he wants me to go away. This whole brouhaha came close to accomplishing that," Samantha protested, trying to make sense of it. Had he been doing her one last favor so he could let her leave with a clear conscience?

"I'd say that this proves otherwise," Gabi insisted. "Wade thinks so, too."

"Or maybe Ethan found out I'd decided to stick around and this was some sort of peace offering," Samantha speculated.

Gabi regarded Samantha intently. "Whatever it was, what are you going to do about it?"

"Nothing," Samantha said wearily. "Ethan made his wishes perfectly clear. Whether I go or stay, he's done."

"And you don't think he's allowed to change his mind, or to wake up and regret what he said?" Gabi protested. "Come on, Samantha. Whatever happened to second chances? You'd want one if you'd done something stupid." She smacked her forehead in an exaggerated gesture. "Oh, wait. You did."

"What did I do?"

"You caved in to Emily's ridiculous insecurities and went to that party inside a cake, putting your reputation and Ethan's at risk." She held up a hand when Samantha started to argue. "I know I didn't help the situation. By the time we finished pressing you, we didn't leave you a way out. I get that."

"Bottom line, no matter who pushed me, it was not a big deal, or it shouldn't have been," Samantha said defensively. "Anybody with half a brain could see it was nothing more than a bachelor party prank. It happens all the time. Nobody ever gets this worked up over it."

"Because nobody else is local war hero and respected physician Ethan Cole or actress Samantha Castle," Gabi reminded her. "As wrong as it was for Ken to splash that picture on the front page with that whole bit about you being a stripper, I can almost see why he did it. People eat that stuff up, especially when such big names are involved. And let's not forget that Boone is a proud son of Sand Castle Bay, too."

"I'm a has-been Broadway and TV actress," Samantha argued. "Even with your excellent prowess at spin, you couldn't have gotten something this silly in a major news outlet."

Gabi gave her a challenging look. "Want me to try?"

Samantha shuddered, knowing full well that it wouldn't be that huge a test of her sister's PR skills. "Absolutely not," she said flatly. "This needs to die down and go away."

"And then what?"

"And then I will go on with my life, build this theater, teach a few classes and create a fulfilling life for myself right here where I can hang out with family."

"Where does Ethan fit in?"

"He claims he doesn't want to," she insisted.

"Oh, for heaven's sake, haven't you heard a word I said?" Gabi protested impatiently, waving the newspaper. "*This* says otherwise. Give the man a break."

"I am not the one who broke us up," she said stubbornly.

"But you are the one who's letting pride stand in the way of a reconciliation," Gabi said. "This act by Ethan, that's *his* apology. Now it's your turn."

"But—"

Gabi's gaze was unrelenting. "Fix this, Samantha. You'll regret it if you don't. And make no mistake, it is up to you. Grandmother, Emily and I can't do it, not with all the clever meddling in the world. You're on your own, just the way you claimed you wanted to be from the beginning."

Samantha regarded her sister wearily. She knew Gabi was right. Unfortunately, this was one of those rare times when she wouldn't have minded a little well-meant meddling.

* * *

Cora Jane had vowed to stay out of the middle of this ridiculous spat between Samantha and Ethan, but with two stubborn wills involved, she could see their whole future disintegrating unless someone with better sense stepped in. She left Jerry in charge at the restaurant and, ignoring his advice to stay well away from either of the injured parties, she drove to Ethan's clinic.

Inside, she nodded toward the back. "Is Ethan with a patient?" she asked Debra.

"No, ma'am, but he doesn't like being disturbed."

Cora Jane smiled. "I think he'll make an exception for me." When Debra reached for her phone, Cora Jane shook her head. "Maybe you should just pretend you never saw me."

Debra shrugged and put the phone back.

Cora Jane found Ethan in his office, a clutter of files spread out on his desk, though his back was turned to the mess and he was staring out the window.

"I came to thank you," she announced, startling him.

He whirled around and regarded her warily. "Cora Jane," he muttered, his tone not especially welcoming. "What brings you by? Everything okay? Did you get cut or burned or something?"

She smiled at his attempt to turn this into a medical visit. "Nope. Like I said, I came to thank you for going to bat for my girl."

"Samantha would have been okay without me," he said. "Still, I figured I owed her a little backup. I understand you did your share of rabble-rousing in Ken's office."

"I did, but I'm not the one who persuaded him to

print a retraction or got to the bottom of who was behind this in the first place. I'm afraid I was too busy ranting to ask the right questions or make the right demands."

"Well, the record's straight now," Ethan said. "All's well that ends well."

Cora Jane gave him an impatient look. "That's it? You see this as the end of things?"

"No other way to look at it," Ethan said.

She studied him for a full minute, then shook her head. "You think she needs to come to you, don't you? You want Samantha to reach out, put her heart on the line again, prove she really wants you."

Ethan actually flinched at what she could only assume was a direct hit.

"She'll never do it," Cora Jane told him. "It doesn't mean she doesn't love you. It just means her pride runs as deep as yours. I hope to goodness one of you snaps out of it before it's too late. Anything else would be a crying shame."

She was halfway to the door when he said, his tone miserable, "What am I supposed to do?"

"You could start by admitting you love her," she said, relieved that he'd asked.

"I do," he said firmly.

Cora Jane smiled and turned back. "Not to me. I meant to her."

"I was afraid that was what you meant."

"For a man who braved death, probably more times than either of us would like to count, why are you so scared of three little words that could give you everything you want?"

When he started to reply, she held up a hand. "Never

mind. I know. You're thinking if she doesn't say them back, it'll be humiliating, maybe leave you with a broken heart."

He nodded. "Something like that."

"You feeling real good with the way things are now?"

A smile played at the corners of his mouth. "Point taken."

She gave a nod of satisfaction. "Good. I knew you were smart. And for whatever it's worth coming from me, she does love you. Not a question in my mind about that, or I'd never have set foot in here."

"Thanks, Cora Jane."

"No thanks necessary. Just do right by my girl."

"I'll try," he responded.

She gave him one of her fiercest looks. "And do it soon, too," she ordered. "Jerry's getting impatient. I can't hold that man off much longer, and we're waiting on the two of you before we set our wedding date."

"Pour on the pressure, why don't you?"

She laughed. "Best way I know to get things done."

And then she left him to think about what she'd said.

Despite his reassurances to Cora Jane the day before, Ethan still wasn't a hundred percent sure what was right. Maybe things had turned out exactly the way they were meant to. Unfortunately that thought left an empty place inside him.

He'd almost convinced himself to live with that lonely destiny when he walked the few blocks from his home to the clinic Thursday afternoon to meet the kids for this week's outing. At the edge of the parking lot, he stopped in his tracks.

There was Samantha, sitting on a bench beside Cass, who was staring at her with the rapt attention of a star-struck fan. Cass's face was transformed. The sullen teen was gone, replaced by an animated young girl. In that instant, all the feelings he'd been denying he had for Samantha—the ones that ran so much deeper than a longing for a quick roll in the sack—surfaced. There was so much about her he had yet to discover, but he already knew just how deeply she cared about people, including—thank God—him.

Drawing in a deep breath, he took his time before joining them, stopping to chat with the parents, bestowing hugs on the kids as he helped them into the van.

A few of the parents had clearly recognized Samantha, but they didn't seem unduly disturbed by her presence now that the situation had been clarified by the paper.

When he could no longer put it off, he walked over to stand beside them—the woman he'd fallen for and the girl who'd been his biggest failure to date. Thanks to Samantha, though, Cass's view of her future was changing.

"What's going on?" he asked, looking from one to the other.

"Samantha's going to start teaching acting classes right here in Sand Castle Bay next week," Cass said, her eyes alight. "And if I'm any good, which we all know I am, she's going to introduce me to her agent."

Then with an impish gleam in her eyes, she added, "And I'm going to star in next summer's first production at her playhouse." She nudged Samantha with an elbow. "I know you didn't promise that, but I am going to earn that lead role."

Cass's delight was palpable, but it scared Ethan even more than her announcement that Samantha was staying. Even though he'd known she planned to stay, this confirmation made it feel even more real. More important, it eliminated any last chance of him forgetting her.

Samantha caught his gaze. "I always keep my promises," she said quietly, clearly understanding his worries, at least where Cass was concerned. "Always."

Hearing the firm, reassuring commitment in her voice, Ethan felt the last of his reservations ease. "Okay, then. You planning to come along today?"

She stood up eagerly, surprising him a little. "Sure, if I won't be in the way. What's on the agenda?"

"Bungee-jumping," he said, just to see the quick rise of panic in her eyes, but it didn't come.

"Sounds like fun," she said, her gaze never wavering.

"We are so *not* going bungee-jumping," Cass said, rolling her eyes. "Can you see Mrs. Gaylord if you took her precious son to jump off some bridge?"

"Darn, and I was so looking forward to it," Samantha claimed.

He laughed. "Just one more thing I need to remember, I guess. You're a daredevil." He glanced at the teenager, whose fascinated gaze kept shifting from him to Samantha and back again. "Cass, hop on the bus. Make sure the kids aren't going wild. We'll be right there."

Samantha grinned at him after Cass had gone. "You know you just ruined her day. She thought she was about to witness what could turn out to be the hottest gossip in Sand Castle Bay, even better than the front-page news in the local paper a couple of weeks ago."

"I'm sure she'll survive the disappointment," he said wryly. "I'm more concerned with whether I'll survive life with you."

"You won't know unless you try," she teased.

He took a deep breath and said, "Then I guess I'd better try."

She smiled slowly. "I was hoping you'd say that."

Ethan took another very deep breath and made a giant leap, one far scarier than bungee-jumping. "Want to elope this weekend? I'm pretty sure there's a beach in Hawaii calling our names."

For the first time since they'd met, he'd surprised her. Her mouth was agape.

"Excuse me?"

"You heard me. I don't think I can handle all that wedding planning and stress again right now, and I don't want to wait. Do you? If you do, I'll cope with it, but I'm thinking impulsive is the way to go."

She still looked a little shell-shocked. "You want to run off and get married in Hawaii?"

"You did say you wanted a destination wedding. If you'll settle for the beach right here, we could probably go that route, too, then take off to any island of your choice for a honeymoon."

He held his breath awaiting her reply.

"I'm thinking you're crazy as a loon," she said eventually. "We've hardly even dated. We've been thrown together by my sisters and my grandmother, but you've not once taken the initiative to ask me out. Not really."

"We have slept together," he reminded her.

"Definitely a consideration," she agreed. Her gaze narrowed. "But maybe I need to be courted properly."

Ethan studied her expression, thought he detected a twinkle in her eyes that contradicted her claim, but just the same he said, "If you want to be courted, I'll give it a try, but I can't promise I'll live up to the romantic scenarios on those soaps you used to be on. I'm a fairly staid, unimaginative man."

She grinned. "Come to think of it, those soap marriages inevitably led to disaster. Maybe you have the right idea about just taking a blind leap of faith, though it seems a little risky given how little I really know about you. I don't even know if you squeeze the toothpaste tube in the middle or leave your socks all over."

"Yes, and no," he said in response. "Is there anything about me you really need to know that someone in this town hasn't already told you? I'm pretty sure my résumé was provided along with your invitation to be your sister's maid of honor. Plus, according to several reports happily passed along to me, you've had a crush on me since high school. That must count for something."

"I suppose," she agreed with a hint of reluctance.

"What's holding you back?"

"I like getting flowers for no reason," she admitted. "And candy. I'm very fond of expensive chocolates. Those usually stop after the wedding, and with us, you haven't yet sent any at all."

"They're yours, every week, if that's what you want," he assured her. "But marry me first."

"Are you afraid you'll get cold feet if we wait?"

"Absolutely not."

"Are you worried I will?"

He shrugged as if that fear were of no consequence. "You say you always keep your promises. I trust you."

"Then what's the hurry?"

"It has recently been brought to my attention that I'm perceived as being slow and stodgy, at least in the romance department. I think my image needs an overhaul. Despite some unwelcome repercussions, that picture in the paper actually spiced up my image. If I throw in an impetuous, out-of-the-blue elopement, that could clinch the deal."

"Is there some reason you're suddenly so anxious for an image overhaul?"

"Yep. Without one, people will never believe I won a woman like you."

She took a step closer, her gaze locking with his. "You won a woman like me by being the best man I've ever met, inside and out," she said, her hand resting against his cheek. "And this weekend works for me."

"What about your life in New York?"

"Over and done with, which you already know."

"I like hearing it again and again. It's reassuring," he admitted.

"Then you should know that the only reason I'll be going back to New York is to pick up my clothes," she said. "Come to think of it, given that look in your eye, it could be a while before I need those."

Ethan sighed, overwhelmed by the feeling of contentment that had stolen over him. He looked deep into her eyes and said the words that had frightened him not so long ago. "I love you, Samantha. I may not say the words enough, but I will show you each and every day."

"You already have," she assured him. "Now we'd

better get in that van. The natives are getting restless, and I'm pretty sure Cass has texted pictures of us to everyone she knows. We could be destined to be front-page news again next week."

"So what?" he murmured, catching her hand and pulling her back. "Ken can run the picture with the announcement of our wedding."

"Our engagement," she countered.

"Nope. We're going for broke," he told her. "Anything less is a deal-breaker."

Surprise lit her eyes. "Boy, when you go all in, you really take it seriously, don't you?"

"I hear it's the only way. Now come over here."

"We should get on the bus," she argued. "Look at all those fascinated faces watching us."

"They can wait," he insisted, sealing his mouth over hers for a kiss that set his heart ablaze.

He'd been right about everything from the very first moment he'd set eyes on her, wearing his football jersey and nothing else. This woman was destined to turn his life upside down.

Amazingly, after all his worries that he'd never find the right match who'd love him for the man he was now, right this second there wasn't a doubt in his mind that he'd found a woman who'd give him a run for his money. And even more amazingly, he was absolutely convinced that he could keep up with her.

And if he couldn't? Well, he knew with a hundred percent certainty that she'd be waiting for him right around the next bend in the road.

Epilogue

"Is everyone here insane?" Emily inquired, looking around at the small group assembled on the beach on Sea Glass Island, where for the moment the sun was sparkling on bits of sand-washed colored glass. "An evacuation order was issued an hour ago. There's a hurricane on the way, people."

"Then the minister needs to hurry up and get here," Samantha said calmly, looking into Ethan's eyes. "We are not budging from this spot until we've said our vows."

As if to emphasize the imminent threat, the sun ducked behind a heavy, dark cloud, the wind kicked up and sand swirled around the wedding party, which included the three Castle sisters, their men, Cora Jane, Jerry, Sam Castle and Sophia, who'd sworn she'd never met such a marrying group of people in her life. Greg was Ethan's best man. Though his folks hadn't flown in for the last-minute wedding, they planned to be here for the reception to be held in a few weeks.

Just then Samantha's veil caught in the wind and sailed down the beach. Boone's son, B.J., chased after it.

"It kinda got wet," he said apologetically when he handed it back to her. "I couldn't get there fast enough."

"It'll dry," Samantha said, unconcerned. "Has anybody checked on the minister?"

"I spoke to him less than five minutes ago," Boone assured her. "He said the boat we sent for him was just offshore." He glanced up. "And there he is, climbing over the dunes right now."

Samantha beamed at Ethan. "No getting out of it now."

"Wouldn't dream of trying," he said. "Though we might want to ask for the short version of the ceremony. Those are some serious storm clouds rolling this way. And the waves are about to overrun the beach. We're going to get soaked."

She laughed. "The short version works for me, though getting soaked isn't such a big price to pay for getting married."

"But getting stranded out here might be more than any of us bargained for," Ethan said.

Even though the service was a bit rushed and threatened by an impending late-season hurricane, Samantha thought it was the most beautiful ceremony she'd been to, and she'd been to a lot recently.

At the end Ethan looked into her eyes and said, "When I left the hospital a few years ago, they told me I was almost good as new. I wanted to believe that. I made it my mission to work with kids who'd been injured to prove that life could be anything they wanted it to be."

He held her gaze. "But it wasn't until you came along that I really felt whole again. You complete me, Samantha, and I will spend a lifetime trying to give you everything you want or need."

Through her tears, she whispered, "As long as I have you, Ethan, I'll have everything I'll ever need. I can't wait to spend my life with you and see what adventures come our way."

The minister glanced up at the sky, then asked, not even trying to hide the sense of urgency he was feeling, "Anything else?"

"Nope. I think that about covers it," Ethan said, never taking his gaze from Samantha's face.

"Then I now pronounce you husband and wife, and suggest we get back to the mainland and get out of town."

"Not before this," Ethan declared, sweeping Samantha into his arms and kissing her.

He took his sweet time about it, too, until fat, cool raindrops splashed on them and waves rolled over their feet. Even then, he clearly wasn't ready to stop. Samantha smiled against his lips, glad that they were on the same page. Some things were more important than a storm on the horizon.

It was the applause and catcalls that interrupted them eventually.

"We need to hightail it out of here, people," Boone said, urging them back over the dunes to the waiting boats some of the locals had provided for the short trip over to the island. Back on the mainland, packed cars were awaiting them. There was no way to know when they might be allowed back in Sand Castle Bay.

While the guests scampered across the beach, Samantha hung back for just a second, relishing the feel of the sand beneath her feet and the warm, steady touch of the man beside her. With the rest of her family nearby, she was well and truly home at last…and oh, so glad of it!

* * * * *

Get 3 FREE REWARDS!

We'll send you 2 FREE Books _plus_ a FREE Mystery Gift.

FREE Value Over $20

Both the **Romance** and **Suspense** collections feature compelling novels written by many of today's bestselling authors.

YES! Please send me 2 FREE novels from the Essential Romance or Essential Suspense Collection and my FREE gift (gift is worth about $10 retail). After receiving them, if I don't wish to receive any more books, I can return the shipping statement marked "cancel." If I don't cancel, I will receive 4 brand-new novels every month and be billed just $7.49 each in the U.S. or $7.74 each in Canada. That's a savings of at least 17% off the cover price. It's quite a bargain! Shipping and handling is just 50¢ per book in the U.S. and $1.25 per book in Canada.* I understand that accepting the 2 free books and gift places me under no obligation to buy anything. I can always return a shipment and cancel at any time by calling the number below. The free books and gift are mine to keep no matter what I decide.

Choose one:
- ☐ **Essential Romance** (194/394 BPA GRNM)
- ☐ **Essential Suspense** (191/391 BPA GRNM)
- ☐ **Or Try Both!** (194/394 & 191/391 BPA GRQZ)

Name (please print)

Address   Apt. #

City   State/Province   Zip/Postal Code

Email: Please check this box ☐ if you would like to receive newsletters and promotional emails from Harlequin Enterprises ULC and its affiliates. You can unsubscribe anytime.

Mail to the Harlequin Reader Service:
IN U.S.A.: P.O. Box 1341, Buffalo, NY 14240-8531
IN CANADA: P.O. Box 603, Fort Erie, Ontario L2A 5X3

Want to try 2 free books from another series? Call 1-800-873-8635 or visit www.ReaderService.com.

*Terms and prices subject to change without notice. Prices do not include sales taxes, which will be charged (if applicable) based on your state or country of residence. Canadian residents will be charged applicable taxes. Offer not valid in Quebec. This offer is limited to one order per household. Books received may not be as shown. Not valid for current subscribers to the Essential Romance or Essential Suspense Collection. All orders subject to approval. Credit or debit balances in a customer's account(s) may be offset by any other outstanding balance owed by or to the customer. Please allow 4 to 6 weeks for delivery. Offer available while quantities last.

Your Privacy—Your information is being collected by Harlequin Enterprises ULC, operating as Harlequin Reader Service. For a complete summary of the information we collect, how we use this information and to whom it is disclosed, please visit our privacy notice located at corporate.harlequin.com/privacy-notice. From time to time we may also exchange your personal information with reputable third parties. If you wish to opt out of this sharing of your personal information, please visit readerservice.com/consumerschoice or call 1-800-873-8635. **Notice to California Residents**—Under California law, you have specific rights to control and access your data. For more information on these rights and how to exercise them, visit corporate.harlequin.com/california-privacy.

STRS23

HARLEQUIN
PLUS

Try the best multimedia
subscription service for romance
readers like you!

Read, Watch and Play.

Experience the easiest way to get
the romance content you crave.

Start your **FREE TRIAL** at
<u>www.harlequinplus.com/freetrial</u>.